T0013139

Just Last Night

Also by Mhairi McFarlane

Just Last Night

a novel

Mhairi McFarlane

WM
WILLIAM MORROW
An Imprint of HarperCollinsPublishers

This is a work of fiction. Names, characters, places, and incidents are
products of the author's imagination or are used fictitiously and are
not to be construed as real. Any resemblance to actual events, locales,
organizations, or persons, living or dead, is entirely coincidental.

P.S.™ is a trademark of HarperCollins Publishers.

JUST LAST NIGHT. Copyright © 2021 by Mhairi McFarlane. All rights reserved.
Printed in the United States of America. No part of this book may be used or
reproduced in any manner whatsoever without written permission except in the
case of brief quotations embodied in critical articles and reviews. For information,
address HarperCollins Publishers, 195 Broadway, New York, NY 10007.

HarperCollins books may be purchased for educational, business,
or sales promotional use. For information, please email the Special
Markets Department at SPsales@harpercollins.com.

Originally published as *Last Night* in Great Britain in 2021 by HarperCollinsUK.

FIRST U.S. EDITION

Designed by Diahann Sturge

Emojis on page 245 and 246 © FOS_ICON / Shutterstock, Inc.
Shooting star emoji on page 245 © Cosmic_Design / Shutterstock, Inc.

Library of Congress Cataloging-in-Publication Data has been applied for.

ISBN 978-0-06-303685-7
ISBN 978-0-06-306042-5 (international edition)

22 23 24 25 26 LBC 9 8 7 6 5

For Kristy,
who loves a Goth dress and a comedy cat as much as I do

But I thought in spite of dreams
You'd be sitting somewhere here with me
—"Being Boring," Pet Shop Boys

After

You were alive again last night.

I wake up with a small startle at sudden consciousness, and lie still in the dark, my brain scrabbling to reassemble reality. It wasn't a nightmare—and I've had plenty of those—it was just another world, exactly like this one, but with a dramatic difference. Your presence. Your presence, which I took for granted.

In this place, we were cheerfully organizing a ski trip, sitting at a school desk, while next to a busy motorway. The cars thundering past made the table shake but neither of us were bothered. *How about Switzerland?* you said. We had plans.

I imagine our messaging, me telling you about it later this morning, entertaining you on your commute. You always replied within minutes.

Hah you'd never go skiing, Eve. "Why would I willingly travel to a very cold place and do any sort of sport and call it a holiday? Who looks at a very steep icy slope and thinks, I know, I'll put things on my feet that will make me fall down it faster?" And so on.

IKR! Obviously my subconscious is trolling me. Also: why are our dreams so interesting to the dreamer and so boring to everyone else? Is it because we're so impressed we created a story, but for them, the plot has no stakes?

1

*Yes and double dull points for the people who think
it's amazing if it's a surreal one, as if your dreams are
going to be logical. "I was staring at the goat but oh my
God, then I realized, the goat was ALSO ME."*

*That sounds pretty cool, tbf. Goat
transmogrification beats skiing any day*

*Argh, why didn't I walk 2 mins further to Caffe Nero,
I am such a lazy sod, even the Starbucks flat white is
a filthy sweet kids milkshake. Pint after work?*

Pint after work! x

I miss you.

I hate inventing you, scripting your lines, instead of having the original. I'm what my mum calls, acidly—because I could do a good impression of her second husband—*a natural mimic.*

But the ease with which I can conjure you up, it feels like a curse. A parlor trick, but it's ghoulish, a parody. It's like waltzing with a mannequin.

I push down under the warmth of the covers, listening to the rain pelt the roof outside. I'm enough of a Goth to relish a downpour when I'm not required to be in it, and it's a good one: really heavy, splashily wet, earth-soaking, you can hear it pinging off the leaves. Only insomniacs, milkmen, the dregs of club nights and early-shifters will know it happened. It's a secret we're sharing while the rest of the city snores.

My heart skips a beat as the curtains move. Roger slithers in the window and mews indignantly. Someone threw cold water at him from the sky, when he was busy staking out rats, having fun.

By the light of the side lamp you bought me—ceramic, in the shape of a toadstool, a Disney toadstool with white stalk and red spotted cap ("As it is a poisonous mushroom, so will twee home accessories be deadly to your hopes of getting a boyfriend.")—I see Roger settle at the end of the bed, his fur in damp peaks.

Someone once said to me birth was the most ordinary and extraordinary thing you'll ever experience, simultaneously, and death is the same. The fact of yours sits there, implacably, being so banal and so mind-blowingly strange at the same time.

It will always be like this, I have come to realize. The ache is permanent, it must be accommodated. It's part of my body now.

I keep waiting to get past it. To "move on," to absorb it, to set it aside, to make sense of it, to process it. For it to be, somehow, "behind" me. *What next?* I keep thinking, with a pain in my stomach like it's been slit open. And—there is no next, stupid. That's the point. Someone has gone, forever, and you have to stop waiting for them to come back. Without realizing it, you are stuck on pause, as if their not being here might change.

This is what I never knew about loss—it's also about what you gain. You carry a weight that you never had before. It's never behind you. It's alongside you.

"Forever": people say it in wedding vows all the time like they understand what it means, but actual forever is fucking huge.

1

Before

"We're going to win tonight," Ed says. "I can feel it. I can smell it. I could slice it like a frittata. The air is thick with the odor of our imminent victory. Breathe it in, my bitches."

He pretends to scent the air.

"Are you sure that's not Leonard?" Justin says. "He had chili con carne for tea. Got up on the counter and had his face in the saucepan before I could stop him, the fool. He's been farting in spicy beef flavor ever since."

"Maybe victory smells exactly like mince and kidney beans working its way through a very small dog's digestive system," I say, as Susie says: "BLURGH."

"How would we know how it smells, after all? None of us have ever been successful," I say, directing this at Ed.

"Speak for yourself. My GP said my hemorrhoids were the most prominent he'd seen in thirty years practicing medicine."

I guffaw. (This is a standard joke format with Ed; I assume his bum is fine.)

4

I reflexively reach out to pet Leonard, who has his own chair, sitting atop Justin's coat, protecting the upholstery.

Leonard is a "Chorkie"—a Chihuahua crossed with a Yorkshire Terrier. He has beady eyes peering out from under a comical fringe of gray-white hair, spiky in the middle like he's had Paul Weller's Mod cut, bat ears, and a lopsided little grin, full of toothpick teeth.

He looks, as Ed says: "Like an enterprising cartoon rat doing some kind of stealthy cosplay as a canine. We've been infiltrated by a rodent master criminal."

Leonard, an omnivorous eater and troublesomely impromptu urinator, is one of the loves of my life. (The rest of them are around, and also sometimes under, this table.)

"You say we're going to win this quiz every week, Ed," Susie says, worrying at a coaster, shredding it into a pile of soft cardboard shards. "And we are always fucked by the same five determined men in Lands' End packable anoraks."

"Describing my best holiday in Wales, there," Justin says. Justin is a self-proclaimed "tiresome show-off and performative middle child" and one of the funniest men you'll ever meet, but you absolutely do not go to him for good taste.

The quizmaster's voice booms out, cutting through conversation, like the Voice of God:

"Question TEN. Who is Michael Owuo? *Who is, Michael Owuo?*"

The usual seconds of post-question hush fall.

"Is he . . . the Labour MP for Kingston upon Hull East?" Ed whispers, faux-earnestly.

"Seriously?" Susie says.

"No," I say, rolling my eyes, and Ed taps the pen on his lips and winks at me.

"You three *do* know who he is, right?" Justin says, doing a double take. "UGH. So we *are* the millennial cast of *Last of the Summer Wine*."

"Did he play the villain in the last Bond?" I ask, and Ed says: "YES! 'Doctor Pardon.' What was his gimmick again?"

"He had bejeweled ear gauges," I say. "And a walker, with tinsel wound 'round it."

Ed laughs. I love the way he laughs: it starts in his shoulders.

"OK, who is joking, and who isn't?" Susie says. "I mean obviously, they are," she grimaces at myself and Ed. "Do you genuinely know who he is, Justin?"

"He's *Stormzy*," Justin hisses. "God, you can tell you lot are thirty-four."

"You're thirty-four, Justin," Susie says.

"There's thirty-four and then there's, like, 'Who are the Stormzys?' thirty-four," Justin says, pulling an "old geezer" rubbery face.

"A '*stormzy*,' you say," Ed says, in a creaky High Court judge voice. "Whatever a *Stormzy* is," and writes "Mr. Storm Zee" on the paper.

Ed has really nice hands; I'm a sucker for nice hands. He cycles a lot and can mend things, and I am now mature enough to appreciate practical skills like that.

Susie takes the pen from Ed, scribbles his words out, and writes Stormzy correctly.

"Don't your pupils keep you up to date with this stuff?" I ask Ed. "Hip to the jive, daddio?"

"It's my job to teach them Dickens, not theirs to teach me grime."

Ed is head of English at a nice county school. You know

how they say some people look like police? Ed looks like a teacher—a film or television, glossy young teacher—with his unthreatening, handsome solidity, strawberry-blond, close-cropped hair. In a crisis in a situation full of strangers, Ed's would be the kind, reliable face you'd hope to see. He'd be the guy offering his necktie as a makeshift tourniquet.

Part of the pleasure of this weekly pub appointment to lose the pub quiz, I think, is it brings out and defines all the roles in our foursome. Ed and I clowning around together, Justin refereeing, with his caustic wit, Susie playing exasperated mother.

Sometimes I stop participating in the conversation and just hum happily inside myself, enjoying our togetherness, reveling in the way we all broadcast on the same frequency. I watch us from the outside.

. . . *didn't she marry the singer from the Mumfords? I'd rather be a Sister Wife. (Susie)*

. . . *this cherry Stolichnaya that Hester brought back from duty-free, it's amazing, tastes like baby medicine. Or so babies tell me. (Ed)*

. . . *he was a right grumpy carrot top. I said to him, do you know why gingerism is the last acceptable prejudice? Because it's acceptable. (Justin, of course)*

"Shhhhh," I say, as I can see the quizmaster adjusting his readers, as he squints at a piece of paper.

"Question *ELEVEN*. The word 'CHRONOPHAGE' is an Ancient Greek word for what is now an idiomatic expression in English. But what does it mean? Clue: your mobile phone may do this. That does not mean you can check your phones, hahaha!"

The quizmaster blows air out of his nostrils in a windy gust, directly into the bulb, and you can hear his spit.

The looks on the faces of our hiking anorak nemeses suggest they're considerably more confident about this than they were about Mr. Stormzy.

"Chrono means time . . . ," Ed whispers. "Chronograph watches."

"Chronological." Susie nods. "In order of timing."

"Phage," I say. "Hmmm. Coprophagic is eating poo. Fairly sure the copro's poo, so the phagic must be eating."

"Eve!" Susie barks, with a potato chip halfway into her mouth. "How do you even know that?"

"I've lived a full life."

"I've been around for most of it so I *know* that isn't true. A quarter full, at best."

". . . *Eating time?*" Justin hisses. "It must mean eating time. Your phone does that. Boom. Write it down."

Ed obliges.

We come to The Gladstone every Thursday. I would say without fail, but we are thirty-somethings with lives and jobs and other friends and—some of us—partners, so there are some fails. But we're here more often than not.

"Question *TWELVE*, before we take a short break. What do Marcus Garvey, Rudyard Kipling, Ernest Hemingway, and Alice Cooper have in common? I'll give you a clue. It involves a mistake."

We stare blankly at each other. Packable Anoraks are frantic-whispering instead of writing or looking sneaky-smug, which means they're not sure either.

"Is it choice of first wife? As in they've all had more than one?" Ed says.

"We don't call people we divorce mistakes now," Susie says.

"My mum does," I say.

"Remember when our religion teacher said, 'People are too quick to divorce nowadays,' and you said, 'I think they're too slow,' and you got a detention for it?" Susie says and I guffaw.

"Ah, there she is," Ed says, as the door slaps open and his girlfriend, Hester, appears, her nose wrinkling in distaste at the slight stench of "armpit."

My heart sinks a notch, but I ignore that it has done this and paste on a strong, welcoming smile.

To be fair, The Gladdy does have a bit of an *aroma* sometimes, what with the sticky floor, but that's part of its charm. It's a dartboard-and-devoted-regulars pub.

I love it, year-round, with its scrappy concrete beer garden with flower planters on the fire escape. I think they are supposed to simulate "verdant urban oasis" in a yard full of lager and smokers. But it's at its best in autumn and winter. Frosted-leaf mulch and dark skies with bright stars on the other side of the steamed-up panes. Serious *hygge* to be had, on this side of the window.

Well, mostly.

Hester moved to Nottingham for Ed, a fact she likes to re-litigate about once a month.

She looks like a colorized picture has walked into a black and white, kitchen sink realism film: skin the color of ripe peaches and shimmering champagne-blond hair. She's like a human Bellini.

Her balled fists are thrust in her coat pockets, a Barbour with a fawn cord collar, as if she's smashed into a saloon in a Western and going to draw two guns.

It's not that I don't *like* Hester . . .

"Are you all drunk by now, then?" she says, bullishly. She glances at me. "Eve looks drunk."

Oh, why do I bother. It's absolutely that I don't like Hester.

"AND ONCE AGAIN for the cheap seats! What do Marcus Garvey, Rudyard Kipling, Ernest Hemingway, and Alice Cooper have in common? It involves a mistake. A *mistake*. An error. OK, back soon."

"Hemingway was in a plane crash, were any of the others?" I whisper.

"Bit of a stretch to call a plane crash 'a mistake' though?" Ed whispers back and I shrug, nodding in concession.

"And Rudyard Kipling's a bit too yesteryear for planes, isn't he?" Justin says. "Not exactly doing his Instagram Story with a Prosecco claw holding a flute aloft in the airport bar."

He mimes trying to photograph his pint glass, and Susie snorts.

"They were wrongly given awards that had to be taken back," Hester says, dragging her coat off her shoulders. "Where's the pen?"

Justin makes a skeptical face and Ed tries to look persuadably neutral as he hands it over. His sense of humor doesn't evaporate, exactly, around Hester, but he goes more *no absolutely of course I didn't mean that* formal.

Hester's late joining tonight as she's been out with friends at a tapas restaurant, and understandably, given the number of babies that the rest of the circle have between them, they wind things up by nine p.m. Hester only joins us at The Gladdy quiz intermittently, anyway. "Sometimes it gets wearying, with all your in-jokes," she says. Even though she's known us all for so long as Ed's girlfriend, I am not sure how there's an "in" she's outside of.

"Are you sure?" Susie says.

"Yes, I'm sure," Hester says. Qualifying: ". . . Well, have you got anything better?"

"Sure, sure—or four-Proseccos-deep-and-we-haven't-got-anything-better-yet, sure?" Susie persists, smiling in a "Wicked Queen with a red apple" sort of way.

She dares with Hester in ways I absolutely do not dare. Susie dares with most people. Most people don't dare back.

Susie has long, thick blond-brown hair she wears in a horse-mane-length ponytail, or loose and bunched up into a scarf like she's Streisand in a seventies film. She has a full mouth with an emphatic pout to her top lip, which looks as if it's being pulled upward by her tilted nose, which I think is a thing called "re-troussé."

"What award did Marcus Garvey get?" Justin says.

"Rear of the Year?" I say, and Ed hoots. Hester's fuming, I know.

"OK, ignore me then!" Hester says. "Pardon me for trying to participate, guys."

"No, no! It's good! I think you're right," Ed says, hastily. "None of us have anything better. Write it down."

I always respect Ed for leaping chivalrously to Hester's defense, while wishing it was for someone who better deserved it.

Hester scribbles while Justin, Susie, and I try not to meet each other's eyes.

"More drinks I think, what's everyone having?" Justin says and gets up to go to the bar.

I go to the loo and, after I flush, I see I have a text from Susie.

11

(Not a WhatsApp, because it would risk appearing in full on a lock screen. Canny.)

When I open it, I see it's been sent to myself and Justin. I know how they're triangulating the signal, next door—Justin nonchalantly studying his handset while waiting to be served, Susie slightly angled away from the couple, feigning picking up her messages.

Susie: *WHY IS SHE SUCH A BOSSY ARSEHOLE THOUGH*

Justin: *She can get away with anything due to the fabulous breasts, darling*

Susie: *I have great tits and you don't see it affecting my personality. That answer is SO OBVIOUSLY WRONG. And why is Ed such a wimp about it. Oh yes write that bollocks down, my precious little poison dumpling. ARGH*

Justin: *Again, boobs*

Eve: *The poisoned dumplings*

Susie: *I swear she knows it's the wrong answer and is doing it to fuck with us*

I lean against the pleasantly chilly wall in the loo and type, grinning.

Having been in stone-cold love with Hester's other half for the best part of two decades means I never know how much of my dislike is plain old envy. Susie and Justin continually—and inadvertently, because they absolutely don't know—reassure me I'd have disliked her anyway. I often play Nice Cop in regards to Hester, to further throw everyone off the scent.

Eve: You wait, she'll be right and that'll show us

Susie: She's not right, she doesn't even know who Marcus Garvey was, you could see that when Justin challenged her

Justin: She probably thinks he won Best Video 2007 at the Grammys

Susie: Lol. And I'd just point out that Eve's suggestion got shot down and she didn't get the hump

Eve: Does this say anything bad about my breasts

Susie: Only that they're not a carbon offsetting scheme for being a horror

Justin: Sigh. Let us get drunk.

2

Justin and Susie are both personality types who, by and large, don't do guilt. It would slow them down considerably. I drink guilt like a smoothie for breakfast, and much as I revel in our regular secret back channel comms about Hester, I know I shouldn't.

As I once reasoned to a colleague, however: some people are intolerable, and life requires you to tolerate them, and there's only two ways of releasing the pressure. One, letting loose at the individual winding you up, or two, bitching mercilessly behind their back.

Option two might not be assertive or noble but it has a lot less impact on the social contract.

None of us have ever really doubted that pushing back on Hester would badly damage our friendship with Ed. You don't get a veto on your friends' and relatives' partners. Don't I know it. Could've avoided my mum's second husband disaster if I did.

When I return to the table, I can sense, at the pace we're drinking, we're beginning a messy descent from general knowledge acuity. Leonard has wisely curled up and gone to sleep. There's only Friday at work to struggle through tomorrow.

"You can tell you're on half term," Susie says to Ed. "Hey. Eve. Did you mention the other day that Mark has had a kid?"

"Oh yes," I say, taking a hard swallow of my fresh Estrella. *Ah, lovely numbing beer.* "He posted the photos last week. Ezra. Cool name."

Mark is my ex and my only serious boyfriend. He went off to be successful in journalism in London when we were twenty-nine and I didn't move with him, we long-distanced. Pretty soon he decided my reluctance to relocate meant I wasn't sufficiently committed—he was right—and finished it. He now works for *Time Out* in San Francisco, is married, an American citizen, and a father. Meanwhile, I got a cat.

Regrets, I might have a few. My gut said we were never quite right, but a nagging voice in my head says that it was as right as I'm going to get, and I was an idiot. Coincidentally my mum says that too.

"Weird to think he used to be in here with us so often, and now he's over there, forever. You're not bothered?" Susie says.

"Uhm, no. It feels very distant to me, you know? In every sense."

"How did you find out?"

"He popped up following me on Instagram a few months ago and I followed him back."

"Aha. He's not entirely over you, then," Ed says. "He wants you to see he's moved on, and check what you're doing. Which is a sure sign of his not having fully moved on."

"Hah. I doubt it. The fashionable neighborhood of Lower

15

Haight, five thousand miles away, is the very definition of moving on."

(Yes, of course I know these things from 1:30 a.m. bleary tap-tap-scroll research.)

"I'm sure of it. Moving on has to happen here and here," Ed says, pointing at head and chest. He looks at me levelly and I blink at him and a tiny, near-imperceptible moment passes between us, and I mentally put it in one of my specimen jars.

". . . I bet he browses photos of you and Roger and thinks, hell, I miss that walking essay crisis with the Cleopatra eyes."

"Crisis!" But I glow, a bit.

"Hey—that's good. 'Walking essay crisis with the Cleopatra eyes,' that's like a Lloyd Cole lyric or something."

"It's funny we use social media to spy on each other really, given everyone's telling some degree of lie on there," Justin says. "There was a photo of a hotel on Trivago doing the rounds because they'd cropped out the nuclear power station behind it. But don't we *all*, in a sense, crop out our nuclear power stations?"

I laugh.

"Yeah, everyone presents their life like it's a holiday destination," I say. "I mean, where Mark's living *is* a holiday destination."

"I always think when an ex is super happy with someone else they should be thanking you for ending things," Susie says. "Clearly you were right to split up. Why is it all 'yeah suck it, in your face, I'm thriving!' No shit, John, that is why I suggested we were both better off apart while you screamed at me that it was the end of your world. Perhaps in fact an apology is in order. Why do they think they've proved their point, not yours?"

I laugh, partly at how quintessential Susie Hart this is.

"Technically Mark dumped me, so he only has himself to congratulate," I say.

"Yes, but only because you chose to stay here."

"Who would leave all this?" I say, toasting the room, and then Leonard. And we laugh, but I know, as we hit our mid-thirties, it's feeling just a trifle hollow.

We can feel ourselves, if not having already made irreversible mistakes, right on the verge of making them. Hester recently observed that we are mutually "idling in neutral gear." And "having each other stops all of you lot looking for more. Co-dependency. You are each other's other halves, so you don't bother with relationships as well."

Apart from Ed and herself, of course. God, she's a joy.

The thing with Hester is, there's a big whistling gap where her niceness is meant to be, but she's absolutely everything else. Good-looking, energetic, high-earning, organized, confident, effortful, sociable, homemaking, birthday-remembering, smart. So I can see how it happened. You'd need to be paying attention.

And Ed's very loyal. Sometimes naturally loyal people fail to spot when they shouldn't be loyal.

"Speaking of disappearing acts. Why are we missing Hester?" Ed says, at her empty seat, and Justin mumbles, "We're not," just quietly enough that Susie and I hear but Ed doesn't.

Conversation is interrupted by a shrieking metallic noise, feedback from misfiring audio equipment, which makes everyone's shoulders involuntarily hunch, and our mouths twist.

"Whoops! Let me fiddle with this. There we are. Hello! Before the quiz starts again, this young lady wants to use my kit for a moment. As it were, haha! Therefore I am handing over . . . to Esther? *Hester*, sorry."

Our heads snap around and we frown in confusion to see Hester standing on the other side of the bar, wielding the microphone with a look of beatific anticipation, as if she's about to belt out a karaoke "Total Eclipse of the Heart" or announce Sweden's scores on Eurovision, as soon as the producer in her earpiece says, "Go."

"Hi everyone," she says, as the saloon bar falls silent. "I'd been wondering for a while about when best to do this, and I had a divine fit of inspiration. It's his favorite place, there's a mike." She waggles it at her mouth like a lollipop she's about to lick and I sense a few males in the room paying keen attention. Hester's presence often has that effect. It's like when you're interested in a lot on eBay and it tells you that Four Other People Are Watching This.

"So . . . that man over there . . ."—she gestures at Ed, who's looking embarrassed, vaguely gratified, but mostly perturbed—"is the love of my life."

She pauses for the *awwwww* to ripple around the room and closes her eyes for a second and nods. My stomach flexes.

"I know, right. Even in that shirt!" Laughter. Hester's giving it the full Gwyneth with her Oscar, in terms of regally commanding the room.

"Yep. We've been together for . . ." She pretends to remember, counting it off on her fingers. ". . . sixteen years! We are right about to age out of the 'youth' demographic, my dear. Thirty-four is the cut-off. I know this because I work in advertising."

Another laugh. *You work for a marketing agency. I've heard you tartly correct people calling it advertising.*

"The autumn I met Ed, we'd only been going out a few months . . . he did something amazing."

God, I am way too British not to find this excruciating. I can't imagine Ed feels any different.

". . . My sister was going through a serious illness and I wasn't sure she'd pull through, for a while. Ed and I were very new. Most guys would've run a mile from the commitment I needed. Not Ed." She looks at him, eyes shining, and the room holds its breath. "He came and stayed with my family that Christmas, he cooked the lunch for us, he took care of my parents, and promised me he'd always be there . . ."

Oh *did* he now. Well, it's possible he didn't, Hester's a great self-mythologizer.

". . . And I knew right then I had found someone very, very special."

The room's part-liquid.

"Now we're thirty-four—what I'm wondering—Ed Cooper . . . after sixteen amazing years, of highs and lows, laughter and tears . . . is—will you marry me?"

A pause, and a roar of male expectation goes up from the steamily packed pub.

Susie, Justin, and I look at Ed in shock, and he momentarily returns it, and gazes at us, as if for our cue or permission. I literally see the thought pass across his face that he's going to get into horrendous trouble if he spends more than a single second weighing this offer up.

"Yes!" Ed says. Then louder: "Yes, I will marry you!"

He stands up and belts over to the bar and leans over, and he and Hester have a quick kiss while the room cheers and claps.

Susie, Justin, and I all realize we should be doing the same, as we look around us, and join in, in mechanical fashion.

"What are you like . . . ? What on earth?" I can hear Ed saying to Hester as she does a "oh you know me, what can I say" delighted both-palms-up gesture, and Justin, Susie, and I drink our drinks and say nothing in the din.

Ed and Hester continue whispering and Ed is clearly expressing his ongoing amazement at Hester's romantic audacity. I tear myself away from the sight and look once more at my friends.

"I didn't see that coming!" Justin says, with a pointedly upbeat, even tone. "At The Gladdy quiz, no less. Keep your gondolas in Venice or your sunsets in Marrakech, this is the way to do it. I will pencil mine in for when we're next getting doners in Panko's Fish Bar. What do you say, Leonard, fancy the job as ring bearer?" Leonard wakes up and stares at his owner and goes straight back to sleep, face down on tufted front paws. I think: *Yep, hard same, Leonard.*

Susie and I make polite murmurs of agreement and it's fair to say, for once, we're both speechless.

Ed and Hester are back at the table and we make nonspecific but emphatic noises of "Wow!" and "Congrats!" and "Oh my God!"

At times like this—OK, there haven't been many times like this, but at times in general when we're meant to show genuine and natural enthusiasm for Ed's relationship—I marvel that someone as perceptive as Ed has tuned out the fact that we obviously aren't that keen. Or maybe he knows full well, and sets it to one side.

Whenever the issue of their marrying arose, he used the fact they bought a "fixer-upper" of a house as a distraction. "We've got better ways to spend twenty grand than that, thanks to Crapston Villas." I hoped against hope his reluctance was about more than the cost.

"Well then! Here we are!"

Hester plonks celebratory Cava down on top of the quiz sheet, Ed juggling five flute glasses, as we croon fake awe at recent events. He's crimson-tinged with shock and glee and booze. Hester unpeels the foil and wrestles the cork out of the bottle and, as it snaps out with a *phut*, the fizz bubbles over, streams down the sides, and splatters our quiz sheet below.

"Whoops!" I move to rescue it, but Hester picks up the bottle and wipes the base with the sheet of paper, the spreading ink turning the writing into indecipherable Rorschach blots. Oh. I pick it up and it's as limp as a tissue.

"I'll put it over here to dry," I say, draping it over the back of the seat.

"You'll need translators from the British Library to decipher it," Justin says, in that quick, light way that gets him away with murder.

I can't help but glance at Susie, and she gives me a quick hard look of understanding and looks away.

We sip our fizz and clink glasses and say "Happy engagement!" as heartily as we can, and Hester says, "It wasn't planned, you know?! I had one of my moments of inspiration. You know my thing is to follow them."

I do know. I remember a story about Hester convincing her in-laws to skinny-dip with her on a family holiday to the Cornish coast that lives on in my nightmares. ("Never trust the physically uninhibited"—only solid piece of advice my dad gave me.)

"Next up, you've got to buy a ring," Justin says. "You should spend a month's wages, isn't that right?"

Ed grimaces. "Luckily my monthly wages are two hundred quid and a bag of scratchings."

"Hah, oh Edward. Best get saving! The one I like is Cartier!" Hester says.

Unplanned, was it.

"Jesus wept, how much are they?!" Ed fires up his phone and Googles. When he finds the relevant page, he mimes mopping his brow with his scarf. "H, the website doesn't even have prices. I have to"—he makes a James Bond face—"*Contact a Cartier Ambassador to Request the Price.*"

Hester's gurgling with delight and I know Ed's in the clear to joke as much as he wants for the rest of the evening. If not the rest of his life.

"If they won't even admit the price upfront then surely it's a real 'going in hard with no lube' situation?" Justin says. (I told you about Justin and good taste.) "Oof."

"Yeah, they'll start well north of five grand," Susie says, someone who knows about posh things more than the rest of us. "Get that kidney ready for the black market, Eduardo!"

Ed mimes queasiness and Hester smooths her hair and lowers her eyes in a mock "Princess Diana" gesture. I feel queasy and it's not even my savings. "I was thinking a spring wedding," Hester says. "I hate long engagements, they're so pointless. They're for people who want time to change their mind, hahaha."

"Or to save up," I say, in a tight voice, my feelings about this finally breaking the surface.

"Eve." Hester turns to me. "Susie." She then turns to Susie. Hester will make a stunning bride. Springtime. It'll be all snowdrop flower crown, flowing backless satin like some medieval princess, tea lights in storm lanterns. "I have something to ask you both. By the time we tie the knot, my best friend back home will be about six months gone and, if her previous pregnancy is anything to go by, she'll look like an egg."

Wow.

". . . And my sister says it's a disgrace and embarrassment for anyone her age who's still single to be a bridesmaid."

A stagey pause, while I think I'm pretty sure her sister's only two years older than us. "I was wondering. Would you two be my bridesmaids?"

A stunned beat before Susie bellows, *"Are you kidding oh my God of course we'd love to!"* and I echo her with as much force as I can muster.

We smash glasses together again and Ed says, "Wow, H, that is the loveliest thing. Two of my best mates, bridesmaids! That's made my day."

I've never seen Ed so uxorious. I admit I've been looking for micro-tells of his being pissed off at this ambush, but I can't find any.

"It struck me as a really nice thing for you two to do, to make you feel part of it," Hester says to me and Susie, as if we're the ones on a school trip by grace of a special hardship fund.

I beam, with a fake banana-size grin. I am so glad to be drunk right now. Hats off, Hester, you've done well.

"And it goes without saying—this is my best man!" Ed says, and he and Justin hug. "The gang's all here."

Through the blurry talk of which venues have enough

outdoor space to host the nuptials, I think about the fact I'll have to go to dress fittings with Hester, with her bossing me in and out of boiled-sweet-colored gowns, free to pass comment on my appearance. I'm known for living in black, wearing my clompy boots, and, as Ed says, sticking to my ageing Goth makeup.

Instead of hiding at the back of this wedding, with a gin miniature, a Valium, and my crushed hopes in my black silk clutch, I will be front and center and required to grin my way through the official photos.

My Best Friend's Wedding might've been a funny film but reliving its plot doesn't feel funny in the slightest.

". . . Question twelve. We asked you what Marcus Garvey, Rudyard Kipling, Ernest Hemingway, and Alice Cooper have in common? It involved a mistake. The answer is: they all read their own obituaries, which had been mistakenly published before they were dead."

"Ah, that was the connection!" I say, but no one is listening. The men in the packable anoraks win.

3

I'm that level of boozed where I'm hovering slightly outside myself, listening to the sound of my feet stamping heavily on the ice-sparkled concrete as if they're someone else's.

The road's asphalt looks so magical when it's white-speckled and has that translucent sheen, like a mirror ball, or mother of pearl. And yet it's so treacherous. Is the pavement a metaphor for marrying Hester? Or am I just drunk?

Everyone in the group is taxiing distance from The Gladstone, Susie in one suburb, Ed and Hester in another, Justin in town. I live in the same postcode as the pub, Carrington, a tiny suburb with winding streets, and red-brick, quirky Victorian houses, some with turrets that look like Correctional Institutions for Wayward Boys, or as if they're made from gingerbread by fairytale witches. Suitably, Fairytale Witch is my look. There are lots of overhanging, mature trees that scatter blossom like confetti once a year.

And cats. It's lousy with cats. Roger is engaged in a bitter ongoing territory battle with the local feral unneutered tom, Dirk. (No, I don't know how a stray has a name either—

notoriety on the local community message boards, I assume. Dirk is a rugged individualist, a white-whiskered supervillain, and no one's going to take his liberty, or his bollocks.)

My phone pings with a text message from Susie. It's not been sent to myself and Justin, only to me, which is intriguing. This suggests deep-dive Girl Talk, and there's very little Girl Talk between us that Justin isn't privy to. He asked Susie to copy him out of her graphic account of her Mirena coil removal, but that's about it.

MAN DOWN. I have opinions on tonight's atrocity, much to discuss. Speak soon. xx

Maybe it's because we're the cursed bridesmaids. I am not looking forward to remembering that dismaying fact when I wake up with a shitty head. Is it possible to decline being a bridesmaid to one of your best friend's brides, without mortally offending them? Could I fake an injury? There's no way Hester would let someone with an orthopedic support boot hop down the aisle, spoiling the vision. Even as I think it, I remember that I'd have been to the fittings by then and be wasting their money. Sigh.

As Justin says, a conscience weighs too much.

I'd reply to Susie, but her message sounds very much like she's about to go to sleep, so I'll leave it for when we're nursing our sore heads tomorrow.

Even though I know this isn't observing safety protocols when female and out late inebriated, in the dark, I turn my music on to the last thing I played. Kylie's "Can't Get You Out of My Head" pounds in my ears, which feels like Kylie knows what's what.

La la la, lah la la lah

It interacts with the alcohol in my bloodstream and makes me feel defiant, and I have an idea.

La la la, lah la la lah

A probably really bad, and yet suddenly irresistible, idea.

I pull my phone out and scroll to WhatsApp, until I find his name, Zack. Susie calls him Baby Yoda. (Susie whispers *"The Child! He should be with his own people"* whenever he and I finish chatting, and I shush her.)

Zack works in a neighborhood bar nearby, the kind of place no bigger than a galley kitchen, festooned with fairy lights and ironic art. Pretend Warhols of Ena Sharples in her hairnet, surrounded by illuminated plastic chili peppers, that kind of thing. Flamingo umbrella-holder stands. The place that you always end up in for the very ill-advised fifth and sixth drinks on an unplanned session.

Zack's got a man bun, a taut stomach, and the level of circulation where he's in a T-shirt with rolled-up sleeves, year-round.

Whenever we are in, he's always pulling up a chair, twirling it back to front, and "explaining" our cocktails to us. Insisting I sip a bit while he talks me through the vital acidic effect of the lemon zest on my olfactory experience. I never have the heart to say, *Zack, I've had a liter of cheap gin already, it could be wheel cleaner to be honest.*

After he finally left us to drink them last time, Susie whispered: "Please have sex with him before I have to get another

Ted Talk on the invention of the Tom Collins, I can't fucking take it."

I laughed this off—me? Him?—but as we left last time, Zack said, with the insouciance of being male and twenty-four and having a taut stomach: "Hey, Eva. Give me your number and I'll let you know when we have that hazelnut liqueur in I was telling you about."

I'm not a hook-ups person, usually. Well, ever, apart from a Canadian guy who looked like a Mountie who I met on a training weekend when I was twenty-three. Straight afterward he made a joke about zipping me into a North Face bag on his floor, which I started to realize wasn't a joke, and left. It was as if God knew I was acting out of character and decided to prank me.

I know this is weak, but, I'm thirty-four, and on the horizon I can see "not being blatantly hit on by twenty-something barmen anymore." Like a sale on Boxing Day, I am suddenly interested in grabbing something that doesn't suit me and I will soon regret, just because I can.

I need validation tonight. I want to do something that says I'm still desirable. That I'm out here on the cool-single-with-options frontier, getting up to spontaneous things. Not still hoping.

A voice says, *You are doing this to tell Ed, to make him jealous. You are doing something just so you can tell him about it and make him feel something back*, and I silence the voice. I don't want to be that person and it can't be allowed to be true, and if I don't think it, it isn't true.

Hi! I don't know if you're working tonight but wondered if you fancied a drink after your shift finishes? E x

God almighty, Eve, you're swimming in drink already and it's midnight. Go home and have a strong coffee and two Advil and realize you're an idiot.

The reply is near immediate, so my fate is written.

Yeah! I am just finishing up actually. Want to hang here? Master mixologist at your service ☺

I'm right outside my house and it'd be a lot easier to hang *here*, but cynically, I'd quite like this to take place off premises, so I don't have to wake up with Zack and kick him out tomorrow. Not a one-night stand, a half-night stand. Eesh. The feminist in me always reacts badly to my mum saying, "Honestly, women are the new men!" but I'm slightly ashamed of my brute calculations.

Zack is impressed by himself, and I'm going to pretend to be impressed by him too for as long as I need to get what I want from the deal. Then we'll be done. That's manipulation, surely. The fact I know he's not remotely interesting to me for anything more is exactly why he's so right for this. I mean, maybe he feels exactly the same way. But it's not like I'm going to check.

I hear Susie in my head: *Eve, offering a man a no-strings hook-up is not exploiting him, fuck's sake. This is your whole problem, imagining you're emotionally responsible for some random dude who's into bouldering and brewing his own kombucha and posts stuff on Facebook like "The new Tame Impala is a vibe."*

I can imagine replying, *It's ambitious to call that my whole problem,* and Susie snorting, *Yes, true.*

On my way! ☺

4

I run into my house for a minute, to brush my teeth, change my pants and touch up my make-up. I thought this was a convenient little confidence booster, until I saw my lopsidedly hammered, sweaty face by actual lighting. In the background, the dressing gown I should be climbing into right now is slung over the shower rail. My silent house is full of reproach.

I've worn my midnight-black hair longish and straight my whole life, but assessing myself pitilessly, pushing it back behind my ears, I fret it's getting too harsh. That I'm drain-circling "crone." As I paint on more liquid eyeliner, I think, is this why you see some old ladies who are gaudy parodies of their younger selves? They refused to disembark from their style, thirty years prior. Failed to heed the signs it was time to lay down the crow-colored dye and poppy-pink blush.

Stripy Roger wakes up on the sofa and shouts "MWOWH?" as I leave again. Which is a legitimate question.

"Enough judging from you, Piecrust," I say, using his birth name as a good luck charm. The old lady who gave him to the rescue charity would only let me adopt him if I promised to keep his name as Piecrust.

"You don't actually have to do it, though," Susie said, as she drove me home with a squirming cat basket. "How's she going to know different, when she sees his name in *The Times* marriage announcements?"

"She had the feel of a mystical hag who could curse me if I don't."

"Well, she's cursed him alright. Piecrust, fuck's sake."

I compromised with Roger Piecrust Harris, which sounds like a comedian who was exposed as a pedophile in the 1970s.

I'm carried on fumes to the door of the bar, but seeing it mostly in darkness, and realizing my friends are asleep—or celebrating engagements, but either way, in bed—by now, brings my folly home to me. My appetite for sexual buccaneering has disappeared. I queued for the ride and now I don't want to get on.

I tentatively rap my knuckles on the heavy wooden door and there's the noise of keys being jangled on the other side. We'll be locked in together. It occurs to me this date is not hugely safe either. I don't know Zack, it's the middle of the night, and no one knows I'm here. Given none of my friends are likely to see any message until tomorrow, it'd help with the investigation more than save me.

"Hi there, Eva," Zack says. "Welcome to my humble hacienda!"

Oh God.

"Hello," I say. "Woah, it looks different in the dark." Creepy. What I mean is creepy. And it's silent.

I step inside and try not to flinch when he locks the door again behind me, though I'm vaguely reassured when he leaves the bunch of keys hanging in the lock.

"Yeah, I'll chuck a few more lamps on, hang on. You don't want to make the place look too open in case you get the drunks banging on your door or the motherfucking popo doing you for an illegal lock-in."

I laugh, without being sure that "motherfucking popo" was meant to be funny.

He throws the place into better light and I relax slightly.

"Sit up there and I'll mix you one of your lavender martinis," Zack gestures at the bar stools, opposite the backlit bar, with its Banksy print of two policemen kissing. "If that's what you're feeling?" he says, and I nod vigorously. I'm not feeling it, I've recovered the few degrees I needed to realize: (1) the last fucking thing I need is a martini, and (2) the last thing I want is fucking, but it's too late now.

It isn't too late as such, I know that. I am clothed, enfranchised, and technically able to leave.

I hate the fact I feel obliged to do anything because I was stupid enough to initiate this. Thinking I'm now committed to some sort of sexual encounter is everything I would hotly and passionately argue against, if it was a hypothetical, and especially if it was someone else. It's one of those unpleasant moments in life you confront the fact your beliefs in theory and behavior in practice can be two entirely different things.

Now Zack is theatrically slapping fresh lavender heads between his hands, clapping to "release their perfume," and threading them onto cocktail sticks with lemon slices, and the complexity of the drink alone feels a debt to pay. I thought once he wasn't working, he'd flip the lids on beers.

"Want music on?" he says.

"Sure."

"Name an album."

"What, any album?"

"Yeah."

"Uhm . . ." Ugh, a coolness test, and I don't want the cringe of anything overtly seductive. "Fleetwood Mac? *Tusk*?"

Zack leans toward the door, talks as if to a pot plant on the bar.

"Alexa, play Fleetwood Mac, *Tusk*."

"Is this your place?" I say, as it starts, struck by Zack's freedom to entertain on the premises.

"No, the owner Ted is in Lanzarote. He lives there part of the year. The cold part. I run it for him when he's away. He's like an uncle to me."

Zack spins a coaster into position in front of me and sets the martini on top of it.

"Thank you!"

"What's your deal, then, Little Miss *Nightmare Before Christmas*?"

"Nightmare before . . . ?"

"The Tim Burton film, like a cartoon? You look like the girl in it. Big eyes and the white raggedy dress. Kinda spooky."

"She's called the Corpse Bride, isn't she?" I say, with a smile as I sip.

"Her name's Sally."

"Ah. My deal . . . ?"

"Got a husband, boyfriend? Girlfriend? Significant Other plus Side Dude?"

"I'd not be here if I did have one?" I blurt, baffled. I then realize how explicit this is in regards to my purpose, even though it's not really my fault he asked such a direct question. I waffle: ". . . In closed-up bars in the middle of the night. Drinking drinks with herbs in them."

"Hey, I'm not here to judge," Zack says, hands up.

He's managed to make me feel like Shirley Valentine cracking on to a Greek waiter, needing a holiday from herself. I feel patronized. Would he have asked a woman of his own age these things, I wonder? Maybe, yes—I have a suspicion that Zack has the gift of annoying people when he isn't intending to annoy.

"Have you got a girlfriend?" I say, hoping my intonation makes it clear I don't care. Although . . . if he says he has, that's an easy out for me. Zack tilts his head in a contemplative way.

"Nah. It's complicated, but nah."

It's complicated means "I'm messing someone around and I think the fact makes me interesting," Susie always says.

"Aren't you drinking?" I ask, as I realize Zack is now rinsing the cocktail shaker under a tap rather than sorting anything else.

"I've got an Asahi on the go." He points to a beer bottle on the counter.

He dries his hands, walks around, and takes up position on the stool next to me.

"Enjoying it?" he says of the martini.

"Yeah, incredible," I say, politely, having some more, really wanting to take the fruit salad out of it so it's more accessible, but not wanting to hurt his feelings.

We chat about music festivals, and hipster restaurants, and some local hoodlums who've taken to drag racing on the main road.

I notice, once again, that company that's not the right fit for you is so much lonelier than being happily alone. I've had no existential moments while sharing pizzas with Stripy Roger.

And Zack's curiosity about me, it seems, began and ended with my partnership arrangements.

When I open my mouth to say something about myself, after a long monologue about the benefits of his possibly moving to Australia—delivered in a slightly weary, rehearsed way as if he's tired of having to explain his life choices to eager fangirls—Zack interrupts. ". . . I'm staying in the flat upstairs. I'm kinda hoping you enjoy that drink so much that you drink it quickly, so you can come up there with me."

He's trying to give me come-hither, hooded eyes.

Clunk. There it is. I knock most of the rest of the martini down in one, and wonder if I'm realistically going to make it to work at all tomorrow.

What can I say to Zack? "Having become two degrees soberer and twenty minutes more aware of your personality, I'm going home"? Yes, I could and should say at least some of this, but I won't. I ponder how many mistakes in life are born of a simple fear of being rude.

"Show me the way," I say.

I feel about as enthused saying that as *Let's Get Brexit Done.*

Zack slides down off his stool with a smirk and gestures for me to follow him up a narrow flight of poky, creaking stairs, through a door behind the bar. The décor budget clearly went on the kitsch joint below: the sitting room he leads me up into smells of microwaved food and sadness, and there are sports socks and pants on a plastic drying rack. A coffee table holds a clutter of vaping equipment, remote controls, and empty Nando's PERi-PERi sauce bottles with candles wedged in them, a version of trattorias and their repurposed wicker wine holders.

Zack points at a puffy pale gray pleather recliner in front of the television.

"Can we do it on there?" he whispers. "I feel weird in Ted's bed. His wife died a year ago."

"Why are we whispering?" I say. "Is she listening?"

"Possibly," Zack says.

". . . What?"

"She *died* in that bed," Zack says, pointing at a room next door, eyes widening. "Freaks me out. I feel Linda's ghost hovering over me. She died of a heart attack and I get this pain in my chest, like she's sitting on me. Trying to give me one."

"A heart attack, I hope you mean?"

"Yeah."

This is so grimly tragicomic and he's so earnest that I have to make an effort not to laugh.

"You know it could be psychosomatic?" I say. "You think of her, and then you feel her sitting on you?"

"I didn't fancy her! She was, like, sixty! Ugh."

"No . . . I . . . OK."

I'm going to copulate with someone who sincerely believes in ghosts, and doesn't understand the word "psychosomatic."

"Other times, I've heard her walking about in here," Zack continues, on a Lore of Linda roll now, hands on hips, casting a suspicious look around the room.

"How do you know it's her?" I say. "This is quite an old building. Could be any number of dead people?"

"Because she had these shoes that made her sound like a clippy-cloppy goat. Heels. Brrr." Zack shudders.

"I don't believe in ghosts," I say.

"I do. It's only science," Zack says.

"I'm fairly sure, whatever else it is, it's not science."

"It is. Principle of physics, a form of energy cannot be destroyed, it can only change form, right?"

". . . Riiight?"

"So when someone dies, where does their energy go? Into another form. Ghosts."

"Well, no, if you're buried and decompose into the earth you're worm food. That's the transfer of energy. Into the soil."

"Worm food energy."

"Yes."

"What's cremation then? What does that energy become?"

"Fire?"

"Woah . . ." Zack pauses. "I still think there's spirit energy. That has to go somewhere."

This is pretty bad foreplay, it has to be said, and my worm energy is seriously on the wane.

I look at the recliner and wonder if Zack always brings women he meets in the bar up here to this seat. I'm grateful for the fact he starts some enthusiastic kissing so I can stop thinking.

I push him down on the cushions and straddle him, a knee on either side of his legs, while he does some unpromisingly aggressive tit-squeezing, as if he's assessing the freshness of fruit at a market. As if he's Jamie Oliver with a couple of pomegranates at a souk in Fez. He'll give them a sniff in a second.

I had forgotten how stressful sex with a new person is, the pressure to perform being a really sexy person who is naturally good at sex, a part-time erotica master. The stupid hair-tossing stuff and the arching of your back. As if there's a panel watching you beyond a one-way mirror, appraising your performance and holding up paddle boards with their scores. It's kind of inimical to enjoying yourself.

Sex is inherently ridiculous. You get better at it once you accept that. Really don't want to be thinking of Ed quotes right now. What if . . . I imagine Zack is . . .

"Oh shit. I should've said," Zack says, looking suddenly worried, catching his breath, his large, hot hands clamped on my seventy-denier-clad thighs.

"It's OK," I say, smiling, moving my hair over one shoulder in a hopefully alluring way. "I have condoms."

Hah, do you seriously think I'd leave that to you, and/or chance.

"No," he says. "I don't do hair."

"You don't do what?" I'd thought that move looked pretty good.

"Hair," he says, and nods toward my black Lycra crotch, the hosiery stretched as taut as a trampoline.

". . . Hair down there?"

"Yeah," Zack says. "Do you wax?"

. . . What? On *earth*? A pre-nup for pubes. Oh God, I feel ancient. I suddenly feel like there isn't ten years between us, but generations. I have time traveled. I'm trying to shag my grandson.

"No?"

"Oh. Sorry, I shoulda said!" Zack says, conversationally, like he's explaining he meant to give me the shortcut directions to the supermarket. "I usually do say up front, on Tinder, but you know. You got in touch tonight. And I was like, yeah, she's hot."

Zack pauses for my reaction. I gather I'm meant to think this is a major silver lining to this cloud. The silver lining, Zack, is how little I wanted to have sex with you anyway.

"Only now I've thought, I didn't say about the hair thing. Yeah sorry, like, no hair for me. I can't do it."

"What, like . . . physically couldn't get it up?"

"Uh. Yeah? I guess. My friend who is into the . . . you know . . . Stepmom Porn likes it. But not for me."

"*Stepmom Porn?!*"

Zack's eyes widen, conveying: wow, you really are antiquated, huh (and proving my point).

"*Jesus.* Stepmoms. That's one for his therapist."

Zack may not be the sharpest but he's caught the edge to my attitude easily enough. He eases me off his lap and as I stand up he says: "It's nothing against you, OK, horses for courses. You do you."

"Yeah, looks like I'll have to, huh."

This is lost on Zack, who blinks.

"But you're . . . sex is sex. Wouldn't you make do and get on with it?" I say. "Where's your Blitz spirit?"

My need to solve this riddle is fighting my need to not sound like I am desperate for him to get on with it, because I absolutely don't want anything from him but answers.

Zack shrugs.

"It is what it is. I'm grossed out by a bush. Like, some guys like blondes. Some guys like . . . guys."

"What would happen if you'd forgot to say and then saw pubes?" I say. "Would you scream, as if I had the *Ratatouille* rat in my pants?"

"To be honest, Eva, uh, I feel like you're shaming me."

"You're the one who called a screeching halt to sex based on my body, so I don't think you're one to talk about shaming."

A pause.

"Do you have hair?" I say.

Zack shakes his head, elastic band slipping from his man bun as he does, and he reties it.

"No, man, I have it all off. Clean as a whistle. Butthole too."

He looks proud, as if this is a great personal achievement. As if he could list *Whiskerless Anus* under "What makes you right for this role" on a CV.

There's not many moments in my life I've managed to assert myself. Susie still talks in awe of the time I got scolded for my cheese scones and told my domestic science teacher she was a complicit instrument of patriarchal control, like Serena Joy in *The Handmaid's Tale.*

Mrs. McNab called me a "smart arse" and I said, *Well, I am smart and I have an arse so I'll take it.* Ten days of detention, ten whole days.

I feel a similar rush of revolutionary fervor coming on at this rejection by Zack.

". . . And what's women's hair, dirty?"

"Yeah, I mean, it's hygiene, I guess. Also the look."

"How mental is it to say you don't like the way women naturally look?"

"Look, I get why you're disappointed, now you're turned on

and all," Zack says. "If you're that upset I could . . . I dunno. Play with your boobs or something."

Oh God. As the horror of this deepens so its anecdotal value sharply increases, like two different colored lines on a chart diverging.

"I'm not disappointed, I'm not turned on, and I really don't want pity boob play. I only think it's grim to want women to look pre-pubescent."

"Loads of girls my age have Hollywoods," Zack says. "It's a thing. It's different for you guys, I guess?"

Gotcha.

"Which 'guys' are those?"

Zack's eyes flick from side to side as I can see he knows he messed up, saying that, and doesn't want to irritate me further. The angry cavewoman stepmom on the premises. "People your age?"

"What age is that?"

"I don't know! Thirty? I knew you weren't my age 'cause your friend had a Credit Suisse Gold card. No need to go crazy bitch on me, OK?"

I laugh, and sigh. Bloody Susie and her affluence.

I came here tonight to proudly assert the fact I could do meaningless wild banging with a near-stranger.

In this dank flat, looking at someone who's seen too much porn, a callow lad who looks damp to the touch, I fully face into the futility. I was trying to diminish the pain of not having who I wanted, by having disappointing intercourse with someone's immature younger brother.

Oh, Eve. All this, staked on that moment in a few weeks'

time when Susie, raucous-drunk, says, *We can't go back to that bar, can we, Evelyn?* and I involuntarily lock eyes with Ed as he involuntarily locks eyes with me, and I see something like pain or conflict. As if those moments are going to add up to something.

Fact check: Ed's getting married, and you could've gone home, cried into a cushion, and allowed yourself to feel despair.

The things we do to avoid difficult things are often worse than the difficult thing.

"I'm not going crazy, I'm just going. I hope Linda sits on you. It's more contact with a woman than you deserve though," I say, with a smile.

I grab my bag, swoop up my coat, and gallop back down the stairs. *Well, Susie,* I think, as I pick my way through the uninhabited chairs and tables, *Tusk* still trickling out from hidden speakers. *You're going to love this.* I know she's going to say I've got one that looks like I'm riding Gnasher, the dog from *Dennis the Menace,* into battle.

"Eva!" Zack says, appearing in the rectangle of light in the opening of the stairway, as I turn the key and yank the bar door open. "Can you pay for your drink, please?"

I whip back around.

"You can't be serious?"

Zack looks genuinely bewildered that I'm objecting.

"Yeah. It's five pounds?" He steps forward, picks up a menu on the bar, and flaps it at me, by way of proof.

In shock, and because I've never skipped a bill in my life, I rummage in my purse for a note.

It's such a dispiriting moment of defeat to end on that as I slap it down, I say, to make it clear I'm not the one who should be embarrassed here:

"By the way, why didn't you check I was alright with bald balls?"

"What?"

"You wanted to know the deal in advance. What if I recoiled?"

"You coulda asked. I've never known a girl ask for nut fuzz though, hahaha."

"I bet you've never known a girl ask for anything in terms of personal grooming, maybe think on that."

"Shhhhh!" Zack's eyes fly wide open. He puts a finger to his lips and jabs an index finger at the ceiling above. "*Linda*," he mouths.

I strain to listen . . . I can hear a soft tapping noise.

I need a decisive exit.

"Alexa, play 'Looking for Linda' by Hue and Cry, VERY LOUD," I say, before slamming out.

5

Being in love with someone you can't have is misery.

Please note: this is not the same as "being in love with some-one who doesn't love you back" because (1) Ed does love me back, or he did, I will show receipts, and (2) while that would sting hard, I am guessing, when it's unrequited, sooner or later an emotional survival mechanism kicks in and you stop howl-ing at the moon.

Nature wants you to pull through and procreate. It dials down the heartsick hormones. When feelings are flying in both directions, you're sunk. Or, I am.

I'm not unique, but it's not something people talk about, not ending up with the one you wanted. Once you're settled down, it's unsayable. It's expressed in our music, books, and films in-stead.

What's that quote? *Ninety-nine percent of the world's lovers are not with their first choice. That's what makes the jukebox play.*

There's a nice lie that the world likes to tell us all, which is: *it's never too late.* It's too late, all the time, for loads of things. We should all be hurrying like the rabbit with the pocket watch in *Alice in Wonderland*.

I think the truth is: opportunities in life are like doors flashing open and slamming closed, for good. You won't necessarily notice when they're open or get any warning they're going to close. If you don't bolt through them when you can, then that is that.

But no one wants to hear that your chance at happiness is time-sensitive. There's very little interest in handling the truth that, sometimes, the diem is no longer the right one to be carped. There's no inspo meme value to that, nobody's going to put it in a curly font next to a soaring eagle.

The story of myself and Ed Cooper is a door opening and closing.

Susie and I were newly minted sixth formers, loafing in the common room. He and Justin wandered in during a free period, one sunny afternoon. I'd only been ever vaguely aware of them as presentable members of the male species, in our large school.

I was curled up with my Doc Martens carefully dangling off the upholstery, trying to concentrate on *Tuesdays with Morrie*. Susie was lying with her back against me, reading her horoscope out from *Heat* magazine. It was an auspicious day for Aries.

"Hi. We don't know you, but you both seem significantly less noisy than everyone else here. Mind if we sit with you?" Justin said. "I'm gay so I'm no threat. He's not gay," he gestured at Ed, "but let's face it, he's no sexual threat either."

Susie and I guffawed, and space was made. We didn't know it yet, but in a single moment, our two double acts had merged forever.

Justin and Ed were good together, Ed as straight man, but both of them very droll in that way boys are when they've spent a lot of time practicing.

Ed said, pointing at my book: "Are you enjoying that?"

"Yes," I said. "Well, it's sad, but it's interesting."

Susie rolled her eyes and said: "Eve has a morbid nature. She likes songs without choruses, all hole-dwelling, vole-like creatures, Mafia-widow fashion, wet weather, and books about people dying of rare illnesses."

"It's not depressing, it's full of uplifting wisdom about making the most of your time!" I said.

"I said I felt depressed once and you said I wasn't a deep enough person to be depressed," Susie said, and everyone howled. I said: "*Oh God, sorry.*" (This was a good explainer of why Susie and I work: pithy in our different ways, but we never took the other one's mockery seriously.)

We had a conversation about middle names and Ed's was Randall. I said: "Edward Randall Cooper. You sound like a 1930s newsreader."

I mimicked a stiff, buttoned-up posh male voice: "*Hello, we are in crisis. The king has abdicated, long live the king. I am Edward Randall Cooper. Good night, God bless you all.*"

"Didn't I say the one who looks like a cross between Little My from *The Moomins* and Winona in *Heathers* would be sassy?" Justin said to Ed, and Ed grinned at me.

I'd never heard myself *described* before. Assigned a character, as if we were in Clue. I liked it.

"What do I look like?" Susie demanded, with the nerve-free confidence of the terminally photogenic.

"Hmmm." Justin narrowed his intense, pale gray eyes. Justin himself had a buzz cut and a rascally handsome face, like a charming Victorian pickpocket. "Jane Austen's Emma meets the Laura Palmer they couldn't kill."

Susie screeched with mock outrage and joy and I swear I saw her fall in platonic love in a single second.

We spent much time laughing in the following hour, our first encounter with four personalities that tessellated perfectly as an ensemble.

"Hey, this works. Ally Sheedy," Justin said, pointing at me, "Molly Ringwald" (pointing at Susie), "Anthony Michael Hall" (pointing at Ed), "and me. Queer Judd Nelson. The Dog's Breakfast Club."

I remember tripping off to my sociology class with a foolish grin on my face, thinking that making friends in adult life was clearly a piece of cake. The thing about being young is, you don't have much else to compare anything to.

But as the months rolled by, I had an inkling we'd stumbled onto something rare, in our tight quartet. There were no rivalries, no real arguments, only magic chemistry where each personality balanced out and complemented the other. The most I'd ever hoped for at school was to be left alone, but I became vaguely aware the four of us were considered both cool and unassailably not to be messed with, now we were a team.

It helped none of us fancied each other.

Justin was not in play, and Ed—well, Ed was a mate.

I only went for wasted, cheekboney, brooding bastards. My infatuation was Jez the premier weed dealer, a bedraggled River Phoenix lookalike at a neighboring college with whom

47

I'd had my deeply unfulfilling loss of virginity with, months prior. ("River Phoenix?! *Canal* Phoenix more like," I can still hear Susie saying. "Canal Pigeon.") I was honestly still in a mild state of shock that an act that was the obsession of ninety percent of popular culture was so underwhelming.

Susie and I once discussed the Edness of Ed, musing that he was, on paper, technically wholesomely good-looking—he'd get a role in *Dawson's Creek*—and pleasingly tall, and we loved his company. So why no "grunt," as we delicately termed it?

"He's too straightforward, isn't he?" Susie said, picking the chocolate cladding off a Magnum ice cream as we sat on chaise lounges in her giant garden. It had one of those lawns like a huge pool of green with an undulating perimeter, the border full of lipstick-pink hydrangeas.

Susie had no truck with any peer group boys whatsoever, and was involved with a twenty-seven-year-old doctor at the time, an age we thought sounded impossibly mature. He let her try some morphine, which we thought was an absolute hoot. Now I look back and realize he was a borderline sex offender who should've been struck off.

"It's like there's no twist, no secret. No *edge* to Ed."

"Hmm, yeah," I said, to Susie's shadowy outline, as I tired of squinting and put on my large sunglasses.

"Plus, he says he's strawberry-blond but, in certain lights, it's very dishwater mouse." Susie wasn't at all equal opportunity, when it came to men and the physical standards they had to meet.

"He's almost ginger in some lights. I like fully red, flame hair," I said. "Young Henry the Eighth was hot, you know."

"Ugh he looked like a Christmas ham! You are so obtuse,"

Susie said, "You are guaranteed to make the oddest choices of men in the future. I bet your husband is a genius recluse who wees in Kilner jars."

We honked.

"He's like an ideal brother," I continued. "He'll make someone a great boyfriend. He's so easy-going and such a good listener. You feel like you can tell him anything."

This was also one of the ways I knew Ed wasn't a prospect—we would share all kinds of embarrassing things and laugh raucously. When I was interested in a male, I tried to be a riddle, I was tense. I didn't admit to having once done a "fizzy poo."

"But you can't imagine ever having your ankles either side of your face with him," Susie concluded, as I screamed in self-conscious horror and embarrassment. That's *Ed*. Our *friend*. He doesn't have sex, and neither did my parents. (Actually, that had turned out to be true.)

6

God laughs when we tell Him our plans, and He also has a good old chortle when He overhears us saying we know things for sure, like who we know we're never going to feel feelings for.

(Yeah, my God is a man, I feel more comfortable blaming Him then.)

The four of us got places at university—all up north apart from Susie, who had to be Susie and go to London—and we were excited and anguished at our separation, homesickness, the big wide world.

Due to quirks of the different institutions, Justin and Susie left days before Ed and I did. Those days might as well have been months of desolation and a montage of trudging with pack ponies through blizzards and deserts for how well Ed and I bore it.

"Left behind, they'll have forgotten us already!" we wailed, having killed a lot of time with coffees, and barrel-scraping action films at the multiplex, and comparing who'd had the most gnomic texts as bulletins from Justin or Susie. (I think Ed won, with Justin's report that only said: "GRAVY AS PASTA

SAUCE!") Our city was a ghost town without our counterparts; all our contemporaries had vanished to halls of residences around the country. There's no self-pity like a teenager's self-pity.

"What are you doing tomorrow?" I asked Ed, before our final day lingering in purgatory. We were eating chips from paper cones, our breath making ghosts, and I thought how grateful I'd been for Ed being around. He was dependable solidity itself.

"Oh, big game with my football team and then we're going to get drunk at The Trip."

"What?! What will I do?!" I wailed, and Ed replied: "Come! Come along. The game won't take that long."

I'd usually not want to be that superfluous at an occasion, or so openly needy, but the prospect of sitting indoors doing nothing but bickering with my mum and my younger brother, Kieran, was worse.

The game was in a park on a hill, north of the city and near where I now live. The field was on a slope, rolling down to the main road, and I languished at the upper end of it with a copy of *Viz* while they ran around.

I watched Ed with his five teammates—his good humor, his natural leadership, his powers of concentration. His muscled legs. Seeing someone you know well in a totally different context is always disorientating and vaguely impressive. You realize you have them on loan from the other lives they lead.

Every so often he'd give me a Royal Air Force–style salute and I'd wave back. Separation makes you value something more and I was acutely aware of how fond I was of Ed, and how badly I'd miss him. It had thrown the big light on, in a room inside me.

I realized, at a subconscious level, I'd complacently assumed my future was full of Eds—what if it wasn't?

Ed changed his T-shirt at the end of the match and I found myself curiously transfixed by upper-body definition I didn't know he had, and the way he yanked the fresh one over his head. Something stirred. Obviously, I must be in a heightened emotional state to be ogling Ed Cooper's milk-pale—if unexpectedly sculpted—abdomen. Susie would laugh when I told her.

We went to The Trip to Jerusalem and drank foamy sour things from casks, served in dimpled tankards, and felt brimful of cheer and anxiety and poignancy, at our imminent parting, to futures unknown. At eighteen, you've not experienced poignancy before.

Ed's mum had insisted on picking him up to check he wasn't too wasted, the night before the drive up to Newcastle. As we walked out of the pub I saw her car pulling in at the bottom of the road. We were too far away for her to see us.

"Sure you don't want a lift?" Ed said. "It's quite late to get the bus?"

"Yeah. No bother. I want the fresh air," I said. The real reason I didn't want their lift was because I knew I was going to cry and I didn't want the audience.

"Ack. This is it, then," Ed said, gazing at me in the twilight, with a sad smile.

I felt the tears rise up and threaten to close my throat, and I said in a thick voice, flapping my hands at my face, as if cooling myself in heat: "Oh God, this is so silly, we'll be home again in a few weeks!"

Our parting hurt so acutely, I realized, not because we thought the geography was insurmountable or that the Christmas break was so far away, but because we didn't know the people we were about to change into.

Maybe we wouldn't be friends anymore, or not close ones. What if everyone returned, being all "had such a great time" and behaving subtly differently, to make it clear priorities and intimacies had shifted? Acting like things were the same, but there was a new distance around each of us, like castles with moats? Name-dropping strangers with whom we'd forged mysterious, exciting, impenetrable new alliances? Nothing held the same power and mystique that the unknown did.

"Fuck, I am going to miss you so much, Evelyn Rose Harris," Ed said. His face had fallen, and his flat tone of voice was not one I'd ever heard him use before. Ed was usually Mr. Laid-back Sunshine.

Not many people knew my birth certificate name. There was a particular tenderness to him using it at this moment.

"I'm going to miss you," I said. "Don't make me cry!"

"Will you? Miss me, I mean."

"Yes, of course."

I swallowed and tried to read his intent expression.

Ed cast a glance down at his parents' car and blew air out of his cheeks. "Give Yorkshire hell, won't you. I don't know why I'm saying that, I know you'll smash it."

He smiled in a sly way, and my insides twitched. Was he . . . flirting? He looked lightly sweaty and also great under the music-video disco-orange of the streetlamp. Ed was classically handsome, really, I wasn't sure why I'd been so keen to neuter and deny that fact.

Uncharacteristically, I was completely lost for words, tucking my hair behind my ears and blushing.

"Fuck. Eve," Ed said, shaking his head. "I love you, OK. As in, I'm in love with you. I'm not sure what I expect you to do with this information. But, there it is. I feel like I can't let you go without telling you."

I was stunned.

"Say something! . . . Are you disgusted?" Ed said, looking simultaneously hunted, bashful, and yet triumphant at his own courage.

Without even thinking, by way of an answer, I stood on tiptoes and kissed him. Ed kissed me back, with the eagerness of it being something he'd been hoping and waiting to do, springing into action. He wrapped his big arms around me, and I'd never felt so perfectly where I was meant to be in the universe as with our tongues entwined.

Wait: *this* was what falling for someone, real passion, was supposed to feel like? With Weed Dealer Jez, I hadn't really fancied him organically. I fancied him on principle. I fancied his persona. I wanted him to fancy me, basically. In a split second with Ed, I understood there was an experience available that was far more instinctive, whole, and multi-sensory.

"Oh my God, I didn't think you liked me like that," Ed breathed, when we came up for air, and obviously I didn't reply, *Well, I didn't know I did until a few hours ago.*

"I didn't know you liked me like that!" I said, which got me out of the trap and had the benefit of being true.

"Oh, me and an army. Loads of us have the 'mysterious Evelyn Harris' crush and I'm no different," he said, which was mind-blowing on two levels. Everyone fancied Susie, surely? There was an Eve Harris constituency? "We don't dare try as you're so smart and aloof. The comebacks would be awful."

I laughed, in amazement at how my world had completely turned on its head in seconds.

BEEP BEEP.

We looked over and his mum was flashing the headlights on and off and trying to peer into the murk over the steering wheel.

"Write to me?" Ed said, urgently, gripping my waist. "You've got my address?"

"Yes, and you have mine. Write to me!" I said.

"OK, I will," he said, eyes shining in the dark. He kissed me again, fast and hard, and raced off to the car. I felt like my heart was going to explode with joy and my groin was going to explode with want.

Woah? What WAS that? I'd decided I was in love with one of my best friends, the night before we both moved to different cities for three years?

That evening, I laughed out loud in the dusk—the timing seemed so comical.

As opposed to what it actually was: catastrophically bad.

7

I still have the letter, the only proof—to be Ziploc-bagged as evidence, or put inside an illuminated glass box in a museum. It's on lined paper torn neatly from a pad. When I'm feeling sentimental enough about old times—or angry enough to want vindication—I open the envelope and unfold the sheets, and I'm right back in my cupboard-size room at Leeds, hands trembling. He'd sent it in the first week, no playing it cool.

There is the inscription, in black pen, that proves Ed Cooper's heart once belonged to me.

Dearest Eve (E.R.H.),

As promised! HI. Wow, I couldn't wait to write to you and now I've got writer's block. Or whatever the equivalent is when you're not a writer, but sat here chewing your pen in the Refectory worrying you're going to sound like a total idiot. OK, so—I picked my moment, didn't I?! Hope you're settling in. Newcastle's great but it's cold, and there's no Eve, which makes it seem colder.

You're probably wondering why I left it until three minutes before

56

we left to say something. I can answer that in a word: cowardice. I've been so terrified of rejection & I couldn't find any clue or hope you felt the same way that I did. (You laugh at my jokes, but that could be sympathy.)

Also, I really cherish our gang. I didn't want to do anything to harm it. I kept thinking: what if you're (somewhat justifiably) repelled and weirded out, and it ruins everything? I knew it would change things between all of us, whether you felt the same way or not. Especially if not.

Then that night in The Trip, I looked over at you. You were talking to Nick Hennigan about his micro scooter, which takes patience and a big heart. I couldn't stop gazing at you—the way you smile and lower your eyes when you start to crack up, as if you're doing something you shouldn't. I live for that smile. (Sorry I'm bad at this. This is how a love letter works, isn't it? You just embarrass yourself horribly?)

And I realized—I couldn't bear to let you leave without you knowing how I felt, whatever the consequences. I had to say it, just once.

By the way, E, I don't want you to think it was some spur of the moment whim, faced with being apart. I've spent two years infatuated with you. (Does this sound creepy? I sound creepy, don't I.) What I'm trying to say is: you're *everything* to me. If you want to be mine, well, I am already yours.

Write back.
Ed xxxx

PS it occurs to me that if you are finding this too heavy and too much, and a quick kiss—after 4 pints of Old Scruttocks Buttocks or Ferret's Achy Hole cloudy cider at 6.5% or whatever it was we were drinking—didn't mean much more than "yeah sure OK, bye Ed"—I get it. I also get that explaining yourself might feel awkward. If you want to go back *to being friends, at Christmas—leave this letter unreplied to, and I'll get the message that way.*

Hah. I had already stocked up at Ryman's for this task, with mint-green notelets, and immediately embarked on a five-page epic. Despite lots of rethinking and rewording, it was on its way, envelope flap tamped down with tape for privacy and security, before the last post.

Ed never wrote again, and while I agonized about this, I already knew how he felt, and how I felt. And I rationalized: maybe he was both swooning, and overwhelmed with First Terming.

It added to the build-up of seeing each other. To be safe, I texted him short friendly updates about uni life, signed with a newly risqué "xx." He always replied swiftly, in kind, an "xx" at the end too. So it was OK? I thought. I hoped.

Sending another letter, when the last had been so febrile and detailed, seemed overkill. Was it my fevered prose, was it too much? No, surely not. I remembered the intensity of that kiss, and the look in his eyes. I was a nervous, insecure teenage girl but not so insecure that I could believe a man in love wouldn't want to hear his bones were jumpable.

Maybe a phone call? I steeled myself on two lager and blacks, and got his voice mail. He rang back a day later and I missed it, though the whole twenty-four-hour lapse had already spooked me. Wouldn't he have returned it when he saw it? Then lots of *What are we like!* texts, Ed flattering me that: *lol, perhaps face to face chat was best?* Still, two kisses.

Thank you for your letter xx

I concluded, hoping to prompt a gear shift, and getting only:

☺ *xxx*

in response, which stopped somewhat short of "F. Scott Fitzgerald to Zelda."

I should take the bull by the horns, I knew it, but I was deeply inexperienced with bulls, horns, and how to take bulls by them.

It was weird. It felt like avoidance, but his tone was affection. It looked clingy to push it. *If you want to be mine, well, I am already yours.* He'd said it, I had my pledge.

The first meet-up back home was on a smoky-cold December night. As I put my eyeliner on wonky and had to sponge it off and redraw it, I finally acknowledged to myself that my anticipation had curdled into apprehensiveness. Something felt badly off.

Shouldn't Ed have immediately asked for a date for the two of us, an emotional homecoming, squirreled away in the corner of a country pub with mullioned windows, doing what tabloid papers call "canoodling"?

Susie arrived before the lads. After we traded stories of freshman year dirt, Susie said:

"I can't believe Ed has a girlfriend already." She wasn't looking at me, absently patting her pockets for her tobacco tin, unaware she had verbally stabbed me with an eight-inch serrated knife.

A girlfriend, a girlfriend, what the fuck—A WHAT?! my inner monologue screamed, deranged.

Susie was busy rolling her roll-up on the cigarette-ash-strewn metal table in front of the chain bar in town we'd chosen for our reunion. It was a "pitchers of Sea Breeze for a tenner" rowdy kind of place that you never see the inside of again after the age of twenty-three. TLC's "Waterfalls" billowed from the doorway.

Funny how trauma gives you a pin-sharp recall for detail.

My heart boom-boomed like the bass from a passing car.

"Girlfriend?" I asked, in a tiny voice.

A vain hope: by "girlfriend," did she mean me? Had Ed presumptuously taken it upon himself to break our news, omitting my identity for a shock reveal? My gut already knew the answer.

I had been frightened he'd cooled on me, but I had been too naïve, too trusting, too *mutually in love*, I thought, to imagine there could possibly be a usurper.

My nervous smile felt like a jagged line on a polygraph as I took a shaky drag on my Vogue Superslim Menthol. (I was trying out being a smoker for six months, until I got a cough and decided I had lung cancer. Susie banned me from then on. "You like to think you're the risk-taking sort but you're not, Eve. You like the uniform but not the hours.")

"Yeah, didn't he say to you too? *Hester.* There's something so very Ed about going off and obtaining a future wife as an undergrad, isn't there. It was written. It was bound to be. Like him ending up president of all the societies."

Hester. *Hester?* I was speechless, I couldn't respond. The casual cruelty had disemboweled me. Ed had my heart, and he'd behaved like Hannibal Lecter with it.

My mum liked to tell me I had no idea what bastards men could be—I thought my dad abruptly emigrating upon divorce had made it pretty clear, but apparently my mum thought being on the daughter rather than wife end of that decision made it less hurtful.

Right now, I felt the full force of that maternal threat, made good.

That someone as gentle, known to me, and, I thought, sincere as Ed Cooper could do this? It was unfathomable. It was *savage*.

"Ah, there they are, our common-law husbands!" Susie said, as Ed and Justin lad-swaggered toward us, through the Friday night throng. *Yeah, my bigamous common-law husband.*

Ed could barely meet my eyes, even as we hugged hello, somehow managing not to make any bodily contact. He radiated pure culpability.

"It's brass bollocks out here," Justin said, blowing on his hands. "Never mind you two's filthy habit, we're going inside." (He started smoking a month later, following the law that anything Justin claims to be censorious about, he is usually thinking of doing.)

"Eduardo, how can you have coupled up this fast?!" Susie said, not missing a beat, once we had drinks. Ed mumbled indistinct, G-rated things about having lots of tutorials together and I stared furiously at the rosy phantom of lipstick mark that wasn't mine on the side of my glass.

"And you're going down to Cornwall to spend Christmas with her family?!" Wow. Ed had sure kept me carefully out of the loop.

"Dum dum dum da-da-dum," Justin hummed Queen's "Under Pressure."

I had a hard lump in my throat, and rocks in my stomach.

"Her older sister's really sick with encephalitis and her parents are up at the hospital all the time. I said I'd cook Christmas lunch for them."

Oh, how Ed. How wonderful of you.

"It's touch and go whether she'll make a full recovery, apparently," Ed said.

He risked looking directly at me, possibly hoping I'd see this was a good and necessary endeavor. I nearly spat: *She could have seven sick sisters and you'd still be a lying arsehole traitor.*

"Do you have a photo? Let's see her! I can't even picture this otherworldly femme fatale who's got you settled down this fast," Susie said.

Susie had no idea how she was ratcheting up my agony as surely as if she was tightening the screws on a rack. I took some small, sour comfort in the fact that Ed was also clearly wishing a whirling portal to another dimension would open up outside, by the bar's happy hour specials A-board.

He reluctantly flashed a wallet Polaroid at us, and I glanced, blank expression, at a blob of pale golden light, a blob that still somehow contrived to have phenomenal bone structure and a sexy broad mouth. She was beautiful, and she looked nothing like me. Of course. Satan wasn't pulling a half shift.

"A Marilyn who's going to be Ed's Jackie," Justin said and Ed replied, "Hah, steady on," and Susie said, "I bet that's true, I bet you marry her," and I couldn't find a single thing to say.

I wanted to howl-weep, I wanted to scream, I wanted to slap Ed—a stinging, full-palm slap like scorned ladies used to deliver in old movies, and the man holds his face and blinks. Instead I went to the loo, when enough time had passed that it looked innocuous, and did a humiliating mini vomit.

It took an hour for Susie to go to the loo in turn, at the same moment that Justin was at the bar, and Ed and I were finally alone.

There was an excruciating moment when Ed glanced at me and tried to speak and couldn't, opening and closing his mouth. I had anesthetized with cheap white wine, which had first helped numb my throat and kept me quiet. Now I felt it unlocking my words, unguardedly.

"You could've told me," I said, when it was clear Ed was going to waste at least half of the precious minute we had for his limp explanation in mute terror.

"Why did you write?" I said, hollow, and blunt. "You could've not written to me. 'I love you' and then this?"

"You didn't write back?" Ed said, guilty head snapping up in surprise, jaw dropping. "I said if you didn't write back, I'd know you didn't . . . want . . . ?"

"What?" I said. "I did write back?"

We stared at each other, uncomprehending. That this had broken my heart was a given. That it could be due to an admin fuck-up, rather than pure evil, was a new room in this hell that I'd not contemplated existing.

"I didn't get it," Ed said, shaking his head, face stricken. "Eve. You have to believe me, I didn't. I wouldn't . . ." He trailed off.

"It was sent the day I got yours," I said. "First class. I posted it an hour and a half after. It should've been there the next day." This eagerness was mortifying and exposing to admit, but essential.

"Where'd it go?" Ed said, and he wasn't going to get any help juggling options from me.

"Wait . . . which month was it . . . ," Ed said, then, clearly speaking at the same rate he was thinking, his hand ruffling his hair as he spoke: "Fuck! There was a flood in the kitchen . . . a load of water-damaged stuff got thrown out and Raf said that there were letters in it. The names had totally blurred so he didn't know who'd lost what. I didn't think you'd write back that quick, or I'd have asked you if you'd sent anything . . . I didn't think for a second I had a letter back from you that soon?"

"Well, you did." I bit the inside of my cheek to stop myself from crying.

"I'm so sorry," Ed said. "I can't believe this. I'd have never . . ."

"Got a steady girlfriend?" I said, mocking, bitter.

"I'm not sure it's serious," Ed said, staring at me intently, reassessing where we stood. But the cause was lost, I knew it was. Any lifeline he threw me was to ease his discomfort, not because it represented a way back to where we were.

"Cheeky Sambuca sidecars!" Justin whooped, at our side once again, smashing down a tray.

That was it. The door with Ed Cooper had closed.

I told myself, in the weeping and the losing of a stone and a half in the following weeks: *You'll get over him, you'll meet someone you feel as much for, who you click as much with. Puppy love. Fish in the sea.* I tried to be my own agony aunt, and responsible adult, and voice of wisdom.

Well, so much for received wisdom—I haven't, and I didn't. There've been times it's hurt less and times it's hurt more, but it's always there and it's always hurt.

And Ed and I have stayed close friends, so my reminders of

our unimprovable rapport are constant. I never told Susie, or Justin, because why make everything weirder, for nothing?

I've asked myself a thousand times whether the missing letter makes it worse, or better.

It's better in as much as Ed was restored to me; he wasn't a villain. But then maybe I needed the simplicity of implacable villainy to move on. Letter or not, he still didn't love me enough, those months later, to end it with Hester. She was a sensational catch. I could see that. The year's convalescence for her sister seemed something Ed should stick around for, and then that was that, they were a done deal.

Every so often, Ed will let his guard drop and I will get a clue that some of his feelings for me are still there, somewhere. Often enough that I can never lose faith.

Holding my eyes seconds too long, after laughing together. Fretting my internet dates might be Ted Bundy. The way his eyes avert if I wear anything lower or tighter than usual, in a way it never seems to around any other female. Or the way he sits it out, silent, if Justin or Susie make ripe jokes in regards to my love life. His general skepticism about, and small but noticeable distance he kept from, my ex, Mark. Calling me to talk about family or work problems, and I know, without a doubt, he's using me as a more reliable sounding board than the volatile Hester. *You give such great advice*, he says.

The way he makes it clear that if I needed him, he'd drop everything. And anyone. Almost anyone.

Sometimes my friendship with Ed feels amazing and beneficial, because it's good to know I can feel that way with someone, and to see him glow with adoration in return. Other times it's like endlessly overperforming in an interview for a job where the position's already been filled.

I know what someone sensible would say about Ed Cooper if I confided in them (though I never have).

If he really was right for you, if he felt what he needed to feel—he'd have left her.

Maybe that's true, maybe it's weakness of character. Perhaps he feels more for Hester than he ever could for me, and after all, there's no nice way to express that?

But believing that if he didn't want me enough, then he can't be good enough to have made me happy—isn't that a fancy version of sour grapes? A way we rationalize that our disappointments don't really exist? "What's for you won't pass you." Everyone knows that's a fantasy to give us consolation and that things that could be for us pass us all the time.

Oh, and the imaginary confidante also tells me that, had shoddy plumbing not done for my letter, and Ed and I had slightly inept, fumbling but thrilling intimate encounters throughout the first term, it would've probably burned itself out by age twenty, what with youthful love affairs tending not to last.

Maybe, maybe not. Or, we'd be the ones engaged right now? Hester lasted. He can do monogamy, and commitment.

My conclusion is this: there's no rule that says the unavailable person you waste your life being in love with has to be the greatest human you ever met.

It doesn't make the loss of him any less painful.

8

The sound of the digital alarm pierces my cranium and hurts physically, as if someone's stabbing a chopstick in my ear.

I have that horrendous split second of not knowing why I feel so abysmal, and then blearily recalling everything I drank and what time I went to bed and knowing every last second of today's agony is my own stupid fault.

I could call in sick, but my job is not super secure, and given it's only eight hours until the weekend, I should soldier through, powered by Diet Coke, Frazzles, and spicy shame.

I work for a website that covers what we loosely term the entertainment scene, called City Nights—long since imaginatively christened Shitty Nights or City Shites by the workforce.

As a user, for a subscription fee, you log in, type in a date, and it tells you what's on around the country and has tickets left, or a table for four free, that kind of thing. "Like Last Minute Dot Com for your social life!" is the ad line. We cover the East Midlands but it's a national service.

There's two members of staff who we could politely call reporters who are, more accurately, twenty-something raw data harvest monkeys, Lucy and Seth, and then two more staff, of whom I am one and Phil is the other, who we could politely call sub-editors or, more accurately, an over-thirty and an over-fifty ex-journo, who have no other way to use a near-redundant skillset.

I check the copy for legal risks and basic English then slap it online with photos and very millennial-wanker, *nudge-nudge, wink-wink* kind of clickbait captions. Like:

My boyfriend says he'd leave me for this peanut dipping sauce at Leicester's newest Japanese restaurant: should I be worried?

Or:

What's better than one Lewis Capaldi date at Nottingham Arena? That's right: TWO (it's not "none," how dare you).

No, I don't have strong self-esteem or record high levels of creative satisfaction, thanks for asking.

I used to be a writer on the local newspaper. As I felt the print industry tanking, I scuttled over to this ship, which was only marginally more afloat.

My ex Mark always said I needed to go to London, to a national, if I wanted to springboard into something better. He was proved right about that. He was right about a lot of things, making me worry he might also be right about other things that I was sure he got wrong.

Stripy Roger has no respect for my fragility and is standing on the kitchen table roaring, to summon me and his breakfast, as I enter the kitchen.

I find his food in the cupboard and try not to gag as an oblong of Whiskas chunks in amber jelly slithers out of the packet and into Roger's bowl, whiffing of liver. He makes Cookie Monster noises as he piles into it.

I trudge upstairs, peel off my pajamas, and stand in a very hot shower. I can't help but gaze down despondently at my apparently revolting tufted pudenda under the running water. I'd heard tell of this hairless breed of men who demanded similar, but I vaguely expected them to live in gyms, and/or the capital's trendy boroughs.

It feels too karmic that a one-night stand that I attempted partly for vanity—*look how easy it is for me to get tail*—has ended up with me feeling like the last old mangy stray at the rescue shelter. I have minge mange.

I pull out a nicer dress than usual because, today of all days, my ego can't take being clad as an "escaped toad disguised as a washerwoman," as Susie and I describe our off-days style.

On the lurching bus ride into town, I consider taking my mind off my nausea by texting Susie a trailer for the Bald Ballsack Zack (ballzack?) anecdote, but I'm distracted by persistent calls from an unknown landline. Only total amateurs answer unknown numbers; you could be tricked into all sorts of unwanted conversations.

My office is in a fashionably bohemian part of the city center, Hockley, but—less pleasingly—in a basement. You don't realize how much humans need daylight until you're without it. Even Goth humans like me.

"Morning, cunts!" says my desk mate, Phil, as I and my

young colleague Lucy walk in. "Oof, big night last night was it, Eve? You're as green as a pea."

"Thanks."

"A lovely pea, I stress. A feminine pea. You're not the 'witch from Oz' sort of green hag."

"A feminine pea. That's me."

I pour myself a black coffee from the filter jug on the sideboard. Phil is in his late fifties and has what my colleague Lucy calls "a council meeting beard," which somehow made me honk with laughter. ("You know, like Bill Oddie's or Jeremy Corbyn's. Not like a 'worn with beanie and sleeve tatts beard.'")

Phil has confused "being crudely offensive" with "a great sense of humor and big personality." Nevertheless, we generally get along, due to my pragmatic decision to take no offense. I would a thousand times rather an abrasive but straightforward Phil, than a snaky, conniving alternative.

"Are you doing the roller-disco pieces?" he asks, and I confirm that I am. Given I'm physically broken, I'm going to lean hard on puns.

Wheels on Fire? Starlight Ex-YES? Oh God that's awful. Rock 'N' Roller?

My mobile flashes with Ed's name. Ugh: this is unusual timing and it must be because he wants to talk about the proposal. I'm the last person who owes it to Ed to make him feel OK about saying yes. Nope. No way. I pop a couple of Advil out of their plastic casing while scowling at the illuminated handset.

"That's a waste of money, you know," Phil says, nodding at the pills. "They're ibuprofen. You're paying that much more for branding."

"I'm a fan of late-stage capitalism and being in debt," I say.

"You must love this job then."

"With all my heart."

"Politicians should study the phenomenon of Advil. People will flush away their money purely for a logo on a packet."

"How do you know politicians haven't?"

Phil keeps squinting at the Advil, annoyed by my lack of taking the bait for an argument.

"Here, listen to this comment on the site," he says, to a roomful of two women who are drinking coffee and not listening. *"An article about BEST RESTAURANTS FOR ROMANCE is very isolating for those of us who are single and makes us feel excluded or unwelcome in such places. Please reconsider your heteronormative focus on coupledom.* Jeezo. Life's hard. We don't all get to shag Beyoncé. Hey, what do you think to this reply: *With your natural joie de vivre it is indeed surprising no one has made you their special companion, Sarah."*

I laugh. "I think you will go viral, and get sacked."

"Yeah, you're probably right."

Missed Call from Ed Cooper appears on the screen. The phone starts flashing with him trying to ring me again. Oh, mate, seriously. Leave me alone.

A text pops up. I slide the bar to open it.

If you're there, I need you to answer. It's not about last night and it's urgent.

"It's not about last night" is strange, and a bit of a mask slip. Ed's tacitly admitting he knows I'd avoid him on that topic?

It immediately rings again and this time, startled as much as anything, I answer.

"Hi," I say. "This best be—"

"Are you at work?" Ed interrupts, without a hello. He's using his teacher voice. A snake uncoils in my stomach. Has he seen our texts about Hester? There are few more unpleasant sensations than being asked to defend your own words where your sole defense is: *I didn't think you'd find out about them.*

"Yes?"

"Can you go somewhere private?"

"What? Why?"

"Can you go outside or to the loo or something, so there's not lots of people nearby? Somewhere you're on your own. Take your bag and coat with you. Please trust me, just do it."

I glance up at my colleagues and both of them are bored enough to already be listening. Funny how the staccato exchange of an abnormal conversation is immediately detectable, despite them only having my side of it.

I'm fully freaked out at why on earth Ed needs me to have my stuff—is he going to drive by and bundle me into an unmarked van?

"OK, hang on." I push my arms into my coat discreetly while keeping the phone clamped between ear and shoulder, gather my bag, stamp up the stairs, and make my way out into the cold fresh air. The office is on a quiet side street, opposite a car park, and there's no one around during daytime, except the occasional parcel delivery man.

"What is it?" I say.

"Are you outside?"

"Yes. You're scaring me, what's this about?"

There's a pause, a windy whoosh of the air around me as I strain to hear any noise from the handset.

"Ed? Are you there?" I say again. "Fuck's sake, say something?" I'm shaky.

". . . I'm here."

Somehow, I know this is momentous, and that these are the last seconds of normality before a bomb goes off. I couldn't possibly say what it is, but I know it's ticking.

"I've got something . . . something absolutely terrible to tell you and I don't know how to say it."

His voice isn't normal. It's a deep pitch and yet wavering and it makes me so scared I could be sick, and that's nothing to do with the units in a lavender martini still working their way through my system. The adrenaline's fixed the hangover, in fact.

"Tell me!"

My body, and time, stands perfectly still. I bargain: is it the wedding, he's called it off? I know it isn't this. I know it's something profoundly bad and my mind has begun spinning a roulette wheel of options but not stopped on an answer yet.

"Fuck, OK. I'm going to say it because I don't think there's a good way. *Susie's dead, a car hit her last night, I am so, so sorry.*"

He says this on one breath and I am, for a second, stunned as if a bolt gun has been applied to my temple. I start shivering, shivering so hard I could be in a meat locker.

I'm furious with him. This is *vile*. You don't go around scaring people, making shit up that's this bad, it's, it's—

"Why would you say that? Why would you say something like that? That's a fucking horrible thing to say, Ed!" I half shout. "She isn't, you know she isn't!"

"Eve, she is, I'm so, so sorry. Oh God." I can hear that he's crying, wheezing on the in-breath.

"No, she's not! She was only with us a few hours ago! Why are you doing this? This is fucked up!"

I realize after speaking that I have no oxygen left. I am suddenly unable to manage talking and breathing at the same time. I suck in air heavily, as if it's through a straw. My knees may buckle. I lean against the wall for support.

"She was walking to her house and a driver veered off on the pavement and hit her. She died shortly after they got her to the hospital."

Information that I, on one level, know must be true, registers as completely false. Thirty-four-year-olds don't die overnight like this, after pub quizzes. Without warning.

It's a level of cognitive dissonance that could make me faint. I'm going to faint. I must still be drunk, or this is a hallucination. I slide down the wall and crouch on the pavement, bag next to me, squatting.

"Are you alright?" Ed says. "I mean, no, you're not alright," he gabbles. "Is there anywhere to sit down?"

"I'm sat down," I snap. "She texted me! This can't be true. This is a mistake . . . I have the text here." *That I can't read to you.*

"When did she text you?"

"Not long after we left the pub . . . half eleven?"

"It happened just after midnight."

My focus on the grimy ground swoops in and then out, in a way that suggests an imminent blacking out.

I put my hand on a wall to steady myself, and wonder why I've never noticed so much about walls before—the heat from the morning sun still in the brick, the rough, porous texture of it against my palm. The way the grainy mortar squeezes out like buttercream in cake.

74

"I need you to come to the hospital and meet me. I'll be waiting outside the entrance of A&E at Queen's Med. Can you get a taxi?"

"Yes," I say, because this is what I'm supposed to say. I have no idea what I can and can't do.

"Eve, this may sound stupid, but I don't care. Walk to the car carefully, sit down if you feel light-headed, and look both ways crossing the road. You've had a huge shock. I want you to get here safely."

"OK."

"I'm not losing you too."

The first hot tears leak from my eyes. My chest contracts and I can't respond. He hasn't lost Susie, we haven't lost her?

"Call me again if you need to. I'm going to wait here until you arrive," Ed says.

"Yes," I squeak, and I drag at my face with my sleeve.

I end the call and stare at the gutter, a chips packet blowing along it in a light breeze. I can hear the electronic dinging of a car reversing in the next street, a song on the radio trickling from its wound-down window. I look up at the dirty paint-water gray of the cloudy sky.

Every single thing about this scene is humdrum, and yet I've been plunged into a dystopian science fiction. They've used the sets from my usual life.

How can all these people be living, how can everything be carrying on as usual, if Susie is dead?

She can't be dead. Susie, *dead*? The single syllable is like a bullet, or an explosion. A profanity. The very idea is obscene, impossible, gruesomely ugly.

Reality has slipped ahead of me when I wasn't concentrating, but I feel certain I can claw it back. If I feel strongly enough that this hasn't happened, I can pull her back to me. This is a mistake. It has to be. But it needs my immediate attention to sort it out. I surprise myself with the strength of this conviction.

The door near me slaps open and Phil emerges. He double-takes at me as I rise shakily to my feet.

"Are you alright? Fuck me, you look like you've seen a ghost with its bollocks out. What were you drinking, Messer Schmitt Herbal Schnapps?"

"My best friend's been killed," I say, trying out this sentence for the first time, even though I think it has zero credibility. Phil's face drops in horror.

"In a car accident. I have to go to the hospital. Can you tell Kirsty where I am if she checks in?"

"Jeezo, I'm sorry, Eve. Fuck! Sure," he says.

"Thanks," I say, shouldering my bag and walking mechanically toward the city center and the taxi stand.

I'm hovering somewhere outside my body, directing myself. I feel like a bag of clothes, held up by a skeleton.

Students from the nearby college pass by, chattering and whooping with laughter, as if this isn't an abhorrent thing to be doing. As if it hasn't happened.

9

Making sure I don't throw up during the ride to the hospital is an unexpectedly useful distraction.

It forces me to prioritize the physical over the emotional and concentrate on swallowing, breathing, gripping the seat belt, and keeping my feet flat to the vibrating floor of the taxi.

Focus on what's real and what's present, worry about the future when it arrives, in a few short minutes' time.

Once we're outside the Queen's Medical Center and start sweeping up the winding roads to the front entrance, and I see the red Accident & Emergency sign, abject terror washes over me. I'm not sure I've ever felt more like a child in my life, including childhood. I want to run into the bushes and simply hide from this. I want an adult to make this alright, to protect me.

"Just here OK?" says the driver, peering at me curiously in the mirror.

"Fine," I say and push a note into the tray in the window between us, before heaving myself out clumsily into the fresh air. I'm going to see Ed and when I see Ed, this will become real.

The thing is, you see, this can't be true. It can't be. But he'd never lie to me.

At first I can't see him and my heart races. This was a prank. This was someone pretending to be Ed?! It hasn't happened, it hasn't happened, it hasn't . . .

"Eve! Eve?" Ed calls to me and I look around. He's rumpled in a T-shirt with his parka thrown over the top. His face twists, and collapses, as our eyes meet. I feel my own do the same. He belts over and throws his arms around me and I sink my face into the waxy cotton of his coat, and sob. I've never appreciated the solid six feet of Ed Cooper more, and I've done a lot of appreciating it. We grip each other as tightly and as desperately as if we're on the deck of a sinking ship.

"I'm sorry, I'm sorry," Ed says absently, on repeat, and I say indistinctly, "It's not your fault," several times.

"I called Justin. He can't get off work until this afternoon," he says, wiping at his cheeks as we disentangle.

"Right."

Of course, Justin. In stark contrast to his irreverent persona and devil-may-care nature in his private life, Justin is a caregiver. He runs a local home for the elderly.

"Who called you?" I ask. I'm cold again, very cold. My teeth are chattering and I have to make an effort to disguise it.

"The police. She'd listed you and I as emergency contacts in her wallet. Apparently her bag was thrown a long way from . . . they only found it searching, later. They said you weren't answering. They went to see her dad but . . ." Ed shrugs.

"Oh God! Her dad." I'd been so busy thinking about us, I didn't think of her family.

"I don't think he understood what they were saying, he told them his daughter should be in her classes," Ed says.

Susie's dad's had the signs of dementia for eighteen months or so. I'd not asked her recently how he was; she didn't like to discuss it. Her mum died several years ago and her brother lives abroad.

"I had no idea it was that bad," I say.

"Neither did I . . . The doctor wants to talk to us together," Ed says.

The word "doctor" hits me in the gut, and yet part of me is still resilient, even hopeful. Doctors make people better. Ed said dead, but he could've meant coma. Her bag was missing, sounds like they could've mixed up the files. This remains negotiable.

Look, this is Susie Hart. People die all the time, but Susie isn't "people."

"Eve? Is that OK?"

"Yes," I say, limp, and take Ed's proffered hand. We have never held hands before. It goes without saying but I never imagined it would be like this, when we did.

Ed guides me through the busy, antiseptic-smelling, brightly lit reception and says something to the woman behind the desk that I don't hear, I think it's just his name. She turns away and makes a sotto voce internal phone call.

She doesn't look remotely perturbed and I marvel at this, that it must be so ordinary for her. She has every day to practice being politely, professionally impassive in the face of people who look as bewildered and shaken as if they've stepped out of a time machine.

In the intervening seconds, Ed turns to me and looks like he's going to say something to me and then doesn't say anything, because what is there to say? Every single remark, platitude, expression of reassurance or hope, or practical discussion of what's ahead, is impossible, null. We've transcended conversation.

I glance around.

Was Susie rushed through here, hours ago, people in uniform running by a gurney, holding a drip aloft, oxygen mask clamped to her face? Or was she never an emergency?

Ed's name is called. A late-middle-aged man with a lanyard appears, and we're ushered through double doors into the rest of the hospital, down a corridor, and into a side room. He wears a fixed expression of rueful, blank respectfulness. Not emotional, but mindful of your emotion. Like the men who drive the hearse, wear white gloves, and never look directly at you.

My stomach muscles seize up as he asks us to sit down, in a featureless room where my sight immediately fastens on the box of tissues on the desk.

When he starts speaking, this will become real. If he tells us it's all been a terrible mistake and Susie is in a bed with a leg in traction, or they're operating right now, then that will be the new truth. This man is the Giver of Life or the Grim Reaper, the one with the power to give her back or take her away from us, forever.

As he walks over to shut the door, I fantasize the words he might use. Imploring us not to sue over their grave error.

Now this has never happened before, but I'm nevertheless incredibly relieved, if ashamed, to tell you.

The rush of relief that would knock us off our feet. Or what if she's injured, but . . . there's physio, we could do anything . . .

"Hello. Ed? Eve." He nods.

I have never dreaded anyone speaking more in my life.

"I'm consultant Gareth Prentice, I'm one of the medical team who saw Susie when she was brought in by the ambulance." Brought in. These strange passive terms, as if Susie is a puppet in their play.

"Who called the ambulance?" I blurt.

"A member of the public who saw what happened and called 999."

I can't imagine Susie helpless.

"I'm so sorry . . . ," he starts, after a deep breath, and I fold immediately, letting go a strangled cry.

"Hey, come on, come on, ssshhh," Ed says, putting his arm around me, and I can tell it's helping him right now to steady himself, to act as my protector. I'm glad of it. As much as I can see anything of the long road that lies ahead, I suspect we will be constantly swapping these roles back and forth.

". . . We saw her during the early hours of this morning with a major trauma to her head. We did everything we could to save her, but her injuries were just too severe. She had a massive bleed on the brain that was simply unsurvivable."

"How? If she was on the pavement?" I say.

"We won't know the full details until the postmortem and the inquest."

There's so much to come I can't contemplate.

". . . If you asked me to guess, and please bear in mind it's only a guess, I'd say the car mounted the curb, hit her, and the impact threw her against a wall, which is when the insult to the brain and skull occurred."

Insult. Unexpected jargon. We're visitors in a foreign country.

". . . The driver is cooperating with the police, as far as I know."

Dr. Prentice adds, with some understatement: "This is an awful lot to take in, I know. Take your time and ask me anything you want to."

He is compassionate, but rehearsed. This is an earthquake for us, a conversation we will never forget, and I think—for him it's the middle of his Friday morning. Something he'll mention in passing to his wife tonight at dinner. *Sad business today, young girl, well, woman, only in her thirties. Friends were in pieces, naturally.*

"What did you do, to try to save her?" I say, and I don't recognize my own voice.

"The paramedics had stabilized her with a neck brace to protect her spine and kept her breathing on the way to the hospital. We put Susie on a ventilator to support her vital functions while we tried to find the source of the bleeding, and ran scans."

"But she died how long after you did that?"

"She had no vital signs within fifteen minutes of arriving here. Attempts to resuscitate her failed."

I imagine the unbroken tone from the machines.

There's no other sound for a few moments, while I heave and weep and Ed makes a gasping noise, like he's trying to breathe underwater.

"Was she conscious?" Ed says. "When she came in."

"No, the impact from the crash knocked her completely unconscious," the doctor says. "She wouldn't have suffered at all."

"You don't know that!" I say, and think, what a time for arseholey teenage Eve to resurface. (Eve Gaddafi, my mum used to call her. "A tyrant.")

"We are as sure as we possibly can be," says the doctor, evenly, completely unperturbed by my snapping at him—prepared and trained for it, just like the unstartled receptionist. "Brain function after that kind of trauma is akin to a deep coma state."

"Was the driver of the car OK?" Ed says, in a clipped voice, and he reaches over and squeezes my sweaty, freezing hands. The idea there is a murderer in this story, a flesh-and-blood still-living person who's violently wrenched Susie from us . . . I don't know how I feel about them yet. I haven't even started trying to work that out. My shock can barely recede an inch to start letting in the ocean of grief, let alone rage.

"He was treated at the scene for his injuries. The police will know more about that."

"Was he drunk?" Ed says.

"He'll have been breathalyzed, I don't know the result."

"Police officers have been to see Susie's father, he seemed in a confused state?" the doctor continues.

"He has dementia," Ed says. "We're not sure how advanced."

The doctor nods. He bows his head, slightly. "We were wondering if, in light of this, you'd be able to identify the body?"

Ed and I look at each other with bloodshot eyes. "No" does not seem an acceptable answer.

"The body." Susie is not Susie, she is an artifact. She has left it behind. She is a thing.

There's a soap opera, unreal quality to this experience, as if everyone other than myself and Ed might be an actor. The phrases we're being given about *take all the time you need* and *we'll be right outside* and *come out and take a break if you need to* and *there's no pressure if you're not sure.*

I feel as if I've seen this scene in blue-light procedural dramas that I had half my attention focused on while shoveling my tea. Except this body will not sit up when someone shouts, "Scene."

I can't accept Susie has consented to leave her body anywhere that her personality isn't. It runs completely contrary to her nature.

Part of me feels defiant—yes, show us this impossible thing you keep saying you have hidden behind a curtain. Death is physical; perhaps it existing in a purely intellectual realm is too much to reconcile. Susie losing her life has been only words, wild claims. Knowing someone wouldn't lie to you, and actually believing them, are two different things, it seems.

I have a firm conviction that if I ignored them, broke free and ran away from this bleach-sluiced place that I shouldn't be in, hailed a taxi and went to Suze's, she'd be there looking baffled at me in the doorway, hair back in one of those cotton Alice bands she uses to keep it off her face.

What's up with you? Course I'm here. I always work from home on a Friday.

The ease and clarity with which I can picture her makes this seem entirely feasible. She's at my fingertips.

They take us into an empty room, with a long, shallow curtained window across one wall. Ed and I hold hands, not looking at each other. My heart is thundering.

"Are you ready?" the doctor says, quietly, more to Ed than to me, and he nods.

On the other side, they briskly draw back the curtains.

I give an involuntary gasp at the sight of her. Ed and I grip each other's hands so hard it feels like it could snap bone.

It's her.

She's there.

Susie's lying on a gurney with a dark blue sheet pulled up to her neck, her long hair pooled around her head, some of it spilling over the edge, her eyes closed.

I expected Susie to look asleep, as much as I could picture this at all.

She doesn't look asleep. She looks like a sallow waxwork of Susie, with a slack expression. Like someone has made a model of Susie Hart from plaster of paris, like something they might put in a modern art gallery.

I've never seen a dead person before and I didn't know that I'd *know* they were dead, if that makes any sense. If I'd suspect a heartbeat hiding under that sheet. But I can tell for sure Susie is dead, that this is what death looks like. If I'd been the first to find her like this, I'd have understood she was gone. We're still mammals, we instinctively know.

Her face—her regal, prom-queen face I know every detail and shadow of—is without animation. I can see the edge of a huge spreading purple bruise at her temple. I guess they have shown us her this way around so it's at the far side.

I turn to the doctor, who's standing with his hands behind his back and his chin respectfully on his chest.

"That's her," I say, voice full of water, and pain. "That's Susie."

The doctor nods.

"I'll give you a moment," he says, and leaves.

I look back at Susie. This is the last time I will ever see her in person, I realize. I try to take every detail in, the extravagant shape of her nose and lips, the brown-blond treacly colors in her hair. I always envied those thick handfuls of her hair, and now it's going to waste? Parts of her are still perfect and she's going to be . . . thrown away? How can her body not be in use, and of use? We've not been asked and I'm not going to ask.

I see her in my mind's eye, in the pub last night, raising her eyebrow at me. Sardonic, witty, unstoppable Susie. From that, to this. *How?*

"This isn't real, Eve," Ed says to me. I sense it's his turn to break down and mine to keep it together. "This is like a fucking nightmare. What is going on? Why did this have to happen? There was no reason for this to happen . . ." His voice breaks. I look at him and he's crying, screwed-up-face crying.

"It's not right," I say, putting my arms around him. "This is not right."

I am holding on to Ed and Ed is holding on to me and I think we're holding each other up.

He strokes my hair; the gesture is so clumsy in his distress that he's catching great hanks of it and vaguely pulling, but I don't care.

Somewhere outside this building, I think, people are having normal Fridays. But there's been a switch around: it's not Susie dying that feels impossible, for as long as we're looking at her dead body—a corpse, she is a *corpse*?—but that ordinary world that is the impossibility now.

I gaze at her for the last time. There's an emptiness to her. The snap-crackle of her, gone, vanished, flown. Her body is a vacated premises. It's like turning up to a house you know well, and finding it emptied and stripped to the fittings.

Have we had enough time with her, we're asked. Yes, we have, we say, blankly.

They close the curtains.

If there's something I am sure of, it's that I will never think I've had enough time with her.

10

On the evening of the day Susie has died—words I am still reeling from stringing together, let alone grasping the concept—something she once told me comes roaring back to me.

Her mum, Jeanette, had a short illness, ovarian cancer that wasn't treatable and well advanced on diagnosis, that left her and her dad shellshocked with the speed of her departure.

We were thirty that year, and Susie was the first of us to lose a parent. As her friends, we thought it was a big, scary grown-up brush with mortality, at the time.

"The strangest thing, Eve, is you don't know how to talk about what to have for tea," she said, when we all gathered at my place, in the week before the funeral. (The quiz wasn't the right mood.)

I was baffled.

"You still need to have your tea, don't you?" she explained. "But it's not seemly. In any other crisis you'd still discuss practicalities like that, they're a relief. And you do talk about funerals and death certificates, all the death admin. *Deadmin*. But on the day you lose someone, you can't go"—she mimed checking her watch—"mmm, six o'clock, who's for a takeaway? Or I think there's leftover chicken in the fridge? It feels so flippant, and like you're drawing a line. As if it's already diminishing in importance if you can think about your appetite or picking one food over another."

"I see what you mean," I said. "You can't be something so trivial as hungry?"

"Not even that. It might only be a Domino's pizza, but the act of choosing toppings feels so frivolous. It's like a statement that life goes on. You're not ready for that statement. You can't find the moment, or the words, without it seeming tasteless. How can they be dead, and you're still preferring pepperoni to ham."

Eventually Justin said: "So what did you have for your tea?"

"Microwaved burgers from Co-op."

"That seems more of a statement that life doesn't go on."

We shrieked, tutted, and laughed, and I knew we were a huge comfort to Susie, in that time. I was the female sympathy and shoulder to cry on, Ed was the calm organizer and steadying backbone, Justin the irreverent clown, puncturing tension.

As Ed and I sit, once more in my small front room with the half-burned pillar candles in the fireplace and the red velvet sofa that Roger has scratched till it bled, we are without Susie, and waiting nervously and miserably for Justin. My stomach growls and as soon as I think: Should I bother to raise eating? Is it an inappropriate thing to say? I remember Susie. I wasn't meant to find out what she meant, this way. I want to tell her, I ache to tell her. I can never tell her anything again. It's inconceivable.

There is a Susie-less space torn in life—and it's only been hours. How do we handle this forever?

The doorbell goes and I feel nauseous. Seeing People for the First Time Since is frightening. It's like having to experience being told, all over again. I stand up slowly and Ed senses my hesitation and answers it.

Justin walks in—my front door opens into the sitting room, I can't afford anything as fancy as a hallway—and says nothing, throws himself into Ed's arms. They stand there sobbing, Justin with his head on Ed's chest, and I think about how I've never seen them cry before. I don't know what to do with my arms, until Justin says to me, indistinctly, "Don't just stare, join in!" and I grip them in an awkward huddle.

The room is silent but for the sound of our weeping. It's quite eerie.

When we break apart, I see Roger in the doorway from the kitchen, ears cocked, frowning in confusion. Noisy humans.

"Fucking hell, Suze," Justin says, when it abates, sitting down heavily. "Always a show-off, that one. Has to be the center of attention. Has outdone herself with this."

We laugh weakly and slightly hysterically, laughs that are half sobs.

"I did not see that coming. And neither did she, clearly."

I wince, while being able to hear Susie's delighted shriek in my imagination. She was the biggest fan of Justin's taboo-breaking. I have a flash mental image of her on that gurney, not laughing. Not moving.

I glance over at Justin, out of habit—he always grins at his own jokes—and instead see him slumped, devastated.

"You saw her?" Justin says. ". . . What did she look like?"

I understand this is a way of asking about her injuries.

Ed opens his mouth and nothing comes out. He looks at me, stricken.

"Exactly like Susie and absolutely nothing like Susie," I say.

"That is . . . well, Eve has always been good with words. Spot on," Ed says.

He looks at his knees. I sense that I needed to see Susie, as difficult as it was, to accept it. Ed found it harder.

"Do you want to see her?" I ask Justin and he shakes his head, emphatic.

"God no, no, thank you. I have seen my share of bodies at the home."

We run through the minimal information we have about the accident and soon stop, because no better answers about what happened will bring her back to us. It makes us think about that moment on the hundred yards from the taxi drop-off to her house, Susie digging in her bag for her house keys, and a hurtling box of metal coming into view behind her. I swallow hard and my heart races, picturing it.

I can't go back, push her out of the way, shout at her to move.

The text. If I had replied to her text, and she'd stopped to read it, or texted me back? It's very hard to absorb that I will be thinking and "what-if-ing" about last night's events for the rest of my life. It has an instant permanence, like looking at a fresh wound and knowing the scar it leaves will always be a part of your body.

If thirty-four is still some superannuated version of youth in our era, I'm aware I've aged exponentially in the space of a morning. That my life has bifurcated into a Before and After and the innocence that I didn't know I had has gone. I'm dis-orientated by it.

"We should check on her dad too," Ed says. "The hospital couldn't make him understand what happened."

"I'm relieved in a way," Justin says. "Because with Alzheimer's there's a worst of all worlds where you understand what's being said and then forget, so you keep reliving finding out, forever."

I fall silent, aghast. No one has ever described hell so vividly to me before.

"What about her brother, has anyone told him?" Justin says.

"Shit, Finlay," I breathe. I'd totally forgotten about him.

"*So have I, and I share DNA with him, so I wouldn't sweat it,*" Susie says to me, so swiftly and clearly I wonder if there's such a thing as an audio-haunting.

Recalling Susie-isms used to make me laugh out loud in the street and now, I guess, they'll always make me cry. A fat tear rolls down my cheek and I wipe it away.

"The hospital had no contact details for him. I explained he's in the States," Ed says. "Is he still in New York?"

"I think so," I say. "She didn't talk about him much, did she?"

Ed shakes his head. We three understood that, conversation-ally, Finlay Hart was a permanent no-fly zone. Susie wasn't really one for gale-force expressions of feeling about people, be it positive or negative, so her vitriol in regards to her brother always took us aback.

"Her phone," Justin says. "He must be in that? Have you got her mobile?"

"Yup."

In the corner of my room, we have a plastic, standard-issue

hospital bag I can barely bear to look at. It contains: Susie's tan Radley handbag, a battered oxblood Mulberry wallet full of bank cards that need canceling (What if she needs them?! What if? She's going to be fuming when she returns), her keys, a pair of stud earrings that I know will be real gold ("As my mum says, I'm allergic to cheap metals and cheap men," she once said, going full Raymond Chandler dame, aged twenty), a roll of hairbands, and a Charlotte Tilbury lipstick, shade "Pillow Talk."

Plus, a white iPhone 8 with a shattered screen that, nevertheless, appeared to be operational when we pressed the power button. Her wallpaper is the four of us, at a music festival, faces posed on top and beside each other, like a Beatles album cover. It had provoked a new wave of sobbing on the drive to my place. As Ed said: she's not here, but a sodding *glass computer* the size of a piece of toast survived.

"Unfortunately Apple makes them impregnable even to the CIA," Justin says. "Probably the way Suze would want it, to be fair."

"I know her passcode," I say.

"Woah, seriously?" Justin says. "Women are mental!"

"Only by chance."

It feels spooky. As if it was intended by some higher power. I've only known it for a fortnight, maximum. Susie wanted me to take a photo of her with a fan of tail-on prawns as a starter in a seafood restaurant. As she was already gripping the rim of the plate and practicing her grin, she gestured with her head at her handset on the tablecloth.

"It's my year of birth but backward," she said. "Don't give me chins."

"I don't need to know your passcode to take a photo, the camera opens automatically," I said, as I wiped my hands of chip grease and picked it up, and she said: "Oops. Don't browse my nudes, will you."

I feel intensely protective of her phone, whether she'd been joking about the nudes or not.

"Someone should ring him, he must be in her contacts," Ed says, and given Ed has broken this news to me and to Justin, I don't think it's fair he calls the brother too.

"What's he called again? Flynn?" Justin says.

"Finlay," I say. "Fin. I'll do it. After you both go."

They both mumble about "not leaving you on your own," and I tell them forcefully that I will be fine and they have to. I don't want them to, but artificially delaying being alone will be worse.

"Tell us how it goes with the brother?" Ed says, as they linger on the doorstep. "I'll call you later."

He looks at me and leans in for a hug, and I hold him for a moment, burying my face in his shoulder. We've always been close but, after today's hospital visit, we're welded.

There is no "later" for Susie and me, I think, as I close the door. I still haven't accepted it. She is just over the brow of a hill, to be glimpsed around a corner. I will never tell her the failed one-night-stand, bald-ballsack story and feel gratified at her gurgling laughter. She will never give me her voluble and welcome scathing opinions on the "atrocity" of Hester's proposal, and soothe my suffering.

I've lost her standing shoulder to shoulder with me, in a matching dress, holding an identical bunch of flowers. The problems I had only hours ago were so minuscule.

You usually say old people are a "comfort" to each other. But that's what Susie and I were, I can see that so clearly, the secret formula: each other's comfort and joy.

The eternity of the silence overwhelms me. The line between us buzzes with monotonous static, a line never to be busy again.

The only word I can think of that comes close to how I feel is: desolate.

11

I Google search: *what time is it New York*. Lunchtime. My hands tremble with the enormity of the task I've taken upon myself with offering to ring Fin and guiltily, although it's seven at night and I lost my best friend today so I am not sure why I feel guilty, I pour myself a glass of white wine to take the edge off. It might be because Susie can't have a glass of wine.

I can't have any more than this, I know that: the prospect of waking up hungover tomorrow is unbearable, because the prospect of waking up tomorrow is already unbearable.

Does the fact that Susie and her brother were estranged make it easier or harder to have this conversation? More complicated, I think, barely easier. I have no gauge of his response. I've never had to break news like this in my life before. I see why Ed was so traumatized by calling me.

After some stiffening gulps of fridge-cold supermarket Sauvignon, I pick up Susie's phone.

What if she changed her passcode? I can imagine her having done that, not because she didn't trust me but because she was fastidious.

Justin is right, she guarded her privacy carefully. Not obses-sively, not much more than average, but Susie had inherited her mum's idea that it was vulgar to let it all hang out in public. Her Facebook was a tightly locked down space for seventy or so people and no one ever knew from such a forum who she was dating. Her longer-term boyfriends were sometimes irri-tated at her refusal to post his'n'hers profile pictures, or change "Relationship Status."

Gobbing away on Twitter or posting bikinis on Instagram were inconsistent, she said, with her being something senior and respectable in finance, which meant she spent half the week in London and earned twice as much as the rest of us.

I press the keypad of her phone with exaggerated care and the screen ripples into the small square tiles of a rainbow of apps. Oh God. I feel the high of successful access, and the prickle of intrusion without permission.

I reassure myself—I'm here for one reason only and that's her brother's phone number. I won't snoop. I'm the guardian of Susie's world in here, and it's a responsibility I take very seriously.

I scroll down to Contacts and go directly to "H." There are a few family members in there, but no Fin, and no one who sounds like a nickname for Fin. Somehow, I don't think she ever called him Brenda.

I try "F." Nothing there either. "B," for brother? Nope. I'm at a loss. Does she hate him so much she erased him from her phonebook?

I feel sure she hadn't taken that step (unless there's been a huge, game-changing fight, but she'd have likely mentioned such a thing). I recall every once in a blue moon her seeing a message, Susie's lip curling and her saying: *Ugh Fin, he can wait.*

However disliked her brother was, not knowing it was him when he called would've only put her on the back foot.

I'm out of ideas about where he's been hidden, so I scroll manually through her list, starting with Annie Butler, Aveda Salon, and Andy Wightman.

I think about the ripples in the pond from this news, the many people who need to be told. I have one person to inform and I'm already failing at the task. I've started to give up hope, having scrolled from A to Z, when I trip over, second time around in the B section:

My Wanker of a Brother

Oh. *Oh.* It's obviously him: followed by a row of digits for a mobile phone number, with the international code in front. I write it down carefully on a notepad and switch Susie's phone off. She's only on four percent battery—or, she *was?*

The absence keeps winding me, the surreal idea these items are without an owner. I'm worried that if her phone dies and can't be revived, even though I'll never browse its contents, I've lost a part of her. I plug it into my charger and watch the lightning bolt appear over the battery icon. If only bringing other things back was as easy.

My Wanker of a Brother. The residual anger that sizzles from her inability to even give him his name.

It's not as if it's news to me that she didn't get on with Fin, but this level of antipathy is still an unwelcome surprise. Susie was plenty open with the three of us about most things in her life.

The two subjects she was tight-lipped about were her dad's

illness and her relationship with her brother. She'd tell me the basics, but in a clipped, obliged, "so you know the score and we can move on" sort of way, making it implicitly clear it was not something she found easy.

She never went into detail about Fin, but gave me to understand he was wantonly nasty to her parents, emotionally frigid toward her, and a disruptive influence in an otherwise happy home. I was upset when Kieran emigrated; she was merely glad to see the back of Fin.

Susie had so few sensitive spots, she was so raucous and confident, that the ones she did have seemed acute and important.

I add Finlay Hart to my phone contacts—I can't call him from Susie's phone for obvious reasons, and I don't feel right calling him without the respectability of a number using his title.

Susie, I wish you were here to tell me what to do. Though I have an uncomfortable suspicion she'd tell me that Fin didn't deserve to be told. *He can stick a row of broken heart emojis on Facebook like every other hypocrite who didn't actually like me.*

The rift after the death of their mum was profound.

She said to me: "Put it this way, I found the bottom of the bucket. If someone doesn't care about their mother dying, what do they care about? No point thinking anything's going to mend it now."

I take a swig of wine, breathe deeply, and hit the phone icon. It takes a while to connect and then rings in that slightly tinny, distant-sounding way of a phone on another land mass. I haven't practiced what I'm going to say. Possibly stupidly, I feared rehearsal would amplify my nerves. Plunge in. As Ed said, there is no good way to say it.

Eventually, a click, and I get a voice mail. The message is British-accented, and efficiently brusque.

Hi, it's Finlay, I can't answer right now, obviously. Leave a message and a number for me after the beep if you want a call back.

Voice mails produce performance anxiety at the best of times, and I flap and feel clammy before blathering: "Hi, this is Eve Harris. I am a friend of your sister, Susie. Please give me a call back when you get this on this number." (Pause.) "It's important."

As I put my phone on the coffee table, Roger settles next to me on the sofa, curled nose to tail in the shape of a furred croissant. I stroke him and feel the comfort of a nonverbal and contented companion.

"Susie's dead, Rog," I say, to his back. "Susie *died*. Can you believe it? I can't believe it. I want her back so much. I want it to be yesterday, so much."

Exhausted tears start to pour forth from me again and my nose runs, adding to a sense that I am at primary school with a skinned knee, wailing for my mum. Mum. I should tell her. But I don't want to tie up the line if Fin calls back. I can imagine him being irritated, busy businessman on the East Coast, hearing the blip-blip and *the caller knows you are waiting*, and being irritated with me by the time we're connected. None of that will help.

What would help? Not more wine.

I get more wine.

Mentally, I pull the files I have marked "Finlay Hart." They're both dusty and slender, figuratively speaking.

I've known Susie since primary-school age and although Fin

was two years older, he always seemed much older to me. Two years in youth is a chasm.

If I went for sleepovers, he was always a scarce presence. He was slight in build, but tall, with watchful eyes and Susie's same enviably thick hair, but much darker brown, like their dad's.

He wasn't unfriendly toward me, but neither was he friendly. He didn't have many mates of his own and I'd hear Susie teasing him about it. Once I heard him reply: *Well, you only have HER. She looks like a sad-eyed doll. One of the chubby-faced ones with a hair ribbon that are found in attics.* I ditched my hair slide with the bow on it, after that.

In our nice suburb, I came from the scruffy end at the far side of it, living with a warring mum and dad. The Harts' address was a spacious, 1930s detached house with a driveway, a garage, a well-tended front garden and a storm porch for boots and umbrellas. Their street did parties with bunting for Royal weddings. My mum called the Royals parasites.

In that way that kids are aware of social castes, I vaguely assumed Finlay Hart, all of ten years old, thought me a little *beneath*.

"SUSIE. IT'S FOR YOU" were his entire words of greeting when he happened to yank open the inner, then outer front door when I called.

One memory stands out, something I rarely think about.

The only thing I did with both Hart siblings was bike rides. In a time when children were still allowed to get on two-wheeled transport and piss off for vast stretches of time, we used to pack a picnic into the satchels on the back of the saddle and cycle out from our suburb to the countryside.

Sometimes we were a foursome, with a girl called Gloria on

their street who had a voice like a foghorn and a helmet hair-cut. (She's a Liberal Democrat MP now.) Susie and Gloria were locked into a ridiculous competition in regards to stamina—their obsessive need to outdo each other carried through to their degrees and careers. Until Gloria got married at twenty-five and had triplets six months later, and Susie was finally happy to hand over the winner's trophy.

On one scorching day, both of them pedaling like maniacs—out of breath, but pretending not to be, keeping up appearances with effortful conversation—I gradually fell behind. Fin was keeping pace with me, possibly because as the eldest, and male, he anticipated a major fury coming his way if they lost posses-sion of the sad doll girl.

Under a large tree by the side of a road, he and I stopped for a rest, my metallic green bicycle with white shopping basket propped against it. Fin had something sharp and racy in black and red, which was more like a couple of metal right angles than mode of transport.

"They have to come back this way," Fin said. "Let's wait for them to pass."

I liked this idea, and we lolled against the bark and picked blades of grass and listened to the bee-buzz hum of distant lawnmowers. We lay down and closed our eyes and imagined we were comfortable enough to sleep. We sat up again, because the ground was lumpy and grass is tickly.

"Have you heard of kissing?" I asked Fin.

I'd seen it on a television program the night before; the woman was in a pink nightie with thin straps and slippers that looked like high heels. I'd been riveted. I'd said to my brother, Kieran, "I've never seen Mum and Dad do that," and he said,

"That's because they don't like each other in the way that man and lady do," and, well, from the mouths of babes.

"Yes," Fin said. "Of course I know what kissing is."

"Would you like to do it with me?"

(I don't think I've ever been as forthright with a member of the opposite sex since.)

He glanced up from under his floppy fringe and gave a non-chalant shrug. "Yeah, I s'pose."

We shuffled around opposite each other and pressed our mouths together. His lips felt soft for a boy, although I wasn't really sure what I was expecting. We repositioned our heads and tried again. It was not a good or bad experience, just a curious thing to choose to do, I thought.

Susie and Gloria reappeared in the distance and Fin and I righted our bikes and rolled them back down to the path. Once again, the girls outpaced us and disappeared into the horizon. As we arrived at the Hart residence, I wondered if I wanted to kiss Fin Hart goodbye.

As I was about to suggest it, his dad came shooting out of the house, demanding to know why Susie had arrived home first and unaccompanied by her brother. A torrent of urgent paternal words regarding his irresponsibility were unleashed in Fin's ear and he was propelled indoors by his upper arm, his mum hovering in the background, arms folded, to continue the scolding.

"Oh, hello love!" his dad said, on seeing me. "Put your bike in the trunk and I'll drive you home." Mr. Hart was always very doting toward me.

Evelyn is such a lovely, clever girl, I'm glad you've made one good choice in life at least, Susannah, he used to say, to much eye-rolling and *DA-AD!* from Susie.

I don't recall seeing much of Finlay after that hot summer, him having crossed that childhood-pubescent dividing line where girls were stupid, girls who were friends with his sister probably most of all, and being seen with them was social suicide.

Later, I remember him being a Most Crushed On at school, wreathed with the unattainability that's only enhanced by a remote and distant nature, and given a rock-star halo that only an older good-looking lad at school and actual rock stars can achieve. Girls would breathe, "Oh my God, *Finlay Hart*," as if the very syllables could get them pregnant.

Then eventually he disappeared altogether, first to London and then to the States. He was very much one of those kinds of people who flit through the same space as you only briefly, and leave in a cloud of jet exhaust fumes and rumor, as soon as they can. The type too otherworldly to have any social media accounts, but in a deep trawl on Google you can find a mention of them in the society diary about an art gallery opening in 2008. Who just seem to move faster, and differently, and have their own laws of physics. By the time you notice them, they're long gone.

"Yeah, he only went to New York because he got model-scouted in Covent Garden and the agency paid for his fare over," I remember Susie scoffing. "*Never* mention this though, he can't know I told you," which was a little theatrical of her, given I'd not seen him in decades.

To my twenty-something ears, this as any sort of embarrassment was up there with "What a loser, he only uses his BAFTA as a toilet doorstop."

"He did modeling? Why can't it be mentioned, did he have his willy out or something?"

"Oh, no idea, it's just too much," Susie said, putting the back of her hand to her forehead in mock faint. I gathered on that occasion she quite liked the theatrics that an evil hot brother in the Big Apple entailed. "The only photos I ever saw were him in a roll-neck sweater and duffle coat looking like a Gap workwear dick, and Mum had to beg, wheedle, and threaten those out of him."

"And he doesn't model now?"

"No, he is a—wait for it—shrink. Ugh. My brother, messing with anyone's head. What a charlatan. He rinses rich old women with neuroses on the Upper East Side who fancy him, no doubt."

Then their mum died, and the long-lost, long-gone, unlamented Finlay Hart was forced to reappear in ordinary Nottingham.

I remember the jolt of seeing adult Fin in an immaculate navy coat at their mum's funeral, straight-backed with an incredible-looking auburn-haired girlfriend, clad in frock coat and spiky black heels. Her mobile went off during the ceremony, the unfamiliar rat-a-tat of a USA dial tone. She calmly switched it off without the slightest facial twitch of self-consciousness. Fin didn't react at all. They looked as if a European prince and princess were on an official engagement to inspect a disaster zone.

I wish he hadn't fucking come, Susie hissed at me, surreptitiously Lime-Drop-flavor vaping by the mulled wine urn in the village hall wake, afterward. When I saw the Harts orbiting each other like satellites, I realized she'd not exaggerated his estrangement. It hadn't dissolved on contact into even a forced friendliness.

Watching from afar, I noticed Mr. Hart making a remark to Finlay, who replied in what looked like a curt fashion and then twitched imperiously at his own cufflink, short of anything more to say. Or perhaps simply uninterested in finding any more to say. They both looked blank, Mr. Hart slightly stunned, and soon moved apart again. No smiles, no tears, no wordless supportive arm squeezes, no warmth whatsoever. It made me inwardly shudder, and my family hadn't exactly written the handbook on functionality.

Susie had seen this too. *Oh, Dad, don't bother, seriously*, she muttered. *He's not gonna change. This hasn't changed him, and nothing will.*

Apparently Fin was incensed by their dad's insistence to have the service in a church because their mum wasn't religious, and it went downhill from there.

"You must be Mr. Hart, Junior," said some nice old boy, pumping his hand and energetically and fearlessly greeting him, in our hearing.

"Hart, an ironic name for someone born without one," Susie said.

12

"Hi, you left me a message? It's Fin."

I jumped as if stung when *FINLAY HART* sprang up on my phone screen.

I don't know why this has caught me off guard. After a half an hour's reverie, he'd started to feel like a myth, not a real man with a mobile.

"Hi! Thanks for calling me back," I say, in the tone of panicked jollity you automatically slip into with a total stranger whose attention you've summoned. Then it dawns on me it's a wholly inappropriate tone to use before I announce the death of a close family member. We've been plunged into extreme circumstances where slight misjudgments equal horrendous gaffes.

Blood pounds in my ears as I say, with excessive formality: "Thanks for ringing back so quickly. I am so very, very sorry to be the one to break this news, Fin . . ."

"I know," he says. "Are you calling to tell me Susie's been killed? I know."

I'm stunned, twice over: first that he knows, and second that he sounds so matter of fact.

"Oh. How?"

"The police contacted me this morning."

"Oh. I'm sorry, I didn't know, I was told the hospital didn't have details for you."

"You were her best friend?"

"Yes. I'm her best friend," I say. Incorrectly correcting Fin Hart on the tense of my relationship to his deceased sister is both ridiculous, and feels necessary.

I don't think Fin is feigning not to remember me; I guess the odds of him recalling the names of small girls his sister hung around with a lifetime ago are minimal.

"How did you have my number, if you don't mind me asking?"

This could sound as if he's being polite but the delivery isn't, at all.

"I have Susie's phone."

"You can get into it?"

This strikes me as such an outlandish line of inquiry I say "Yes?" in an affronted way.

"I wondered. I'm glad you called me because I want to talk to you. My father's no longer capable of managing something like a funeral . . ."

It crosses my mind that this might be a point to say his father's not capable of managing this development whatsoever, but I don't feel on sure footing.

". . . And I'm over here. I can't be in the UK for long. Would you be alright to start the funeral plans and I will get over there as soon as I can to help? Contact undertakers and so on."

"Yes. Sure," I say.

"You'd have a better idea of what she'd want than myself or my father anyway."

"OK," I say, trying to hide my general amazement. Fin sounds like we're planning her a baby shower.

"The need for an inquest will delay things slightly but they should have the findings of the postmortem soon, and then they'll open an inquest, and release the body."

The body.

I gulp. I don't want to extend this interaction, but Fin obviously has information that I don't.

"Do you know any more about why the driver hit her?"

"The guy had a stroke at the wheel, he went to hospital afterward. The breathalyzer was completely clear. The police say there won't be any charges."

"Oh."

I'd not prepared for this and don't know how I feel. I was sure anyone driving on a pavement and killing best friends had a case to answer.

Once again, I ask myself—is it better or worse not to have an enemy, other than Fate?

"Having to live knowing he killed someone is no doubt worse than anything a court could impose anyway," Fin says, evenly, and while I see the logic, I can't believe his attitude. He's so *detached*. "I'll be back in touch with a date that would work for the funeral. You're in Nottingham, aren't you?"

"Yes."

"OK. Bye then."

Ed calls not long after and I relay the news about the driver, and the distinctly unsettling manner of Finlay Hart.

"He'll be in shock. You can't expect everyone to respond the same way."

"No, but . . . it's absolutely consistent with the person Susie described. Not the smallest sign he was upset, none."

My blood heats. If I need a nemesis, he'll do.

"It does sound nuts. Rich and strange families, huh?"

"I guess better than fairly broke and strange, like mine."

"Hey now! Don't misspeak Connie, please."

Did I mention Ed has completely charmed my mum? Sigh.

"Do you want to go 'round to Susie's house tomorrow morning and help me do some sorting out?" Ed adds. "I know it sounds weird, but it needs doing and I can't bear the thought of sitting around doing nothing. Justin's on a morning shift. I already know I won't be able to lie in."

"Sorting out?"

"I don't know what the status of her dad's mental state is, but he's still next of kin."

"Along with her brother," I say. I should visit her dad.

"Yes, when he's over here. They'll have rights to do the house clearance." That her house needs clearing makes me wince. So soon? So fast? Her property not belonging to her. "I'm thinking, as her best mates, she might want us to do some preparatory tidying up for her? Take away anything she might find . . . compromising, not want her family or other authorities to see?"

"Oh. Yes."

My brain plays a clip of me looking quizzically at a giant dildo.

"Thing is, E . . . are you OK to see the corner? Where it happened?"

"Oh!" I'd not thought of this. I'd not considered the scene, by daylight, still existing. "Yes. I think so. She's not there."

"Yeah. But thought I'd flag. Pick you up at eleven?"

"Yes, sure."

Given where Ed lives, picking me up involves driving miles past Susie's and back south across the city again. He is being solicitous and caring in a *taking charge* kind of way, and I'm hugely grateful for it. He's not making me jump through the hoops or agonize about whether to say I want looking after, he's just looking after me. Which is Ed.

13

I don't recommend the sensation of emerging from fitful rest, face so sodden with tears that you have wet collarbones, momentarily wildly elated that your best friend dying violently was only a disturbing creation of your subconscious. Before the murky world of four fourteen a.m. on your digital alarm clock swims into focus, and you remember that she has.

Ed looks as tired as I feel when he knocks on the door.

"Morning," he says, balefully.

"Hi. Coffee?"

"I want to get going with it, you?"

"Same."

We exchange sleepy monosyllables on the way there, lulled by the familiar drive. Everything's the same and everything will always be different.

"I suppose in the modern world we should each of us nominate someone to do this," Ed says. "Wipe our browsing history. Get rid of *the secret shoebox* we're directed to under the bed. Without opening it."

"Hah. Yes."

"I'll be your nominee if you'll be mine," Ed says, smiling, and I say, "OK, deal," while squirming at how it reminds me of his ill-fated letter. Also, why isn't his fiancée that person to him?

Why indeed.

"Hester wanted me to give you her love, by the way," Ed says, flipping the indicator.

"That's nice of her," I say, blandly. "Say thank you for me."

"I will."

"She and Susie clashed antlers from time to time, but Hester was very fond."

Like hell.

"Yes, of course."

"I didn't want to say on the phone, I don't know why, but—Susie liked *recreational pharma* sometimes, didn't she. With her sister wives."

"Huh?" I say.

Ed swings a look at me. "Lauren? Aisha? *Jennifer-Jane?* Who has two forenames outside the mid-West, that always got me, such a snob."

"Oh, the cokey idiots!" I say. "The Teacup Girls."

Those nicknames for Susie's work friends are Justin's. The former is self-explanatory (Justin loves his ironic revival of exasperated dad words) and the latter—the Teacup Girls—is because he said they'd had so much Botox, if they want to express amazement they'd have to drop one.

Susie kept this gang entirely separate from us, and only dipped in and out of it herself, not a core member of the cast, a guest star.

They all had cosmetic work, huge kitchen extensions, white off-roaders they drove to the hairdressers, handbags with logos, wealthy husbands, took skiing holidays in Whistler, and drank rosé when the kids were in nursery. And sometimes they put on things covered in sequins to get smashed on champagne cocktails, get off with men who weren't their husbands, and do lines in the bathroom.

Susie would tell us about their antics, and we'd revel in a good gasp and tut. She gloried in their excesses and, sometimes, she partook in the Class As.

"Any idea if she has any in the house, or where she'd keep it, if so?"

"I don't think she bothered unless someone else brought it to the party," I say. "I'd be amazed if there was any in the house, honestly."

"Hmmmm."

I was the keeper of Susie's secrets, and she was the keeper of mine. All bar one.

WHEN WE ROUND the corner by the cricket ground, nearing her house, Ed inclines his head and says: "It was there."

I twist around to see an otherwise unremarkable street corner, a tree with a gash in its trunk and some cellophane cornets of carnations lying at its base, in a modern shrine. Who are the people who do that? I can't imagine Susie even knows her neighbors.

I imagine the scene, the sound of it, the squeal of tires and the startled cries of people loitering outside the fish and chips shop opposite as the vehicle came off the road, trying to warn Susie. Wrong place, wrong time. The sickening thump of a human body on the bumper, the crack of Susie hitting a hard surface at speed. Her lying prone, like a toy thrown across the room in a tantrum.

"Why did she get out of the taxi on the main road?! If she'd been dropped at her house, she'd be here now. This was so meaningless," I say, suddenly furious again, this time, with her. The phrase *banging your head against a brick wall* has more meaning now than I ever want it to.

"She'll have been vaping," Ed says, who's obviously thought about this as much as I have, albeit from different angles. "Dying, for the sake of those bloody tampon-holder things and Skittles-flavored steam. Mr. Kipling fog."

"Ohhhhh," I say. Of course. We'd applauded Susie moving on to e-cigarettes in our late twenties. Good to see you taking your health more seriously, we agreed. It was still going to kill her.

"I wish I'd smacked it out of her hand," I say, trying to keep the ragey hopeless tears back.

"Well, not to be Mr. Logic from *Viz* . . ." Ed glances at me as he pulls in to park. "You still read *Viz*? But she'd have stood there like a chimney with real cigarettes too."

"Oh. Yeah. Duh."

He turns the engine off.

"I've started doing this too," he says, into a quiet that seems larger than it is, with the sudden absence of engine noise. "Playing variables, worrying about what if Hester and I hadn't got engaged, we'd have left the pub earlier. We can't, Eve. We're going to go mad if we do. What happened, happened, and our only job is to live with it. Which is enough of a fucking job, frankly. Not beat ourselves up."

"Yeah, you're right."

Ed squeezes my shoulder before we get out of the car and I'm so grateful I at least have him and Justin to share this loss with. No one else can understand.

I contemplate how hard it'll be to be in Susie's house, without Susie, as we walk up the path. Her home can seem like nothing much to the untrained eye, but I promise you that solid red-brick Victorian semi-detacheds in this postcode are a pretty penny.

Not a starter property in an area with "drinkers' pubs," petty crime waves, and trash bins with Wite-Out warnings like "*No. 22s!!!! (DO NOT FUCKIN ROB AGAIN TWATS.)*"

"I want an investment and Dad's not getting any younger, it's walkable to his," she said, back in our twenties. I think she was rationalizing that she felt more comfortable among her own, MacBooks in Caffè Neros and Marks and Spencer's nearby. After all, she didn't walk to her dad's, she got in her racing-green Mini Cooper, with 6 Music cranked up high. (Her Mini, that we averted our eyes from as we passed it outside: how is it here, when she's not here? It will have to be sold. She's going to be raging when she comes back and finds out it's gone.)

I use the key and let us into her narrow hallway, pushing against a small drift of mail that's already built behind her door. On the other side, the familiar smell of Susie's house, the pungent laundry detergent she used, blindsides me.

"I'll take those to the kitchen table and look through to see what needs canceling, utilities, et cetera," Ed says.

"I think you need a death certificate for that?" I say.

"You might be right."

I'm not sure how I know this. Standing in her house, discussing registering her death. Surrounded by Susie's décor choices, her things, so many coats of hers I remember nights out with her wearing, hanging limply on the back of the door. Soon to be decorating the local branch of Oxfam, on plastic hangers with handwritten price tags.

I'm choked. This is the most difficult thing I've ever done. Second most, after the hospital.

Why are things, abandoned things, so hard to bear? They didn't have that quality before. And compared to the living thing you've lost, they're without value.

When I was a teenager, the family cat, Horace, died. He was a grumpy old bruiser, prone to biting the hands that petted him, and my "complacent young person" grief wasn't great. Yet a while after the vet's trip where my parents returned with an empty carrier, I noticed a fur-covered moldy grape by the television stand. He'd been rolling it around and jealously guarding it, for weeks prior. Horace had a thing about grapes. All other small spherical objects were ignored, but grapes were his fetish.

At the sight of the fur-covered moldy grape without its protector, my heart cracked.

I HAND ED the sheaf of letters and say: "I'm going to see if there's anything needs 'tidying up' in the bedroom."

I have something particular in mind. During the KonMari craze for banishing clutter, I told Susie I'd completed the "sorting personal mementos" hardcore level for the aficionados.

"I could never do that," she said. "I've kept all my diaries and all my letters. Every last one. I'm anal like that. Not many people ever wrote to me, though. I am not the love letters type."

"You kept diaries?" I said. Susie didn't seem the diary-keeping type either.

"Yeah, I gave it up eventually but when we were younger and into my early twenties. I was being precious. They're full of trash, obviously. *Wah wah I'm so fat wah wah my brother's being mean. Wah wah my mum won't let me buy a crop top.* The usual."

Something I know, as I heavy-tread up the stairs and think about when she made me rub thick swatches of a dozen near-identical oatmeal fabrics to choose this carpet, is: I will never read these diaries.

Telling myself I have the right to because she's no longer here to stop me, to "feel closer" to her somehow, would be an ultimate betrayal. If she'd never been moved to show me them alive, there's no cause to think she'd want the contents shared now she's not.

What I can do for her, though, is stop other people reading them. I push open the door to her bedroom with trepidation. Susie's taste was very different to my love of dark walls, big plants, and kitsch trinkets. Her bed is a white four-poster and the whole space is a symphony of neutrals, and order. The bed is unslept in, neatly made, pillows plumped. I stare at it.

Imagine if Susie had known when straightening that duvet that she'd never be in that bed again. That she'd come back not to this room, with her foam earplugs on the nightstand and her pajamas folded on that chair, but instead would be wheeled, flesh chilly, into a morgue.

This lack of warning is another aspect of it that I can't accept. Susie didn't know her last day was her last day. She got no ceremony, no sense of occasion. Life life life . . . and in an instant, dead. Like a brutal edit in a film, a jump cut. Over. Finished.

I see now why those who lose loved ones young become risk-takers. They're not reckless, they just see the stakes differently from the rest of us. More clearly. They don't have the same blithe trust in *tomorrow* that we all do, they know it's all up for grabs. Ignorance is bliss.

I tentatively open her built-in wardrobes, sweating like a burglar, and riffle through the clothes, trying not to look at any one item, not able to cope with the tsunami of memories they'll unleash. For a second I stop, paralyzed every time I get a stab of recognition, a specific memory attached to a particular coat or a dress.

There's odds and ends in the bottom of it, pieces of empty luggage, and a box, made of a felt material. It has a lid, and holes in the sides for handles. I drag it out, put it on the bed, and open it.

Well, that was easy. Praise be to Susie for being so organized, and, this box aside, no sort of hoarder. Inside are several small bundles of letters, fastened with elastic bands, all of them still in envelopes, and addressed to Susie at her rented flat back when she lived in the Lace Market. And underneath those, girlish diaries with pastel, patterned, foamy covers, the kind with clasps but not locks.

A quick poke about in a set of dresser drawers with glass handles, and a sweep under the bed, turns up absolutely nothing sensitive whatsoever.

I pick my way carefully back downstairs, box balanced on both arms, and find Ed in the kitchen.

I announce: "I'm taking this. I'm not going to pry through anything in it, on my mum's life. But it's old letters and diaries, exactly the sort of thing she'd want gone."

"And I'm taking this, but not in the sense I'm taking it."

I lean my head around to see what he means, and Ed's flapping a tiny packet of white powder at me.

"Where the hell was that?!"

"In the spare teapot. Which looked like she'd inherited it from a granny. Susie's in heaven right now having to explain herself."

I laugh, while feeling ever so slightly perturbed that as her best friend and keeper of her secrets, I wasn't the one to predict its presence.

14

"Ey up me ducks," says Justin, unwinding a snazzy silk maroon scarf from his neck. Ed and I mumble greetings. "Nice day for it. Anyone want anything from the bar?"

We demur and Justin goes to order his coffee.

Uncharacteristically, I cringe at Justin's playful manner, in the direst of times. It's been just over a week since Susie died and we are gathering to discuss her funeral plans. I know he's nothing but good intentions, I love his general iconoclasm. He gives the impression of recklessness for the purposes of his comedy, but he's emotionally intelligent.

When we were at sixth form, Justin did work experience at an old people's home. He took a man in a wheelchair out to see a lake and produced homemade sandwiches and KitKats for them to enjoy alongside the view. The man cried and said it was one of the nicest days he'd had in years, as his family didn't visit.

"That was that," Justin said, at the time. "I knew I couldn't do any other sort of work."

That's who Justin is.

However, today I don't trust a total stranger to realize Justin is entirely benign, and that goes triple when the total stranger is Finlay Hart. I am additionally unusually relieved that Justin left Leonard with his sister today, as I can't see his yappy interventions being taken as comic.

It's been just over a week since Susie died and Fin got in touch to ask to meet. I explained it was a group effort between me, Ed, and Justin, and Fin said, "Well, bring them."

I asked if he wanted to choose a venue and he said, "Anywhere in the city center should be easy for everyone?" and I nominated the Caffè Nero by the Brian Clough statue, as straightforward to find.

"Are you coming in from Bridgford?" I said, not to be nosy, but because I was edgy and didn't know how best to spin the conversation out to something of conventionally polite length.

"No, I'm staying at a hotel in town," Fin said.

I didn't know what to say to that other than "Ah."

Now we're here, on a Saturday afternoon, with a gang of twenty-somethings near us bellowing and playing music on their laptops, it feels a lumpenly stupid choice.

Ed and I bump into each other outside, and in the pin-sharp white sunlight I notice how drawn and shadowed he looks, after only a few days apart. Like Ed, but sketched in charcoal. From the way he squints at me before heaving the door open, I suspect I look much the same.

I once again allowed myself to believe the cosmetics industry's lies that you can cover under-eye circles, and spent a while dabbing on three layers of beige. Then caught my reflection in a shop window and saw a very tired woman with ochre raccoon markings. Her expression is set to "embattled, and vaguely concussed."

We choose a table upstairs with a view, looking down on the buskers and the shoppers and the people whose lives are continuing. Lucky foolish unwitting bastards. How can they make being alive seem so easy, when it wasn't possible for Susie to stay that way? Do they not know how precarious this all is?

I feel scared, to the point of being in a secret sweat under my winter parka as I unzip it, even though there's nothing to be scared of, exactly. I suppose I'm scared constantly, now, of this completely altered reality I'm expected to manage.

There's something so counterintuitive in planning a funeral—the one person it's for can't attend. Dispensing a Lifetime Achievement award, but with no cutaways to their delighted face in the audience.

It's not for Susie, it's for everyone else, my mother said.

She made me strong cups of tea, sitting at her kitchen table, and rubbed my back as she said things like "Oh my God, how awful" and "That is no age, no age at all" and "I know you two girls were thick as thieves" and "I am so sorry, darling" at intervals as I heaved and near-retched, talking about what happened. I wasn't holding my emotions in check for anyone else's sake, I could let it out with my mum. She talked fondly about how she'd always thought Susie looked like Carly Simon, and I got a bittersweet pang of gratitude at a familiar observation that only days ago would be pleasant but mundane. The value of memories of Susie had shot up, like the hiked price of a rare autograph.

But how does that advice work, in practice? It's for Susie and not for Susie, at the same time?

"How is everyone?" Justin says on his return, setting his cup down, spoon rattling in the saucer.

"Terrible," I say. "You?"

"I look like I'm in prosthetics to play Winston Churchill, I'm that puffy."

I laugh weakly. I wish Susie's laugh was echoing mine.

"You brought notes, Eve?" Justin adds.

I look down at my gnawed-looking scrap of paper. "Uh yeah. Things we discussed previous."

In truth, I wanted to look as if I have homework if Fin gets testy about the fact we've not sorted much. The delay in the body being released after the postmortem means we can't book the funeral yet.

The body. *The remains*, as someone said to me. It made Susie—whole and beautiful, if extinct—sound like a shard of bone found on a dig in a forest.

"You kind of wonder what aesthetic Manhattan restaurants use, now that even coffee chains in Britain have ripped it off, huh?" Ed says.

"Mmm?"

"The Edison light bulbs, exposed brick walls, and the knacked-up brown Chesterfield sofas in here. I mean, that was cutting-edge cool, once."

"Hah. Yeah."

"The Teacup Girls have got in touch with me, by the way," Ed says. "They want to offer their input into Susie's send-off. Also, they want to know why we haven't changed her Facebook page into an In Memoriam. She has her wall locked down."

"What?!" I say, chest immediately aflame with indignation.

"Firstly, no way are they having input! They'll give her horses with feathers on their heads and a Snow White glass coffin and 'Wind Beneath My Wings.' Played by Boyzone. On kazoos."

"That sounds pretty rad and status quo disruptive to be fair," Justin says. "Make a note now: that's what I want."

"Also her page isn't set up for lots of 'rest in peace our princess' posts because Susie would loathe that."

I know why I'm incensed and protective. If attempts are made to rewrite who she was, to rival my claim to her, I'll lose her by another degree. My Susie is the real Susie.

"Why did they go to you, and not me?" I add.

"Given your reaction, I can't begin to imagine," Ed says, tipping his cup to drink with little finger aloft, and Justin guffaws.

I harrumph and say: "Yes, well if they know her best female friend would cockblock them doing it, then that tells them they shouldn't be doing it."

"I'll ask them to message me their thoughts and we can decide whether to use them. I have a feeling they'll lose interest as time goes on. No one has the right to get across you, Eve. Everyone knows that. You two were practically a marriage."

I nod and try not to cry for the thousandth time. I will never have a friend like her again. Not only because of our affinity, the sheer timescales. You can't make new old friends. Doors in your life, open and closing.

Ed sips his Americano and glances across to the staircase. ". . . Oh, speak of the devil. That could be Finlay . . . ?"

I look over.

It's definitely Finlay. Even if I hadn't recognized his features, the ink-dark expensive clothing and pristine white Adidas

Superstars signal money, and Otherness. And yes, "the devil" seems apt.

He scans the room. I raise my hand, as if in class, to say "Here."

IN THREE PURPOSEFUL strides across the room, Finlay Hart is at our table.

My first thought is: he's taller than I remember. My second thought is: I'm surprised at how easily I recognize him. You know when someone asks you to picture a person you've not seen in years and you can't, and therefore you think you wouldn't know them? Then you see them, and *bang*, there they are, you have no doubt? Pattern recognition?

He still has the solemn, dark blue eyes, and straight brow. His nose is different to Susie's uptilted one—how is it possible that nose has ceased to exist?—neat and straight, and those are Susie's lips, just smaller, with the defined Cupid's bow.

I trace similarities to Susie like I'm piecing together a facial composite—he also has her pronounced cheekbones. But their coloring was very different, so you'd never have put them together as siblings. I remember Susie saying: *I'd love to think he's adopted, and no doubt so would he, but sadly the documentation is in order and my dad's dad was the absolute spit of him.*

My third thought is, as Finlay pulls a knitted hat from his head and riffles his dark brown hair back into place: he's intimidatingly well put together, if not actually appealing in any way. His face looks like a plasterer could sculpt it in a few quick swipes of a trowel: fierce geometry.

It suits his nature. No softness.

"Hi. I'm Finlay."

I vaguely recall he had floppy *Brideshead Revisited* hair last I saw him; now it's slightly shorter and neater and he's got *just got off the red eye* stubble that's pretending to be a beard.

Fin's not smiling at us, but then, being fair, it's not a smiling occasion.

"You must be Ed," he says, sticking out a hand for a handshake. "And Eve?"

I give him my hand. It's like we're meeting for a job interview. He gives it one firm small downward yank.

"I'm Justin," says Justin, who's too far away for a handshake, so he waves.

I can't stop raking Fin's features for resemblance to Susie's. It's the tingle of having a shadow of her returned to me, her genes in someone with even less body fat, and more testosterone.

But though he has her lips, it's interesting how character comes out as you age, because they are set in a superior sort of pouty sulk. You can *see* he looks down on everyone around him, no acquaintance needed.

Don't they say they have the face you deserve by forty? *Tick tock motherfu*—

"You don't want to get a drink?" Ed says, of the space on the table in front of Fin.

"I'm not keen on the coffee here. I'll get one somewhere else after we're done."

Wow.

"Do you want to go somewhere else now? It's no trouble," I say, my arse rising, if not literally.

"No, it's fine."

"We all loved your sister very much and we are all so, so devastated about what's happened," Ed says, partly by way of diverting us from subpar roasting beans. "It's horrific. But I don't need to tell you that."

"Thank you," Fin says, levelly. For a frightening second I think he's not going to say any more, then he adds: "There's a complete meaninglessness to it that is tough to process."

We three nod vigorously and mutter agreement, as much in relief that he's given us something to work with, I think.

". . . Though what meaning does any death have, I guess? It's not as if a fatal illness has intrinsically more significance," he concludes. I can't say I'm surprised that Fin doesn't do cozy platitudes.

"No . . . ," Ed says and I suspect, in the brief silence that follows, we're all mentally sifting potential responses and discarding them.

I could say that the difference for me is that if you're going to get sick, you're going to get sick. There is an inevitability, a mystery.

What tortures me is that there were so many tiny but necessary contributory factors in that evening that cumulatively brought Susie to be standing in the way of that car, in that single second. Playing variables, as Ed said. She wouldn't have been there if the taxi had taken longer to arrive. If it had stopped at more red lights. If the quiz had been shorter, or longer. If we'd gone back to mine for a nightcap. If the person in the car who had the stroke had chosen a different route, or if that bulging blood vessel wall in their brain had held out a moment longer. There was chance upon chance to survive, and she didn't.

Our environment is so extraordinarily perilous. That's what I can't unknow, sitting in rooms abuzz with ignorant noise.

Nothing is for granted, and everything you know can be taken away in an instant.

Nevertheless, even if I didn't suspect Fin to be both hostile and toxic, *I can't stop obsessing that your younger sister could've so easily escaped her untimely end* is not a remotely comforting or acceptable thing to say to anyone.

"So. Regarding the funeral," Fin says. There's no trace of transatlantic in his voice. No Midlands either, but then the Harts are from the sort of postcode where everyone's accent sounds posh-neutral to the point of southern. "You said you've not been able to confirm a date for it yet?"

"Yes," I say, feeling the onus on me to take charge. I explain we should be able to, very soon. I describe the readings and the music choices and a rough order of service, and Fin nods, neutral, throughout.

"I didn't know if you wanted to do a reading?" I ask him.

"No, thank you," Fin says. I try not to judge this, without knowing his reasons, though obviously I'm judging it hard. It doesn't help that he doesn't elaborate why, beyond that curt confirmation.

"As to the venue for the wake, there's a hotel at the top of Derby Road called The Waltons. It's chintzy and pretty, but not too stuffy. We thought that'd be fitting? It has a bar and we could put out a buffet. I don't want it to be too youthful and like a party, but Susie would've hated something . . . fogeyish? For want of a better word."

Fin nods. "The family will pay for this, obviously. Give us costs and if anything needs paying upfront, I'll transfer to you straightaway."

I nod back. Just as I think this is going to pass off without controversy, I say (congratulating myself this is a thoughtful touch, he will appreciate it): "We called the church about the churchyard where your mum was buried, and they have a plot free for Susie."

I can't believe I'm saying these words. She is arriving fifty years ahead of schedule.

"It's not right by your mum, but it's very near. Under a tree, which seemed . . ." I was going to say nice, and realize that there's nothing nice about this whatsoever. "A good idea."

"I don't want her to be buried," Fin says. "Absolutely not."

I startle. "What? Why?"

"It's how I feel," he says, fixing intense eyes on me. "I hate the thought of her rotting in the ground. She'd agree. Cremation only."

"I think . . . Susie would like the thought of being near her mum, though," I say.

Fin's eyes focus harder upon me. He clears his throat.

"I don't think Susie would've *liked* the thought of any of this. Imputing 'liking' things to her seems slightly mad, given the situation. There's only least worsts. The least worst to her would've been cremation, in my opinion."

I am horribly stung by being called "slightly mad," which would be hurtful any time, but in this context is like he kicked me while I was on the floor.

Only a pass the size of his loss can stop me openly losing it, in return.

"Erm, OK, but I knew her well too, and I am sure she'd . . . want burial."

"With all due respect—" Fin starts.

A phrase that only ever means "which is none."

". . . You can't be sure. Did you ever discuss which method of disposal she'd prefer, should she die suddenly?"

"No, *obviously* not, but . . ."

"Right, well. Neither did Susie and I. But we aren't a religious family, and we aren't a burials family. My mother's was something of an anomaly."

Oh, of course. The fight. He's rerunning it. People don't change. *Bastards gonna bastard,* I hear Susie say.

I'm left uselessly opening and closing my mouth. Purely at a debating level, it seems to me Fin should've picked a lane—he says it matters he'd rather she was cremated, while also saying Susie would agree. *Which is it? Especially as you two disagreed on what color the sky was, from what I can gather.*

I hadn't—stupidly, perhaps—expected him to pull rank. I feel as if I'm letting Susie down by allowing Fin to prevail, and that feeling is powerful.

"But . . . ," I begin.

"If you want cremation, and you're her surviving relative, then that's what should happen," Ed interrupts, with a pointed look at me that communicates *let this go.*

"Her surviving relative who's compos mentis, anyway," Fin says.

As I'm about to ask if he's checked in on his dad, and what state he's in, Fin's phone rings and he says: "I've got to take this. Thanks for everything you've done. Call me if there's anything else."

He picks up his phone and says a brisk "Hello?" into it, puts his hand up by way of farewell, and strides away across the café.

We sit in stunned silence for a few beats. Ed with clenched teeth, me lightly seething, Justin quizzical.

"*Well*. He puts the strange in estranged," Justin says. "Was it me, or was there some hateration and holleration in this dancery?"

"Not a complete mystery why he and Susie didn't see eye to eye, is it?" I say. "Not up there with the Bermuda Triangle and who built Stonehenge. Fucking hell."

"Ah dear . . . I don't expect him to be cheerful," Ed says. "That did seem unnecessarily confrontational." He pauses. "But maybe he has particular reasons regarding not wanting a burial."

I roll my tired, eyelinered eyes at Ed.

"Oh come *on*, Ed. Even you don't believe that. That was about a show of strength. It was testing how it felt to get his own way, when Susie's not here to stop him. He's not even fussed she's gone, from what I can see. He's a monster. A walking Voight-Kampff test in spotless sneakers."

"That's the check to show whether or not you're a replicant in *Blade Runner*," Justin says to Ed and Ed says "I know!" indignantly.

"Should I have insisted on burial?" I say, doleful.

"Wait, that wasn't you insisting?" Justin says, with a sly expression.

"You know what I mean."

Ed shakes his head, emphatically. "No. Even if he's secretly a robot, it's his call. We're only getting to do as much planning as we are due to Fin allowing it. He could be owning every last detail."

"It's only as he doesn't want the hassle and didn't know her.

Can you imagine him having an insight on anything she liked since the 'Barbies' age?"

"Whatever the reason," Ed says. "Don't piss him off. You only have to tolerate him until the end of the wake and then you'll never see him again."

"Imagine. He might sack his dad's funeral off entirely," Justin says.

"Oh no, he'd come back for that, and you know why?" I say. "Little thing called being a sole living heir."

"Unless his dad disliked him so much he wrote him out of the will," Justin says.

". . . And the unscrupulous long-lost son reappeared, when his father was infirm and mentally unsound of mind . . . and got him to change it?"

"Woah," Justin says, and we boggle at each other at the eminent plausibility of this being Fin's current, concurrent project.

"Alright you two, this isn't an episode of *Inspector Morse*," Ed says. "Concentrate on the tasks in hand."

15

We decide, after Fin's flourish of a departure, to sketch out the order of service before I go to the printer's.

A Celebration (??) of the Life of . . .

"Are we going with 'celebration'—yay, look on the bright side?" I say, looking skeptically at my own words. "I see no cause for optimism." I add another question mark.

"It's not saying there's an upside. It's saying we won't only weep and lament but also remember why it was so good to have had her here," Ed says.

"Yeah, I agree with that," Justin says. "We're celebrating Susie, not celebrating her death. That's a category error."

"But 'In Memory of' seems more neutral?" I say. "With celebration I worry people will think they're meant to wear jaunty colors and all that jazz."

"It feels like 'In Memory of' is more for old people," Ed says. "Not so much for Susie."

"Nothing about this feels right for Susie," I say, instantly raw.

"So it's . . ."
I write, carefully:

A Celebration of the Life of
Susannah Carole Octavia Hart

"She hated her middle names," I say. "No one was allowed to know them! I can hear her now saying 'Strike that shit off there, you're showing me up!'"

"Yeah, I used to call her 'Cocktavia' and get hit with her knuckle-duster rings," Justin says, and I laugh, and for once it's not just a weak teary laugh. I sense recovery may be buried somewhere in laughter. Partial recovery.

"Her mum loved Carole Lombard," I say. "You know, married to Clark Gable? I can remember Susie fuming that Carole was not a film star name by the 1980s, it was a 'can I speak to the manager' name."

"Where did Octavia come from?" Ed says and Justin says, "Škoda."

As they guffaw, I think about how there are still things I know about Susie's origins that they don't, having had ten years' jump on them. Octavia was her gran.

We've chosen a photograph for the cover of the order of service. The useful thing about our social media era is that profile pictures on Facebook provide a nest-clutch of images you know for sure the user liked, or at least was happy enough with to make public. Susie had very definite ideas about things; she was very certain of her own mind.

We feel reassured that the snap of her on a ferry, blond-brown hair whipping around her face as she grins stoically through rain, complexion rosy in the cold, was as attractive to her as it was to us, if it had been available viewing to everyone on the internet in years gone by. It's from her late twenties, but she looked no different. There was a younger one at a wedding that we pondered, before deciding it was too "puppyish pre-twenty-five" to those who knew her face well.

They're quite strange, the calculations you find yourself making. There's no rule that says the photograph has to closely resemble the person at the point they passed, but it feels as if there is.

If I stare at the picture too long, I go slightly light-headed. She is right there, and yet not here.

"Maybe use the initials for her middle names then, like on official documentation, or your bank card?" Ed says, not entirely serious.

"We can't call her 'Susannah C. O. Hart.' That makes her sound like a 1950s movie studio mogul," I say.

"Or Irish, *to be sure to be sure*. Susannah Cee O'Hart, so it is," Justin says.

"What about Susannah Hart?" I say.

"If you're giving her the full first name but not the middle name it feels unbalanced, somehow," Ed says.

"Susie Hart? Too casual?" I say. "It's how everyone knew her. Except maybe in close family."

"Yeah, that's my fear. Her dad also chose the names Susannah Carole Octavia," Justin says. "I'm not sure it's OK for us to erase that and go 'The S Dog, The Susiemeister General' nicknames on her order of service."

"Without being either flip or nasty," Ed says. "How much will Mr. Hart Senior know what's going on anyway?"

"Hmmmm." We collectively stare sadly and contemplatively into the foam on our second round of coffees—the one you fancy and know you don't need, that leaves you too wired.

"I think Susannah Hart," I say. "That's her birth certificate name and the name we knew her by. If there's a benefit to your friends doing your order of service, it's that they knew your taste in a way your parents didn't. If we put her full name on there, everyone's first minute will be spent whispering 'Carole Octavia lol?' and we know she'd loathe that."

"Motion carried," Justin says. "One point: what if her brother objects?"

"Hmmm, he didn't seem the type," Ed says, and we all laugh, and I'm glad we can still clown like we used to. It feels like fortitude.

". . . Can I raise a practical point if he does," Ed says. "Finlay's signed off on us putting together the order of service. If he doesn't like the names we chose, he's going to see that at the same time as everyone else, as they're being handed out at the crematorium. *So what's he gonna do, huh?* You'd have to be a psychopath to start finger-jabbing and shouting at a funeral."

"Oh yeah? You need to meet my mum's family up north," Justin says.

"I wouldn't rule psychopathy out," I say. "That's an inactive amygdala if ever I saw one."

"Wasn't that just the way he was sitting?" Justin says.

"Can you translate that from the Eve?" Ed says.

"The bit of the brain that doesn't function in scans of serial killers. How can he be a psychiatrist? He's like Harold Shipman, posing as a doctor."

"Shipman was a doctor," Justin says.

"Well, regardless of how many people he's murdered, if he kicks off, that's on him. We're in the clear," Ed says, sitting back.

"Edward, you crafty ferret," Justin says.

"I think he lets you and I blaze out in front as the bad guys while he's actually the worst," I say, and Ed makes a "straightening the brim of an invisible hat" gesture.

"Other point of controversy," I say. "We're definitely going with the *Twin Peaks* theme to play us out at the end? I didn't mention that to Fin, I'm quite glad now."

"I love it," Justin says. "She loved it, it's so her. She went to that Halloween night as Laura Palmer, didn't she?"

"Yep," I say. I helped her with that costume. A plastic wrap, blue hair dye, glittery robot face paint, and a sign that said *She Is Filled with Secrets* on the back. I refuse to dwell on the fact that I daubed silver highlighter down her signature Hart family cheekbones to simulate alluring rigor mortis.

"If she can see us from anywhere, when that comes on, she'll laugh out loud. And do a fist pump," Justin says.

"That's what matters then," Ed says. "We're honoring her, not some snark in the third pew."

"Amen!" Justin says.

"Amen," I agree.

"And give her brother a break too," Ed says to me, trying his luck.

"Sure," I say. "Leg or arm, lol?"

Heart isn't possible.

After a pause, I say to Ed: "And you definitely want to do the reading? Whatever I write?"

"Without a doubt." He squeezes my hand.

This is what we agreed, through a vale of tears. I can write about Susie but can't bring myself to perform it. Ed says he can read something, but can't steel himself to write anything.

Justin has offered to critique it all afterward.

Ed keeps hold of my hand and I squeeze back again, to make it polite to release it. He gives me a meaningful look as I withdraw my fingers.

"You'll be great at it. You know that, don't you? Don't be scared of it."

"Thank you," I say. Ed is right, I am scared of it. It feels so good to be understood.

"Ooh, er. I've just realized something spooky," I say. "You know how you always said Susie was Laura? The penny's dropped who Fin reminds me of. Agent Cooper."

Both Ed and Justin tilt their heads, think, nod.

Justin clicks on an imaginary recorder, leans in: "Diane. Met three more assholes today."

16

The countdown to the funeral is awful. "Awful." What a limp word for this experience. Queues at the supermarket on Christmas Eve are awful. Banging your elbow on a hard surface is awful. My sliding scale for "awful" has completely changed and I need an enhanced vocabulary to deal with it. You don't realize the flippancy of your generation's attitudes and language until you grasp for the terminology that conveys the impact, and it's not there. It's been shopworn by silly jokes and ironic hyperbole.

Reliving the morning I found out, which I do, constantly, compulsively, is harrowing to the point of some sort of PTSD. Yet the word "harrowing" isn't enough.

I can see myself and Susie in my mind's eye, sitting in sleepwear at her house. Susie in a cricket sweater over her pajamas, hair like Beetlejuice and with brightly pedicured feet up on the coffee table, describing our aftereffects from shotgunning rosé wine in a local bar as "harrowing."

"This is an ordeal," Susie would say. "We're going to need Uber Eats KFC, and possibly dips from Domino's. We've been to war. We have been through the wringer and in the trenches."

When you've used those words to mean "got sick" and "wish you'd not kissed a man whose Twitter handle is @DoctorPenis" it feels wrong to apply it to seismic, disturbing, stuff-of-darkest-fears that have changed you forever.

It took me two and a half hours, and pauses for whimpering and bawling, to write my eulogy for Susannah Hart. I sent it to Ed, who replied: *That's me broken into pieces.* And then a few minutes later. *It's beautiful. I can only hope to do it justice. Xx*

Then I went back to work on Monday, accepting everyone's curious pitying looks with a wan smile, fielding the volley of questions with polite but peremptory answers. *Yes, hit by a car. No, they weren't a drunk driver. Funeral next week. Yes, it was no age. No, she wasn't married and didn't have kids. Thanks, I am bearing up.*

Satisfied they have the intel, Phil, Lucy, and Seth go back to staring at their monitors.

I feel like I'm playing dress-up at normal life. As if I've put on armor in a battle reenactment game with a bunch of fellow geeks in a field. Oh, are we doing the one where it's life as usual and we write for a website?

I sit and type:

There's hotdogs, then there's THESE hotdogs. Find out why people are going crazy for the dirty loaded sausages at Who Let the Dogs Out?

"Are you doing the trashy frankfurters piece?" asks Phil. Phil has been tentative around me, as even he doesn't think his bombastic mode of jocular insult works with a newly bereaved person.

"Yeah," I say. Defiantly calling them "frankfurters" is so Phil. Coke is still "fizzy pop."

"Bloody horrible, aren't they. Who wants fried prawns on a hotdog? Filthy bastards. We're not in America."

"It's hipsters," I say. "They'll put anything on anything."

"There seems to be a glorification of things you only used to eat when you were steaming at three a.m. in my day."

"Modern world, Phil. It's not for us," I say.

"Ah stop, you're young!" Phil says, and I can see by his face he's awkward at being even that complimentary. *Is this that thing called flattery*, he's thinking. *Am I doing it right?*

"Well, thank you."

Phil looks at the page I'm on.

"Can we call them 'dirty'? Isn't that a bit contrary to health and safety?"

"It's accepted to mean 'calorific stuff dumped on top,' now. Marks and Spencer do dirty fries."

"Oh. Right you are."

Phil shakes his head in dismay at his monitor.

I drag an image of the El Gringo Dog—jalapeños, avocado, and crushed tortilla chips topping—onto the page and wish I did a more useful job, like Ed teaching kids or Justin caring for old people. It's pretty hard to tell yourself to soldier on so that the region gets vital information about the Triple XXX Ringstinger Chili Dog.

What would Susie want me to do? I ask myself, as an antidote for feeling useless. I know the answer immediately. She'd want me to check on her dad, beyond one stilted phone call. It's intimidating, given I'm unsure about who I will encounter.

I remember when she first mentioned he was struggling,

a couple of years ago. She said: *I caught my dad looking up "ice cream" on Wikipedia. I was like—"Dad, are you thinking of a retirement business, churning your own?" He said, "It's the darndest thing, I can't remember what ice cream is. Is it ice, and cream?"*

Susie talked him through mint choc chip and vanilla flavors and cornets by the seaside, and he laughed and said, "Of course!"

At the time, we brushed it off as a slightly worrying but ultimately quirky bout of senior forgetfulness.

It sounds ridiculous, but Susie's dad used to run his own engineering company and was an amateur tennis champion. Iain Hart, with his soft Caledonian burr, was a self-made, old-school, head-of-the-family type, with a bristling mustache. He was a very involved governor at our school, a member of the Masons, a bootstraps Tory who brooked no self pity. It didn't feel as if he could get dementia. We were sure he'd kick dementia's arse until it apologized.

In my early twenties, I was briefly in a house share with two others where my female housemate was never there due to shift work, and my male housemate was a lunatic and a creep, given to throwing furniture around and warning me he'd pursue me if I tried to leave.

Susie told her dad. In absence of me having a dad (in the UK) to do the same for me, he barreled around in his BMW 5 Series, parked right outside with a noisy screech of brakes, audibly pulling the handbrake on so hard it was like he was cocking a gun. He banged on the door, marched in, and told me to pack my things in front of the perp. Mr. Hart then calmly informed him if he touched a hair on my head, he'd find himself floating in the Trent. My housemate suddenly wasn't such a bully, and insisted meekly that I'd misunderstood. I'll be forever grateful for that intervention.

After work, I catch a bus heading the other way out of town and walk the short distance from the bus stop to the Harts' family home. It's too cold for kids to be playing out—and possibly too much in the age of Minecraft—and the streets seem eerily quiet, compared to my less expensive postcode.

These houses with their bay windows and neatly delineated, walled territories used to seem like imposing castles to me when I was small, in the long summers of childhood. They're far more quotidian suburbia in my thirties. Which is ironic, really, given I'm even less likely to inhabit one after piddling away my career chances in my twenties: they're further out of reach than ever.

The cost of this area means the demographic skews older—not within the reach of young professionals and families, who, if they do take on this size of mortgage, would probably go for something more fashionable they could stick bifold doors and a marble kitchen island into.

I walk up to the Harts, No. 67, and as I do, I think: *How many times did I stand on these very paving flags as a kid and think nothing of it?* Looking forward to a swimming trip, or tossing gaily about in Susie's huge bedroom, gossiping and trying on lip glosses, the consistency of runny honey.

The wrongness of all this hits me once again.

Life's veered sharply away from the script. We're traveling a branch of an alternative future we were never meant to be on. Some other Eve, in a parallel place, is having after-work drinks with Susie right now. Not only is that Eve a different person, so is the one at the pub quiz. That night was the last night of The Past, and we had no idea.

My heart speeds up as I press the old-fashioned button doorbell that ding-dongs dimly in the hallway beyond. I guiltily hope Susie's dad's not in. But within seconds the inner door opens and he appears.

"Hello, Eve!" he says. He looks a little more sunken in his sweater than I remember, a little thinner on top, but otherwise incredibly well and unchanged, all considered.

"Hi!" I say. And "I wasn't sure if you'd remember me," which is meant as politeness and, I think, maybe not what you say to someone with Alzheimer's.

"Of course I do. You're Susie's lovely friend."

I am momentarily so wrong-footed I can't speak, both by him knowing my connection to his daughter, and the mention of his daughter.

"Yes!" I say. "Well. Hope I'm lovely, haha."

"Come in, come in, good to see you." He hustles me in, seemingly with real enthusiasm and pleasure.

The hallway beyond is a time capsule to me—the same round table by the side of the wide stairs, with the cream plastic rotary landline sitting on a doily kind of mini tablecloth. The thick plushy pile beneath our feet is the color of a hamster.

Fashions of all kinds passed the Harts by. Susie's glitzy, ritzy mum liked Dubonnets and lemonade, a *Dynasty* blow-dry, and her downstairs loo to be a symphony of shrimp-pink. Adolescent Susie declared it all "tacky"; I loved it as pure exotica.

"I wonder if you wanted any shopping getting in, see how you're getting on?" I say.

"Hah, thank you, I'm not that useless yet! The only drive out the car gets is to Sainsbury's."

My plan with Mr. Hart was simply: make him this non-specific offer, which, if he seems entirely lucid and announces he has no need of such help, I can row back from without too much embarrassment. It didn't seem worthwhile plotting out a strategy when I had no idea what his state of mind would be like.

Now what?

"No, I'm very well, thank you, Eve. But how are you? I've not seen you in ages! Susie never brings you 'round."

I flinch at the mention of her. I had guessed he wouldn't have held on to the fact she's dead, but it's still a shock for him to demonstrate it.

"I've been busy," I say.

"Sure you two haven't had a falling-out?" he says.

"Definitely not," I say, and then, haltingly: "Close as ever." As I say those three words, my voice suddenly thickens and my throat closes up, and I pray he doesn't notice.

"Would you like a cup of tea?" he says, and I accept, thinking, *I will get a look at the state of things, domestically.*

Susie insisted that while her dad didn't have a grasp of which year it was, or correspondingly, his time of life—thinking he was off work, marveling that his holidays felt so lengthy—he was absolutely himself in regards to every practicality. She'd been through his bank statements, made sure his clothes were clean, checked the fridge. There was never anything to do. Chunks of his memory had fallen away like masonry, but tasks right in front of him were fine.

I follow him through to their sunshine-yellow kitchen with

its frothy white blinds—tart's knickers, my mum used to call that style—and watch Mr. Hart fill a kettle, get a polka-dotted cup from the cupboard.

"Has everything been OK with you?" I say.

"Not too bad," he says. "Some aches and pains, you know, but that's age, isn't it. I'm still managing the garden. Eric still comes over once a month for the heavy lifting."

"Oh yes!" I step forward and peer out the window at a garden that's every bit as manicured and brochure-perfect as I remember. "It looks wonderful."

"How are things at college?" he says. "Not too worried about your exams?"

Aside from the lack of understanding about Susie being gone, he's not said anything overtly odd until now and I try not to look startled. I'm pretty sure Justin's told me that with dementia, following the person into the delusion is preferable to fighting it and upsetting them.

"No, no. I've done my revision," I say. "Feeling confident."

Extra confident given I got my three As and two Bs, sixteen years ago.

As Mr. Hart's finishing dunking the tea bag and is about to hand the cup to me, the doorbell goes again.

He trots off to answer it and I hear male voices in the storm porch in a conversation that becomes, in pitch, if not a quarrel, then certainly more fraught than a chat.

One line becomes distinct:

"Look, I've told you. You've got the wrong house."

Finlay Hart looks as overjoyed to see me, hovering behind his father, as I am to see his moody visage in the darkening evening.

"Can you tell this young man who I am, please, Eve?" Mr. Hart says. "He's convinced he's some relation. I've never seen him before in my life. Oh, hang on, your tea will be getting cold."

He disappears back to the kitchen and Fin steps inside and closes the door behind him.

"What are you doing here?" he says, in a low, forbidding voice.

"I came to see how he is."

"And what do you think?" Fin says, though there's no genuine inquiry in it.

"He seems OK, I think? Not distressed, anyway."

"Well, he's . . ." Finlay stops as the door moves.

"Here you go," Mr. Hart says, reappearing with the Tetley's, which I accept. He seems momentarily taken aback that Fin is now in the door and says to me: "Ah, I see—do you know this man?"

"Uhm, yes," I think, sipping. The whole "busking it and playing along" thing feels like it's unraveling quite fast.

"A boyfriend?" he says, looking from one to the other.

". . . Yes," I say, gritting my teeth as I glance at Finlay, whose jaw flexes in cold fury. What else would he have me do? *No, he barged his way in, call the police!*

I realize Mr. Hart is waiting expectantly for an introduction. "Finlay," I add.

"Oh my goodness," Mr. Hart says, and Fin and I stare at each other, as we know what's coming. "My son's called Finlay. Fin, more often."

We stand in silence and I sense that Finlay, above and beyond his deep irritation at my unexpectedly being here, is embarrassed. My seeing his father like this is a privacy invasion and he feels exposed. Fin is about the iron-clad façade, the KEEP OUT sign he has hung on himself. This is weakness and vulnerability, if only by proxy.

"Tell you what, I've got some nice biscuits, with fruit in them," Mr. Hart says. "I'm going to find those, then let's chat about what you've been up to. Go on, take a seat through there and I'll join you."

I carry my cup of tea to the sitting room, Fin right behind me, near-closing the cream gloss painted door with its floral enamel handle behind us. The Harts' home belongs to an era where the wife made all the interiors choices. It always blew my mind they had a sitting room they watched television in, here, and a posh front room next door with a dining table with a runner tablecloth and candelabra, where they received guests. (Not scrubs like me, I mean dinner parties.)

"You shouldn't be here," Fin says, in a loud whisper. "He doesn't need the disorientation of strangers from Susie's life turning up on his doorstep."

"He knows who I am! He greeted me as Eve!"

"He thinks Susie is seventeen years old. He has no real idea who you are."

"You're here, and he has no idea who you are?" I say.

"I'm his son," Fin says, eyebrows shooting up. "I have a right. You have no right."

"You wouldn't be in the door if it wasn't for me."

"Here we go, they're pieces of crystallized ginger, I think," Mr. Hart says, pushing the door open, bearing a plate, which he sets down on the coffee table. "Delicious. Would you like a cuppa, young man?" he says to Fin. "I do apologize. I've forgotten you."

Indeed.

". . . Yes, thanks," Fin says, after a pause, where he no doubt realized it'd be a useful prop to extend his stay. "Milk, no sugar, thanks.

"Have you been into Susie's house?" Fin says, after his father leaves. "I thought it looked like someone had tidied up."

"Yes," I say, sitting up straighter, spooked, thinking, *Thank God for Ed.* Thank God for him being the kind of person who spotted that we needed to attend to that straightaway.

Finlay Hart was clearly at Susie's with the locksmith as soon as he'd got out of the airport transfer from Heathrow.

"Did you take personal effects from her room?"

My skin prickles.

"A box of personal mementos, nothing of financial value whatsoever."

"Can I decide if they're of value? What things, specifically?"

I have no idea whether I should dissemble and I don't quite dare stonewall him.

"A box of letters and diaries."

"Right. Can I have that back, please?"

"No, they're private." I had not, for a single moment, thought her brother would either know these things existed or identify their absence, and I've been caught off guard.

"They were private, to Susie? They're not yours."

"I'm keeping them private for her."

"But not private from yourself."

"Yes, actually. I'm not going to read them."

Fin does a double take.

"You've got something you say I can't have, that you're not going to look at?"

"Yes. It's about protecting Susie."

"Er, OK, noble as that is, you don't get to appoint yourself guardian of her possessions without asking me."

"Why do you want her diaries?" I say. "You were hardly close."

"I don't have to justify my motives. How do you justify doing a smash and grab?"

"As her best friend, who knows the last thing she'd want is her brother"—I vainly try to be more diplomatic—"or anyone, reading her old diaries."

"It's not for you to decide."

Pretending to get along with Finlay Hart, I've decided, is a jig that is up.

"Actually, it is. As I have the box, and that's the end of that."

"Do you want this to turn ugly? Do you want me to lawyer up? Because trust me, I will."

"Knock yourself out," I say, panicking that if he does this, I have no idea what his rights might be. As he pushes and I panic, the more defensive I feel. Should I burn them? Is there a destruction of property case he could then wield against me?

". . . Are you pretending that you and Susie got along?"

Fin's face contorts into restrained contempt: "I didn't say anything about us getting along. I said that's irrelevant to you effectively thieving, because you've decided her things belong to you. They don't."

I could tell Fin he was filed in her phone under a stinging insult but, in the teeth of his loss, in his old family home, and with his diminished dad in the next room, I don't have the stomach to be that unkind. Nevertheless, I'm absolutely sure if he had the same on me, he'd use it.

Mr. Hart reappears, bearing a cup of tea for Fin, and the doorbell's ringing again.

"I'm ever so sorry," he says. "I meant to say, my cleaner's due tonight. I hope you two lovebirds can entertain each other."

The door closes again and we hear a female voice. She's speaking in that pointedly upbeat, firm sort of way that suggests she's well aware of Mr. Hart's challenges.

"I fly back the day after the funeral," Fin says. "Return Susie's things to me by then or expect a nasty letter."

"You don't have any qualms about disrespecting her wishes, do you?" I say.

"You don't have any qualms about using her speculative wishes to do whatever suits you."

"*Suits me?*" I hiss. "You think I'm doing this because I'm enjoying it?"

"I said it suits you. Only you know why that is."

We blaze at each other, at an impasse, and I don't want to have this fight when it might upset a newly bereaved dementia patient. (Are you still bereaved when you're unaware you're bereaved?)

I drain my tea, head to the downstairs loo for both urination and reconnaissance, and find it pristine.

As I leave, receiving a cheery farewell from Mr. Hart, I see Fin has ducked into the front room to talk to the cleaner.

I wilt at leaving a vulnerable senior citizen with an enemy combatant in the house, but what else can I do?

17

Perhaps unsurprisingly, the first thing I do when I get home is check the box is still there.

Do you want this to turn ugly? Do you want me to lawyer up? Because trust me, I will.

Finlay Hart isn't just dislikable, he's frightening.

I hammer up the stairs, drag the box from under my bed, lift the lid, and check everything's still there. Perhaps I should move it from here? It's a very standard hiding place and I feel like Finlay Hart is capable of breaking and entering. In a balaclava and bright white sneakers, clambering out of a window as he hears my key scraping in the lock, Roger mewing his confusion. These are febrile imaginings, but I'm not able to be rational about this or anything to do with Susie.

This second poke through the contents of the box is when I notice it. As I rearrange the bundles of letters, I see a hole has been ripped in one of the envelopes by the way Susie's torn it open.

It reveals feminine handwriting that's not Susie's and, quite clearly, the words:

around Eve, she might

I stare and stare and drop it, dully, putting the lid back on. My heart is racing, my face suddenly warm. Me. There's a letter that talks about me.

Around me, "she's not." I'm not, what?

The desire to read it is considerable, to the point of overwhelming. I'd been so firm and genuine in my conviction not to snoop, but this level of temptation is unexpected.

The angel on my shoulder says: *Your initial instinct was correct. Eavesdroppers hear no good of themselves. This is still a letter marked only to Susie, and as far as you know, she'd never discussed its contents with you. Do you really want to see something that might be jarring or upsetting, the day before her funeral?*

The devil says: *You didn't ask to see this and now you have, it'll scratch at you until you know what it is. It's almost certainly nothing. And look at the date! It's from ten years ago. You were in your early twenties. It'll be trivia. Can you remember anything you might've written down about Susie a decade ago that would have great significance now? Well then!*

I hypothesize outcomes. If it's mindless bitching, meanness, disloyalty, suggesting Susie's been misspeaking me to a third party, how will I feel? It will hurt, yes.

However, Susie and I were close enough that we were able to snap and complain to each other and about each other, and it meant nothing. The air between us was always clear. It was part of what made us such formidably good mates, there wasn't that residual build-up of unspoken gripe that seemed to end up clogging the pipes of lots of other female friendships.

(This, for example, describes Hester's. She has an array of moral objections, jaded observations, and historic grudges about everyone she's supposed to count as close. If you meet a Hester pal and say something like "Verity's good company, isn't she, lots of anecdotes," immediately she'll fire back, "She's SO exhausting, and FYI, none of that stuff about that tabloid editor she dated was true. She's very *colorful*, if you know what I mean." No wonder she was short of bridesmaid ideas.)

Then I think, Eve, what the hell—what could possibly be anywhere near as bad as what you've already been through? What could touch THAT?

Open it, read some shit that was merely replying to Susie fretting that she didn't know how to tell you that you didn't suit a dress (that you can't even remember owning, and she's not here to jog your memory, and that will hurt just as much), and move on. Laugh, and get a stiff gin and tonic. Then commence internet searching whether Finlay Hart can legally compel you to hand these effects over.

I open the box again and pull the letter out from under the elastic band. I knew as soon as I saw my name I was going to read it.

I unfurl the paper, shaking out the pages and turning them first to check it's to Susie—*Dear Suz!!*—and then to check who it's from.

Becky. Hmmm. Becky was Susie's closest friend at university, from her accountancy degree. I never liked her, which could sound like it was a consequence of simple rivalry, but it really wasn't. Susie and I were so fixed as best-friends-who-also-had-other-friends, I never feared Becky taking my place.

In fact, it was the other way around. I think Becky very much wanted me out of the picture, which is where some of our wariness of each other came from. She and Susie went traveling together in Europe after university and it was documented in a way that subtly yet clearly laid claim to her "gorgeous number one super bff" in every caption. I found Becky a bit tiresome, fakey, and super girly. She probably found me misanthropic, sweary, and super not interesting.

These days Becky and her husband have a grand pile in Cheltenham and Becky's husband is something important in a picture agency for news wires. When we've met on her Susie visits to Nottingham, she's never wasted an opportunity to say, "Declan could get you an interview, you know, just say," in regards to journalism, as if it isn't rude to offer professional help to someone who never said they needed it.

She messaged me her lavish apologies that they can't come to the funeral due to a family holiday in Marbella: "It's a luxury villa we booked through Mr. and Mrs. Smith, has a heated pool and use of a speedboat, we'd literally lose thousands," Becky told me, amid her tearstained odes to her love for Susie. I said yes, absolutely, don't worry. Your gorgeous number one bff would've understood. And the thing is, Susie would have. She'd have said nonrefundable deposits and whirlpool tubs trumped sentimentality any day.

I start scanning it from the beginning.

Sorry for taking ages to write back, work's been mad. Wow, so—you fair blew my mind with your news—you and Ed! Not so much a slow burn as a no burn? And then a blaze. Hahaha. WOW. You sly dog! Dog(s) plural. I had no idea you two had the horn for each other and sounds like you didn't either.

What. What? *What?* No. I feel my gorge rise. I reread this passage seven times before I'm able to read on. The back of my neck is cold and I can't feel my feet.

So to answer your concerns, I can see why you're worried. The thing is, if you and Ed don't tell anyone what happened then no one's going to know, simple as that. Ed's not going to confess to his L/T girlfriend, he's not stupid, is he? Why would he?! As for your issues around Eve, she might be besotted but she's not his girlfriend. She has no right to get upset with you, but yeah if she feels as strongly as you say about him, *don't* tell her. I don't see why you need that aggro. Are you absolutely sure there's nothing more between you & Ed though? It sounded torrid. Gonna need the full debrief over margs and Doritos next time you're down ☺

My life is SO boring by comparison, remember that promotion I told you about that my . . .

My hands now glistening wet with sweat, I speed-read through the rest of the letter and ascertain there's nothing else about the Susie and Ed tryst in it, or about me. I sit down on the bed heavily and read it again and again, hoping for the words or meaning to change.

Ed and Susie. Susie and Ed. Could Becky mean some other Ed? Perhaps it's too indicative of my psychological state that I spend almost a minute trying to stand that theory up, though it requires Susie not only to know another Ed, but for him to have a long-term girlfriend and an Eve who's "besotted." She knew. My most closely guarded, painful secret, and even fucking Becky Speedboat Villa Holiday knew.

When people say, "My whole life has been a lie," it sounds like purple scriptwriting, like something they'd shout in the Old Vic on Christmas *EastEnders*.

Yet I can't think of any more accurate way to describe how I'm feeling, as I sit stunned on my bed, tears rolling down my face. All my cherished ideas of what Ed and I felt for each other, separated by cruel circumstance, our Tesco Express version of a Shakespeare tragedy—a lie. Who I thought Ed Cooper *was*—a lie. (Fuck, is it possible he DID get my letter, back in the day, but Hester was just too big a temptation?)

My best friend, who I thought kept nothing from me, who I thought I knew the very bones of—nope. Her greatest secret imaginable, and Becky was someone worthy to share it with, not me.

Our friendship group, which I set so much store in, people I'd go to war for—the whole time had this subset within it, people who'd shagged and hidden it, specifically from me. Did *Justin* know? How big a fool have I been made, here? I'm woozy.

And finally, my firm belief that no one knew how I felt for Ed, except perhaps, obviously, Ed. This revelation might be harder to accept than the sex. Susie knew all along. Why did she never say? Because she wanted Ed for herself? The closest person to me was busy outmaneuvering me, over the thing that mattered to me the most? *How did she know?* I thought I'd given nothing away. Did Ed tell her? Pillow talk?

There's no one I can talk to about this. I love Justin and vice versa, but he's still Ed's best friend. The only person I could tell—my best friend—is firstly, the person who's most hurt me and, secondly, dead.

To take first place on the podium ahead of Ed Cooper in the most-hurting-me Olympics is an absolutely awesome achievement, here. The only latitude available was Susie not knowing how I felt, and evidently, she did know.

I lie on my bed, stare at the ceiling, and ask myself why I set a bomb off by reading that letter. I have shattered everything.

Ten years ago, Ed and Susie, two people I thought had never so much as shared an intimate glance, slept together. My best friend and the man who I thought was my secret soulmate, destroying my image of, and trust in, both of them, in one fell swoop.

And the worst part of it is, the very worst part: Susie knew I was in love with Ed, and she did it anyway.

No. That's not true. The worst part is, I never get to ask her why.

18

"Where to, love?"

"Wilford Crematorium."

"Ah, shame. Not a nice day for you, then?" the cabbie says, looking at me over his shoulder, trying to pitch this as sympathetic, as opposed to quite nakedly prurient.

No, of course it isn't you dick, what kind of question is that?

"No."

"Anyone close to you?"

"Yes."

Actually, I don't know if that's true. That's how bad I feel. That's how humiliated and betrayed I feel. I can't even say goodbye to Susie today, the way I thought I would, as I don't know who exactly I'm saying goodbye to.

"Oh. Sorry to hear."

The taxi reeks of a large and turnipy burp he did right before he picked me up, but I'm too British to roll the window down and thus communicate: "You smell."

". . . D'ya want the radio on?" he says, after deciding perhaps on balance he won't inquire into my loss further, and I mumble: "Sure, OK."

"Do you listen to Radio Two, ever?" he says, once it's blaring out. I gather he's in a chatty mood. Despite picking up a woman with gray-pale skin, wearing a black coat over a black dress, eyes red-rimmed and puffy from much crying and scant sleep, who has asked to be driven to a place where they incinerate dead people, and answering him in clipped monosyllables, he's still going to press on with the banter he fancies having, in the guise of trying to cheer me up.

"Not much," I say.

"See how many of these you can get for me in the pop quiz, I'm rubbish at this," he says, twiddling the volume knob upward.

I rest my head on the car seat, close my eyes, and think: this could be annoying but, actually, the burble of T'Pau is better than thinking about the destination.

"'China in Your Hand'!" the driver says.

"That's 'Heart and Soul,'" I say.

"The answer is 'Heart and Soul'!" says the presenter.

"Very good!" the taxi driver says, visibly impressed.

"They only had two hits," I say. "Process of elimination."

I've successfully dodged any conversations with Ed since I read the letter. I've accidentally missed his calls by being "in the shower," answered WhatsApps in a way that didn't invite lots of back-and-forth. He no doubt concluded I'm in a state of agitation before the funeral and decided to let me lie low.

"Elastica," I tell the driver.

"Sorry, Dave, that's not right, it's not Sleeper. It's Elastica. *Elastica*," says the presenter.

"You're brilliant at this!" says my driver. "Can I pick you up every day? We could win a yacht."

I can't manage a yacht, but I tip him well when we reach the top of the hill, whereupon my stomach lurches as I see people milling outside the crematorium chapel.

I wonder who they are, what their connection to Susie is—like some dismal photographic negative image of a wedding. They're from different areas of her life, and there will be plenty I don't know on sight. The one tour guide I need isn't here.

And plenty I do. I spy Justin.

I feel the grief bubbling up uncontrollably at the sight of him looking handsome and adult and slightly uncomfortable in a narrow-cut, dark suit. It's as if we're playing characters in a drama.

He sees me and comes straight over. We hug, Justin muttering into my hair: "You're OK, gal. Hang on to me."

At this moment, I can tell he and Ed have had various conversations about how I'm coping, and I should feel good about their support. I don't. I feel good about Justin's, assuming he wasn't in on the "torrid" (torrid, *torrid*) banging.

Right behind Justin are Ed and Hester.

"Eve, my darling, how are you! I've not seen you," Hester says, throwing her arms around me.

She's had a blow-dry that is ruffled by the slight breeze, golden-corn waves against the navy of her coat, and black leather gloves. She smells of roses.

"Alright, you," Ed says, tenderly, and I submit to an embrace, blank-faced, thinking: don't bother with your faux-adoring chummy bullshit. It's been a long, long con, but it's over.

Hester starts fussing with Ed's tie under his overcoat and

I think, a strange aspect of my new knowledge is that I may revile her, but she's the one who's been wronged here, more than me. Ed and Susie only broke unspoken promises to me. He fully cheated on her.

But what a hypocrite I am—I never minded the idea of Ed being unfaithful to Hester, but it had to be with me. It had to be about love, and it had to promise a future together. Was the other unfaithfulness about love?

"Holy moly," Justin says, with a low whistle, indicating to look over our shoulders.

Approaching over the brow of the hill I see the Teacup Girls. in black body-con dresses, pill-box hats with birdcage veils, and four-inch heels, two of them with crimson Louboutin soles, and fishnets. Despite the freezing weather, they've clearly opted to carry their coats to better show off their outfits.

"They look like mistresses attending against the wishes of the family," Justin says.

"Do you know what, Susie would've loved it," I say, with a tightness in my chest about what she did and didn't love. *Torrid.* "Why not."

I see Finlay in the distance, immaculately suited and booted, chatting to elderly attendees unknown. I can't see his dad.

The hearse with the white coffin comes crawling up the path toward us and I breathe in, and breathe out, and Justin grips my arm tightly to let me know he knows how hard this is, but doesn't try to speak to me, and I'm incredibly grateful for his getting it right.

The somber-faced undertakers perform their rituals with the arrangement of the car and another terrible moment arrives, Justin loosening his grip on me and stepping forward to join the pallbearers. We agreed it would be Ed, Justin, Finlay, and one of her friend's husbands.

Being a pallbearer, and concentrating on not messing it up as they shoulder the weight of the coffin, looks less difficult than watching them do it, which is a sight I will never forget. It leaves scorch marks on my soul.

To my chagrin, Hester is suddenly by my side, grasping my hand and dabbing at her eyes.

I don't doubt Hester is upset; you'd need to be an alien life-form not to be. I also know she'll bounce back in no time, because Susie was a familiar feature of her life courtesy of Ed, but not anyone truly vital or valuable to her. They pissed each other off. Hester is performing a proprietorial sadness in public that won't smudge her mascara. Now she can't, in this moment, be Ed's elegant fiancée, she has to be Susie's best friend's comfort. I don't mind her not hurting as much, but leave me in peace to hurt more.

We follow the coffin inside to the classical music we chose, heads bowed, mourners who recognize each other murmuring hellos. The coffin, the celebrant explained to us prior, will sit in the chapel space in this room and the cremation takes place elsewhere on site afterward. I'm glad, as the "pressing of a button, coffin sliding out of view to the oven" section has always struck me as faintly bleakly comic.

We take an order of service from the box—*oh, her face, her joyful, smiling, unwitting face*—and I choose my seat carefully, knowing Ed and Justin will slide in alongside myself and Hester.

I pick the opposite side from Finlay and other distant family members, and a few rows back, so as not to overstate our importance.

I glance across at the Teacups, at others from Susie's office. Something bothers me, and at first I can't figure out what it is. As I watch them riffling through the service card, craning to see who's here, and if anyone's about to take to the lectern, it hits me—they're *excited*.

Not in a malicious way, or that in they wished this upon Susie. But a premature, dramatic exit like hers—it's plot. It's a major narrative twist. It's like a famous person dying and everyone's smartphones lighting up with the newsbreak, people scrabbling to post it first online. You know of them but don't really care about them, so are free to enjoy the thrill of the event.

I finally understand why my late gran used to scan the obituaries column in the local paper with such relish, despite her enhanced odds of ending up in it herself.

"Welcome, everybody, to this service to remember the life of Susannah Hart, a person I know was very dear to many of you gathered here today."

And yet not very dear to one.

I look at the back of Finlay Hart's head, staring straight ahead, and wonder what he's thinking.

A Celebration of the Life of Susannah Hart

I focus on these words until they're no longer the English language. It feels like they've bored holes into me.

The celebrant's recitation of the key dates and events in Susie's life, reiterating her value to all of us, a poem, "Life Goes On" by Joyce Grenfell, read by Susie's Auntie Val.

"Nor when I am gone / Speak in a Sunday voice."

A piece of music, Billie Holiday, "The Very Thought of You." We wrestled with this choice: Vivaldi and Val Doonican are so easy to slot in when a pensioner passes, crematorium-appropriate, but Susie's love of the Pet Shop Boys wasn't quite so useful. Much as we loved them too, it was hard to imagine everyone trying to remain impassive and pensive listening to "Paninaro."

"'Being Boring'?" Justin said, but although there was consensus it was great and apt, we couldn't imagine the poppiness of it working.

Thankfully, I remembered how much Susie loved Billie Holiday sound-tracking a late bar we found in Rome, her seeking an album out and playing it endlessly when we got home. It's a catalyst, and as soon as it starts up, I'm back getting drunk on Aperol spritzes with her, in a bar lit by a jukebox and tealights, making plans for a future she barely got to see. My face is a flash flood.

Then, it's Ed's turn, I see him stand up at the end of the row, his notes in his hand. Listening to Ed read out my tribute to Susie was going to be extraordinarily agonizing, before last night's discovery. Now I don't have a way of categorizing my emotional response.

At the lectern, he coughs into a curled fist and looks up at everyone. The sight of him momentarily blurs in my tears as I blink them back.

"Morning," he says. "I may only be thirty-four years old, but I'm going to guess this will forever be the toughest public speaking gig of my life. As a teacher, I include the time fifth years smuggled a dozen two-liter bottles of Magners Cider in on the last day of term."

He gives a thin smile. It's not as if audiences at funerals can give you much encouragement by way of laughter.

"What I'm about to read to you has been written by Susie's best friend, Eve." Justin squeezes my knee as Ed looks toward me. I would squeeze back, but I will primal howl.

Who are you, Ed? I never needed to rely on you more than now. The rug has been pulled from under me. I can't imagine ever trusting you again.

"Eve was not only one of the people who Susie loved most in this world, and vice versa, she's also very good with words," he says. "We thought it fitting she say a bit about Susie from the perspective of her friends. Eve can write, I can read, so this is a team effort."

He coughs again and I tense, waiting for my words in Ed's voice. Whatever else, I'm very glad I didn't try to read it myself. I wouldn't make it through a sentence.

"Eve met Susie in primary school in the 1990s. The first photo of them together is in a nativity play. Susie was the Virgin Mary, always natural casting as a lead, and Eve was the back half of a camel. Always a natural to cast as a dromedary's arse."

Ed looks up and says: "Just to remind you again, Eve wrote this."

He gets an actual laugh.

"There followed what was to become a notorious incident at Saint Peter's C of E Primary, where the front half of the camel passed out and vomited into the head of the costume, and the back half of the camel struggled out and stood there dressed in vest and pants, and some vomit spray. Other children screamed. Susie Hart, ever the one to make lemons from lemonade, shouted, 'Look, the camel also gave birth, like me!' and incorporated it into the storyline."

This too gets a ripple of amusement.

"From that day on, they were an inseparable duo. On the face of it, Susie and Eve were a total clash. Susie was the captain of netball, whereas Eve wore a fake bandage so she could sit PE out and read *Sweet Valley High* books.

"Susie didn't much care for rules and would do anything for her friends. Susie was one of life's winners, until a split second of horrendous bad luck took her from us. Yet she could never pass by on the other side. She strongly identified with the underdog, while being a straight-A student who succeeded at everything she tried to do. That was her particular magic. Eve remembers a time when a girl in their class was getting bullied for having cheap shoes and Susie not only stuck up for her, she bought the same pair and came to school in them the following week. When Eve said she was heroic, Susie shrugged it off and said: 'Ugh, I just hate bullies. And anyway, I think I look quite good in gray patent.'"

Another laugh.

"That was Susie. Sardonic, audacious, confident, with a humanity and humor that always shone through. When Eve came to write this, she says she realized that all of Susie was contained in that moment, aged eight years old, when Susie anointed her as God's vomit-covered baby camel. Confidence and compassion and a metric ton of sass.

"There's no way to explain how much our group of friends will miss Susie, or how we can begin to calculate how much has been taken from us. From everyone. There's something exceptional about friendships with friends you've known since you were young. They know all the versions of you. They know how you were built. They have a map for you. There's a shorthand between you, and a love that is as strong as any blood tie." Ed's voice wavers and he pauses to gather himself.

"I'm going to read Eve's summing up in her own first person:

"What I didn't expect, after Susie died, was to feel this panic. A panic she'd be forgotten. Not her name, or her face, or achievements. The official things. The panic that her voice, the way she spoke, her attitude, all that was unique and specific to her, would pass into history. I wanted her to be here, and for her contributions and opinions to still be with us. That she is past tense feels so impossible, when she was so vividly alive. As I wrote this tribute, I asked myself, what would Susie say if she read it? Hers was the only opinion I wanted, and the only one I couldn't have.

"I pictured her scanning through it, chin on hand, chewing the drawstring on that terrible rowing club hoodie she wore. She'd giggle at the camel anecdote, and say something about 'God, do you remember that games teacher though? Put the "hun" into Attila the Hun.' Then she'd say, at the end, mouth going a bit wiggly and wiping a tear: 'Oh, you sentimental oaf, give me a hug. I'm not sure, it's so sweet. Does it make me sound a bit like a cross between Mother Teresa and Samantha from *Sex and the City* though? I can't even remember the shoes thing, are you sure? Oh well, if you say so. You can be my official biographer; you've got the job. Someone else can write the scandalous stuff about me singing "Happy Birthday Mr. President," and then bunking up with him.'"

Ed pauses.

". . . I hope I never stop hearing Susie's voice or keeping her memory alive. So, the final line is delivered fully in the spirit of Susie Hart, as we knew her—Susie, you were always too much. But we wanted more. Thank you."

Ed closes his notes and steps down from the lectern.

People clap, which I'm not sure usually happens at funerals and which I will take to mean we did Susie justice.

Justin puts his hand on my leg, and says, in a strangled voice: "Perfect, Eve. Perfect."

I barely hear the celebrant's wrapping-it-up speech.

As we file out to the *Twin Peaks* music, all I can think of is Susie's costume that said: *She Is Filled with Secrets.*

19

"The quiche is really good, actually," Hester says, and I know it must be as she does not dole out praise willy-nilly, or indeed ever. "Want my other slice?"

She's done the buffet drive-by heaped plate load, where you pick things up for the sheer hell of it and share your scavenger's bounty when you get back to the table.

"No, thanks. Does look nice though."

"Can't eat?" Hester says, and I shake my head. "Well, at least think of how skinny you'll get. Every cloud."

This is such tone-deaf classic Hestering I can't be bothered to mind. There's no Susie to text, no 4G in heaven.

Your violent death had a silver lining, I now fit that
Whistles dress. You know, the zebra-print one with a
waist so tight it was like a religious test of penance.

Wait, you mean if you'd bought a size up, you
vain crow, I wouldn't have had to die?!

As Hester pokes through the potato salad, I look curiously at the top of her head, her immaculate platinum parting, thinking: I was so jealous you had Ed, but *did* you have Ed? What's been going on all this time, exactly? What would happen if I told her he'd cheated? Would she dump him?

The wake is in the kind of kooky, plushy boutique hotel surrounds—chandeliers, mismatched crockery, and colorful Chesterfields, open fires—that would make for a great "do" at any other time.

As it is, it's a peculiar, energy-drained sort of sub party. All the trappings of a get-together without the bonhomie. When a person goes "at their time," as my mum says, you can find solace in that. You're allowed to brighten up after the main farewell. Yet as much as we're supposed to be "celebrating" Susie, obviously, we can't. *Dearly beloved, we are gathered here today to get through this thing called death.* The volume level rises with inebriation, but it's still half-hearted.

My mum wanted to come but she had a walking break planned with her friends, and I didn't want her to miss it. Losing a holiday to a funeral didn't seem fair, given the number of things she has to enjoy.

After we arrived, we found a table in a corner, territory with walls behind us so we could more easily defend it. Justin bought a bottle of Veuve in an ice bucket, declaring he couldn't care less "if Uncle Rod from Chepstow disapproves." (This is a generic relative, I don't think Susie actually has an uncle Rod from Chepstow, disapproving or otherwise.) "It was Susie's favorite drink and she'd not give a stuff that you don't usually drink champagne at wakes. In fact, that's precisely what would appeal to her."

I still keep my back carefully turned to the room during the telltale phunk-splut-fizz noise of the cork emerging.

"To Susie," Justin says, holding his glass up. "Our dearest girl. Not here, but as far as we're concerned, never not with us."

We hold ours up and mumble: "To Susie."

I think of her on that gurney. Not moving.

"What was that daft thing she used to say when she got 'one for the road' in?" Ed says.

"A brandy for the reindeer," I say, and Ed laughs, and I look away quickly in case he tries to make it any moment of connection.

Our dearest girl, not here. Her Not Hereness gives me a low hard stomach pain, what she and I used to call the *empty suds.* I lost a lexicon with her, a shared cache of things only the two of us understood.

If Susie was returned to me, though, would we have a friendship-ending size of fight? I would have to know the answers to things that I doubt we'd have fully recovered from. She's died twice.

"Ed, want some quiche?" Hester says.

"No, thanks," he says, with a smile. "Gorged myself senseless on the sausage rolls."

Incredible how one revelatory discovery can completely change your perception of someone.

As we're the primary group of mourners, aside from Susie's saturnine brother, people have approached us to pay their respects. Instead of sitting down, Ed stands up, satellite to us throughout the arrivals—greeting people, thanking them for praising him for the reading, pointing them to the complimentary drinks, directing the traffic.

Before I'd have thought: oh, how good of Ed, both promoting and protecting us.

Now, it's: I see you're making yourself important again, being our ambassador, who asked you to do that?

Is it because Susie mattered more to you than any of us realized?

"Excuse me, are you *Eve Harris*?"

A thirty-something man is tapping me on the shoulder, using my name as if he's pronouncing something exotic he'd like to order from a menu. "I'm Andy. I was in Susie's team at Deloitte. That was a beautiful reading. You wrote it?"

I say yes and thank him, and we chat about anodyne professional things and every so often Andy shakes his head and says, "Terrible thing, such a dreadful thing," almost as if he fears I'll think he's forgotten if he doesn't.

I think, *I must tell Susie I met Andy*, and then remember that I can't. Whatever summary or insight that Susie would offer about him is a forever unknown. I imagine the machines in the hospital, with their unbroken tone. I want to go home and be alone.

"She talked about you a lot," Andy says, and I reply, "Oh really?"—vacantly, so I don't think about this, and crumple.

"Oh yes! She quoted you endlessly, said you were inseparable since school! *We are exact opposites who are completely alike* was how she described you." Andy beams, he means so well. I can see he thinks he's being comforting. Each word is like a screwdriver jabbed in my shins.

I thank him effusively and excuse myself to go to the loo. I bump into Finlay Hart in a doorway, in a way that necessitates some sort of interaction. He looks as delighted about that as I feel. He's clean-shaven now, and there is the glimmer of those Susie genes again. It's interesting how his forbidding attitude leaks out of every pore: despite his evident pretty boy credentials, I sincerely doubt even the Teacup Girls are giving him sidelong looks. Well, OK, maybe they are, and getting nothing back but radiation sickness.

I have a hideous flex of resentment that God chose the sister to die and the brother to live. God didn't choose anything, of course. Any more than He or She chose what I'm drinking.

I always thought that anyway, but I'm more sure of it than ever, no chance of me finding religion in this. No wonder we play the *what's for you, won't pass you* mind games with ourselves, when the brutal senselessness is so hard to swallow.

"Thanks for organizing this," Finlay says, formal, bloodless. "It's gone off well. As well as could be expected."

The king of qualified praise.

I nod and say: "Thank you."

The redheaded girlfriend with poor etiquette from his mother's funeral is nowhere to be seen, but that could be because she decided that when it came to meeting his British relatives, once was enough.

"Is your dad not here?" I say.

Fin shakes his head. "He couldn't be made to understand Susie was gone, so it wasn't possible."

"That's a shame," I say.

"It is and it isn't. He's spared the pain of it," Fin says.

"I suppose so."

Whenever you say something blandly sympathetic to Finlay

Hart, you get batted back as if you're a juvenile intellect, as opposed to saying the comforting, polite things people say. It riles me.

"Is it possible he'll understand at some point in the future, and be upset that he missed the funeral?"

"That's not how his illness works. He's not himself on Tuesday and dementia sufferer again on Wednesday."

"No, I know, but I thought his memory might come in and out, like the tide. Susie said he could be completely lucid?"

Fin stares at me, appraisingly, weighing his response. "That's not my experience of how it is with him. Some things are fixed. Susie being a teenager seems that way."

"And you? He thinks you're the same age?"

I know this is nosy and possibly unfair. It's hardly a comfortable subject. I feel myself doing that thing with someone I dislike: baiting them into saying something that proves my dislike is justified.

"I'm—I was—two years older than Susie, so in London at that age, I think."

"Right."

"While we're discussing your interest in my family, I've consulted a lawyer over those letters. In absence of a will, Susie's house and possessions belong to myself and my father. What you did was illegal. You'd be much better off returning her things to me now, rather than letting this turn official and expensive."

"We're really doing this at her wake?" I say, feeling a lot more rattly and intimidated than I let on.

"I don't want to be doing this at all. It's your choice that we are."

"Finlay? It *is* you! My goodness!" A sixty-something friend-or-relative joins us and I'm very glad of the interruption.

I walk away before I say anything more, which would definitely not be in my Sunday voice.

"What were you having intense confidentials with the sinister brother about? I'm starting to get a crush, you know. He flounced into that Caffè Nero like Dracula returning to his crypt at two a.m., after drinking his fill of virgins."

"Ugh, you have always had the worst taste. Apart from Francis."

"True."

Justin conceding this immediately shows he's in a reduced state. Francis shone briefly for a matter of months, a year ago, as a rare Justin official boyfriend and general joy to have around. Until Justin declared that *sorry, that much nice is just too much pressure!* while Susie nodded her firm understanding and Ed and I boggled at each other. ("You *want* a massive arsehole?" "Poorly phrased, Edward!")

Justin's rosy-eyeballed with champagne and crying and is clearly finding it hard to be his usual ebullient self. Every so often he pats my arm absentmindedly: to wordlessly convey, once again, *what on earth has happened, how has this happened?*

We're dreading life on the other side of this day.

When there's a sense of *that's that, then* and "normality" resumes. We've agreed we're not honoring the pub quiz tradition for the foreseeable, to show our respects. In truth we're fighting shy of it because the empty chair, the comeback that never comes, the bag of chips we don't need to buy, is going to debilitate us that much more. When this strangeness is over, the Not Hereness will truly land.

"Thing is . . ." I glance over to check Fin's safely on the other side of the melee. "He wants me to return a box of diaries from Susie's house. Remember when me and Ed played clean-up squad? He says anything in Susie's house belongs to the family."

"How did he know it was there?"

"He asked if I'd taken anything and I blurted it, like an idiot. Now he says he can lawyer up and make me give it up if I won't."

"He wants her diaries that much? Why, for God's sake? Who wants to know who fingered their sister in the third year?"

I nearly spit my wine out at this.

". . . That's all it'll be!" Justin says. "God bless our Sue but they won't give Samuel Pepys any competition. She once said to me, why would I read a book when I could watch *Steel Magnolias* with a tub of Chubby Hubby again?"

"I don't know what's in them. I'm not going to read them," I say, uneasy.

"There I was thinking the nose bag was the controversial discovery. I'd give them back to him, E."

"*Really?*" It seemed so morally obvious to me to resist.

"Yeah. If it's going to turn nasty. You don't need that."

"But . . . she'd hate him having them."

"She'd hate a lot about this but it's not in our power, huh."

This surprises me. Justin is much more of a pragmatist than I am. He was also much more like Susie than me, which makes me think even she might agree.

"She was his sister, Eve. He's entitled."

"Yeah well, you're right there."

I glance over at Finlay and the clenched set of his jaw, sequestered in his corner of the room. I bet he despises everyone here. I bet he wants to run from this place straight to the jet bridge to board his 747, shuddering with repulsion and pity. We're the small town he escaped. Well, city.

"They hated each other," I add.

"Maybe. It's not for us to play judge and jury though."

"But it was Ed who thought we should protect her reputation."

As I say these words, I realize their full meaning, and their irony. If it was to conceal this information, however, he didn't seem interested in Susie's personal effects. I don't know what to believe anymore. I don't know who he is, who my best friend was, or why the world's become unrecognizable to me in a matter of days. I can't surmount a sensation that I've been hugely, horribly negligent, to allow this whole timeline to happen.

"I'm going to be frank in order to shock you, now. It doesn't happen often, admittedly, but Edward Cooper is capable of error."

Justin slides a look, seen only by me, in the direction of Hester, who's rearranging strands of hair around her face while gazing into a hand mirror.

"Heh. I'm going to get some air," I say, with a smile, picking up my glass and, as an afterthought, one of the many bottles too, because I need a proper escape from company.

The hotel has a terrace with canopied wooden tables. The paved space is lit by fairy lights and heat lamps, as the winter sky's darkened. I know the doors are unlocked as I've seen smokers sidling through them, in furtive ones and twos, grasping lighters.

God, I wish I smoked right now. Susie demanded I give up that vice and then hers contributed to her getting killed.

I head out and adjust my body language to *do not speak to me please,* which is contained in the determined scowl, the tension in my shoulders and the lack of eye contact. It works, in part at least as I think people know not to hassle a solo mourner.

I find a table at the edge of the terrace and set my wine down. The bitter temperature is a sobriety aid and the view of the city rooftops at nighttime is quite lovely. Aided by a deep swig of white wine, I try to find some sort of inner calm.

I briefly imagine standing on the wall, like I'm a swimmer on a diving board, and plunging into the ink-dark tangle of bushes below. Rolling and bouncing down the hill toward the road, until I hit something hard enough to stop me. It feels more appealing than it should.

I glance back at the wake, staring resentfully at the throng beyond the steamed-up windows. What I hate is, yes, of course they're sorry this happened, but their lives will resume, seamlessly, as soon as they leave.

Nothing for us will ever be the same. It's like losing a leg and everyone coming to gather around the hospital bed, consoling you over the fact you only have one left, and walking out doing a hop, skip, and a jump on their two again. I'm envious of these people.

"Hey you. Taking a break?" Ed says at my elbow, giving me a startle.

"Oh? Yeah."

I wish I'd planned for his approaching me, thought of something to say that could icily dispatch him without revealing anything. One on one, Ed can't be avoided, the way my injured feelings require. I can't bear to pretend warmth toward him.

"It's gone alright, I think? We did her proud," he says. His black tie's been removed and his dark gray suit looks good with his sandy coloring. May he shrivel and perish.

I shrug.

"I hope so. Hard to judge. It's not for people who knew her, this thing, is it?" I gesture back at the hotel with my glass and pause. "Actually, it's worse than that," I say, vaguely picking a fight. "It's for people who don't really care."

"They care," Ed says. "Just not as much as we do."

"This isn't the time for your super-reasonable balanced perspective. Let a shit thing be shit."

"I'm not saying it isn't shit."

I hunch my shoulders and turn away from him, looking back at the cloud-streaked ink sky.

"We've got to look after each other. That's the only way to get through this," Ed says, thickly. "That's the only conclusion I've drawn."

I don't respond.

"Are you angry with me about anything?" Ed says, hesitantly. "Did I mangle the eulogy?"

"No."

"No to both questions?"

I didn't know I was going to say it, until this moment. Amid turmoil and inebriation and not knowing what else to do, whomp, it tumbles out of my mouth:

"You slept with Susie."

The actual words spoken feel jagged. It's as if I swallowed something sharp and metallic, and it tears up my insides as it makes its way out of me.

20

"... What?"

I look at Ed, his stunned expression. And I know, once again, it's true. Even the near-imperceptible split-second beat before the "What?"

For an innocent person, it'd be an immediate: *Wait, what?!*

Not: "[Oh-my-God-how-does-she-know, hard gulp, response required] *What?*"

"You heard."

There was no way it wasn't true, of course, but somehow the confirmation is still shocking and dramatic. Some truths, like Susie's passing, are too large to be digested in one go.

Ed's already pale skin is the color of a fish's belly. The people nearest to us, though still beyond earshot, have finished their cigarettes and trooped back inside, making this moment of inquisition even more deathly quiet.

"What do you mean?"

"What do I *mean* by 'slept with'?"

"I mean, why are you saying that?"

"Because you did."

Ed stares at me, desperately trying to read my expression.

"When?" he says, though not with composure. I can see his fear.

"You need me to specify which time period? How many times were there?"

"No," Ed says hurriedly, trying to get control of himself, to work out how to handle this.

A combination of alcohol and incredible, soul-flattening misery has given me a malign superstrength. Every other expression of anger in my life, I realize, always came restrained with concerns about how it made me look, or how it affected the other person, or if I could get fired. Consequences, basically.

I don't care! is often said but rarely fully meant. But I don't. I have nothing left to protect or worry about in attacking Ed over Susie. From where I'm standing, I've already lost everything. I'm the origins story of a dangerous comic-book villain.

"OK," Ed says, visibly heavy breathing. "OK. Look. This isn't the place . . ."

"Hah!" I give an evil, boozy snort. "I should've picked the many other occasions it was appropriate to raise you being a lying cheater who exploited our late friend . . ."

Exploited? I have no idea where that concept came from, but in for a penny. Once again, under stress, my mouth is galloping ahead.

"Unfortunately I only found out last night, so."

Ed is chewing the inside of his mouth, forehead furrowed, trying not to further incriminate himself. I am grimly satisfied at throwing a grenade into the wake for him, now he has to deal with it too.

After what looks like brief and fraught internal deliberation, he says in a small voice: "*How* did you find out?"

"A letter. In the box I took from her house."

"I thought you weren't going to look at them?"

"So did I. But one had already been opened, it was right on top, and bingo."

We stare at each other in the low lighting. A breeze is ruffling us and neither of us are shivering. I'm deliberately resisting any of the heavy look of shared understanding that Ed is trying to impart. That is over for good. Talk your way out of this one.

He opens his mouth.

"Aren't you two absolutely freezing?! What are you doing out here?"

Both of us turn to see Hester, arms folded over her chest in her navy wiggle dress.

"Don't mind me, what were you talking about? Looked intense."

"Just the reading . . . ," Ed says.

"What about it?"

There's a pause.

"I see Eve's fully equipped," Hester says, eyeing my bottle.

Not now. Not here. No way.

"Yes, I'm having a drink after my best friend's funeral, if that's alright," I say to her.

"Justin's getting them to make him negronis in there. Bletch," Hester says, ignoring me. "They taste like travel sickness medication."

Ed realizes he's gone from one incendiary situation to an even more flammable one, if I decide to share my news with Hester, and says hastily: "It's more than allowed, I might get myself another pint actually."

"You're going to have a hangover," Hester chides.

"Yeah well."

I have absolutely no interest in filling the dead air that follows with chatter, though I'm aware that if it continues, Hester may fully realize she's interrupted something. I sense Ed is grasping for something to say but that options are limited in the circumstances.

"Hey, so—while I've got you," Hester says to me. "I wanted to let you know, as a bridesmaid. After thought and discussion, Ed and I are going to press ahead with the wedding on schedule."

I reply: "Oh?"

"It can be something for us to look forward to, amid all this grimness."

"Right."

Like me getting thinner, the wedding is rebalancing the scales. It's one thing to know someone's insensitive, and another to have them demonstrate just how insensitive they can be when you're at your most sensitive.

Ed is staring at the ground.

"I'm going to see if Verity will take Susie's place as bridesmaid. Don't mention to her that Susie was the first choice at any of the fittings, will you?! I don't want her to get huffy at being on the reserves bench. I mean, just you watch, she's going to fight me every inch of the way on the dress design. She's gorgeous but there is *no one* vainer, haha."

I nod and drink some drink and Ed is avoiding my gaze, in new depths of torment, I'm sure.

Well, you got engaged to her.

Silence.

"The show must go on. It's what Susie would want," Hester says, catching herself, I think.

As a coup de grâce, her eyes well up with Disney tears. I can imagine a man rushing to put his jacket around her as she trembles. Ed remains frozen still.

Hester has found my breaking point. I've never said a word of challenge to her in all the years I've known her. But a dam has burst.

"What she'd *want*? What she'd want is to not be a pile of fireplace sweepings in an industrial furnace in Wilford right now."

"Sshhhh, Christ, Eve." Hester looks around, eyes like saucers at my tastelessness. "It's not the time for your . . . unique turn of phrase."

"Not the time? You're the one talking about bridesmaid fittings for her replacement."

"Hang on, it's fine for you guys to crack jokes, but the moment I talk about something else, I'm in bad taste? Is that it?"

"What I mind is you using Susie's imaginary wishes as your excuse. She'd not care less about whether your wedding went ahead. Leave her out of it."

"Wow, 'excuse'?" Hester says, face twisting. "Alright. Thanks. I don't see why you've attacked me. So you think out of respect we should cancel, and lose two grand . . ."

"I don't care," I say, with sufficient force she looks genuinely startled. "No one gives a shit about your wedding tonight, Hester. Sorry to be the bearer. In terms of hitting the right tone, you might as well walk around playing a tuba."

I find I'm not scared of her. I feel like Bette Davis gene-spliced with a cobra.

Hester's unused to being called on her behavior and it shows. Like an unfit person suddenly asked to run a mile, she's out of shape when it comes to taking negative feedback, huffing and puffing. Whereas I feel like I've been in training for this moment for years.

"Talking about my wedding—our wedding"—she shoots a look at Ed, who she suddenly realizes should be backing her up—"is about 'life goes on.' You agreed we should still go ahead with it. I don't hear you agreeing now though?" She looks at Ed again.

There's a painful pause.

"I did agree. But you didn't need to bring it up now. Eve's right," Ed says, and I swear I feel Hester lift two inches off the ground in fury. "Leave it."

"You're taking her side, after the way she's spoken to me?" Hester says, pointing at me, to identify the culprit for the jury.

Ed doesn't answer.

Her eyes narrow. "I am so, fucking, sick, of the way you lot are with each other, your cliquey little gang and your . . . *superiority*. Don't twist my words and take this out on me, because you're sad and bitter," she says to me.

She wipes at her suddenly streaming eyes and stalks off back into the hotel. She might as well have said "Heel!" to Ed, for the obviousness of the expectation that he follow.

I don't feel regret, or triumph, or worry at the repercussions from that spat. I don't feel anything. I'm numb.

"Sorry," Ed says, turning to me, looking like a man who's aged a year in minutes.

"What for?" I say. Usually that is a response to an apology that exculpates someone, but here it's accusatory.

"Hah." He rubs his temple. "I'll call you," he says, in a low voice, and heads indoors to find Hester.

As my eyes follow him, I see Finlay Hart, leaning against the wall in the shadows, a glowing ember of a cigarette in one of his hands. I near-physically twitch at recognizing him in the gloom, plenty near enough to have caught every word of the altercation.

How long has he been there?

He smiles at me, drops his cigarette butt, and grinds it under his heel. It's the first time I've ever seen him smile. Might've known he only enjoys malign triumph. And Marlboro Gold.

"Can I help you?" I say.

"Take the positive from that," he says.

Ugh.

". . . Which is?"

"Doesn't sound like you'll have to be a bridesmaid anymore."

21

Three weeks later

Hot Yoga!

Get Bendy with Wendy (yes really, that's what it's called) in Loughborough

There's shock and then there's grief, and there's the simple tiring unending chore of life afterward. These are all different things, I've learned.

It's the forgetful twitch that's the worst. *Oh I'll text Susie if . . . Oh I wonder if Susie wants tickets to . . . What did Susie say about that, again? I'll just . . .*

Each time, the whiplash of remembering, like the spike of nausea you get coming to a very sudden halt aboard a moving object. Then the abyss of "no Susie ever again" opens up beyond it. It doesn't change, this being gone. Who knew that the most obvious thing about it is the hardest part?

It's boring too—the relentless grind of it, getting on with

things without the person who punctuated life's work and obligations. The person who made sense of me.

I'm grateful for the distraction of going into the office but equally I can't pretend the job itself is some sort of nourishment. Life is a pantomime. Once again, I am the back end of a puking camel.

I put on an outfit this morning that Susie recently said "is the epitome of you. You have become the epitome of yourself": a long polka-dot dress with puffed sleeves, and Grenson boots. "It's your personality in textile form. Sweet and appealing with a hard punchline."

I should've asked Susie if I delivered the punchline or if I was the punchline.

Phil sets a coffee down for me this morning and says: "Your friend. It was a cremation?"

I nod. There's been no discussion among my friends of who collects the urn. Ed might've quietly gone and done it. Bloody Ed.

"Johnny Depp paid for his mate's ashes to be put in a rocket. Cost him three million, the silly sausage."

Lucy and Seth look up and hold their breath, to see if I react badly to this. Classic Phil.

"Did he?" I say, conversationally. "We didn't stretch to that."

Lucy and Seth visibly relax.

"Seems odd to me, firing remains over a field," Phil says.

"I suppose people scatter ashes in all sorts of scenic places. Arguably just a more dramatic delivery system?"

"Good point."

I find Phil's brash manner strangely soothing. Not for him the eggshell-walking that most others give the newly bereaved.

He had that subdued week—possibly influenced by the fact he was the one to find me after the news, and saw its effect on me—but, funeral past, had judged it to be business as usual. Which I guess it is. Phil is what my mum calls "a wind-up."

He's squinting at Wikipedia on his monitor now.

"Oh, my mistake, it was a cannon. Rich people, eh? They're a different country."

Ed's peppered my phone with attempts to contact me since our showdown. I've managed to hold him off—without too much suspicion from Justin that something specific is afoot—by saying I want time to myself to come to terms with the new world order, and the pub quiz cannot be contemplated for the time being. Hester no doubt thinks I'm sulking. Oh, and Ed had to go on a weeklong school trip, so that helped—he lost a week to shepherding truculent preteens around Chichester.

But I know that clock's going to run out soon, and my avoidance of them all will be classed as worrying, rather than self-care.

Once Ed's back from the trip he calls, he texts asking if we can chat, he calls again, he WhatsApps, asking if I'm going to ignore him indefinitely.

Halfway through the morning, my WhatsApp blips with Ed again. I open the message and scroll through a large amount of text.

Alright, this is a long one for WhatsApp and I only have seven minutes before the next lesson starts, but—I get why you are very, very angry and very, very shaken, Eve. But part of that might come from not knowing much about what happened, beyond the stark main fact. If you don't want to give me the chance to explain because you don't

think I deserve the chance, I get that. I think you might feel better hav-
ing heard me out though, and you get to give me a no holds barred
response too. I'm not pretending this is selfless, there's plenty of self-
interest in here too. I hate that you think this badly of me, and I hate
not having my best mate around at the worst time in my life. Which is
what you are. Not Hester, not Justin. Not Susie. You're my best friend
and if that still means anything, then let's at least discuss this. That's
probably shameful emotional blackmail, I'm too ragged to judge at
this point. It's also the truth. Ed. X

I'm not sure telling me I'm his fondest-ever friendzoning is
the winning suit he thinks it is.

After an hour of knocking back black coffee like it's hard
liquor, I force myself to message Ed back.

I've been going back and forth, over and over, what I say or
do next, and I still don't know.

My only firm conclusion is: if I hadn't wanted this conversation with Ed, I shouldn't have sounded off at Susie's wake. (Her
wake? Wakes are for the dead.)

And there's a glaring problem with holding Ed to account
for this—Becky's letter showed Susie knew how I felt. If Susie
knew, then she and Ed must've discussed it. The fact neither of
them told me proves *something* was said. How far do I pursue
the humiliation of getting Ed to spell it out? *We agreed that as*
you're patently a lovesick wreck . . .

Yet their knowledge is central to my betrayal, can't raise one
without the other. I don't know how to navigate that.

I concede out of sheer practicality. I have to see him, though.
It's Justin's birthday soon.

OK, you can come round to mine tonight at eight. I'm checking in on Susie's dad straight after work.

The day passes in a listless stress haze, wondering what Ed will say tonight.

There should be a German word for both dying to know something and, at the same time, being sick with terror at the prospect of hearing anything about it whatsoever.

Dying to know. Susie is dead. I rehearse that fact for the hundredth time. It rears up and punches me again.

"Why are you wearing those docker's boots with a nice frock?" Phil says, as I get up to leave at half five. "What do you look like?" He pauses and I gather this isn't rhetorical. "You're reminding me of something. I know! One of those Art Deco lamps. My mum's got a repro. A graceful dancing lady with a long swirly dress, stood on a big heavy base."

Despite myself, I laugh.

As I queue for my bus home, my phone pings. Finlay Hart. A name to spark loathing and dread. As it once did for his late sister, I guess.

Hi Eve. I'm in the UK again next week to sort the sale of Susie's house, and I've still not had the diaries and letters returned. Can we make an arrangement to meet for you to hand them over? Thanks. Finlay

I thought that was going to involve lawyers?

This is a last chance to avoid that. Up to you.

Hmmm, I smell bluff. Surely if he was going to do that, he'd have done it by now?

My intransigence with Fin could look like hardball but, in truth, my silence comes from the fact that I don't know what to do. I'm scared of myself around that box. What if I'm compelled to pry, and discover yet more?

Susie wouldn't want Finlay to have them, that's my only certainty. But am I creating a real-world problem for the sake of some abstract notion of her honor? You can't embarrass the dead. The living have to pay solicitors, and I'm perpetually broke.

I try to hear Susie's voice, but on this matter, she's silent.

22

I'm not fully sure if Iain Hart wants or needs my calling around, but I absolutely can't not do it, so I'm glad he seems to receive my visits with pleasure, albeit with a slight air of courteous bafflement. I make a peculiar busybody, but so far he's not busy enough himself to mind.

Once a week I turn up on his doorstep, usually with biscuits—having usefully discovered Mr. Hart is a biscuit fiend—announce I was "in the area," and ask if he "needs anything." We have a cup of tea, a chat about this and that, and I reassure myself he seems safe and well enough to keep buggering on.

Today he seems edgier than usual, forgetting to eat his plain chocolate biscuits, wanting to tell me about the professional hierarchies at his long-since-sold company. I get the feeling he has a nagging sense of leaving things unattended, but isn't able to articulate what or how. Up until now, his dementia has seemed quite benign, if sad. Because he's outwardly so cheerful and functioning, it wasn't too startling. Now I see more clearly that it's a living prison.

"Anyway, I mustn't run on and bore you," he says. "You

young people have got more exciting things to be doing. I was young once too, haha! Look, here . . ."

He picks up a picture on the mantelpiece, a 1980s wedding, full of leg-of-mutton sleeves, artificial flower crowns, and estate agent suits, and points to himself, more luxuriant in mustache. He has his hand on the head of a small, somber-faced, dark-haired boy, who must be Finlay.

"That's my brother Don's wedding. He lives in Edinburgh. A beautiful city, it's where I grew up. Have you been?"

"Once as a kid, but not for ages," I say.

"Oh you should, you should! I should visit Don actually; it's been too long."

"I'm sure he'd like to see you," I say, wondering if Don was at the funeral. My only point of introduction would be Finlay, and he was hardly likely to bother. Had Susie told her uncle of her dad's infirmity? She never spoke about her wider family, even when we were kids, really. If only we'd known we'd need handover notes. If only we'd known lots of things.

I get home with only half an hour to spare before Ed arrives, and find that I can't eat for nerves. Wine for dinner it is then.

He arrives right on eight, and Roger's at the door wailing his excitement as Ed steps into the room, the stripy traitor.

I hate that even now, at the sight of him in his raincoat and rain-damp hair, I want him to hug me. You cannot reason with what your senses crave, it seems. *Everyone's a fool for somebody,* as my mum says.

"Alright, Rog, she not been feeding you again? Guess what Uncle Edward brought you!"

He produces Roger's favorite beef-flavor chew sticks in front of him, and flaps the packet, at which point Roger's vocal pitch

moves from "girl at a Bay City Rollers concert" to "actual sei-
zure."

While he's gnawing on Ed's insufficient peace offering, our
eyes meet fully. Ed is glowing with exercise.

"Drink?" I say, brusquely.

"One. I'm on my bike, don't want to fall off."

"Take a seat. Beer?"

"Yes, cheers."

I go to the fridge, pour myself a large Sauvignon, then crack
the ring pull on a can of Staropramen and hand it to him.

There's no appetite for small talk and Ed, always one to read
a room, says, businesslike: "Firstly, I've been wanting to say for
ages, sorry for Hester being a dickhead at the wake. She's pretty
mortified at what was said. There's no hard feelings. Or, not
from her end."

"I can't believe she admitted she was out of order."

I'm not going to be overtly rude about Hester to her fiancé,
but equally, I'm not going to be so scrupulous about hiding my
opinion of her behavior, from now on. Some truth has broken
through. It can be the new normal.

"Yes, she has," Ed says, with a forehead-creasing, hard frown
that makes me think he came out of his corner fighting, once
they were home.

"She was wasted"—she wasn't, I think, but whatever
works—". . . and she's got so consumed with the wedding.
When I pointed out she was blithely talking about Susie being
replaced, to her best friend, she got it."

"Ah, OK."

I think I see how the trick was worked. Ed, the man who
could broker any peace. *Don't you see how devastated Eve will be*

not to have Susie by her side that day? Swinging the spotlight back to Hester, the sun that we planets revolve around.

What's the betting his version also made Hester think I'd see the error of my ways and be shamefaced at insulting her, once sober? A truce where we both think the other surrendered.

Ed clears his throat. "As to the other . . ."

I sip my wine, look at him levelly. He sets his can down and pushes forward, hands on knees.

"I'm so sorry you found out about this when you did, Eve. Believe me. That day was hard enough without that on top. I can't imagine how difficult it was."

The empathy card. Or is he implying this is only sordid because Susie's gone?

"When you keep secrets, you never know when they're going to come out, I guess," I say.

My voice sounds tight.

"I'd almost forgotten it'd happened, you know. We'd dug deep to bury it."

"Sounds like you're pretty rubbish in bed, then," I say. "Most of us would have a memory of banging one of our best mates."

Ed flinches.

Yes, bad luck. I'm not going to play along with any *I tripped up, fell on her, I'm so haplessly clumsy that penetration occurred, memory very fuzzy* minimization game.

"It was ten years ago, that much you know, I think."

I've never seen Ed look this discomfited.

". . . It was a Friday night. We decided at the last minute we were both bored and wanted to go out. Hester was in Switzerland doing the au pairing."

I'd forgotten that. Hester was working full time but took

a summer sabbatical to teach English to a brood of rich kids. She's one of those people who needs to staple extra pages to her CV as opposed to bumping the font size up, like me. Mark once said mine had EVELYN HARRIS so big it could be a flypast banner.

"Justin was in London that weekend on one of his bacchanals."

I'm waiting for Ed to know where I was. *You . . . we didn't call you.*

"You were off somewhere in the early days of Mark."

Ah. This throws me, for a moment. I should've spotted it was that era.

"We went to the Tap and Tumbler, played pool, drank loads on an empty stomach, got accidentally wrecked, had half a pill each. Then we went to the club at Rock City . . ."

I wait. I can feel the rising heat of my sweat under my clothes.

"Remember they always played Rage Against the Machine? 'Killing in the Name' came on, and somehow"—he blows air out—"one thing led to another . . ."

"Oh don't 'one thing led to another' me, Ed," I snap, in my embarrassment as much as his. "You're not telling the kids in class that your wife's having a baby."

Ed flushes.

I'm a paper tiger. I'm interrogating a man who is engaged to be married to someone else, not me, about sex that happened a decade ago, with another someone else who is no longer here. My rights here are far from clear. It wasn't me who Ed cheated on, yet I feel jealous, betrayed, and gut-twistingly angry. I'm presenting as indignant and righteous but, in actual fact, I'm drowning in shame and confusion of my own.

This is why you don't stay in dysfunctional unspoken love with spoken-for people. A few chess moves later, it looks completely mad. I guess it always was completely mad.

"You know, drunk air-punching during the chorus, turned into hugging, then woah, somehow, without knowing who started it, we're kissing," Ed says. "It was one of those spur-of-the-moment total pieces of insanity that seems to make sense to you when you've had five pints of lager on an empty stomach and you're twenty-four-years old."

"So you kissed, and . . . ?" I say.

"We went back to Suze's to get drunker. Remember when she had the flat for debauchery in Lace Market? It was a getting-smashed escalation where doing the next thing, and the next, seemed a good idea, we were almost daring each other. We were off our faces. Neither of us left the house that night intending it."

I prepared for tonight, as much as I could, and I force myself to ask (or I'll be condemned to forever wonder): "Susie's description of it was 'torrid'?" Well, Becky's. Same-same.

Ed's face has gone from shrimp pink to shrimp pink tinged with sickly white. I really hope he's not about to admit to an act I'll have seared on my imagination's retina forever.

"We did it in the loos at the club," he says, after a pause, and I swallow.

The severe crush I have suffered for ten years is dealt a body blow. A two-body blow.

I will always have to have this as part of my mental landscape of Susie and Ed: a frantic coupling in a graffiti-strewn toilet stall, Arctic Monkeys pounding through the walls. As a definition of torrid, I suppose it's preferable to some degenerate activity I'd never heard of involving orifices and water-balloon animals, as if the world is some huge gangbang I've not been invited to. If I'm placing it on the great sliding scale of "the best to worst sort of unusual sexual activity for two friends to partake in, when breaking a third party's heart." A third party. That's me.

"Susie led me into the ladies. We did it again at hers. We passed out. We woke up in the morning to the worst hangovers of our lives, absolutely crucified with horror by it. Believe me, a huge motivation for hiding it was how badly we both wished it had never happened. We agreed not to tell you and Justin . . ."

"Justin doesn't know either?"

That's something. I'm not alone.

"Yeah, he does. I told him, down the line. Susie didn't know that."

"*What?!*"

"Man-to-man, late-night-confessional kind of thing. To get it off my chest when I felt guilt over Hester."

"Great, so I was the only one. Susie never told me."

The sense of having been made a fool of, sitting there as the sole member who didn't know this thing, who wasn't mature enough somehow to be told this thing, gives me a feeling of intense rejection. It's like what Ed did when we were eighteen, squared.

"She bottled it. As time passes it gets harder and harder to come clean. Bottlings only get bigger. It's the cost of cowardice. The price of making the wrong choice at the outset."

Ed stares at me heavily, as if there might be a double meaning, and I'm grateful for Roger's sudden screech for a second chew stick, breaking the tension. Ever resourceful and charming, Ed has another one, of course.

Amid the noise of eager feline mastication, Ed continues: "After Susie had finished throwing up that morning, we discussed what we stood to damage or lose entirely by being a pair of twats. I'd been unfaithful to Hester. We'd potentially upset this—" Ed says, gesturing at me, but meaning our group. "For what? For something animal we'd done after drowning our frontal lobes in Heineken. We could barely look each other in the eye. We didn't remotely fancy each other and, in the cold light of day, that made it simpler, but also much worse. I've never known self-loathing like it."

I strain to remember any time when I'd come back from seeing Mark, when Susie had been different. I can't. I remember larking around in that flat, Susie smoking with her arm held out of the sash window. She was seeing people, on and off, but never anyone significant.

With some effort, I remember her once saying to me, uncharacteristically pensive: "The thing about you and men, Eve, is you fall very rarely and very hard. I fall often, but I'm over it in a week."

She must've meant Ed—so she fell for him too? Why did she never confess? Did she think I'd explode into a shower of dry leaves? I pick up my glass.

"You let Hester carry on being friends with Susie, with no idea?"

"That was utterly shit of me, yes. But I only had shit choices. If I confessed and our relationship survived it, I wouldn't have been allowed to still be mates with Suze, so RIP our gang. She's always been messed-up about how close we all are, as you may have noticed. The cost-benefit didn't seem worth it, and it still doesn't."

"The cost-benefit," I say, witheringly. "It wasn't about balancing books. It wasn't going to benefit you."

"No, exactly, who would it benefit? Hester deserves to know the truth, in principle, but it wouldn't benefit her, quite the opposite. There's no way of discussing this without sounding terrible, because it was. It was a really gross thing to do and I'm ashamed of it to this day. I offered the ugly truth and, yes, it's ugly."

I'm randomly reminded of my mum and dad arguing over Bill Clinton's impeachment. My dad saying: "You ask a man if he fooled around with someone who wasn't his wife, he's going to say no, isn't he? What man in the world when put on the spot would say, 'Ya got me'? I don't see why him lying was a big deal when anyone in his shoes would." My mum replying: "He shouldn't have fooled around!" My dad: "Yes, but that's a 'I wouldn't start from here' when someone's asking for directions, Connie, isn't it?"

Am I unreasonable, asking Ed to be better than a president? Ed's lies have only been omission.

Roger, offstage, slaps at the door on his cat litter box.

". . . I've asked myself, apart from alcohol, why I did it," Ed says. "I've never come up with a better answer than 'because I could.' You can't disown your own character under the influence. Suze used to taunt me for being staid, a lot. I think showing off might've been involved. When I realized what she was intending, me feeling I had to meet the challenge and show I could be wild too. Ironic, given there was nothing to be proud about in what happened, the opposite. I couldn't have made myself look or feel more ridiculous."

"Oh, it was her pushing for it, was it?" I say, rolling my eyes.

"As I recall, yes," Ed says, looking dog-tired all of a sudden. "I can't be sure, given how drunk we were. But I wouldn't have dared drag her to the women's bathroom."

There is, at the heart of this explanation and apology—if that's what it is—a problem. All this might be true, but the connection I thought Ed and I had—it can't exist. Or not in the way I thought it did, if he could do this. Anyone but her, the closest human being to me. I weathered the treachery of Hester, as I could follow how it happened. Not this.

"This isn't the person I thought you were," I say, bleakly. And although, in my head, this wasn't a killer line, only a spasm of pain that I couldn't help exiting my mouth, Ed visibly crumples at it.

"Yes, I know," he says. He takes a deep breath. "It's not who I thought I was. Your opinion is everything to me."

The most difficult part of this for me is upon us, and I have to tackle it, even though it makes me feel like I'm sitting here naked.

"Susie said in her letter she didn't want me to know, in particular?" I hold my breath.

Ed breaks eye contact for a moment and says: "She was aware there was . . . something between us. She felt she'd let you down, because of that."

I writhe, and maintain a false composure. "Did you tell Susie about the letter you sent me? At university?"

"No! Why would I do that?" Ed, wide-eyed, thinks he's scored a point here, kept my confidence. But I know what it means—he let it all rest on me.

"Then why would she think there was something between us?"

This is a question I would only dare ask under extreme duress, and to someone with Ed's size of motive to be tactful right now. *Did I really make it obvious?* is one of the world's most agonizing inquiries.

Ed lifts his hands from his knees in an *I don't know* gesture. "I'm not sure."

"What did she say?" I ask.

"Do you really want me to go into this?" he says.

"No, Ed, I don't!" I say, temper breaking, in my fierce blushing. It's a funny combination. "I don't *want* to hear a word of it, but thanks to you, it happened, I found out, and Susie's dead. I'm going to have to spend the rest of my life wondering why she kept this from me, otherwise. It's 'need,' not 'want.' I'd have thought that was pretty obvious."

"She said she thought you were in love with me and it would destroy you," Ed says, in a rush, and looks at his knees.

I'm damp with sweat. I don't change expression.

"Erm, OK. Wow." This is good and ambiguous, I think. It could mean *Wow she knew?* or *Wow she thought that?* "Then you said . . . ?"

"I agreed it wasn't a good idea to tell you."

"But you didn't say oh hey, I told Eve I was madly in love with *her*, a few years back?"

"No," Ed says, frowning. "It wasn't the moment and I kind of assumed you'd have told Susie about that at the time, anyway?"

It hadn't occurred to me he'd think this. I suppose he would've thought that, what with girl talk and gossip. The truth is, it was first too precious, and then too painful, to let any sunlight in on it. And as usual, the group was to be protected at all costs.

I only say: "Nope."

I wonder why he thinks I didn't tell Susie.

"Eve," Ed says. "I know 'speaking for Susie' keeps tripping us up, but she'd be crushed to think she'd hurt you by keeping this from you. Nothing mattered to her the way you did. *Nothing.*"

This rings hollow, after talking about a night when my feelings definitely didn't matter to her. She knew I was in love, and it would destroy me, and she still did it. "Destroy"—her word, not mine.

For nothing more than an ungainly, sloppy one-night stand. She was Susie Hart—she could've gone home with any man in that club if she'd wanted to.

What would she say if she were here? I can only imagine some version of Ed's "We were drunk, we were idiots." *Much stupid, so regret.* What other excuse is there? She wasn't the person I thought she was.

"Would Hester still marry you if she knew?" I say, making it clear there's no point to any more mollifying speechifying from Ed.

"I don't know. It would be an apocalyptic fight. It being Susie would make it a thousand times worse, of course, compared to some anonymous woman. I don't want her to think less of Susie." Ed holds up a palm as he sees my jaw drop. "Yeah, you can call that a really slimy thing to say, it is, but it's true. You think Susie would want that, in her memory? Us splitting up over some decade-old embarrassing transgression? Or Hester being tormented by the thought of it? You've found it gruesome enough."

"Well, I'm implicated now," I say, interrupting, before we get into measuring of what I'm feeling versus what Hester would.

206

"Because in your vows there'll be that bit about *if anyone knows any reason why these two should not be joined . . .*"

"You'd not be the first person to sit through that part of a ceremony and know something about the bride or groom that either one of them doesn't."

Ed tries for a small rueful smile, and I stare it down.

"It's not funny."

"It's not. I'm not saying you can't tell Hester if that's what your conscience tells you to do. I've never cheated on Hester, apart from that one time."

"Oh, paging Pride of Britain awards."

"No! I mean, it's not habitual, this isn't the tip of an iceberg. You're not letting another woman walk unwitting into a marriage with King Rat."

"Hmmm."

I'm not going to tell Hester. Given how little I think of her, it would be nothing but revenge on Ed, and, as my mum says, revenge is throwing piss in a strong wind. She should know.

"Thanks for hearing me out. I know none of this is easy."

I agree it isn't, and feel the emptiness I knew was on the other side of this groveling. Now what? Accept it and carry on.

Ed leans down to pet Roger, who's winding himself around his ankles and clearly pondering a bid for Chew Stick 3: The Enfattening.

"You've been off the radar a bit since the funeral . . . are you OK? Apart from the giant things that aren't OK?"

I raise my shoulders and drop them. "Yes and no."

Ed nods. He's temporarily lost his rights to be emollient Ed, and he knows it. He scrunches the sides of his empty can, making a small crackling noise.

As he leaves, he says: "You'll come to Justin's birthday, though, right?"

"Oh? Yes. Has he planned anything?"

"Not that I know of. It'll be low-key, obviously. As much as anything involving Justin is low-key."

Ed smiles, clearly in relief at the status quo returning. The explosive device, defused. I don't smile back. He knows I'm not going to tell Hester, so we're back to how it was, except we aren't and never will be.

"Can you do me a favor? Don't tell Justin we had this conversation? I'm hoping you haven't filled him in on any of this," I say.

"None of it," Ed says.

He looks at me and realizes he can't risk so much as a pally shoulder squeeze.

"Bye," I say.

After I close the door, I feel flattening disappointment with myself, as well as him, and I know why.

I didn't have the guts to ask: did *you* think I was in love with you?

23

I nail the rest of the bottle of white wine in a dark red mood.

The rain that spat at Ed earlier becomes a downpour. It's the only thing I'm capable of appreciating, alongside the Nick Cave album, the candle I put on, and the alcohol in my bloodstream. The insistence of water hammering against the window panes is almost soothing.

It's not lost on me that Susie would ordinarily be the one to spring me from this sort of trap. She'd survey the scene, eyes focusing on the telltale flickering Diptyque tubéreuse candle (too expensive to light during lesser trauma), and say:

What's up with you? Ugh, I can't stand that miserable singer, he's got a booming voice that sounds like he should be down Annesley Woodhouse Working Men's Club doing "My Way." "WHAT IS A MAN / WHAT HAS HE GOT / IF NOT HIMSELF / THEN NOT A LOT . . ." Wait, did he just say he's got the "abattoir blues"?

Yup.

Who'd be happy if they were in abattoir?!

It's a metaphorical abattoir.

He can leave it, then, can't he. He's what my dad calls a moaning Minnie. Oh, I'm in imaginary Pork Farms, poor me.

I'd dissolve in laughter at *imaginary Pork Farms* and she would say *where is the lie* and pull her *you think I'm silly, well I'm not* chipmunk face, pushing her lips out in a parodic sulk, so like petulant child Susie. I would sense how pleased she was to have amused me.

Except, even if she was here, she couldn't fix this. Why did she do it? I know she was drunk but . . . had someone she knew stopped her, when her hand was in Ed's hand, weaving in and out of the crowd in Rock City, and said, "Oh my God, you two, together, can I tell Eve?" she'd have said *no, no, no, don't you dare.*

Someone who can fumble with the fly on a trouser can remember who her best friend is. Alcohol doesn't erase who you are, it gives you license.

We didn't knowingly hurt each other. We would never have competed for the same man. No Becky, with good or bad hair, could come between us. There were a few unspoken sacred rules, our foundation stones.

And what was with Ed giving me the come-to-bed eyes, at his words: "the cost of cowardice"?

If he *did* do that? Am I projecting? Have I been gaslit into grudge-filled madness?

The trouble is, we think of being in love, romance, in active terms—a pursuit. We're working to outdated models. We need new concepts for modern fuckery. Ed is not in pursuit of me, by any measure, nor vice versa. Yet he's always *there.* We're forever romantically adjacent. But how do you emotionally detach when they're one of your best mates? I don't recall any agony aunt advice on that score.

Roger rearranges himself on my stomach as I stare at my "docker boots," dangling over the arm of the sofa.

Why am I the only one clinging to the past? The only one caring? Everyone else takes what they want and moves the fuck on. Even Susie, rocketing into the afterlife.

She's not here, worrying about anything. Her problems, old and new: the Ed secret, the antagonist brother, even her vulnerable father, they've all been left to me. She died "intestate," as the wills and probate guy told us, but that only referred to who inherited property and money. Maybe I don't want these burdens, Susie? Maybe I didn't deserve them? Can't I push the responsibility aside, like you all did?

I think these thoughts as a form of self-harm, taking a vicious comfort in the intentional cruelty. I'm angry at Susie, I realize, and not only about Ed. For not glancing the right way up a dark street, for not moving fast enough, and leaving me with this much pain. For just leaving me.

After I've wallowed in this, I dislike myself.

If my life was a box-set drama, I guess this would be the moment a portion of the audience would say: *I tried to get into it, but she was so self-pitying, you know? Ugh, your friend is killed, but you're the unlucky one?* (Or maybe they'd have bailed after HasPubesGate. "Can't cope with cringe comedy, two stars out of five.")

I'm seized by an urge to do something destructive and definitive . . . The letters and diaries? Eighty-five percent of me says: yeah do it, get rid of them. Fifteen percent of me whispers nervously: you can never undo this decision.

The eighty-five percent bellows back: yeah there's a lot that can't be undone, haven't you noticed that? At least if this is a mistake, it's one I bloody chose and controlled. Instead of being Fate's piñata.

She said she thought you were in love with me and it would destroy you.

There you are, she was prepared to destroy *me*, never mind some of my sophomoric doodlings.

Before I can change my mind, I place Rog to one side, bolt upstairs, and grab the box. Once back downstairs, holding it, I realize incinerating the contents presents a problem. People only have metal bins—trash cans—for burning things outdoors, in American films. Our plastic pedal versions aren't fit for this purpose.

Wait, instead of fire, what about water? I have a deep trough of Bristol sink that cost me an arm and a leg. My mum observed its installation with the words: "Isn't it odd how we end up fetishizing the ordinary things our grandparents had? That said, I never wanted their outdoor loo."

I upend the box into the basin, grateful the cursed letter is on top, and will therefore be at the bottom. Now I'm looking at the jumble of envelopes, like a tombola, what I'm doing becomes real. Susie's words, her thoughts: about to be lost forever. I twinge, I wonder if I should sit here, read and commit their contents to memory.

Then when Finlay has me tied to a chair in a garage, holding a petrol can, I can spit out a mouthful of blood and say: *If you kill me you'll never know.*

The diaries present a different problem, with their protective spongy covers. I have to open them and brutally rip the pages out from the glue of the spine, so I can't avoid seeing the sloping script of Susie's girlish handwriting in blue pen, catching stray words even though my brain doesn't want to. Mostly excitable, context-free adverbs and *"chicken nuggets for tea!"* (supporting Justin's theory, and Susie's claim, that there's no creative loss to the world here). I pause, only for a moment, when a shredded piece bears the word "FINLAY!!" in capital letters, underlined, with a ☹ face.

Not my business. Not his business—Susie would've writhed at the thought of him picking through this.

It has to be done. Temptation needs removing, privacy needs protecting. *Is that really why you're doing this?* a voice asks. *Or is it revenge, Evelyn Harris?*

I turn the tap on and watch the water gush out onto paper, ink melting and blurring, the paper becoming transparent, fragmenting, making a dun-colored soup. When I turn the tap off, the remains can be squidged into a strange, soggy snowscape.

I pick up handfuls of now unintelligible correspondence and chuck it into the bin with a damp thud.

Roger wanders in and lets go a pealing mew of confusion, which I interpret as: *but what are the legal ramifications of destroying the hotly contested artifacts?*

"Dunno," I say to him, thick with wine, triumph, and defeat.

A stray memory—a few birthdays ago, Susie got me some nostalgic joke gift extras, some Vogue Superslim Menthols, a bottle of Dolly Girl perfume, and a bag of mini Daim bars. Kitschy "what were we like!" talismans of times gone by, insights only old friends have.

I find them in a hat box in my bedroom, scooping them up before the memory can hit me—recalling her expectant face as I unwrapped them in a Greek restaurant, in that giddy past, where we didn't know we were born, and that she was going to die.

I come back downstairs, dump the haul on the counter and spray the perfume at my collarbones, open a Dime and gnaw on it. God, that's face-twistingly sweet. Susie and I used to eat bowls of vanilla ice cream using the Dimes as scoops. It's a wonder we have any teeth left.

That *I* have any teeth left. If you identify people who died in fires by their dental records, what do crematoriums do with teeth?

I unwrap the cigarette packet and light one with a kitchen match, dragging, inhaling, exhaling, and coughing. Oof, this is horrible, did I really used to do this?

Badly, I hear Susie say.

The rain's abated, so I open the back door and sit hunched on the soaked concrete step in my tiny yard, water seeping through the seat of my dress, blowing plumes of smoke into the damp air.

I feel like a cowgirl for a moment, like a tableau in a film.

Without knowing I'd started crying, I feel a tear drip from my chin.

24

I could've waited my standard, if arbitrarily imposed, week to visit Mr. Hart again, but I've got an expensive brand of Florentines in a cardboard box that I think he'll love.

So four days later, I walk up the street to the Hart home, listening to a true crime podcast about an unsolved murder that changed one small mid-American town forever. This isn't only about being the Good Samaritan, though I'm glad to do it. Seeing Mr. Hart makes me feel connected to Susie, it helps me fill this time that I suddenly have so much of, and so little use for.

I pause my podcast and ring the bell. My stomach does a revolution as moments pass, and the interior door is wrenched open by Mr. Hart. Junior. Oh shit. I should've anticipated Finlay might be here—his texts, the ones I'd left unreplied to, said: *Next week.* Here we are in next week, and unfortunately, here he is. The letters. My rash move. My stomach now feels like a cake's being mixed inside it.

He has the hollow-eyed, stubble-shadowed, and slightly swollen look of the jet-lagged, and yet has the kind of bone structure where dishevelment only enhances him. The way a fresh haircut looks better when riffled by wind. The T-shirt and hooded zip-up top say "came straight from the plane."

"That's odd, I've just this minute been trying and failing to phone you," Fin says, without a hello. His expression: sardonic *j'accuse*.

"Oh," I say, taking my AirPods out like I'm removing clip-on earrings with a flourish in *Dynasty*, "I didn't hear, I had these on, sorry."

I feel guiltily grateful this is evidently true, even if absolutely nothing's going to get better for me from here on in. *I don't have the letters, shit. I don't HAVE them . . .* I remember how angry he was I was simply holding them back.

I hear Justin saying: *It's not for us to play judge and jury.* I played judge, jury, and executioner.

I hard swallow.

"Come in," Fin says, standing back. "My dad's not here."

"Oh, I'll not bother you then . . . ," I say.

"We have things to discuss," Fin says.

I expect he's going to round on me about the letters and start wielding frightening New York City law firm names. *Unless you want to hear from Carver, Cutthroat & Strank.*

What do I say? Do I come clean? Do I spin him along, until a moment I'm not in front of him?

Instead Finlay heads off to the kitchen and comes back with a piece of paper. He holds it out to me, mouth a straight hard line. I take it, and read:

Ann, Sorry not to see you this week, but I'm on a jolly, as we used to say.

*That nice friend of Susie's with the black hair—name escapes me—
suggested I visit my brother, Don, in the motherland, and I thought,
why not! Reckon I'll do the tourist spots first and see the old family
pile, then call in on him. Here's the cash and don't worry about the
ironing in the spare room, nothing that can't wait. See you next week.*

Iain

"Oh no . . . ," I say, limply.

"You encouraged my dad to travel to another country? Can
I ask why?" Fin says. He's not out-of-control angry but he's on
a war footing, in his black Converse boots.

"I didn't encourage him," I say, uselessly, in the face of hard
evidence. "He showed me a wedding photo of his brother and
I asked if he'd seen him lately . . . and your dad said no, and I
said, erm." Finlay's gaze lasers holes into me. ". . . I'm sure he'd
like to see you."

Spoken out loud, in the silence of the hallway, I can hear
how foolish I sound.

"I asked you not to visit, not to confuse him further," Fin
says, glowering intimidatingly from under his mussed sweep
of private-school, pretty-boy hair. (Even though he wasn't privately educated. Is that what he really hates me for, knowing
where he came from?)

"I didn't think he'd take me literally," I say, gabbling, feeling oily with heat under my coat. "It was a figure of speech,
like, oh perhaps it would be nice to . . . Not, absolutely, yes,
crack on, go to Scotland immediately."

"My father has Alzheimer's. He doesn't have the same responses to social niceties."

Neither do you, to be fair.

"Is it really bad that he's in Edinburgh, if he gets there safely? You could call your Uncle Don and explain he needs care . . ."

"He and Uncle Don didn't speak to each other," Fin says.

"Oh . . . right. Maybe your dad will have forgotten why, and Don will sense he's not himself . . ."

"And Uncle Don's dead," Fin says. "So I'm not putting much hope in a reconciliation."

"What?! Shit . . ."

"Are you going to be there when my dad finds this out, for the second time? Or the first, as far as he's concerned."

Oh God.

"I'm sorry," I say, and Fin shakes his head.

He's not a person you want to be in the wrong with.

"How long ago did he die?" My voice is small, the house is quiet.

Fin folds his arms.

"About five years."

"How do you think your dad will react?"

"I don't know. I don't know how he'll respond to the disorientation. He's rationalized and explained his surroundings to himself, here. This is traveling back to a past that he's living in and expects to find unchanged. It's his present."

"Have you told the police?"

"Yes, and they've notified the police up there, but being realistic, given my dad's unlikely to be visibly out of his senses, they're most likely to identify him if he walks into a police station. Nothing I've seen in my father, so far—and I include his life, pre-senility—makes me think he's going to be telling any stranger in a uniform he's not in control of a situation."

Finlay Hart is very bright, I concede. Coupled with his nature, this makes me wary, rather than impressed.

". . . Even if they pick him up because he's confused, there's not a lot they can do other than talk him down and alert me," Fin continues. "He's not been committed. He's free to go if he wants to."

Finlay pauses and blinks those dark blue, opaque eyes at me.

"I was supposed to have a care worker come and give him a mental capacity test this week. That's not likely to happen now."

"You really think he's not alright to be here?" I say, gesturing at the house.

"I'm not sure. That's why I want the tests. The cleaner found a kettle in the bath on one visit."

"What? In water?"

"No, the bath was empty. She says he said he'd gone to fill it because the downstairs tap wasn't working and forgotten about it. I think my dad knows something is up and is working hard to cover for himself. I've been researching dementia and this can be a thing. Verbally adept patients presenting as more 'with it' than they are, thinking on their feet, talking a good show. He'll need a care home or assisted living at some point and so I have to set the wheels in motion now. It's not fair on the cleaner to be my eyes and ears, as it is."

I nod.

"I'm going to go up to Edinburgh to look for him. If he ends up in a pub, talking to a stranger at the bar, they may spot he's not in his right mind. Aside from his personal safety, my father has a house, a car, savings, a working credit card, he wears a Patek Philippe watch. He could be taken for a lot."

Hmm yes, also, that's your inheritance, I think, ungenerously.

"But no mobile?"

"No. He had one years back and never turned it on and now it's missing entirely, probably in a drawer somewhere with fifteen defunct cables."

"Ah."

"However, when it comes to recovering him if I find him, he has no idea who I am. He thinks I'm a neighbor who's got him mixed up with someone else."

"Yes . . ."

"And if this annoying neighbor turns up on the Royal Mile, saying hey, how about you come home with me, I don't envisage that going at all well. To the point of hostilities breaking out."

"Yeah . . . ," I say, in a sympathetic tone.

"If I pay for all your costs, your hotel room, could you come to Edinburgh and help me look for him?"

"What?" I say, face heating. I hadn't anticipated this. "How would I help?"

"He responds really well to you. That note shows he even remembers your conversations after you've left. That's a power pretty much no one has."

"I don't know . . . ," I say. I know I have to get out of this, I'm not sure how. "Can I think about it?"

Finlay's eyes narrow. He's way too smart for *Can I think about it?* ploys.

"OK, look. You helped create this problem. I'm asking you to help fix it, at no financial cost to yourself. That's not unreasonable? You involved yourself, when I asked you not to. Uninvolving yourself at this point is pretty selfish."

I make an indignant gasping noise at the word "selfish," even though it is more or less a fair summary.

"Plus, if you do this . . . ," Fin says. "I'll let the diaries and letters thing drop."

"Really?"

He has me. The appeal of escaping that drama, when I've obliterated the items of value, is undeniable.

"Yes. I'm upset about it but I'm willing to let it go, if you help me."

I lick dry lips.

"When do we need to go? For how long?" I say.

"Tomorrow. I'll hire a car, drive us up, book us rooms somewhere central for a few days. Ann, the cleaner, has my number to call me if he appears back here in the meanwhile."

"Tomorrow?! I have a job."

"You can't swing time off?"

"Hmmm. Maybe?"

Actually, our area manager Kirsty has been giving us strict orders about one of us booking holidays this month. No one wants crappy November when they could have party-filled December, and we'd been eyeing each other, wondering who'd break first.

And my neighbor Greta is always delighted to feed Roger, in return for a bottle of Prosecco and a box of chocolates.

I chew my lip.

An old-fashioned grandfather clock ticks behind us.

"I guess I could help. If it's for a few days."

"I'll pick you up tomorrow. Message me where's best."

I WALK BACK to my bus, deep in thought and, possibly, second thoughts.

Why is Finlay Hart, born without a heart, the man who didn't care about his mother dying and couldn't bring himself to exchange more than a few terse words with his father and sister at her funeral, exerting himself to find Mr. Hart? He lives in New York, he could respectably wash his hands of this, leave instructions for his father's return. As he says, his dad doesn't know who he is.

In the minutes it takes for the bus to pull around the corner, I think—if it's not love, could it be money?

Is it to get the will changed, if he's been disinherited? Fast-tracking Dad to a home, house straight on the market, and no Susie to object or interfere? Or indeed, claim half. It seems possible.

If that's the case, am I being an accomplice, by retrieving his dad? Putting a smiling friendly face to the plot? I rationalize: if it *is* that, I'm still better placed by his side if I want to prove it and prevent it. If Mr. Hart's happy and safe at home for now, who is Fin to hustle him into care?

Ghost Susie's voice swims into my head, immediate and unbidden.

You know what they say, Eve. To catch a thief, you have to climb into his rented Mercedes Benz S-Class.

25

The immutable law of my workplace is that you are always in the wrong, somehow. When I ask to be granted the holiday allowance that we were being strong-armed to take, it turns out I'm still a troublemaker.

"Yeah, it's *wunderbar* you're miraculously complying, Eve, but does it have to be, like, *today*?" Kirsty drawled, when I requested it, having emailed the evening before. "Has *Brad Pitt* swung by in his *Gulfstream* and said 'Get in, loser, we're going shopping'?"

Kirsty is a pretend-posh person. She could come from Cairo or Kettering.

"Yes, ideally today, please?" I say, ignoring the sarcasm. Kirsty does a windy sigh and leaves me listening to the tap-tap of her mocha shimmer Shellacs on her keyboard, as if she's calling up a vital spreadsheet when she's almost certainly continuing an email to a friend. "Hmmm . . ." She draws it out. "Hmmmm . . . if you can work a half day and take the afternoon off, I can *just about* swing it. Call me your Fairy Godmother," she says.

I got off the phone to her and explained my exceptionally fortunate dispensation to the rest of the office.

"Fucking hell, the fuss they make over leave. You're not Obama, are you," Phil says. "It's not like the irreverently captioned clickbait farms will be in chaos, and the financial markets racked with uncertainty until you return. Death to our neoliberal overlords."

"They have to create a narrative, Phil," I say, playing to his gallery. "Where we take liberties and they're endlessly patient and understanding. That way their punitive measures are always in the context of being harassed, exhausted parents who finally snapped."

"I think they're just twats," Seth says.

Ed messages to tentatively ask if we're ready to reinstate the pub quiz yet, and I say no. When he tries to message again asking how I'm feeling, I reply that I'm up north for it.

My phone rings.

"Edinburgh, why?"

I explain.

"The *fuck*?! You're going to Scotland with him?"

"Yes?" I'm troubled by the strength of Ed's reaction.

He couldn't fake this, simply to act the good guy protector for much-needed brownie points—he seems genuinely astounded.

"You don't know this guy from Adam and what we do know is unpleasant. How is this remotely safe, for one thing?"

I hadn't fully thought it through, and I don't want to admit this.

"He's back to New York soon, I don't think he's likely to . . ." I trail off.

"Commit any offenses when it'll mean extraditing him to charge him? Solid reasoning, five out of five."

"What are you suggesting? I know he's never going to win Personality of the Year but I didn't take him for any sort of sex predator."

"No, if I recall rightly, you more liked him for serial killing. Plus hoodwinking his decrepit father out of a fortune."

"If he is doing that, this way, I have a ringside seat for the plot . . ."

"What?! Are you Jessica Fletcher now?"

Ed leaves an aghast pause.

". . . You're not yourself and you're not thinking straight."

"I appreciate the chivalry, but I know what I'm doing. Life isn't risk-free and I caused their dad to do this runner. I have to help or I won't sleep at night."

Ed says, "Hmmm. He was certainly happy to blame you, wasn't he? What does that tell you?"

I mutter noncommittal things. He twisted my arm, but I have to admit that had he not done so, I would've said no.

"If you're doing this, can I ask you to do something? For me?" Ed says.

"Which is . . . ?"

"Message me every day, at nine p.m., in such a way that I know it's definitely you, and let me know you're alright? Don't say it's an arranged check-in, in so many words. Then if anyone else has your phone, they won't know to do it on your behalf. If I don't get the message, I'll be calling the police, and on the first train up there. Send me a photo of the license plate of the car too. Don't let him see you taking it."

I laugh. "Seriously? You don't have to turn white kni—"

"Yes, I'm serious!" Ed says, with vehemence. "You're about to skip to another country with a dubious man you don't know, on a wild goose chase where he's running the show and picking up the tab. This has Very Creepy Interlude all over it."

I agree I will send proofs of life and Ed calms down a notch. Yet when I end the call, my insouciance evaporates.

IT'S TWO O'CLOCK in the afternoon by the time I'm waiting with my packed bag outside my house, ready to climb into Finlay Hart's waiting car. It's a dark Audi, you called it wrong there, Susie.

He gets out and opens the trunk, takes my bag from me. He's wearing a fine-knit sweater under a navy trench coat, which he shucks off his shoulders and throws across the back seat. I notice his clothes have that quietly expensive quality where they're un-showy, yet hang perfectly. If I bought a black sweater and a blue coat, they wouldn't look like that.

There's no opportunity to slyly paparazzi license plates. First fail.

"We should be there by dinner time," he says, after hello. "Five hours, I reckon. Give or take."

"Dinner is the best time to arrive anywhere," I say, in a hope-fully amicable tone, as I get into the passenger seat. ". . . How come you don't sound more American? There's only the small-est hint."

I'm trying for friendly irreverence. It has belatedly dawned on me that never mind danger, I furthermore have hour after tedious hour in the company of someone with the conversa-tional charm of a wooden actor playing a Nazi guard.

"I thought I did," Finlay says, neither sounding offended or especially animated. "I moved to the States when I was twenty so your accent and vocabulary is pretty fixed by that point. Plus, a lot of friends are expats."

A lot of friends. I struggle to picture them, but maybe he's the life and soul, over there.

Once in the driver's seat, he fiddles with the radio. "Do you want music on?"

"Sure," I say.

"You choose," he says.

I poke at it until 6 Music blares out.

"What's playing? I'm so out of touch these days," Fin says, checking the wing mirror as we pull into the flow of traffic.

"It's 'This Is What She's Like' by Dexys Midnight Runners," I say, pleased that I happen to know by complete chance because I'm pretty out of touch myself these days. Justin loves Dexys. "You know, they did 'Come On Eileen.'"

"Yeah, I know that much," Fin says, with a smile.

He navigates out of the city and to the motorway with reasonable ease, punctuated by a stentorian male GPS voice, barking instructions.

"Only to get me to the motorway and I'll turn it off," Fin says, and I say "Sure" again, like a little robot. The car is comfortable and smells of valeted leather. I stretch my legs out in the footwell and feel grateful at least that I'm not writing about getting bendy with Wendy.

I've always liked this part of any trip, the sense you're escaping. Whenever a plane lifts off, I think about what a tiny piece of the planet I inhabit, how limited my horizons are.

I can hear Mark in my head saying, "Yet I couldn't get you to Stoke Newington." And his line in our break-up fight: "You know what fucks me off the most? You'd move here for Susie and the gang."

He was probably right.

"Don't judge me for the automatic, it's years since I've driven stick, as they say," Fin says, as we zoom past the postwar houses that line the ring road.

I smile at the idea that of the things I might judge Finlay Hart for, it would be his not using manual gear change. A bonus—comfortable silences are easier when you don't have to stare into each other's faces.

I steal a sly look at Fin at the wheel, grudgingly admire the hard, leading-man jaw—clean-shaven once more—the arms with rolled-up shirt sleeves, and classy, rather than showy, leather-strap vintage watch.

No one said evil couldn't be attractive. It's how evil gets a lot of its workload done, in fact.

I amuse myself at the idea of him talking into a recorder, like Agent Cooper. It's an imperfect comparison: Cooper looked like baby-faced FBI. Finlay Hart looks like the clean-cut assassin who nobody can remember clearly afterward.

"Whereabouts do you live in New York?" I ask.

"Park Slope. A gentrified but still almost affordable part of Brooklyn, if you don't know it."

"Do you like it there? New York as a whole, I mean?"

"Yeah . . . mostly. I'm not sure I want to stay for good. Put it this way, when I get together with friends all we do is moan about how awful it is, which is the point you know you're a native. How about you? Do you like Nottingham?"

For once, Fin's determinedly neutral tone sounds like something approximating grace.

"Hahaha. New York . . . to Nottingham. Big Apple to . . . tiny oranges. Big cats to bin raccoons."

Fin smiles. "I like it."

Of course he does, in that gently patronizing way that cool people, who have nothing to prove, feign approval of uncool things.

"You left it," I say, also smiling.

He loosens his collar and peers up at a road sign. "Sometimes people leave places they like. Sometimes people leave people they like."

"You're a therapist, aren't you . . . are we into therapy now? Can you charge for this?" I say.

"No matter how many years I've done my job, this being said to me never gets old," he says, still smiling, but it's thinner, and I make a mental note he doesn't want to discuss his work.

"Do I like Nottingham. Yes in some ways, no in others," I conclude.

"That's every adjusted person's view of anywhere really, isn't it?" Fin says. "I'd mistrust anyone who said, 'Yeah where I live, *best place ever*, it's perfection.' I would suspect it's more about their choices having to be the best ones."

I steal a sidelong look at him. This sort of cynicism, I can work with.

"You say that, but my dad lives on a sheep farm in Australia and I think you'll find it's literal heaven on earth."

"Do you mistrust him?"

". . . Yes," I say, and in mutual surprise, I laugh and Fin grudgingly smiles. His face looks completely altered in amusement, like he was never the other person all along. It freaks me out a little.

God, it's come back to me: Susie conceding he was probably a good model because "he looks different in every single photo. Not like a different photo of the same person, or another angle, a different person. Brrrr."

That now-familiar hard pang that I can never tell her any of this. With the added psychic blockade of the fight I can never have with her either.

After over an hour of intermittent, low-key small talk, Fin sees a blinking on a mobile he has in a holder and says: "Ah. Romilly's calling me."

"Romilly?"

There's no time for further explanation as he prods "Accept Call."

"Hi, Rom." Fin frowns. "You're on speakerphone, I'm in the car. I have someone with me."

Crackle. "Who?"

"Eve. She was a friend of my sister's. She's helping me find my dad. Remember he absconded?"

"Oh. Hello, Eve?" says a crisp, East Coast, *Sex and the City* voice. A Charlotte one, or actually—Miranda.

"Hi!" I say.

"I wanted to let you know that Ethan's appointment went fine. They want to see him again in three months, but they don't think there's any damage to his hearing."

"That's great. Is he happy?"

"Oh yeah, he's back to being a little jerk again. I took him to Balthazar to celebrate and he ate half the breakfast menu. The waiter couldn't believe it."

"Good! Tell him I'll bring him something back from here."

A pause. Hard to say if it's a transatlantic connection pause or a loaded pause.

"Call me when you get to Scotland. On a private line," Romilly says, eventually, which I take as a forthright dig at me. Or maybe it's merely Big Apple directness?

"Your girlfriend?" I say, once Fin's pressed to end the call.

"Ex," Fin says.

"Ah."

From her frostiness toward me, I intuit that Fin ended it and she's not over it, but who knows.

"She has a little boy, from a previous relationship. I like to know how he's doing," Fin says. "We stay in touch about him."

"Was she at your mum's funeral? She had red hair?"

Fin looks surprised. "Yes. Were you there?"

"Yes."

"I didn't see you."

This strikes me as a peculiar thing to say. If he didn't know me in adulthood, he wouldn't have known me by sight, so how would he know if he saw me? That event doesn't strike me as one to pry into further, however.

"Romilly," I say. "Unusual name."

"Her parents are French Canadian. Why did you make that face?"

"What sort of face?"

"A kind of 'huh typical' face."

I realize I did do this. "It's just. 'Romilly.' So cool. You were never going to date a Doris."

"Given Dorises are over eighty, no, probably not."

"You say that, but it's becoming trendy again. Middle-class nurseries are full of Dorises and Mauds."

"I wasn't planning on dating a five-year-old either."

"Everyone calls their kids grandma names or silver-screen film star names now."

"Isn't Eve an old movie name? *All About Eve.*"

"I'm Evelyn, actually."

"Evelyn. That's nice."

I can't tell if Fin being pleasant is him being pleasant, or being pleasant is a tactic of some sort, which I'm not *Wolf of Wall Street* enough to grasp.

"Thank you. It is nice. Even if it sounds a bit like I listen to *The Archers* and keep dried lavender sachets in my pants drawer."

"You're fond of saying whatever's in your head, aren't you?" Fin says, throwing me an accompanying smile to defuse the accusation.

"You're fond of never saying what's in your head," I blurt, with a return smile.

Despite the fact he's driving at eighty-two miles per hour, Fin manages to give me a stare of mild consternation. Is the shrink not used to being shrunk on?

The moment is interrupted by a seriously peculiar and unfamiliar sensation. All of a sudden, the car's lurching and bunny-hopping down the road, with a nasty clanging sensation, as if the underparts are banging directly on the tarmac. "Underparts" is the extent of my automotive expertise.

"Ah fuck, I think we've got a blowout," Fin says. I brace my palms on the dashboard in front of me as he signals and moves rapidly across the road, his expression not flickering as he checks the mirror.

I'm glad he's in charge because if I was driving, and this sickening pitching had started, my response would likely involve high-decibel screaming.

We clank down the slow lane, onto the slip road, and into services, the car handling like we're in a cartoon. When Fin pulls to a halt near the entrance to Burger King, I heave a huge deep breath, and can feel a high tide of moisture at my hairline.

"Overall, I didn't enjoy that," Fin says, sounding typically composed, but when I look at him, he's as ashen as a lunar landscape. I'm glad I didn't realize he was as frightened as I was, until now.

26

"Any minute now, they promise me," Fin says, pushing his mobile in the pocket of his coat as he approaches me. "Though that's probably the cab company's 'Just 'round the corner.'"

I'm perched on a cold hard curb by the petrol pumps, under guise of "guarding the luggage," eating Haribo Sour Cherries, as BreakdownGate enters its ninetieth minute. I crumple the bag and stand up, wiping sugar from my hands, to try belatedly to look efficient and involved.

The "dismayed inspection of the vehicle" and the "lengthy technical conversations with people on the other end of a phone" phase has been run entirely by Fin. I initially sat in the car feeling useless, then stood around by our luggage feeling useless, then dawdled off to buy sweets.

I gathered it was worse than a tire blowout, and our Audi was in fact, to quote a passing mechanic who'd given us his off-duty opinion for free: "fucked."

"Mini break was it? Hope it's not an anniversary," he added cheerfully, as Finlay and I stared blankly, there being no acceptable social shorthand to describe what it actually is. *We have formed an uneasy temporary alliance to hunt down a senile senior citizen.*

The car has been towed away in disgrace.

"Ah, wait, could that be . . . ?"

Another gleaming set of wheels, this one silver, sweeps onto the forecourt. Fin strides over and has a brief consultation with the driver. He accepts keys and a piece of paper and there's lots of exclamatory head-shaking, palms-up gestures from the hire car man and *what can you do* shoulder shrugging from Fin, presumably discussing the fate of the last one.

I pick up Fin's duffel bag with one hand and the handle on my suitcase with the other, and roll it noisily across the concrete, toward what I notice is a Mercedes-Benz.

"Is this . . . an S-Class?" I say, hairs prickling on the back of my neck.

". . . I think so?" Fin says. "Why?"

I stare some more. I mean—it's nothing, is it? It's a daft coincidence. "No reason."

"Never had you down as a petrol head," Fin says, with a smile, taking my bag from me. "If it gets us to Edinburgh in one piece, that'll do me."

I'd obviously never mention Susie in reference to anything supernatural, but I climb in wondering how much mentioning of Susie is either tactful or astute, full stop. I have no idea what's going on inside Finlay, what's behind that attitude.

I can hear Susie in my head:

Less than you think. True of all men. It's so very Eve to be script-writing them vivid inner lives.

"Another car to get used to," Fin says, as we crawl onto the slip road. I push back against the head rest and Fin turns the radio on.

"Wheels feel good and solid," I say.

"We're getting a free ride out of them trying to kill us," Fin says. "Just so you know. I'll put the proceeds toward choc ices at the zoo."

I guffaw. "Wait, you're serious? We're going to the zoo?"

"My father said in his note he was doing the tourist stuff first, so I guess so."

"Right." It's hard to imagine how we'll find one man in a sightseeing throng but perhaps it'll be like Denholm Elliott standing out like a sore thumb in his panama hat in *Indiana Jones and the Last Crusade.*

"Choc ices," I say. "Britspeak."

"Oh yeah. In American it's *Popsicle.*"

I smile and we settle into a courteous quiet, with New Order's "Regret" filling the space.

Observing Finlay's alleged psychopathy up close is a disorientating business. I don't sense menace, as such, but Finlay has a motive to keep me onside.

As we flit past beautiful mountains to Scotland, Fin says, apropos of nothing:

"I appreciate you doing this. I know it's a lot to ask. Thank you."

"Oh . . . it's alright," I say, caught off guard.

"I don't want you to feel like we have to be adversaries, because we had a rocky start," he says. "OK for me to put the traffic news on?" He reaches out and prods at the radio, and I nod.

I'm reassured, but I'm also spooked. What if this is a ploy? What if this is key to Finlay's particular menace? He plays at being a nice, adjusted, kindly human being for a time, then when it suits him, rips the rug from beneath you? So when he does something whiplash-nasty, it makes you feel ridiculous for having trusted him? What if trying to get along well with Finlay Hart is like trying to walk backward in heels on a travelator, holding a martini? Like watering a plastic plant?

If so, Susie wouldn't have told me this.

I remember once when Becky Fucking Villa Holiday stung Susie for the whole cost of their luxury accommodation on a girls' weekend in Bath. Susie paid up front for the place they rented, for convoluted reasons of convenience given by Becky. Susie had been surprised to receive a thank-you card from Becky afterward saying how wonderful it was for Susie to treat her for her thirtieth, especially as she was spent up due to her forthcoming Nile cruise. I read it and snorted.

"Translation: I have mixed in my birthday obligation with a hint of 'I can't afford to pay you anyway' to create the maximum inhibition and discouragement to ask me for the money. Hi, I'm Becky Bramley, I have massive clanking balls of brass."

Susie guffawed but stoutly defended her and insisted the agreement to go dutch must've slipped her mind. I was incredulous that arch cynic Susie could be so naïve in the face of an obvious heist, and concluded she was soft on Becky. With hindsight, I can see it was more about Susie being unwilling to admit that anyone had got one over on her, than thinking the best of Becky. "Being taken in" wasn't a thing that happened to Susie; it was totally off brand.

Was the intensity with Finlay not only that he was her brother, but that at some point, she'd been utterly blindsided by him?

IN WHAT FEELS like not much time at all, we're into twilight Edinburgh, car crawling along more densely populated roads, past Georgian sandstone houses with white-framed windows. The GPS now issuing commands every thirty seconds, after its long nap on the motorway.

We inch down Princes Street and come to a halt in front of The Caledonian, a red sandstone Victorian façade with Corinthian columns, white-gloved doormen, and gilt logo-ed awnings. A Union Jack and the Scottish flag hang at angles on poles, and there are neat box hedges and revolving doors.

I wait patiently for Fin to drive past it and on to the reasonably midpriced anonymous option we're booked in at, while the GPS intones: "You have reached your destination." Fin's car door is opened for him by a liveried footman. As is mine.

"This is where we're staying?" I say, having clambered out, as Fin hands the car keys over.

"Yes?" he says.

"It's The *Waldorf*," I say, squinting at the signage. Everything is lit up, so the edifice glows honey-yellow against the blue-black sky.

"As in the salad, yes."

"But . . . Wow. OK."

"The Waldorf is where we went when we came up as kids. More my mum's taste, to be fair, but I thought my dad might've homing pigeoned back here."

"This is a fair step up from what I'm used to," I say, looking back at the car, which is having luggage removed from it before being taken away to be parked, without our involvement.

"I can book you the guest house in East Lothian where the top TripAdvisor review said there were Minion toys on the bed and cryptic graffiti in blood on the shower wall, if you'd prefer?" Fin says.

I step into the revolving doors, laughing.

Oh God—I can withstand flash, but flash and witty is too much.

In the gleaming curved marble lobby with white napery, we have to wait behind tourists in loud shirts with Nikons, in Velcro-fastening sandals. Fin checks his watch.

"It's pretty late to find a restaurant," he says. 'Shall we each get room service tonight and then head out to the sights tomorrow? Meet you down here at nine?"

"Sure."

"Each" meaning "not together." I suppose I could be offended at Fin's lack of wanting to spend any more time with me, but a burger eaten on a bed, while I'm in what Americans call a "waffle robe," is too appealing.

"Put anything you want on the tab while you're here," Fin says, then hesitates, his face coloring in a way I've not seen before. "I mean, I don't want there to be any awkwardness or confusion over it. I asked you to come here. It's my responsibility and therefore my bill. Obviously."

"Thank you," I say. Then, at a loss of what else to say, looking around, trying to ease the tension: "This place, though! I top out at the Radisson Blu for a spendy weekend."

There's possibly a creakingly obvious subtext of *I didn't know you were loaded!*

Fin puts me on edge anyway, so I'm possibly not judging the line between playfully irreverent and rather crass very well.

"Did Susie not give me shit for having money?" Finlay says, having read it as I predicted. I twinge a little.

In the quiet of the lobby, the murmur of voices echoing, his asking me this feels potentially significant. I'm the guardian of Susie's estate now, intellectual if not literal.

"No," I say, glad I can at least be honest. "She never mentioned that at all."

"Wouldn't have predicted she'd miss that opportunity, but perhaps, thinking about it, I should have."

"Why?"

"Because she'll have given me shit for absolutely everything else?" Fin's manner is light-hearted but there's a weight behind this that makes it feel threatening to me. Not to mention a history.

"No, I meant: why should you, having thought about it, predict it?"

His eyes narrow, quizzically. "I know the legend has it I'm horrible. 'Has money' is only going to be used if there's an angle in the case for prosecution. As far as I'm aware, there wasn't one. I'm not an arms dealer, I don't buy corporate boxes at Ed Sheeran gigs."

I laugh. Fin humor is delivered with a curt precision, and so straight-faced that I only realize it is humor a second or two after he finishes speaking.

I'm all of a sudden awash with curiosity about Fin's side of their war, while simultaneously certain it'll be a heavily biased fiction.

No one gets a reputation by accident, a favorite truism of Justin's. (I seem to recall I once argued against this, from a general vague sense of injustice, and Justin retorted: "When you can show me the exception, I'll start making exceptions." I have yet to show him an exception.)

Fin steps forward to the reception desk and I fidget while he checks in, feeling very scruffy in the surroundings.

"Do you know if your dad's staying here?" I say, under my breath, as Finlay hands me my key card in its paper sleeve, room number written on it.

"No, but there's no point asking. I'll get Data Protection, blah blah."

"Hmm." I rub my chin. "They won't tell you if he is here, but I bet with some light wheedling they'll tell you if he isn't."

"How do you mean?"

"Let me try," I say. I move forward to the available person behind reception, who, probably helpfully, is a man around Fin's father's age.

"Hi, I wonder if you could help me. Myself and my brother"—I nod back at Fin, in earshot, looking perplexed—"are here to surprise my dad for his seventieth birthday. I don't suppose you could call up to his room for us, and tell him there's someone down here to see him? Please don't say who we are though!" I flap my hands nerdily at the two of us, make a mouth-zipping gesture.

"What's his name?" says the man, smiling indulgently.

"Iain Hart," I say. "That's Iain spelled I-A-I-N."

The man taps a keyboard and looks at his screen. "I'm afraid we don't have a guest at the moment under that name."

"Oh! That's fine, he's maybe arriving later tonight then?" I turn and address Finlay who mutters: "Yes, must be."

"Thank you anyway," I say.

"I shouldn't strictly do this"—the man leans toward me—"but if you give me your room number, I can let you know if anyone does arrive with that name. I wouldn't be able to tell you his room number but I could contact him on your behalf, once he's settled in?"

"Oh sure yes, definitely," I say. "Thank you! I'm Evelyn Harris in Room 166 and this is Finlay Hart. Room . . . ?"

"312," Fin supplies.

"Got it." The man beams, marking it down on a notepad. "Have a lovely stay."

As we walk to the lifts, Finlay says: "That was genuinely impressive. I'm impressed."

"I used to be a reporter at the local paper. The base machinations and grubby audacity never leave you."

"Probably helps to have charm too," Finlay says.

"Oh . . ." I startle a little at an unexpected compliment. He thinks I'm a presumptuous irritant, doesn't he? "All part of the . . . routine."

"If it's an art, I've never mastered it," he says, with a twitch of lips, as we step into the lift. He punches the first and third floor buttons respectively.

"Thing is," Fin says, after a short silence, "I'm not criticizing your methods. To me this makes it even more impressive. But why would you turn up for your dad's seventieth as a surprise, and then have a receptionist tell him you're in the lobby? That'd ruin it, no? You do the big reveal when dinging a champagne glass with a fork, in some restaurant, surely?"

"Aha, any card sharp could answer this. Cons don't work because they're clever, they work because they're fast."

The lift doors slide open at my floor.

"You're full of surprises, Evelyn Harris," Fin says, as I step out, and I wonder what the other ones were.

My room is the size of a London flat, a tundra of cornflower-colored carpet and milky coffee-colored expensively hewn fabrics, a bed the size of Italy with starchy, crease-free, snow-white pillows in upright rows. When I twitch the curtains, I have a plum view of the illuminated castle. It's Instagram brag crack cocaine, except I'm not minded to advertise this online and be asked why I'm here.

I try not to be so vulgar as to dwell on the cost, but I have a sense that consecutive nights here, multiplied by two, must be six months of my mortgage payments.

I must remember to text Ed. But . . . on reflection, what right does Ed have to make me feel, albeit subtly, with the cover of good intentions, as if he has some sort of ownership of me? He's engaged to his long-term horror and he slept with my late best friend.

Late best friend. I stare at the remote controls lined up on the walnut side table and, for once, I'm shocked at these words, not because they are surprising to me, but because they aren't.

Susie's deadness has crossed an invisible line, passed into an unexceptional fact I can rehearse as part of my mental furniture, as much prosaic scenery as the mini fridge and the safe for valuables over there.

I know this is only true right now, in this particular moment. It'll astound me again, at another time in the near future. But gradually that will happen less and less, and this will happen more and more, until it's simply always ordinary.

One day, I might be looking at photographs with my currently unlikely kids, and they'll say, "Who's that?" and I'll say, "Oh, that's my dear friend Susie, she got hit by a car and died really young." They'll peer with renewed interest due to this macabre backstory, and then, because she was never Auntie Susie and they never met her, turn the page in the album. I feel an indignation that's almost anger at this prospect. It's a lie, that obituary. Susie is not a sad short story. Susie is not a tragedy. She was a long lively story, cut unnaturally short.

With some secret chapters I hadn't seen. Footage left on the cutting-room floor.

I unzip my suitcase and yank my toiletries bag from it and have a shower that's long and scalding enough to make up for the lack of one earlier. I raid the complimentary toiletries and dry my hair section by section on a big round brush in front of a vast mirror, rolling my wrist as if I'm in a salon. I've not thought about my appearance for months. All of a sudden, I want to look nice. I think it's the surroundings, and being here for my fake father's fake seventieth with my fake brother. I wish I were living her life, the goofy, loaded, carefree liar.

A knock at the door and my dinner arrives, thrillingly under a silver tureen.

As I dip the last French fry in the dainty ramekin of ketchup, my phone lights up with a message from Ed . . . Oh God it's half nine!

Hi! Remember me? Remember that thing we talked about?

I wipe my greasy hands hurriedly on the thick linen napkin.

Argh sorry sorry it's been crazy—the car broke down and we've got to the hotel late, but the good news is, it's The Waldorf 😜 🌟

*Wow sounds like my worries were misplaced! One big
suite is it?* ☹ *Michael Bublé on the Bose and roofie
fizzing like an Alka Seltzer in the Laurent Perrier* 🤞

I should've known he'd equate the outlay with a Finlay Hart
scheme to lay me. He's *met* Finlay, how can he seriously think
"desire" features?

Uhm no, separate rooms. ☺ *Sorry I forgot
to say hi, I'll remember tomorrow*

Mind that you do. N'night, Harris x

My phone blinks with light again.

*PS: I'm sure you know this, but. If you need me to come and get you
as a matter of urgency at any point—call me. I will be straight there,
no questions asked. Do not let pride stand in the way of help. X*

Of course, thank you. (you would ask questions though) x

OK yes I would X

By the light of a lamp, I lie on the bed and gaze up at the
ivory ceiling's cornicing, pristine and unblemished, like a roll
of marzipan icing.

Ed is jealous. I repeat that evident truth to myself. I'd sensed
it during his previous tirade, but not so clearly registered it until now. I try to work out what to do with it.

27

After unwinding a croissant and sipping the sort of black coffee that reminds me how coffee is supposed to taste in a metro-tiled breakfast room that was absent of Finlay Hart, I go back up to my room, brush my teeth, and head down at nine.

Finlay's an imposing, ink-blue figure against all the wedding-cake white—unsmiling, hands thrust in pockets in his trench coat. He's not unfriendly, exactly, but seems a little antsy, brisk, eager to get on. I shouldn't mistake the splendor of our hotel for any pleasure he's taking in this.

"Tourist traps, then the family addresses, is the plan," Fin says, sounding stiff and somewhat disenchanted, as we emerge into the cold snap of Princes Street. "Following the plan set out in my father's note."

"Gotcha. How about a sightseeing bus?" I say, as one rolls past outside. "Cover more ground."

Finlay looks up at the Coca-Cola-red, logo-emblazoned ve-hicle, skeptical. His profile is momentarily strongly redolent of Susie's, against the morning winter sun, and I get a sharp pang, that stupefaction, remembering her loss. I'm perversely glad it's a shock again.

"Hmm, really? Would we recognize my dad in a crowd, from a pigeon's vantage point?" Finlay says.

"We'd get off at the stops," I say. "How are we getting 'round them any faster, on foot?"

Fin shrugs his reluctant agreement and buys two tickets from the man in the lanyard, accepts tour leaflets, and we step on.

"Upstairs?" I say, to his shoulder.

"If you want," Fin says, glancing back, wearing the look of a tolerant weekend dad with visiting offspring. He picks seats near the front. It's almost empty, as you'd expect from the roof-free top deck of a sightseeing bus in a rainy country at a cold time of year.

Mercifully, it has optional headsets where you can plug yourself in for an audio narration, so we get to experience the city without the soundtrack of someone bellowing jovially into a microphone about Greyfriars Bobby, as we lurch corners.

Everyone else on the deck brandishes their phone aloft on portrait mode, with both hands, taking pictures or filming.

"Do you think any video taken on holiday ever gets watched?" I whisper to Fin. "People will film *anything*. How does it work, do you go home and then on a boring Tuesday say: get the beers, let's watch three minutes of shaky footage of the Royal Mile? Or do they subject friends and family to it?"

"I don't know," Fin says. "I'm not a fan of the way the technology's turned everyone into an amateur documentary maker. I saw an argument in The Bagel Hole the other month, and another customer stood there as if it was their kid's nativity play." Finlay mimes holding a phone and staring intently into it.

"Yeah, and it's mad the way people act like they become invisible when they hold a phone up."

We lapse into silence and Fin still looks tense. Does he anticipate a messy scene, if we do find his dad?

A shoal of French teenagers in rucksacks stream onto the bus, exclaiming "Edinbourg, Edinbourg!" in excitement, as if they expect the identity of the city they're craning over the bus's railings to look at might change. Then, confusingly: "Skiffle! Skiffle!"

"Skiffle?" I whisper, with quizzical expression.

"*Skyfall*," Fin corrects. "The Bond film? Had a whole sequence in Scotland."

"Oh hahaha. That makes more sense than love of The Quarrymen."

Fin smiles back, but he's indulging me, and the smile doesn't reach his eyes.

I decide to relieve him of the burden of small talk by putting the headphones on, wrestling them out of their small plastic packet.

The Grassmarket is one of the most iconic views in the city. The market place lies in a hollow, well below surrounding ground levels, directly below the castle.

The bus judders to a halt and we climb off.

We wander past the lollipop-brights of the shop doorways, across the worn-shiny paving, scanning the passersby. We wander, but with secret purpose, and I find pleasure in the strangeness of it. Usually you're obliged to enjoy this sort of activity; today we're almost obliged not to, which is kind of freeing. Humans are irrational.

"It's such a handsome place, isn't it," I say, blandly, wondering if I'm replicating bad date levels of chat.

"Would you want to live here?" Fin says, after a pause.

"Yes . . . I don't know. If I could bear to leave the things I care about, back home."

"What are they?"

"My friends, my mum. The really good fish and chips shop."

As soon as I've said that, I immediately wonder if, especially post-Susie, this is sufficient reason, or if it's an alibi for standing still. I know what my ex Mark's vote would be.

"I believe Scotland's pretty strong on chips," Fin says.

I look around, breathe the damp air and try to picture myself in a grand new setting. It would be exhilarating. Scary, but exhilarating.

As soon as I've pictured escape, I think about how Susie has no more choices to make. I remember her in that last pub quiz, gaze bright over her bundled scarf, all the unspoken urgent communication flying between us that we had no idea would stay forever unsaid. My eyes well up. Whatever changes and dulls, I know this will be the case for the rest of my life, the ability of the thought of her to turn me to tears at a second's notice. They don't put that in the eulogies, do they: *They will live on in your hearts, and in the way you find yourself weeping like a freak in Birds Baker, because you inadvertently recalled how much she loved an Elephant's Foot pastry.*

I blink rapidly to regain control and see Finlay's noticed all of this. "It's alright, you know," he says, quietly. "You're allowed."

"Allowed to what?"

". . . Be alive. Carry on."

I don't trust my voice to reply, so I simply nod. I'm spooked to be read by him so effortlessly, but I feel comforted too. He's so assured. What are his feelings about his sister's loss?

"Ah, the castle," I say, in relief, as we find ourselves in a clearing with an impressive view. "That's worth a photograph."

I wrestle my phone out of my pocket and train the camera. I notice Finlay is in the far right of the frame. At first I covertly snap him gazing across at the castle.

Then a tableau of him waiting for me to finish: looking away, down at the ground, pensive, running his hands boredly through his hair, then looking right at me. I shift the center of the frame so he's more in shot and run off rapid-silent snap-snap-snap extra pictures. I don't know why I collect this stealthy memorabilia, and I'm amused at my own hypocrisy, after criticizing the disinhibited nosiness that comes with camera phones. I tell myself it's the modeling thing: I'm curious to see if he's as casually photogenic off-duty as he was for money.

When he's in danger of sensing my eyeline isn't on the "historic fortress," I stop. Hah, Finlay Hart is a historic fortress all of his own.

WE MUST GIVE bored school pupils a run for their money with our workmanlike efficiency in getting around the National Museum, powering through the light-filled, vaulted central atrium with the dinosaur bones, separating to cover different galleries.

I text Finlay:

Can confirm it's just me and the giant Panda Ching
Ching in the animals section. She was embalmed
in 1985 and still looks better than me

Yep drawing a blank in Art, Design & Fashion, though tbf I doubt
18th century corsetry is my dad's thing. See you outside

"Feels strange not to have middle-class guilt at binning off the antiquities exhibition, doesn't it," I say, as we clatter back on the bus, lower deck this time, as the weather looks threatening. "My dad would be appalled."

At John Knox House, I get a nostalgic rush at the combination of the respectful speed-shuffling from room to room, and musty, woodsy smell of interiors. I'm disorientated not to have a worksheet to fill out on Protestant reformers of the sixteenth century afterward. It's only lacking the teacher asking if anyone needs to use the facilities before we get back on the bus and telling us we have fifteen minutes maximum in the gift shop. I'm almost tempted to buy a pot of unsharpened pencils and a rainbow eraser.

I sense Finlay's mood plummeting further, each time we reboard the bus.

"Is it worth prioritizing things your dad would find particularly interesting?" I ask. "Is he a devolution junkie, would he be interested in seeing the Scottish Parliament buildings? Or . . . the café where J.K. Rowling wrote Harry Potter?"

"I honestly don't know, it's second-guessing someone I'm distant from, who is ill," Fin says. "I think imposing old buildings are probably his taste."

251

"Stay on for Holyrood Palace, then?"

"Yeah."

Finlay can read me, but I can't read him. Something's bothering him and I can't identify what it is. This was his idea. I'm here because he demanded I be here. Anyone watching would think it was the other way around.

We disembark at Holyrood and Finlay buys entrance tickets.

"Christ," I say, surveying its colossal magnificence and general vast spread. "You take the west wing and I'll take the east wing?" I make a grit-teeth face.

There's an ominous grumble of thunder and as the heavens open, correspondingly, Finlay's mood breaks fully.

"This is all we fucking need!" he splutters, both of us holding the hoods of our coats in place as we dash for cover across the manicured lawns.

"Let's take shelter in the ruined abbey!" I say. "It's a little further but this is *just* the moment to appreciate it."

"How do you know about that?" Fin says, and I'm quite pleased with myself that I do.

"Like a Goth, I always research evocative ruined abbeys."

I lead us there at a jogging pace, and on arrival, Fin says: "Not to be a nitpicker, but the place you've brought us to has no roof."

I start laughing in that slightly helpless way you do when the weather and circumstances are attacking you.

"It has a beautiful façade though. Here, this part still has a roof."

We huddle in an archway, watching the rain beat down on ancient mossy stonework, interiors that are now exteriors. We've stumbled into a peculiarly unforgettable few minutes.

"Let's just settle in for three hours of this then," Fin says, eventually.

"I love it. Wish we'd brought a hot thermos."

When Ed called this a Very Creepy Interlude, he might've underrated how much I like creepy interludes.

"How are you so perky? To the point of . . . revolting effervescence."

Finlay says this unemotionally, in his usual crisp manner, face splattered with water. I get a squirm of pleasure in my stomach at this teasing, as I watch him yank his hood back down and try to pat the water out of his hair, which only spreads it around. He'd only dare be this familiar if he's feeling comfortable around me.

"Am I perky?" I say.

"Yup. Dragged against your will to another country, by a man you don't know, to look for another man who's not in his right mind. Being drenched in what looks like a *Game of Thrones* set. And it's like you've been handed a Coco Loco at a swim-up bar."

"Sad is happy for deep people," I say, and I'm rewarded with authentic Finlay laughter. I realize I'm talking to him like he's Susie, and somehow I don't know if I'm doing it on purpose or not.

"Is that original?"

"No, I nicked it from *Doctor Who*."

"I don't even know when you're having me on."

"While we're being personal, why are you being a mardy arse?"

"A *mardy arse*?" Finlay says, speaking the words as if smelling a stinky local delicacy cheese.

"It means grumpy—"

"I remember," he says. ". . . Agh, it feels so futile and foolish. We're a day behind him, if not days, we're not going to find him doing stupid sightseeing buses. Not that I had any better ideas," he adds, remembering it was my suggestion.

"Yeah. I reckon in a new place, he'll stick to his former points of reference," I say. "Where was his family home? Where he grew up?"

"Portobello, the seaside. Lovely day for it."

"Let's go back to the hotel, dry off, get lunch, and try that this afternoon."

Finlay nods. "I think the forecast is actually dry, later."

"I might get a photo of this before we go," I say, looking out at the rain pelting down.

I pull my phone out and unlock it, and with sickening inevitability, the last thing I had open appears, my camera roll. Finlay Hart glowering at me, unaware he was my subject.

Fin isn't quite close enough to see the full screen, but he can still spot himself well enough.

"Is that . . . me?"

"Yeah," I say, re-angling my phone, glad that my hood is partially obscuring my face, and that I can legitimately not meet his eyes, shrinking into the fur. "You wandered into my compositions of the castle."

"When I was standing still?" Fin says, with his infuriatingly sharp thinking. I'm momentarily without a comeback, sizzling with embarrassment, pretending to concentrate on focusing in on an archway, pushing at the screen with finger and thumb.

"I wanted general mementos of the trip," I say, the pleasurable squirming now writing internally.

"Mementos of people who don't know they're being photographed," Fin says. "Do you also take locks of hair from your sleeping victims?"

I look at him in shame and his face is lit up in amusement.

"Oh, *now* you stop sulking, in your malicious glee!" I blurt, faux-indignant, but glad he's not outright calling me sinister. "I'll delete it if you're that bothered."

"No, don't. I'm touched you'd want to remember a single second of this," he says, in a diplomatic tone.

I put my rain-speckled phone away.

"Can you get rid of any of the ones where I have a double chin though?" Finlay says, with the insouciant flirtiness of someone who's never been troubled by a double chin, and has slyly correctly guessed there's photos, plural.

"It's a deal. Though I'd remind you, vanity is a sin."

"And I'd remind *you* that creepshotting is not ethical."

The storm billows around us as we smile at each other under our hoods and I feel inexplicably . . . what's the word? Soothed. I feel soothed.

Back at the hotel, I scroll through a series of unexpectedly luminous, sulky pictures of a man with dark hair in a blue coat and feel something that I wouldn't call *soothed*, exactly.

28

Although I appear at ten to one, in hopes of being first, Finlay is already sitting at the bar. He's toying with the spoon in the saucer of a cup of tea, amid lots of young shiny people in 1920s costumes, buzzing from high spirits and midday alcohol.

They join in a lusty round of *"Happy birthday Dear BOBBY!"* while a pleased-with-himself-looking cherubic lad with a side parting in a white tuxedo and lopsided bow tie raises a coupe glass to them. I notice the women, in feather headbands, dropped waists, and kiss curls, are in badges saying "East Egg," the dapper men branded "West Egg."

"It's one of those passage of time ironies, isn't it," I say, quietly, after greeting Fin and ordering a Diet Coke. *"The Great Gatsby* was about how wealth and glamour and social climbing will hollow you out and destroy you, steal the love of your life away. So naturally we appropriate it for *hey, let's get wrecked* costumes for parties that unironically celebrate those things."

"Haha. Never mind Jay Gatsby, I could tell them wealth and social climbing as a mysterious nobody in New York doesn't lead anywhere good. My culture is not your prom dress, Bobby," Finlay says, with a knowing smile, looking up from under his brow. I'm momentarily floored by his exceptionally quick and self-aware riposte, combined with looking like a sodding film star. I can practically see the fireworks going off behind him.

"A 'passage of time irony' . . . is a good phrase. I'm a walking 'passage of time irony,'" he says.

I laugh in admiration, and Fin and I share a confidential look. I get the distinct impression he's trying to make a connection with me, but I don't know why he'd do that. I've lost my bearings and need to recover them, swiftly.

"I wasn't aware psychology was lucrative and social climby," I say, carefully, steadying myself. "But then I don't know any psychologists so I'm not sure what I'm basing that on. Also, psychiatrists in films look old as wizards. Wait, which are you, and what's the difference?"

"I'm a counselor-psychologist. In essence, the difference is that psychiatrists prescribe drugs. I don't prescribe drugs. Lucrative, it depends," Fin says. "If you go into private practice and you're successful. I got a lucky break early on."

"What sort of lucky break?" I ask, sipping my drink.

"Hmmm . . . ," Fin says, appraising me. "I have these thoughts about what I want going back to Susie, then realize it can't."

"Me too," I say.

"What, you'd have ever worried I'd talk to her?" he says, raising an eyebrow.

"No, in general. The impulse to refer back to her and realizing you can't anymore."

"OK. Please don't repeat this anyway, but . . . when I first began treating people at my own practice, after my residency, a friend sent someone with a profile to me."

"With a profile?" I repeat, blankly.

I think of Finlay as sharing a lexicon with me, and every so often he sounds like an *NYT* Long Read. As if he's going to start using words like "storied" and" preposition" and "luscious plums."

"They were working on a big-budget film and not able to carry on and needed therapy, someone to talk to."

"Oh God, you mean they were *famous*?"

"I did sessions with them, they felt able to return to work, the studio saved a lot of money and the film won Oscars."

"Shit!"

"Then the person I helped told their friends about me. That formed the basis of a very strong client list."

Fin drinks the last of his coffee.

"You're the head doctor to a bunch of neurotic A-list actors, so can set your prices at 'totally mad bilk' level? And you know all their secrets?!"

"I'm good at what I do, my clients are human like you or I, and my prices are competitive, thank you," Fin says, rolling his eyes, but with no real ire. "Patient confidentiality is inviolable."

"What made you want to go into it?"

"I had some therapy myself," Fin says, and I feel like his background plus his Statesideness meant I should've anticipated this. "It was really interesting to me, unraveling why we behave the way we do. I wanted to help people in the same way. Not to sound too *Miss Universe*."

"Susie never knew this thing about being 'doctor to the stars'? You really wouldn't tell her?"

"I tried to tell my family as little as possible," Fin says, and the shutters visibly come down, in his tight expression.

I push my luck with Finlay, but I can feel the danger well enough to not joke or poke anymore.

"Can I ask something?" he says, putting the spoon in the cup. "What was the *Twin Peaks* music about at the end of Susie's service?"

"You didn't like that?"

"I didn't dislike it, I thought it was a curious choice, that's all."

"Why? She loved the show and its atmosphere fitted somehow, I guess. She liked to say she was Laura Palmer."

The Laura Palmer they couldn't kill. That has aged badly.

"A series about a blonde homecoming queen with a demonic side who died tragically young?" Fin says. "Her life a seething mass of sex, drugs, and dysfunction behind the apple pie, charity bake sale surface? It honestly didn't occur it might look like some sort of . . . comment?"

I open my mouth and for once I'm lost for words.

"For it to be a comment, any of that would have to resemble Susie?" I say.

Fin sits back and contemplates me.

"Ready to head off?" he says, eventually, with a nod at my glass, and I say yes and neck my drink.

What on earth . . . ? Did he know about Susie's few grams of coke, or what?

"I NEVER THOUGHT of Edinburgh as having a seaside," I say on the fifteen-minute drive, adding, "Despite it being a port, obviously," in case Finlay thinks I'm full airhead.

Fin ordered an Uber to take us to Portobello, saying he

doesn't fancy city-center motoring on what feels like the "wrong side of the road," for the time being, which seems fair enough to me.

"Apparently, Sean Connery worked as a lifeguard at swimming baths out here," Fin says, as we emerge from the car into the freezing gray of a wintertime promenade.

"You'd want to be covered in whale grease to do that in Scotland, wouldn't you?" I say, shoving my balled hands deeper in my parka pockets.

"I'm an idiot, aren't I," Finlay says, as we wander down the street, past the railings and the band of pale deserted sand that must be thronged in high summer. There aren't many people out and about, the odd rollerblader whizzing past us, a pleasant tang of fish and chips in the air, the occasional gull cawing.

"Why are you an idiot?" Uncharacteristic of Finlay to self-criticize.

"As you said. I've come to a city of half a million people on the basis I'm going to bump into one confused man who himself is following no real rhyme or reason. Someone who won't even know who I am if he sees me. I don't think this makes much more sense than the penguin enclosure."

"Hah. It must be so incredibly hard to have a parent treat you like a stranger," I say, thinking about it for the first time. "Like . . . abandonment. Even though it's not, it's an illness, obviously."

Finlay looks at me and, I feel, is really focusing on me. He pauses a few seconds before replying.

". . . I didn't expect Susie to have someone like you as a friend," he says. "I'm glad she did."

"Thank you," I say, while feeling there are dots to connect

that I haven't connected, in why these two things followed on from each other. Maybe they didn't, maybe it was a way of not discussing his dad's dementia.

"There were women at the wake who seemed more what I expected," Fin says, hesitantly. "Vampy kind of clothes?"

"Oh . . . the Teacup Girls!" I exclaim. "That's what Justin called . . . never mind, another time. Yeah, they're quite different to us. That speaks well of Susie, really, though. She had different friends from different parts of her life, but she wasn't snobby. Susie was socially mobile. But not a climber."

We walk on.

Fin seems to have changed his opinion of me from "dreadful" to "acceptable," much to my quiet astonishment.

"Don't lose faith," I say, distracting myself. "If these are places your dad might go, we stand some sort of chance. It's a huge place, but the likely locations we are searching are not huge."

"He's not staying at The Waldorf, though, clearly," Fin says. "Strike one for my being able to anticipate his movements."

"Like the IRA, you only need to be lucky once," I say, and Finlay bursts into laughter.

"They wouldn't quite know how to deal with you in New York, you know," he says. "I can see this from having been away and come back again—you're a very British kind of bad taste."

"Bad taste!" I mock huff.

"Bad taste, but amusing," Fin says. Under my artificial fibers, I glow. Even if these compliments are a device. Tools, to do a job. "Unserious outerwear."

My parka has a giant doughnut of deep red faux fur around

the hood, the color of devil's food cake. No mockery by men with high cheekbones and even higher IQs will make me love it any less.

"OK, let's find the historic family seat." He produces his iPhone and studies a map. "It's quite something. I wouldn't have minded inheriting it, even with all its noisy ghosts."

I shudder, not with cold. The wind ruffles his hair and a passing pair of thirty-something women throw Finlay a wolfish look, and then me a wary glance.

Oh, be my guest, gals. You have no idea. Might as well build yourself a snowman, it'd be warmer, and you'd have the carrot nose for sustenance.

I look out at the sea and take a deep breath. Didn't the Victorians prescribe sea air for patients? I feel like I'm convalescing.

"Right, eleven minutes in this direction, I am promised," and we set off.

"Mind if we walk along the beach for a bit?" Fin says. I agree, though after we've headed down to it on the concrete shallow path and started tramping through the sand, I regret it. These boots were not made for beach walking.

"You OK?" Fin says, and I say, "Fine, fine," while concealing my effortful semistumbling because it's one thing to be Whimsical Coat Girl and another to be And Packed the Wrong Shoes Too Girl.

"There's a method behind my madness," Fin says. "We'll get a better view from here."

"A better view?" I say.

"There it is. The original Hart family residence," Finlay says, drawing to a halt, pointing across the road at an incredible detached sandstone villa. Its main trunk is like a huge rounded tower with a pointy spiral for a roof, flanked by giant bay windows and a huge curved front door with metal hinges, like they have in fantasy dramas. It's colossal, like a mini castle. If I'd not been told it was someone's home, I'd have assumed it was a new Michelin-starred restaurant serving daring fusion dishes, too elegant to feature its name prominently, or a jazzy church.

"It's stunning," I say. "*This* was your dad's family home?"

"Yup. Alright, isn't it."

"Alright is not the word."

Fin's hands are in the pockets of his coat, shoulders hunched against the wind, face very pale in the chill wind.

"It feels so strange looking at it now. You know, the last time I'd have been standing here, my dad would've been pointing out this and that about the architecture, reminiscing about him and my uncle Don smashing a downstairs window with a football during the '66 World Cup. My mum would've been complaining the wind was messing up her hairdo. Susie would've been in her plastic tiara and tutu."

"And what would you have been doing?" I say.

"Listening to my dad, I guess, or else no one would've been. Looking awkward, with my pipe-cleaner legs."

I almost remark, *I remember you at that age*, but given we've never broached encounters with each other back in the day—not that they really matter—it feels odd to start now. I block out the memory of the kiss, and I hope he has too. He must've had many, many women, since.

"It's a gastropub with rooms," he says. He nods toward the cavernous bay window on the left. "That's the bar."

"Really? It does look too massive and splendid to be someone's house."

"Want a drink? It's not impossible Iain's ahead of us on that."

"Yeah, why not?" I shrug, with the slightest shiver of nerves at the prospect his dad is in there. I've been given a room in a five-star hotel, with expenses, on the basis he will respond positively to me. Fin wouldn't blame me if he didn't, I'm sure, but I'd still feel like a freeloading fraud.

Hang on, I ask myself: once he no longer has a use for you, how are you so sure about what Finlay Hart would or would not do? *No one gets a reputation by accident.* I have a suddenly powerful, disorientating sense of Susie watching me trot obediently after Finlay, banging on the glass that now divides us, screaming *"Stop."*

29

"If I could afford this, I'd turn it back into a home but leave this room kitted out as a pub," I say. It's charming and cozy as hell in here, spartan but homely, half-melted pillar candles on wrought-iron stands and a crowded bar area selling packets of chips and wedges of brightly iced cake with silver ball sprinkles under glass covers.

We choose pints of the real ale on draught each and a seat in the window where we can see the sea. As the light dims outside, the lamps inside seem warmer. A scan of the room has produced no sightings of Iain Hart.

Fin himself likes to move around unnoticed, I notice; he doesn't carry himself in a way that draws attention: subtle, almost stealthy. Being beautiful must be an inconvenience.

"Can you believe this was ever someone's sitting room?" I say, casting a look around.

"To be perfectly honest, the Hart dynasty are sufficiently crazy . . ." Finlay pauses. "Professional term, don't quote me." I smile, and once again, I can tell he's making a special effort with me. "That their house being so large it's now used as commercial premises is the least of it."

"How were they crazy?"

"My grandad had a shop, then a chain of successful pharmacies. He sold them, retired at forty-eight, set about drinking, gambling, and womanizing. He and my grandma loathed each other in that way you loathed each other in a toxic marriage in the 1950s, but never dreamt for a moment you'd leave. Or that your poison might infect the kids. When my grandad was home, he chain-smoked so many cigs, there was a nicotine patch on the ceiling above his chair."

"Woah!"

Finlay casts a look upward at the ceiling. "My dad would be able to point to the spot."

I try to imagine this space, like a television device "star wipe" effect, dissolving into a vision of the Hart paterfamilias dragging resentfully on endless cigarettes, the mother offstage banging pots and pans, little Iain and little Don playing with a train set.

Fin drinks his pint and I drink mine and I think of the utterly terrible and bizarre set of circumstances that led to me sitting here, as the sky outside turns from deep blue to paler purple. What *would* Susie think of me being here? Hotly resentful of me for getting along with Finlay, of that I'm sure. Almost as if I was showing her up, by showing it can be done. And I get a peculiar sense—given we never kept much (well, so I thought) from each other—she'd be nervous that I was prying.

"What's the story with your family? Your dad is Down Under?" Fin says.

"Yeah, he emigrated when I was sixteen," I say.

"That's a difficult age for your dad to leave you?"

"Hah, yeah it is, and thank you for calling it leaving, because that was a very controversial word, at the time. *I'm not leaving, Evelyn. I'm only ever twenty-four hours away and there's internet and the phone and in many ways I think I'll be more present than I was before.*" I pause to eye roll. "'I'll be more around on the other side of the planet than I was when I was in the same house' is quite the self-justifying crock of shit, isn't it? If I ever get married, I'm going to offer him a video link to walk me down the aisle, which I'll tell him is more like being there. I'll kiss the screen of the laptop. Thanks, Papa!"

"Why did he go?"

"He met a woman online who he'd dated at college. Remember when Friends Reunited was a thing? My parents were unhappy anyway, but instead of Relate, my dad got into late-night emailing with 'the one who got away,' then left my mum for her. She was in Adelaide."

"That is . . . well, ouch," Fin says.

"Quite. It gets better, by which I mean worse, obviously. My brother, Kieran, goes out there aged twenty, my dad sets him up with a bar job. Kieran meets a girl, drops out of university, and stays. Can you imagine my mum after that phone call?"

Finlay is frowning, impassive. I get the impression he's gone into professional mode. *And how did that make you feel, Evelyn?*

I drink more beer. I will want more beer, I can tell.

"I've only been out to visit twice," I say. "It's not very comfortable. My dad spends his whole time on salesman mode, showing off about what a great life it is. It was like he's making a tourist board ad. His second wife, Amelia, has two sons in their twenties, who my dad seems to manage to be a very involved father to. So that's nice, isn't it? Glad to have been his practice slope."

"Has he never acknowledged how difficult it must've been for you?"

I shake my head. "When I cried or ranted at the time, I got told it was terribly hard for him too, but he wasn't happy, and didn't I want him to be happy? My dad's pretty skillful at putting his feelings first."

"How did your mum manage?"

"She rushed headlong into a short-lived second marriage with Nigel, a man who I can only describe as a human burp."

"A what?!" Finlay says.

"Like the personification of an egg belch. You'd have to meet Nige to understand it. I wouldn't recommend it though. For the five years of their marriage, mother-daughter relations were strained. She ended up agreeing with me, but it somehow hasn't made up for it. 'Thanks for pointing out my spouse was awful, turns out you were in on the ground floor on that one'—things you're never going to hear."

Fin smiles, with sad eyes.

"It's just lost time we spent fighting. You should see me in the wedding photos. I wore a black lace birdcage veil. It's like they invited the Babadook."

I cackle.

"You haven't seen much of your brother since, then?"

"No. We Skype every so often. I feel bad for him. He feels permanently guilty about going. It wasn't his fault. He was never very academic, struggling at his degree, goes out to visit Dad, and suddenly it's sunshine, beers, a wage from bar work, a girl. Of course he stayed. Now his life's out there, and that's that. Mum feels he chose Dad. And that Dad not only betrayed her, he stole her son. It's not good for her to see it like that, but equally I can't blame her, given that's in effect exactly what happened."

Hmmm, didn't I once tell Mum she had to let go of her justified bitterness about things she couldn't change, to be happy? Or else "her demons would eat her"? (Always the dramatic Goth.) Who needs to take that advice now, I wonder? Never try to be wise at age twenty-five, it will bite you fully on the ass later.

"Divorce is a shitshow of competing interests," Finley says, "Kids often end up being the brokers."

"Tell me about it."

"It must've felt like every single member of your family deserted you, one after another," Finlay says. "Including your mum. Into that marriage."

I stare at him, for a second, stunned. "Yes. *Yes.* That's exactly how it felt . . . I'm no longer surprised at you being an in-demand psychologist not psychiatrist."

Finlay smiles and runs his hand through his hair. How many women fall in a version of God-worship doctor love with him, after he fixes their feelings? Or feel their feelings, however this works.

"That was just basic empathy," he says. "It's a helluva tale."

I nod. "Thanks, I've not told it for a while. I'd kind of forgotten that it was. I'm *allowed* to be a damaged loser."

Fin smiles, but ignores this. "How do you think it's affected you? I will admit that's a bit of a therapy session question. No charge, however. Except another one of these." He points at our drinks and my spirits lift, as I'd been hoping we'd stay.

"Deal! Hmmm, how's it affected me." I'd actually never

asked myself this. "I think . . ." I pause, as a pain has appeared under my ribs, without warning. "I think I stopped expecting good things to happen to me, after all that."

Finlay looks at me intently. "I know exactly what you mean."

"Do you?"

We exchange a look.

"Let's have more beer. Damn, that Uber was a good call," Fin says, and the moment is broken.

Over second drinks, we chat pop-culture trivia, and I'm relieved.

As we leave, Fin shows a photo of his father to the bar staff. The man pulling the pumps peers, shakes his head, calls his wife over to double-check.

She takes the photo from Fin, between finger and thumb. Yes, he was in, yesterday! He'd wanted to describe to her at some length how it looked when he used to live here. He had a cup of Earl Grey and a slice of walnut-coffee gateaux. No, he never said where he was staying.

We leave, buoyed by the trail going hot, but, once the thrill fades, twitchy on the drive back.

If Mr. Hart's definitely here, then we're definitely failing at this task.

30

"By the way, if you've got the energy, I've booked a place called Café St. Honoré for a meal tonight. It's been there years, we went there every time we visited, back in the day. Possible my dad will be there, tucking into Stornoway black pudding, telling the waiters what's what about Scottish independence. I thought it was easiest to combine a visit with eating, given we need to eat."

Invites to dinner have been warmer, but I agree.

"See you in the lobby to leave at half seven?" Fin says, as we prepare to part in the lift of The Waldorf.

"Is it super posh?" I say, warily.

"No, more of a buzzy bistro kind of thing."

"Nice. This is turning into O.J. Simpson's hunt for his wife's killer, isn't it?" I say. "I will leave no golf course or beach resort uncombed!"

Fin boggles at me and then bursts out laughing.

"Oh my God," he says, as he recovers.

"What?"

"You're . . ." Fin shakes his head. "You're so constantly out-rageous, and yet somehow get away with it. If I said half the things you did, I'd be in prison."

"Thanks," I say.

"It's not exactly a compliment," Fin says, as the lift doors roll closed, and I say: "I know."

In my room, I pull out the one vaguely smart dress I packed, unsure why. It's black—of course—fitted around what you'd call the bodice, requires a balcony bra, and has a flared skirt. The last time I wore it, Justin accused me of planning to "marry his dad and steal his inheritance."

I remember my suspicions about Fin, who's since turned out to be a man of means. That makes him chasing any change to his dad's will less likely, surely?

By some sort of cosmic ordering, after I pull the dress on and drag the hard-to-reach low zip up my back with some effortful pushing and pulling, my phone rings with a call from Justin.

"Hello, Ed says you've been kidnapped and sex-trafficked. Is this true, and if so, can you ask Finlay Hart if he'll sex-traffic me?"

I honk.

"Hello! It's good to hear your voice. Nothing of that nature, sorry. God, what is Ed like?"

"He's going to become a Tory MP by forty, at this rate. Will start booming about degeneracy and scroungers and how tanga briefs aren't proper underwear," Justin says. "Seriously, I think he's hyper and ragged in the way we all are. But yes, he is fretting."

I describe the situation in Edinburgh and Justin sighs. "I

know this sounds inappropriate—but then I am inappropriate, so that's what's going to happen—but I envy you."

"Why?"

"Being in a different place with no memories attached to it sounds so good. I keep thinking, oh I'll tell Suze this, oh I'll see the gang at the quiz, I'll WhatsApp her. Oh wait, hang on, no, I won't. Life now is horrific. I keep wanting to go back to those minutes before I got that call from Ed."

I hadn't thought of that, of the value of my escape, but I know exactly what Justin means.

"Yes!" I say, gripping the phone handset in gratitude. "God, yes. Forgetting and then remembering again is so awful. It's like hiring someone to follow you around to kick you, every time you relax."

"What's the brother like? He seem sad, or is being up north yet more time away from his home planet? Planet of the Tall Sexy Rude Men?"

"Sad, I don't know. I think he was already sad. There's more to him than we thought, I think."

"Oy oy! I knew you were stupid, but I never thought you were blind. Plumb those hidden depths, definitely."

"Yeah yeah." I heavy sigh at Justin, smiling.

"Listen, I didn't call you up to insinuate lewd things, though it's enjoyable. You know it's my birthday next weekend?"

"Yup."

"I was going to forget about it altogether, stay in and drink myself into a stupor. But I've decided to go the other way and drink myself into a stupor at a second location. What do you think to me, you, and Mr. and Mrs. Ed in a cottage in

Derbyshire for a weekend? Thursday, Friday, Saturday nights? It speaks to my need to be out of the house and around people, but not out of a house and around people, if you know what I mean."

"Oh. Me and Hester in close proximity?"

I blurt this before considering he presumably knows nothing about what went off at Susie's wake. Fortunately, Justin seems to take it as a reference to the standard antipathy.

"Yes, I know, as ever. But, drink through it. I think Ed must've read her the riot act about being a Bridezilla as we're hearing a lot less about the merits of blush ranunculus versus peach peonies in springtime bouquets."

"Argh, OK. I doubt I can swing another day off so soon though. I'd have to get there for Friday night?"

"Good. That way we'll have unpacked the groceries, made the ice cubes, and found the firelighters."

Justin asks what I'm up to and I tell him about dinner.

"What are you wearing? Can I see?"

I switch from the call to the camera, take a selfie, and send it to him.

"I think you've correctly judged the mood of the nation there," Justin says, after receiving it. "Hair up, maybe? Knock him dead. If we're still allowed to use that phrase after Susie. She'd squawk at that!"

"She would." I smile, and get the solar plexus punch of happy-sad, lemon juice with sugar.

After I ring off, I spend time in front of the mirror in the gleaming marble bathroom, sticking pins in handfuls of my lightly backcombed hair until I have an acceptable bird's nest that I *think* looks sort of French chanteuse in smoky speakeasy.

Within half an hour and one Kir Royale, it will no doubt land as more "It's fine if she doesn't want to be found, her family just want to know she's OK."

In the lobby, I can't see Finlay at first. I pick my way very carefully across the marble floor, which resembles an ice rink in my precarious footwear.

Annoyingly, as I've had my tongue poking out in concentration and I'm holding the sides of my coat for balance while I thought I was unobserved, I spot Finlay leaning against a wall, watching my progress with an expression of indulgent amusement.

"Still not giving up on those boots, huh," he says.

There I was thinking my hobbling on the beach had gone undetected.

"I'm very loyal," I say.

We walk to the Café St. Honoré in a glacial dusk, me trying in vain to pretend I'm not walking like I've got two hip replacements on the steep inclines of New Town.

I wonder what lives are being lived behind the smart blank blinds in the sash windows.

At one point, I slide-stumble and Finlay catches my elbow and says, "Got it?" and I say, "Hmm mmm, yep ta," and feel furious at myself for emulating some Bambi-legged ditzy cliché. It's fine to go arse over tit around your friends (well, if you must have an audience) but with Finlay Hart I want to stay in control.

When we get to the restaurant, my feet are sore but my heart lifts.

"This could not be any more my thing if it was named

Evelyn's Actual Thing," I say, under my breath, looking around once we're seated, waiters having politely shaken their head in unfamiliarity at Fin's discreetly proffered photo of Iain Hart.

The floor is black and white square tiles, the walls are crammed with artfully tarnished mirrors. There are glossy black curved chairs, the pendant lights are glowing orbs that throw everyone into moody, woozily drunk half-light. It's a pastiche of 1940s Paris that makes me feel as if I've fallen face first into a date in a romantic novel.

"Lollipop bay trees in box planters outside, those fairy lights above the wall of wine . . . it's my Moon Under Water of restaurants," I say, as we open the menus.

"Let's hope you like the food then," Fin says. "It's got a lot to live up to."

"They could put a slab of Morrisons chicken liver pâté onto a plate with some Ritz crackers and I'd be happy," I say and Finlay smiles a small smile and asks my approval of the red he's ordering.

"What originally took you to the States, did you go there to study psychology?" I say, as we finish the bread.

Finlay shoots a look at me. "Susie would've told you that."

"She did."

"Then why ask?" he says, evenly.

"Because"—I feel myself becoming less afraid of Finlay; how much of that is familiarity, and how much is Côtes du Rhône, I don't know—"the polite way is to ask. Not confront someone with something you already know, which obliges them to tell you."

"That's merely a longer way around to the same destination. I think we call it fishing."

"God's sake!" I say, in exasperation. "I'm making conversation. Whatever you told me the answer was, I'd accept. Including 'It's none of your business.' You act as if there's landmines and tripwires everywhere, when there aren't."

Fin sits back, fiddling with his wineglass stem and surveying me, and seems to come to a decision.

"I'm sorry. I've had so much shit when I'm here, I come into the ring with my boxing gloves up. I don't always know when to lower them."

"OK."

"I got model-scouted in London and taken onto the books of a place that also had New York offices. I only did it for a couple of years, I hated it, but I made enough money to pay me through my degree. I find it hideously embarrassing." He shrugs.

"Why?! If I'd ever been a model, you'd not shut me up about it. Even when my grandkids were like: seriously, Granny, because you look like a warthog."

"I had to stand there as if I didn't exist, while people discussed if my arms were too thin, or my profile photographed as well from the left-hand side." Fin tilts his face accordingly and my stomach flexes, as all I see is slightly bristled jaw by candlelight. Pretty sure I could take a good photograph of it.

". . . Or if my look was too 'catalogue generic' et cetera. My only talents being utilized were the ability to stand still, or walk down a ramp. It was the very opposite of an ego pump."

"Wowee. Who knew?"

"If you want to be told how good-looking you are, pay for someone's drinks all night at a bar. Model bookers and clients will tell you how good-looking you aren't. I would honestly flip burgers before I'd go back to it. Not that they'd have Dumbledore here, aged thirty-six."

"What did your family say, that made you bite my head off?" I ask, with a smile for safety.

"You spoke to Susie, right?"

"Yes. She said you were very oversensitive about it."

"Hahaha. If you want a perfect nutshell of how they turned the effects of their behavior into my problem, you couldn't do much better than that. My dad thought it was synonymous with me coming out as gay, my mother and sister thought it proof of preening vanity. 'You? A model?!' So yes, I was 'sensitive.' The same way someone makes a noise if you hammer a nail into them." He pauses. "Do you know why Spanish flu was called Spanish flu?"

"Because it started in Spain?"

"That's what everyone assumes. In fact, to protect the morale of troops in the First World War, they underreported people dying of it here. Spain was neutral and free to broadcast it, leading to a belief that Spain was worse affected than everywhere else. Hence the name. They found themselves landed with the rep for being the flu hotbed, purely for being more honest. That's me in the Hart family. I was the one who complained, and so I got blamed as being the source. The Finlay flu."

"What did you complain about?"

"Long story," Fin says, after a pause, in a way that says *not now*. I don't know what else to say.

"Sorry, you did ask about the *Zoolander* years, and here we are. This is why I usually don't want to talk about myself," he says, face drawn again.

The starters arrive.

For the first time I wonder properly if the ballad of Finlay Hart is a story of his being done wrong. It's seductive, especially when he's sitting opposite with rolled-up sleeves and those forearms in this lighting, but my instincts still rebel against it. It was three votes against his one, and I've seen for myself how icy he can be.

"Fair enough. Susie always said you were a lot, when you were younger." I say this in a throwaway, rather than accusatory way. "That's all. But I'm ignorant on this, compared to you, obviously. I only had her side."

"I was a lot," Fin says, dully, spearing a cornichon with his fork. "Or I got that way. She wasn't making everything up. It was more what she left out. How's your terrine, is it good?"

I have a mouthful of it so have to do a one-handed thumbs-up.

"What did she leave out?" I say, after swallowing.

"Can I ask you something?" Fin says, as if he hasn't heard me. "You knew my sister very well? The best of all, I think it's fair to say."

I nod.

"How do you think she'd have acted, had I died? How do you think—if she'd flown to Manhattan to sort the funeral and walked into a room of my friends who, if not hostile, had negative preconceptions of her, given the bad terms we were on—she'd have handled it?"

"Uhm . . ." I'm glad of the wine. I take a stiffening swig. "She would've . . . she'd have been Susie, I guess. Irreverent and tough. She'd have . . ." Oh, this is tricky, wanting to honor truthfulness while not being offensive. "She'd have probably said it would've felt different if you two were closer."

To put it mildly.

Finlay nods. "Yes. Exactly. She'd have assumed my friends were the enemy, informed them of her rights, shed few tears about me, and got the hell out. My friends would have thought she was, how did you put it? A lot."

He goes back to his rillettes. His point's been made decisively yet effortlessly.

It's not like me to be at a loss for words.

How had I not seen this? How had I, someone who prides herself on thinking hard on things and being a sharp judge of character, never seen Finlay and Susie were, in fact, very alike?

31

Aware things have got heavier than we want them to be, we manage to steer back to discussing the joys of life in Park Slope and matching it to my scant touristy knowledge. I tell him about Mark's job in San Francisco to try to sound like more of an internationalist, hoping I'm eloquent enough that he doesn't notice I'm piggybacking on my ex-boyfriend's accomplishments.

As we decide we're having a cheese board instead of dessert, another diner interrupts us.

"Excuse me . . . ," says a woman with gray hair in a bun.

"Beverley, don't!" says a well-spoken man standing behind her. "Leave them in peace."

"I want to let you know, you're the loveliest couple I think I've ever seen." She puts a palm to her chest in a theatrical swoon. I suddenly remember the girls at school and the smudged ink initials 'FH' on their books.

"Really . . . ?" we both say, simultaneously, looking at each other in surprise.

Although I'm sure my surprise is the greatest. I'm not anything like an equal to Fin aesthetically, I don't think, all false modesty aside. Shows what sitting opposite him can do. Like when film crews hold up reflectors.

"I've enjoyed watching you." She leans down and squeezes my arm, resting on the table. "Have a long and happy life together, won't you. For me."

She picks up my left hand, sees the ring finger is ringless.

"Ask her, you fool!" she stage-hisses to Fin.

"Forgive my wife, she's had a lot of Bordeaux," says the man, and we laugh, and they leave.

An awkward pause ensues.

"OK, since Bev's brought it up, we can't avoid it any longer. Will you marry me?" Fin says. "We don't know each other but we can't make a worse mess than most people who do get to know each other first, right?"

"Since you put it like that."

I laugh gratefully, and we clink glasses. I initially took his words as a graceful way of breaking the tension, but he's gazing at me in a way that might, just possibly, be construed as flirtatious? Nothing thus far has prepared me for Finlay Hart, flirting. Had you asked me the one thing he'd never do, I'd have said flirting.

It's not fair, in these surroundings, in his white shirt, with his bone structure, after Jesus has dropkicked me through the goalposts of life.

"Can I tell you something weird, without you thinking I'm weird?" Fin says.

"Probably depends on it not being too weird?" I say, trying to reassert some sass, as I feel vulnerable and a little bit . . . what would my mum call it? *Squiffy.*

"Years back, maybe five years ago, I was in a bar in the East

Village. The kind of self-regarding place that plays Yo La Tengo and Whitney Houston and the barmen have sex-offender mustaches. There's a dog walking around and it serves melon-flavored cocktails in jelly jars . . . The dog's not serving."

"Jelly?"

"*Jam* jars, sorry. See, I've got some American in me now. And 'Catch' by The Cure came on, you know it?"

"Yes, this is my wheelhouse! Kind of a ditty . . . ? *'I'd see her when the days got colder'*—that one?"

"Yes!" Fin's the most animated I've ever seen him.

"That song came on and all of a sudden, out of nowhere, I got this pin-sharp image of you standing at the door when you used to call for Susie. A big bow in your hair. Your solemn eyes."

I gasp. "I didn't think you remembered me! Or any of that. Or I'd have mentioned it."

Finlay frowns. "Of course I do. I've been away for a while but I don't have amnesia. Listening to that song, thousands of miles away, so many years after: I realized what it was about you that felt so unusual."

"Was it the Edwardian ghost hair accessory?"

"You always looked so worried. For a kid."

"Did I?"

He plays with his wineglass stem again and looks at me, and I feel seen, though I'm not fully sure why.

"Yeah. Well, to me. Maybe it takes one to know one."

I puzzle.

"Shall we get the bill?" Fin says.

"FANCY A NIGHTCAP?" I say, when we get back to The Caley. "On me too! I don't like not paying for anything."

283

"Why not," Fin says.

Its bar is a narrow, galley space so we have to sit side by side on high stools at a counter, which I always like.

I watch the barman rattle ice in a shaker like a maraca after we order two smoked old-fashioneds.

With minutes to go, I remember my nine p.m. check in with Ed, and apologize while I hack out an EVERYTHING FINE, SITUATION NORMAL bulletin, without explaining that's what it is.

"Sorry, meant to reply to my friend Ed about something," I say.

"Is Ed the fair-haired guy at the funeral, who did the reading?"

"Yes!"

"He's your ex, right?"

"Ed? No, no, no, not my ex. Nope."

"Ah."

"Is this what we call . . . fishing?" I say, and Fin smiles back.

"No, it's making conversation, when you politely ask a question and the person is free to respond, 'None of your business,'" Finlay says, the quote marks clear in the intonation.

He sips his drink and I cast my eyes upward.

"Oh, very clever. You're asking as you overheard our argument at the wake?"

"It was quite heated but I'm not sure I followed what had gone on. You read a letter? A letter from the box of personal items you weren't going to look at, but, hey, that's not important right now . . ."

Fin does a comic *look into the middle distance while tilting the glass to his lips* pose and I guffaw, my stomach clenching with guilt. I'm still slightly stunned he has such levity in his repertoire: like your mate sitting down at a street piano and bashing out a fluent *Moonlight Sonata*.

"Apart from that one moment of weakness," I say, hastily. "Which, as you clearly bore witness, fully, karmically repaid me, so you don't need to bother shaming me."

"Right. So if he's not your ex, why is it an issue he slept with my sister? Don't tell me if you don't want to."

I hard swallow both at the amount he knows, and his asking a question I've levelled in great embarrassment at myself.

"It's complicated . . ."

"We're in one of those intense situations where we see each other every day for a few days and then never again in our lives, so what would usually be indiscreet, isn't, right?" Finlay says.

"Yes! This is like a holiday romance with no holiday and no romance," I say, with the boldness of a woman who's half a centimeter deep in orange-flavored paraffin.

I describe the letter to Ed at university going astray, Hester, the engagement, the sense of understanding between us, and my discovery regarding Susie, in context. I summarize everything Ed said when he came around and gave Rog chew sticks. It feels good to purge it by telling someone, so much so it outweighs any hesitation and my self-consciousness.

Fin listens to it and says at the end: "I see why you were upset."

I breathe out. "Thank you."

"Want my take?"

"Yes," I say, and brace, as Finlay is sufficiently clever that even if he gets it wrong, he's going to sound right.

"Your boy Edward has had his cake and eaten all of it."

My eyebrows rise.

"He's had exactly what he wanted from each of you, hasn't he? Adoration from you, steady commitment from his fiancée, casual sex with Susie. It's hurt all of you in different ways. Susie only in terms of her memory, as far as we know. But who knows? Must've torn her up, keeping it from you."

"Yeah, I guess so?"

"He chose to start things with you, he chose to let them drop, he chose to start dating someone else and let you find out the way you did. And he chose to cheat. Yet he doesn't own those as choices, but as pieces of bad luck? Beware the Nicest Guy in the Room, who doesn't think his failures are the same as everyone else's."

I suppress a smile at Fin having definitely not put himself at risk of being accused of "Nicest Guy in the Room–ing."

"Hmmm. I mean, I'm sure he didn't set out *intending* it . . . with me, with Susie. Even with Hester, given he thought I'd not written back . . ."

God, I can hear myself. Let it go, Eve.

"That's not a particularly useful measure of your enemies' motive. If there's one thing I've learned, it's that harm done with explicit conscious intention of doing another person harm accounts for about two percent of all harm inflicted. That descriptor pretty much only applies to dictators in banana republics, serial killers, and PE teachers."

Finlay pauses, to the relief of my whirring brain. I'm not sure I've ever been given this much in one go to think about since history A-level cramming.

"These are good, aren't they? Strong but good." He takes another sip of old-fashioned. "You had no idea whatsoever about the thing with my sister?" he says.

"No. What breaks me is that I can never ask why she did it, given she knew what I felt. She'd say she was pissed, I guess? What else could she say? It doesn't feel like the whole answer. She could've pulled anyone. She went for him."

"I think I know why she did it."

"Why?"

"Jealousy."

"Really? But she never fancied Ed in the slightest."

"Jealousy of you, not of him. Jealousy of the feelings between you. Jealousy and envy manifest in many ways. Plus, if there was action of any sort around, my sister wanted a slice." Fin smiles. "Take it from one who shared a toy box with her."

I feel my disloyalty, using Fin as a sounding board, and being dissected like this; it's too efficiently on point to be comfortable.

I can't believe you're listening to my wanker of a brother trash-talk me! UGH . . . please tell me you don't fancy him?! That's it, I'm gonna barf.

Ed, in a toilet? I say to her, sternly. She falls silent.

I pick at a drink coaster. "She'd have thought my tragic love for Ed was exactly that though, tragic. Why would she envy it?"

"If you don't mind me saying, based on a very short acquaintance—you seem to take people at their word, which is a really good quality, but maybe leaves you short of an answer at times. Susie mocked plenty of things, but it wasn't necessarily representative of how she felt, deep down. As far as I know, she never fell in love with anyone. You were in love, and that would've fascinated her. What happened with Ed . . . she was probably trying to find out why. She was exploring, trying to feel what you felt. She was rifling through your closets when you were away."

I sip my drink and think I have amateur-hour tangoed with an absolute ballroom professional here. His analysis is a series of controlled explosions.

"She was snooping?"

"Yeah, emotionally, experientially, snooping. You were with your ex throughout the Ed thing? The one who's now on the West Coast? How did that work, given your hang-up?" Fin says.

I gulp and shrug and feel ancient guilt.

"Like any torch you carry over a very long time, I suppose. I put the torch in a cupboard for the duration and there was still a faint glow. When Mark and I fell apart, it was still there. Mark accused me of not being willing to leave the group behind and move with him to London. He principally meant Susie, but I'll always wonder if Ed was a factor too. He must have been, I suppose."

"What was your reason for not going at the time?"

"Well . . . Mark was this laconic, funny, super-talented, and ambitious hack type. I admired him more than I ever felt feelings for him. I turned office banter into going to the pub and the pub into a one-night stand and a one-night stand into a fling, and a fling into a relationship. It was all powered by wishing and hoping for the love of my life to have arrived. But at the point he wanted me to give my life up for a life with him, it was too much. The jig was up. I'd conned myself first and Mark second. It was shit of me. But I didn't intend it . . ."

I trail off and break into a grin. "Hah. Like you said. God. It's so clear, when I look at it now."

Fin smiles back. "Yes, relationships. So obvious what was going on in hindsight. Especially when described to third parties in hotel bars, over some sort of classic drink with four units of alcohol and a curl of fruit peel in it."

My phone blinks with a WhatsApp message from Ed. I slide to open it.

Good to hear from you, Harris. Justin tells me you're going on dressy dinner dates?! Is the brother's idea that you might find his dad down the leg of a pair of silk stockings? X

It's so lumpenly manipulative, in the black and white speech bubble of text. That is the possessiveness of a boyfriend, with a built-in plausible deniability of Concerned BFF if I called him on it. I feel something approaching contempt.

What space does Ed imagine making for me, on the other side of his wedding, their having kids? It's like he's got me trapped playing the Janeane Garofalo role in a *Will They Won't They?*, which he knows, in his heart of hearts, is already a *They Never Did*. He's going to marry Uma Thurman. It's the hope that kills you.

"What about you, then?" I say, thinking I have a clear run at nosiness, now. "You and . . . Rowena? Romilly!"

"Ah." Fin smiles an eye-creasing, sheepish smile, and looks into his drink as his hair falls forward a little, and my heart goes boom, whether I like it or not. "She's my ex, as said."

"I got a sense from her call she is a semidetached ex."

"Yes, your senses are correct. I ended it in the spring, but she's convinced I'm going to change my mind."

"Are you?"

"Oof. More of these, before I can do that? Same again, thanks," Fin says at my nodding, and gestures to the barman. "No, I'm not, but I have a relationship with her five-year-old that I'm finding very hard to walk away from. Also, she said a thing in our final fight that I can't forget. I've lain awake in the dark, thinking about it."

"Was it . . . *life is one vile fuckin' task after another*? Al Swearengen, *Deadwood*."

Fin laughs, fully corpses, and I know I've definitely broken through the hard carapace with him. Susie would've found that funny too.

"She said . . . ah, thanks." Fresh drinks arrive. Fin waits for the barman to move away. "She said . . . you don't want me because I remind you too much of yourself."

". . . Oh."

"Mmm."

"What did she mean?"

"She means—well, she said as much—I'm tough and I'm cynical and my faith in people is broken. But I want an optimistic, kind, more gentle person to restore all that. Someone who, if I actually got, she said, I would eat alive and pick my teeth with her bones."

"*Oh.*" On my bare knowledge, Romilly sounds like she might have him sussed.

"Plus, she said, 'That sweetness and light girl has *no chat*,'" he grins.

"No chat?"

"No wit, no comebacks, no spark. Can't make me laugh."

"Did she have someone in mind?"

"No. It was very Romilly to be disgusted by even the *thought* of the next person I might date."

"Why does it keep you awake?"

"Because I'm forty in four years' time, and I worry she's right. When you pass on something that has good things about it, but isn't good enough, you're gambling that something one day will feel better, aren't you? Stick, or twist. I'm getting old enough to say: I might be wrong about that."

I pause. "Fuck, you sound like my mum! Don't tell me mum was right about Mark!"

"Well. She remarried a 'human burp.' Equally you can be too accommodating."

I honk loud enough that the barman looks over.

Fin's phone, lying on the bar, bursts into light. Not only a call, a full-screen picture, a FaceTime. Featuring first a red-haired woman, then jostled by a small red-haired boy. I think: bit late to have a child up? Then remember New York is hours behind.

"Oh, speak of the devil," Fin says, with a startle at Romilly's features. "I best get this."

"Of course," I say, swigging the last of my drink and pushing down off my stool.

"Meet at nine in the lobby for the grand tour of Leith?" Fin says.

"You're on!"

Upstairs, I get into my room, pull my pajamas on, tease my

hair out of its pins, and brush it smooth under the bathroom light.

As I pad through to the bedroom, I see my phone flashing on the nightstand. I pick it up—it's an unknown caller, an international number with mysterious digits.

Out of the sheer intrigue, I answer it.

32

I lie prone with hot tears coating my face, my mobile handset still a warm slab of glass in my hand from the recent call. A green light unexpectedly winks on the landline by my bed. For the second time inside twenty minutes tonight, I break my own rules and answer blind.

"Hello?" I say, blearily.

"Hi it's me," Fin says. "I didn't wake you?"

"No."

"You wouldn't have a spare iPhone charger, would you? Mine's frayed and the battery's inching up by one percent a half hour."

"Oh," I sit up and glance at my open case. "Actually, yes. Think I do."

"Mind if I come get it?"

I have to heave back a sob and say, "Sure," which comes out as a squeak.

"Are you alright?" he says.

"Not really," I gasp.

Fin pauses.

"I'm on my way."

A soft tap at the door moments later and he's outside, in his T-shirt and sweatpants. Even with hiking socks, it's a good look for him.

"What's the matter?" he says, as I hand him the charger. I try to speak and instead I burst into fresh tears, clamp a palm over my face. Fin steps into the room, shutting the door quietly behind him.

"Mark called," I say, when I get the power of speech back. "My ex? In America. He'd seen something on Facebook today about Susie and called me to see how I was. He was so shocked, and his shock made me shocked all over again."

Fin nods, face grave. "Yeah. Telling people, talking about it, is a series of aftershocks."

"Yes! He was so sympathetic; it really did for me."

During our conversation, I could hear the snuffling and occasional ragged cry of a newborn in the background of the conversation, an unknown female voice shushing. The connection had that slightly echoey, windy quality of long distance.

Standing in the anonymous surroundings of this grand hotel, it was what Susie and I used to call a "searchlight in the prison yard" moment. When you're caught in the bright, unforgiving glare of an inspection you've not prepared for.

I didn't want to be with Mark. Yet somehow, his being so distant in sunnier climes, and my being here in cold, lonely dark ones, amid such grief—it made me feel my life had comprehensively fallen apart, since I declined to share his. It felt like judgment, by a higher power.

"Mark's memories of Susie caused me to think, you know, in a way I hadn't, about how we all were." I hear my tremulous voice in the quiet of a plush, noise-proofed hotel room. "About a time gone past. Racing around in our twenties, when things were hopeful and choices were unmade and Susie was with us. When I could've warned her not to get out of taxis early to smoke. It's all gone," I say, looking at Fin with streaming eyes, wiping my face ineffectually with my pajama sleeve. "It turns out that nothing worked out. My friends were the bit of my life I'd got right and now everything is sick and strange and fucked up forever."

Finlay is frowning in concern but letting me talk.

"I feel like I got old overnight. I know how indulgent that sounds when Susie only got thirty-four years. All I have is pain and regret and a shit job where I type stupid things into boxes."

"It won't always be this way, Eve," Fin says, quietly. "Life has harder parts."

"What's going to change for me?"

Fin smiles, sadly. "That's largely up to you."

"Yeah. I don't have much faith in Future Me. Past Me is a twat." I pause for a strangled breath. "I miss Susie so much," I say. "I miss her so much, and I've spent this time being uselessly angry at her . . . and you were right, she was snooping with Ed, like I snooped on her reading that letter. Oh God . . . I just want her to be here to say sorry, so I can tell her *I'm* sorry. For everything. And that I love her so, so much and nothing matters except that fact. I can't, I won't speak to her ever again, Finlay. Game over."

I sob openly, and Finlay puts his arms around me.

I make a decision, in the embrace, to lean into it. I'm not going to stanch my tears out of embarrassment. I'm not going to stop and choke this back into something feminine, and picturesque. I ugly heave-sob into his T-shirt until it's wet enough to stick to his skin. He feels hard-bodied and lean under the fabric, a stark contrast to the squish of my chest. I've never been this physically close to an athletic type before. My partners, however narrow they looked when dressed, were always softly British-pudgy from beer and curries. Like me.

"I miss her too," he says, into my hair.

"Really?" I look up at him. I blink and focus enough to see he has tears in his eyes. "I wasn't sure if you did."

"Yes," he says, voice very low. "Very much. Not in the same way you do, I can't miss a relationship I didn't have. I'd been missing her for a long time. But it's like I've lost a part of myself, my past. So many things only Susie shared with me. I already was pretty isolated, but now I realize, I wasn't. Not like I am now. And like you, there are things between us that will always be unfinished. After the police called, I sat in silence, before the tears. I wasn't ready. This wasn't how it was going to end. I know you only saw the anger. I think there was still some love, underneath. Or a bond at least, whatever you'd call it. I know there was on my side. I found out I'd always been clinging hard to a notion of a point in the future when we could reconcile. The way things were between us wasn't ever going to be forever, you know? And it turned out, it was."

I've never heard Finlay, or indeed anyone, sound this raw.

"I'm sorry for being like this," I say, in the deep silence that follows.

"Why?"

"I didn't mean to suggest my loss is greater."

"I know you didn't. Come and sit down," Finlay says, and

guides me to the edge of the bed. "How about a cup of milky tea with a large sugar in it? It's what my mum would suggest."

"Sounds perfect," I say, smiling. It actually does. I watch as Fin goes to fill the kettle in the bathroom, rustles around in the stash of sachets and plastic pots of UHT milk, clanks the china cups.

"Why have you got the television on, on mute?" he says, noticing the dancing picture in the gloom.

"I turned it on and I didn't know how to turn it off."

"Silent rugby at Twickenham is oddly hypnotic."

Fin hands a cup to me, demonstrating good manners in twisting it so the handle is nearest. From his bearing, you'd definitely think he went to a posh school, not my school. He is a bit of a Gatsby.

"Thank you."

"Want to be alone, or shall I stay for a while?" Fin says.

"Stay! If that's OK."

"Of course."

Fin pours hot water onto a tea bag, dunks it and casts it aside, and walks to the bed. It's so huge that he can lie on it and channel surf without it feeling as if we're in bed together.

As I drink, I realize that as well as being emotionally unsettled, I was half drunk and dehydrated. Halfway down the cup, I feel significantly steadier.

Finlay holds the remote aloft and clicks through channels rapidly. For a few seconds, a male model with goatee and top knot in huge trousers swings down a catwalk and holds a jacket off his shoulder, before pulling it up, wheeling around, and stalking onward.

"Oh fuck's sake. Where's the off button on this thing?!" Finlay points the remote while pretend hammering at it in straight-faced ire, and I gurgle with delight both at the incident, and Fin having a sense of humor about it.

I have a tiny revelation: I like him. I'm not sure I trust him, but I do like him.

"Oh my God, can you do that?" I say.

"What, walk? Yes. Thank you."

"Can I see a modeling picture? Are there any online?"

"No, too old, I'm afraid. Archive material. They were still using Box Brownie cameras."

I gurgle some more. This was the brightener I needed.

"Did you do any famous 'campaigns,' as I believe they're called?"

In laughter, I've unintentionally rolled closer to Finlay. Our arms are nearly touching, and neither of us are moving away again.

"Hmmmm, not telling you. You'll look it up."

"You said there's no photos of you anywhere!"

"I was lying, as people do when they do not wish problematic women to know things."

"Problematic, haha."

He lifts his hips off the bed, pulls his phone out of his sweatpants pocket, turns it on, and presses a few buttons, careful to angle the screen away from me. "Think there was one for a whisky brand that was quite *Mad Men*, that I didn't hate . . ."

My heart rate jumps a little, as it dawns on me he's doing this not only to oblige me, but to impress me. I didn't think for a second he'd actually show me anything, in my teasing. But I have more power than I realized.

Fin holds the phone, screen side to his chest.

"Alright, I'll show you this, but the search term *has been obscured for a reason!*"

He barks this in a mock "schoolteacher when the bell rings" voice and I'm weak with giggling as he turns the phone toward me and I hold it steady, my hand over his, and examine the image. It has such an effect on me, I almost wish I hadn't started this.

Finlay Hart in a slim-cut, dark brown sixties suit, one arm thrown over the back of a leather booth, the other holding a lowball glass with ice, staring straight down the lens with a *come shag me then* petulant challenge in his eyes. His hair is coal black and short; his skin looks lit from within.

"You look *phenomenal*," I breathe. "Seriously. I don't know why you're embarrassed. I'd have this shit framed."

"If it's cheered you up then maybe it was worth it," he says, charmingly, repocketing his phone and sipping his tea.

"You're an enigma, Finlay Hart," I say.

Fin sets his cup down and turns his face to me, and we gaze at each other in the flickering moon glow of the television.

"I don't want to be an enigma."

"What do you want to be?"

"Isn't that always the big question."

We both pretend to watch people hanging out of rolled-down windows and firing guns in the police car chase through nocturnal Los Angeles streets in whatever film is playing, after the rugby. I don't think either of us are thinking about it.

"Do you ever wonder what it would be like, to drop all . . . this, with someone?" Fin says, eventually. He makes a gesture up and down from his face to his shoulders and down to his waist that leaves me nonplussed. "The defenses and the deceptions and ways we have of impressing people. To fully be yourself, with no . . . no fear, I guess? Of how you're coming over. No management of the impression you're making. Total honesty."

I get an unwelcome flashback to being astride Zack, getting ready to pretend to be someone who would please him.

"No," I say. "Maybe I should."

"For what it's worth, if you could see yourself through my eyes, I don't think you'd think you were a busted flush at this 'living,' Evelyn."

"Really?"

"Really. I see a person who has everything going for her. The only thing you lack is self-belief."

"Thank you," I say. I parcel this incredible compliment up, mentally, to unwrap and fully enjoy after he's gone. "You're not doing badly yourself."

"Hah. That's what I told myself. It's so strange being back here. I realize I left part of myself behind. Like pulling yourself out of a bear trap and half your leg not coming with you. You're free, but you limp."

"Why was it a bear trap?"

"I said had you ever wondered about dropping this." He motions at himself again, smiling. "Not that I was ready to."

"Haha. *I don't want to be an enigma*, said the man who spoke in code."

"I think what I really meant was: I don't want to be an enigma to you."

"Why?"

We're side by side on a bed and he's looking down at me,

steadily. I'm accosted by an urge to pull his T-shirt upward. Wait wait wait . . . are we going to kiss . . . surely not? I'm very nervous, yet, I discover, receptive to this turn of events, looking at his outline in half light and being close enough to smell his shower gel. I lean in closer so our sides are touching, my right breast pressing against his arm. It's as encouraging as I can be, using nerve endings, without seizing him. He's still too intimidating for me to risk that.

"I should go to bed," Fin says, pulling back and sitting up straighter, voice a notch louder.

". . . OK."

Finlay pauses, swings his legs over the side of the bed, and stands up.

"See you in the morning, Eve."

He pads across the carpet and the door closes with a snap-click behind him. Well. That de-escalated quickly.

I turn the bedside light out and lie still, listening to the ambient, offstage noises of Edinburgh city center, late at night.

What was that about? Lots of intense staring, photos of him as Don Draper, *I don't want to be an enigma to you*, and then, gone.

Maybe he wanted to know he could have me if he wanted.

I remember our first kiss when we were kids, my asking, *Would you like to do it with me?*

I got a direct answer in the affirmative, back then.

How have my skills with men degraded in the intervening twenty-five years?

As I'm drifting off to sleep, I think: In the actual Waldorf, surely reception would've had a spare iPhone charger? Did he want to see me again, tonight? Was he heading down here

301

with—surely not—any amorous intention, and then I burst into tears? If so, why just up and go, later? No. That's the cocktails telling me flattering lies.

I imagine relaying what he said about a reconciliation never being off the cards, to Susie. I picture her picking at her sleeve, face set in grumpy consternation, except the pout and the frown not for comic effect this time. She'd resent being asked to feel something that wasn't ire, I think. The hurt and sadness would make a fleeting appearance.

Believe it when I see it, Eve.

Then she'd change the subject.

33

The morning after the night before, and I'm apprehensive at seeing Finlay. Following any awkward encounter, nothing's as hard as the second your eyes meet, before the hello, and you give away everything in the discomfort of your expression.

Will he get all "American therapist" and discuss it? I hope not. I want the British version: squash it into the glove box, so to speak, and never mention it again. Finlay Hart dolefully explaining to me why I'm not someone he wants to kiss—even in glorious splendor, after smoked old-fashioneds, with no strings, when someone else will be washing the sheets and we'll be on different landmasses within a week—really isn't a clarification I want or require.

Time ticks past in the lobby and my edginess increases: is he trying to make an alpha male point by keeping me waiting? When it's almost half nine, I decide something is up and call his mobile. It rings out. I ask reception to contact him in the room.

"I'm sorry, madam, I'm getting no reply," says the brightly lipsticked woman in the pussy-bow blouse.

I check my watch. 9.35 a.m. Did I get the time wrong? That still doesn't explain the lack of response. Did he get a tip on his missing father and rush out at dawn? But why not answer his mobile, if so? Or message me? I conclude there's nothing left for it but to go up there myself, hammer on the door, and see if he's fallen asleep or something.

I cross the lobby, catch the lift empty. Seconds later, the doors slide open on the third floor with a ping, and I follow the arrows to the correct section of the rabbit warren of corridors to find 312.

I turn a corner and almost bark out loud at the sight confronting me. Which is Fin Hart, back against the door of his room, naked but for a scrap of towel being held taut across his groin to protect his modesty. The cotton covers the essentials but stops short of his bare hip, making it clear he's got nothing else on. I realize the rest of the towel is on the other side of the door, leaving Finlay with these half measures.

"Eve!" he shouts and holds up a palm like he's stopping traffic.

"What on earth?!" I turn my eyes upward and shield them with a hand. "And good morning to you, sir!"

"Someone knocked at the door when I'd got out of the shower, I answered it, there was no one here. I got my towel trapped in the door and it locked shut on me!"

"That's called knock down ginger," I say. "Knock down definitely NOT ginger it seems, hahaha."

"Har fucking har. Please can you get another key card from reception so I can open this bloody door?"

"OK, will do. First, I have something to say, and I'm about

to make eye contact—my gaze strictly staying at head level again. Are you ready?"

"Where else would you make eye contact other than at head level, fuck's sake?"

"Hahaha. Well now you're asking."

I risk a glance at Finlay's furious, blushing face. He must still go to the gym as I've not seen a chest like that anywhere except in magazines bought by Justin.

"What was it you want to say?"

"Do you want my coat?" I say, tweaking at the red fur hood.

"No, I do fucking not! Key card, now!" Fin says and I guffaw. The more indignant he gets, the funnier this *Carry On and Don't Try to Glimpse My Willy* skit gets.

"If you say so, it was a generous offer. It'd be me landed with the dry-cleaning bill if you rubbed your goolies on it," I say, hooting as I turn and retreat the way I came.

I snigger all the way down in the lift, across the lobby, and even when I'm asking for another key card, and explaining the contretemps.

"We can send a staff member to open it," says the lipstick woman, dubious about casually running off spare room key cards.

"I think it had better be me, or he'll go off on one about his privacy. Seriously, please don't get me in that much trouble," I plead.

After a short negotiation where she needs to be reassured that Fin and I checked in together by tapping on keyboards and calling up records, and I'm safe to be given access to his room, she produces an envelope with a card.

I head back up again, still smiling.

"Where did you go for it, fucking Delhi?!" Fin shrieks as I round the corner and I collapse, bent double laughing.

"Stop being angry while naked, it's too funny, ahahahhaa." I pass the card to him and Fin snatches it with his free hand.

"This is going to be a dance of the veils, eh," I say, as I realize Fin's got to somehow twist around to use the card while staying behind his towel. And when he opens the door, the towel will drop?

"Yes, which is why you're going to turn around, please," Fin says.

"We are all naked under our clothes, nothing to be ashamed of." I mock sigh, while turning my back.

A moment later, I hear a small commotion, swearing, and a female shriek behind me, and turn to see two sixty-something women clutching each other. There's a fraction of a second's blur of pink, as an unclothed Fin disappears into the room and the door slams shut behind him.

"That was an unexpected treat!" whoops one of the women. "Better than dress circle seats at *Mamma Mia!*"

"What a lucky girl you are," says the other.

WE DRIVE TO Leith in a terse mostly silence with the radio blaring Pulp. It's a shame it's "Do You Remember the First Time?" as it immediately feels like discomfiting commentary. Nevertheless I suspect Fin and I are in the kind of atmosphere where anything other than "Hi Ho Silver Lining" would seem loaded with subtext. Probably even that.

We park up and Finlay's phone points us to his uncle's old

place, a five-minute walk. It's much smaller than the family home, a simple, boxy but appealing stone two-bed terrace. It reminds me of my house.

I comment on the disparity with the last property.

"Yeah. Remember my grandad's addictive personality? Uncle Don had it worse, and with less money to squander," Fin says. "Horses were his thing. Leith's taken off since he bought here so his house probably shot up in value."

"He didn't marry? Or have kids?"

"No, used to say he couldn't afford to. He was probably right."

We've knocked the brass knocker on the mint-green peeling door but the occupants of Uncle Don's former residence either aren't home or don't want to speak to us.

"What did he and your dad fall out over?" I ask, as we walk back to the main street.

"Money. My grandad predeceased my grandma, and there was an almighty ruck between the siblings about which care home she should go into and whether she even should go into a care home. Don inevitably had a very keen eye on what he expected from my grandad's estate and was in favor of my gran going budget. The siblings always seemed a tinder box, to be honest. I don't remember being surprised when we stopped coming up to Edinburgh in the school holidays."

We wander down the quayside and I ooh and aah at the interesting-looking independent shops and trendy places to eat and drink. Finlay walks with hands thrust in his coat pockets, engaging with me only when he's prompted. A drizzling rain starts, and I put my hood up.

"Are you in a mood with me?" I say, from under a halo of blood-red fluff, after the fifth or sixth failure of an observation to spark conversation.

"No."

"You're very quiet?"

"Maybe, all things considered today, I'm not feeling noisy."

"All things considered today?"

"Oh, I don't know, Eve, of all the things I could mean today. I wonder?"

"TowelGate?!" I say.

Finlay glowers at me.

"That's hardly worth sulking over!" I say.

He really cares about that? He was a model, aren't they always waving it at anyone and everyone?

"I'm not sulking, I'm just not in a high-spirited, chatty mood. If you had flashed me this morning, how would you feel?"

"Er . . ." I pause. "Embarrassed, I guess . . . but I'd—"

"There you go. Embarrassed."

"OK. I didn't think you'd be embarrassed."

"Of course you didn't, because you don't think I have normal emotions."

"I do." I frown.

"You don't. You think I'm some sort of Cyborg war machine, sent from the past to attack my sister."

"Is that a reference to *Terminator*?"

"Obviously."

"He was sent from the future. He was naked when he arrived though so . . ."

I grin and Fin slow-claps, with his leather-gloved hands. "Thanks."

"But why would you care?"

"I'm SHY," Fin exclaims. "I'm a shy person, OK? About a lot of things. Why is that difficult for you to grasp?"

"I didn't realize."

"Evidently."

Am I not allowed to be shy too, given last night featured a reasonably clear rejection of a fairly obvious advance?

"Let's talk about embarrassment, shall we," I say, about to vindicate but also embarrass myself, but needs must, can't make an omelet without breaking an egg. "You're acting like this is such a big deal, I didn't even see your nob, not so much as stray pubic area . . ."

I pause as the question about whether I said that too loud is answered by a couple of bundled-up passersby, who are boggling. Fin is studying the middle distance in a silently furious way.

"I saw, like, two inches of your very important VIP hip—"

"VIP means 'very important person' so that doesn't even make sense," Fin mutters, and I ignore him.

"And none of it was my fault. What about the fact that last night, we—"

I'm interrupted, mercifully, by the sound of Finlay's phone ringing.

"Hi, Ann?" he says. He walks a short distance, just out of earshot, to hold the conversation.

I kick my heels until Fin rings off.

"That was Ann, Dad's cleaner. My dad's been in touch with her. She couldn't get him to be precise about where he's staying but he says he's been to see my aunt Tricia."

"Your auntie? You never said you had an aunt up here?"

"That's because I don't, really."

"What does that mean?"

I'm really starting to tire of Hart family riddles.

"She fell out with my dad years ago. When Susie and I were teenagers. A couple of years before my uncle did."

"Your family is one long string of fallings-out, huh?"

"Tell me about it."

"But your dad's been 'round?"

"Apparently so. Which means she must be still at the same house."

"Why do I have a horrible feeling this is going to turn into a *let's call on the auntie who hates us* outing?" I say.

Fin grimaces. "She might have softened with age. Sounds like she let my dad across the threshold. And he might've told her where he's staying. So . . ."

I raise my shoulders and drop them.

"Sounds like we should go see her," I say, pulling a face.

"Look, I'll level with you—yes, Auntie Trish is fairly terrifying. But I think she'd like you. She liked Susie. She'd think you also have a thing she calls 'moxie.' If you wanted to be your most charming self, she *might* give up my dad's whereabouts to you. Let her believe she's got you onside, whatever she says to me."

"You want me to be an iridescent beast," I say, without thinking.

"A *what?*" Fin says.

"Oh, sorry. A private joke I had with Susie. I had a fixation with F. Scott Fitzgerald's wife, Zelda, when we were in sixth form. I read this story about Zelda being a wayward Southern Belle socialite at a party. It said she was at her 'iridescent best' and I misread it as her being an 'iridescent beast.' So Susie and I used to say, whenever we were going all out to impress in a situation, that we were going to be iridescent beasts."

Fin shakes his head in a *if you say so* way.

"Riiiight. Yes, please be an iridescent beast, Evelyn."

34

Finlay cranes his neck over the headrest to reverse park while the car's sensors go blip-blip-blip. The sweeping curve of Georgian crescent with its luxuriant, rain-soaked mature trees is a strikingly elegant address and I feel a commensurate foreboding about what we're walking into. I don't think you bullshit and bluster your way past the kind of individuals who dwell behind these glossed doors, in their giant tax brackets.

Our conversation on the way here has done nothing to allay my fears.

"Just *how* bitter was the falling-out?"

"Put it this way. Last we heard she was having a pacemaker fitted. My dad said: 'I hope her surgeon has shaky hands.'"

"Oof. Whenever I'd say about someone, 'I wouldn't wish that on my worst enemy,' Susie used to say, 'I fucking would, that's why they're my worst enemy.'"

"Hah. Sounds Susie-esque. She and my father had quite a lot in common in outlook."

"Do you think your dad remembers he and his sister had fought?"

"No idea. We're about to find out."

Fin rings the bell on the canary-yellow door in the town-house, which, unlike the last door we stood in front of, is in perfect condition. The tall edifice feels like a personification of Aunt Tricia, bearing down on me. We hear footsteps beyond and the door's thrown open by a woman with close-cropped silver hair. She's in the semiofficial uniform of middle class, "liberal arts college" women over sixty: outsize coral and turquoise Tibetan-style necklace, neutral floaty jersey top with draped jersey cardigan, wide linen trousers.

"Well well," she says, in a silver-spoon kind of English accent, folding her arms. "Après the father, le déluge! Why would you be moved to call on me, after all this time, Finlay? It *is* Finlay, isn't it? You were in an under-fifteens football uniform, last I saw you."

"Yes. Hi, Aunt Tricia," he says. "I'll explain. This is my friend, Eve. Susie's best friend, to be strictly accurate."

"Wonderful to meet you," she says, brusquely, with a quick appraising stare at me, pushing reading glasses up the bridge of her nose. "What's that got to do with me?"

"We're looking for my father. We'd heard he'd been to see you and wondered if he'd said where he was staying in Edinburgh?"

"So you thought you'd simply turn up on my doorstep, after . . . let's see. How many years is it?"

"Twenty?"

"Twenty-two, but who's counting? Apart from me. Why not call first?"

"I didn't have a number for you."

"I'm sure I'm in the phonebook."

"Sorry, it just didn't seem a conversation to have on the phone."

A moment develops, where our welcome hangs in the balance.

"Come in, then," she says, with an exasperated sigh, and I wilt in disappointment that we're getting an audience with her. I'd hoped, once she demonstrated her hostility, that this was going to be bloody but brief.

We follow her down a hallway painted with so much brilliant white it's like stepping into a modern art gallery. The floor is treacle brown and there are moth orchids in glass jars with pebbles on a dark side table. In the high-ceilinged sitting room beyond, everything is again white, apart from two squashy linen-covered sofas, a royal purple. There's virtually nothing else in the room, bar a wicker basket full of logs for the open fireplace, and a huge floor standing lamp, its bowl-shaped shade a bright chrome.

I have only known Auntie Tricia forty seconds to judge, yet the house already seems a convincing expression of its owner. Blinding migraine-inducing blankness, punctuated by furniture that shouts at you. We're not offered a drink.

"Terrible business about your sister," Tricia says, though without much sympathy.

"Awful."

"I spoke to Susie a few years ago. After your mother died."

"Right."

"She said you hadn't bothered to visit when your mum was sick."

I glance worriedly at Finlay, who doesn't flicker.

"That's not quite true."

314

Tricia snorts. "Oh, come on, Finlay. Susie said you didn't make the trip until the funeral."

"It wasn't that I didn't bother, I didn't know she was ill. Maybe Susie didn't know what my parents had or hadn't told me, but I didn't find out about my mum's terminal diagnosis until two months after she'd been given it. Why would I lie?"

"Oh, er . . . let me see. To not look like a heartless brute in front of a pretty girl?" She gestures at me. "You're saying your sister wouldn't have lifted the phone and talked to you, when your mother was dying?"

"As I say, I don't know what Susie thought I knew," Fin says. "Perhaps she thought I was ignoring her. But no, she wouldn't. She and I weren't close."

"*Indeed*. Now you're haring after your father, from whom you are similarly estranged. Why?"

"I don't think he's safe to be traveling alone, and I want to get him assessed for care home living before I go back to the States."

"Do you," Tricia says, crossing her legs. "*Do you?* The house would be sold in this scenario, would it?"

I shift in my seat.

"I guess so. What state was he in when he came to see you?"

"He seemed with it for the first few minutes, and it slowly dawns he's quite gaga. He thinks he and I are still young."

"Yes, that's it. He's present when it comes to practicalities that are in front of him, but in terms of his . . . broader mental architecture, it's like he's lost twenty years."

Fin pauses. "Did he say where he was staying?"

"I wish I could trust your intentions, Fin. I really do," Tricia says, picking away imaginary lint on her knees.

"How does this judgment upon me work, exactly?" Fin says, frowning now. "You had a feud with my father, you cut my family off. But you still blame me for not getting along with them? I'm guilty of exactly the same thing you are?"

"I couldn't tolerate your father. I had no argument with your mother and sister. But unfortunately for you, I still have insights into what you put your parents and sister through."

Fin runs a hand through his hair and looks like he's concentrating efforts on keeping his temper.

"You didn't care about your parents. That's a fact, I'm afraid. Now that you're the only one left, if you're insisting on organizing your father's life, I do wonder if this is about your father's will."

Fin goes murderously pale. "It isn't, but it doesn't look like my word is worth anything."

I remember my mission. "Please excuse me, I don't know any detail of the historic family conflicts, Susie never told me about them . . . and neither has he . . ." I gesture vaguely at Fin. "I'm definitely not in any will, nor do I want to be. But if we don't find Mr. Hart and make sure he's OK, he could come to all sorts of harm wandering around a big city in his condition. I know Susie would want me to get him home. That's the only reason why I'm here."

"Good cop, bad cop, is it?" Trish says.

"I'm not a cop," I say, somewhat stupidly. *And I don't understand metaphors!* "Of any kind. Every word of that is the truth. I only want what's best for Mr. Hart's welfare."

Tricia looks at me with pursed lips and I assume I'm going to get hosed with scorn too. I'm taken aback when she mutters, with reluctance: "He said he was staying at a hotel, the name escapes me, that's the truth. Give me your number and, if it comes back to me, I'll let you know."

She's speaking specifically to me. She gets up, roots around in a drawer, and hands me a pen and pad.

I print my number on it carefully as Finlay gets up to leave. As I move to follow him, Tricia discreetly catches my arm. Finlay disappears out into the hallway, and she's still holding me back, with a steely grip.

"Do *not* trust him," she hisses, releasing her grasp. "I mean it. If you have anything about you at all you'll run as fast as you can in the opposite direction away from that boy."

"Why?" I say, quaking a little.

"He destroyed that family. I saw what happened. He's poison. Even his parents said so. *Poison.*"

"OK . . . Why? I mean, why would he treat them like that?"

"Some people are just born bad," Tricia says. "I don't doubt he's talked a good game to you, and he's got the looks. But looks can be deceiving."

"Right."

She shakes her head at me, with a sour expression. I read it as *you won't listen to me, I'm sure.*

My mind is racing and my heart hammering as I walk to the car, its engine running in its parking spot. I'd been so dismissive of Ed and his concerns, but right at this juncture, I take it back. I came here as Finlay's guest, and I gave away a large degree of my power in doing so. I did it, not knowing who I was ceding that power to. What if I really have been colluding with something—or someone—sinister? He doesn't seem that way, but perhaps what I'm feeling is the arrogance of anyone who thinks their powers of detection can't be bypassed. We all think our internal security systems are foolproof, until they're not. Everyone thinks they know when they're being lied to. I didn't spot it when Susie did. Have I missed it with Finlay too?

"What did my aunt say to you then?" Fin asks, as I swing my legs into the footwell.

"Not to trust you," I say, putting my seat belt on, hoping my hands aren't betraying the volume of adrenaline washing around my system.

"I did warn you she's venomous."

"*Is* she?" I say, turning to Fin, nerves breaking the surface. "What was that stuff about your mum?"

"Bollocks?"

"I don't know anyone else that's followed around by so much bollocks."

"Lucky them."

"Or accused by their nearest and dearest too."

"She's not near or a dear."

"Who *is* a loved one?"

Who gets through thirty-six years of life without a single good character reference?

Fin's jaw flexes.

"As I said. In my family, I'm the Spanish flu."

"Here's the thing about the Spanish flu, Fin—it still killed millions of people."

"Let me get this straight, did the woman we met there strike you as a reliable narrator? Is she someone you'd ever pick to testify in your defense?"

"No, obviously. But . . ."

"But, what?"

"She warned me against being around you, in the direst terms."

"You're not going to be for much longer."

Finlay looks back out the windshield and I have an odd sense that I've hurt his feelings. I expected anger, or contempt, or even threat—not to wound him. I didn't think he could be wounded. Or, is this an act?

There's a loud rap on the driver's side window that makes us both jump out of our skin.

It's Aunt Trish. Fin electronically lowers the glass with a *zeeeeeep.*

"The Waldorf," she says. "It's come back to me. The Waldorf, up on Princes Street."

"Thank you," Fin says, but Tricia's already turned to walk back into the house.

35

At least wondering about how on earth Mr. Hart was staying at the same hotel as us is a diversion from dwelling on Auntie Tricia's verbal IEDs.

I don't know quite why she's frightened me so much, when it's nothing Susie didn't say already, using more expletives, over pints in The Gladdy. I think it must be due to growing closer to Fin. Before, he was a folklore take, a changeling, the goblin swapped for the real baby son in the crib, who they then raised by mistake. Not the man at the wheel of a rented Mercedes at this very second, a man who I might have been stupidly growing fond of, and yes, even crushing on. I had predicted that when the old version of Finlay resurfaced it would be jarring. Is that this?

But, Aunt Tricia was so sure. No one would be that excoriating of a nephew without cause, would they? Was it true his mother didn't tell him she was dying, and Susie didn't contact him either? That's such a huge accusation and the women who could contradict or explain it are dead. His father is incapable.

I scour my memory banks for a Susie reference to Tricia, and can only recall something about "a right pterodactyl," but her aunt had fallen out with her father too so it's not necessarily an endorsement of Fin's opinion.

"If my dad is staying at The Waldorf, of course," Fin is saying as I zone back in, checking his mirror at the lights, "he may have been shaky on the detail."

"His sense of direction seems completely sound though."

"True."

"My man on reception was going to warn me if he appeared!" I say, for the sake of something to say.

"Except your friend was one of at least five working the desk, on that shift alone. We had a one-in-five chance. Depending on the shift."

"True."

We pull up and Fin hands the keys over and he nods at the revolving door to indicate *you first*. For the first time in this trip, the tension feels as if it's between us, no longer about its objective.

"Where should we start?" I say to Fin, as we survey the lobby, and Fin says, "Right there."

Mr. Hart is ten paces away in his coat, packed bag at his feet.

There's no time to wonder if and how to introduce myself, as his face breaks into the warmth of instant recognition.

"Eve?! Goodness, what are you doing here?" he says, face wreathed in smiles.

It's a sad irony that he's losing his mind but physically he's worn so well. He's so little changed from the Central Casting, tall, responsible Mary Poppins father of my childhood memories. "And your young fellow," he says, acknowledging a mute Finlay.

"Uhm . . . I'm Christmas shopping!" I say, off the top of my head. "You?"

"Came for a trip to see family, but I'm checking out now."

"You saw your brother?" I ask, stupidly.

"Yes, my brother and my sister are here. Couldn't raise my brother at all, he seems to be away."

"Ah . . . How was your sister?"

"Oh, same old, same old. What was that line from *Frasier*? You'd get more warmth from a wedding buffet's ice sculpture. Patricia could certainly keep the shrimp cold."

I laugh, as much in surprise as mirth—his having Tricia's number and remembering lines from old sitcoms. This is also the Mr. Hart I remember—shaking out his paper and making affectionately acerbic remarks to Susie and me as we disappeared out the door, up to no good.

"Now you're back down to Nottingham?" I say.

"Yes, yes, I am . . ." He checks his watch. "If I get a clear run I think I'll be back by tea time."

"Oh. What a coincidence, so are we?" I say to Finlay, who nods. We'd expected to have to do some persuasion; we'd thought we'd be ahead of Mr. Hart in this whole Edinburgh encounter game plan, and the reversal has left both of us gawping.

"Race you!" Mr. Hart says, in jolly fashion. "Ah, thank you!" he adds, as Waldorf staff appear.

"Drive safely!" I say, and watch uselessly as a white-gloved doorman signals he has his car keys. I look to Finlay for objection or confirmation and he raises, and drops, his shoulders.

"Well, 'Visit Scotland, Operation Recover Iain Hart' was a thunderous success?" Fin says, as we watch his dad head for the revolving door. "I dread to think what would've happened without us being here."

"Should we try to stop him?" I say.

Finlay shrugs. "He's got a valid driving license and the wish to go, and how are we getting his car back anyway? The main aim was to get him home again in one piece and having not signed up to any pyramid schemes. As far as we know, that's going to be the case."

The detachment in his tone tells me that the Finlay Hart who told me I could boss my life if I wanted, and showed me old photos on his phone, he's gone, at least for now. The shutters have come down again. I took Tricia's side by doubting him, it seems.

"I guess so."

There's a literary word for what I'm feeling: bathos. Anti-climax. This is the end of our pursuit, but it doesn't feel the way it was meant to. Did I want a struggle, a sense I'd saved Mr. Hart from harm? No, thinking it through, of course I didn't.

"Can you pack fast, and meet back here in fifteen minutes?"

"Yes," I say.

"OK, you go ahead, and I'll check us out."

As I get the lift up to my room, I should feel lighter.

Instead my stomach has a stone in it, a rock, like a dragging weight.

I keep hearing that word, over and over again. Almost like a taunt, asking me if I'm going to believe it or not. Asking what I'm going to do with it.

I jab the button for the first floor.

Nothing. I'm going to do nothing with it, because I'm hours away from never having to see Finlay Hart again in my whole life, and this is a puzzle I will never solve. I feel sure Susie took the last pieces to her grave. The lift pings, first floor.

Poison.

THE MOOD ON the journey back to England is suitably subdued. We don't have to meet each other's eyes, and we have a shared purpose, at least. I fiddle with the radio, or the air con, and Finlay makes the occasional banal remark regarding the traffic, and all in all, the satnav probably says as much as either of us.

"I feel ridiculous at having dragged you all this way for a two-minute chat with my dad," Finlay says abruptly, as we pass Leicester, and I know what he also means is: you saw all that dirty washing, and for what?

I recall how much he hated me being in the family home, that week before Susie's funeral. Trips to nice restaurants were making a virtue of necessity.

"Honestly, it's fine," I say. "I don't have tons of amazing uses for my holiday allocation from City Nights anyway. Change is as good as a rest, as they say."

"I don't think when they said 'change' the meaning was so elastic as to encompass getting a full-bore blast of my dysfunctional family," he says, with a grimace.

Oh, he's still dwelling on the aunt encounter the way I am too. That has to rate as one of the strangest fifteen minutes of my life.

"Think you'll stay at . . . what's it called? City Nights?" Fin says.

"I will for now, I have a mortgage and a cat to raise. It's more whether City Nights will stay at me. There aren't many ways to make a living from typing snappy things these days, are there?"

"What would you like to do? What's your dream job? Writing, presumably?"

"Yeah, you know those Long Reads in the *NYT*, or like they used to have in *Vanity Fair*? Thousands of words, really brilliantly written, and the journalist got months to research the subject. You know, like old Hollywood scandals involving the Pickfair Mansion, or some true crime investigation thing. The sort that ends up getting turned into a book. Like the one about the Golden State Killer."

"You've got a sunny nature, eh?" Finlay says.

"Well, there are Cure songs about me," I say and then regret it.

Fin looks gratified, but pinkens slightly. I wonder if he wishes he'd not told me that. I wonder what he's said and done out of spontaneity. I wonder where all that *do you ever wish you could drop the act* conversation came from.

"Seriously, yes, I do know what you mean," he says. "About the writing. That sounds really good. So how do you get into that, then?"

"I have no idea," I say. "Plus, you'd need a time machine for a golden age of print media and proper budgets."

"I have uses for that time machine," Fin says. "Does it seat two?"

"I'm not sure I'd trust what you'd do with it," I say, and smile, to defuse any insult.

"I'm not sure I trust what I'd do with it."

A meaningful silence ensues. I feel I have to break it, especially given this is likely the last time I'll ever see Susie's brother.

"We'd both head back and tell Susie to look the other bloody way though, right?" I say, bluntly, the pain of this thought making me graceless.

"Yes," Finlay says, throwing me a glance. "We both would."

After another brief silence he says: "Thank you."

"What for?"

"Assuming I didn't want my sister to die."

"That's . . . obvious, isn't it?"

"The relative of mine we met, prior to my father, would beg to differ," Fin says, as he adjusts his grip on the steering wheel, and narrows his eyes at the road. He made such a good model in that picture because of his ability to turn into a hardened blank. You never know what he's thinking.

"She accused you of neglect but she wouldn't think you'd want Susie to . . . ?" It's such a grotesque idea, I can't finish the sentence.

"Yes, the bar's really that low," Fin says, voice thick. "I thought this was the basis of our conversation afterward. *The Spanish flu still killed millions of people.*" He takes his sight line off the road to give a wry smirk as he says this.

I begin to heat at my words in emotion being repeated back to me, out of context.

"That was your analogy, I didn't mean you were literally capable of murder! I've never thought for a moment you wished harm to Susie," I say, glad this at least is true, if not the "Finlay Hart's a killer" insinuations, made in coffee shops, only half in jest, and only a few short weeks ago. I was privately likening him to an assassin on the drive up here. "That's mad."

Fin glances and smiles, sadly. "As I say, sorry to expose you to my family," he says, diplomatically drawing a line, as he changes lanes.

I feel a twinge of complicated affection, and a distinct sensation of regret.

"Can I ask something, personal?" I say quietly. "Tell me none of my business, usual rules apply."

"Yes," Fin says, eyes still on the road.

"Why did your mum not tell you she was dying?"

There's a dreadful pause where I worry this is a terrible thing to have asked.

". . . Because I was the last person she wanted to see with the time she had left, I guess," Fin says. "Quite literally, as I was only informed when she'd been moved to the hospice. I was so angry and hurt, I waited a week before I flew over. And then she'd gone. My aunt was right. What Susie said was true. I only came over for the funeral."

I risk a quick glance at him and, for a split second, his eyes shimmer with what I think could be tears, but in one blink, they're gone.

"Sorry," I say quietly, and insufficiently. I want to ask *But why didn't she care about you?* but that is too great a question to level, if an explanation's not being offered.

I now know why there was such an emptiness to Mr. Hart turning up—he was the point of our mission, yet he ended up feeling like an interruption. I was unraveling something, and the process came to an abrupt halt. I'll spend the rest of my life wondering what was behind the screens with Finlay.

Count yourself lucky then.

For the first time, I'm irritated by the interjection of imaginary Susie. I want to challenge her—I can't fit her Fin together with this Fin. There's something missing in this story, and I'm going to commit to an opinion: I don't think it's his heart.

"This you?" Fin says, as the car rolls along my street, toward my house.

"Yeah, this is me," I say, in resignation. He pulls up, turns the engine off and for a second I think he's going to say something, but he's snapping his belt out of the lock so he can get out of the car, handing me my bag from the trunk.

"Thanks for your help," Fin says, after he slams the lid shut again.

"I didn't, did I? Sorry about that."

"You really did."

"Thank you."

"Take care of yourself, Eve. And if you're ever in Brooklyn and need a place to stay . . ."

"Ditto, Carrington," I say, motioning toward my house, and we both laugh.

"Careful, might take you up on that," Fin says, and I hope my expression stays steady and neutral as he looks at me from under his brow.

I put my hand out for him to shake, as much to find a moment to end on as anything. Fin looks at it, takes it, uses it to draw me into a quick, hard hug. I can't put my other arm around him due to my luggage, so I submit by pressing my face into his shirt. He smells indecently fragrant for someone who's been driving for five hours, I think. Why is he grateful to me? Ostensibly it's good manners, but I know in my guts and bones that it's more than that. Is it because getting along with Susie's best friend is the closest he'll come to reconciling with his sister?

He leaves without another word, or a look back, and I'll never know the answer.

36

Edinburgh's awkward timings mean I return to work on a Wednesday, like no one, ever, and have to act like that was the plan, without discussing what "the plan" might be.

"I thought you weren't back until next week!" Lucy says, innocently and inconveniently. Fortunately, my mumbling "We got the hotel deal on Wowcher, so we couldn't pick the dates" seems to do the trick.

"Which hotel?" says Lucy.

". . . The Waldorf."

"Fuck my boots, The *Waldorf*'s on budget deals?" says Phil.

Phil's beadily meerkatting at me over his monitor, which is edged with tinsel, and, from oversize trouser belt up, he's in a joke shop costume as an elf. As soon as the calendar hits December, Phil—in strange defiance of his otherwise ultra-curmudgeon persona—embraces every piece of comedy seasonal rubbish available and insists on a drum of Quality Street candy on the go at all times.

"Airbnb must've really impacted the industry," I say, with a faux wise professor nod.

"Go with a boyfriend?" Phil says.

"No, a friend."

"Not sure I'd waste The Waldorf at Christmas on a girl-friend," Lucy says. "Could be just as pissed sleeping in a Trav-elodge, and spend the money on shoes."

"It wasn't a girlfriend, Lucy," Seth says, throwing me a grin. "He's just not a boyfriend, am I right?"

"Oh, well deduced," Phil says, looking from one of us to the other. "Don't take us for fools, Harris!"

"Phil, you're wearing a striped hat with a bell on the end, a large pair of pointed rubber ears, and a top that reads I'm SHINNY UPPATREE."

I open today's screen.

TEQUILA! It makes you happy. Or it makes you very sick. No in between with tequila, is there?

New margarita-making classes with the "Marg Masters"

My God, it's stultifying. So much so that I Google *creative writing courses* in my lunch break and try to pretend I'm still on holiday at night, ordering Indian takeaway and fighting a losing battle to keep Roger's nose out of foil trays of curried chickpeas.

I vacillate about messaging Fin about how his dad is, but everything I draft feels awkward, contrived, and not much of my business.

It's strange: it's as if the trip up north blew fresh air into my life, and I have heightened awareness of how stuffy its rooms are, now. Finlay Hart may have all kinds of faults, but failure to move forward isn't one of them. Even my home feels like it has lower ceilings. Maybe that's the inevitable effect of The Waldorf.

At Friday's end, I walk down the hill from the office to the train station, dragging my suitcase and laboring with a bulging shopping bag, thanks to a midafternoon WhatsApp from Justin, regards the birthday cottage logistics:

EEEEEEV! Can't wait to see you later. If possible can you bring a large corn-fed chicken, long matches, slimline tonic (guess who's been put on a wedding diet? Clue: not the bride) and two pints of double cream? LOVE YOU ETCETERA. xxx

I have to get a rush-hour train to Derby and then stand shivering waiting for a taxi to take me to the cottage in the middle of nowhere. I'm bad at judging distance and I didn't think to Uber, so the local minicab costs me a ton of cash and takes forty-five minutes.

By the time we pull up in a squelch of mud outside a horse fence gate, I'm starving, and silently cursing Justin for not going to Pizza Express for his birthday like a normal person. I could be pleasantly mullered on the house white and full of doughballs right now. Justin had warned me they'd probably eat before I got there, due to due to the relative lateness of my arrival, which was just as well, given I was catastrophically late in the end.

The cottage is four hundred years old according to Justin, and accessed down a perilous slope after you've unlatched the gate and relatched the gate—and why the hell is there no outside light?!

"Fucking knackers!" I shout, as I trip over and mud-slide down to the door, sledging on my arse.

"Hark! I know the sound of a Cheltenham Ladies' College alumna when I hear one . . ." A burst of light has appeared in the pitch black beyond (I always forget how proper dark the countryside is) and Justin is framed within it, wearing a bobble hat and holding a large glass of red. "It's a bit *Withnail and I*, innit? Welcome to Crow Crag! Calm down, Leonard, it's only Eve!" he says, at an as yet unseen but audibly excitable canine.

"You best be pouring me one of those, right the fuck now," I say.

I struggle in the door, kick off my filthy shoes, peel away my coat, and hand the heavy shopping bag to Justin.

"Oh, you darling. Charles and Diana are through there, you'll see wine bottle and glass in the kitchen on your way. Follow the handbag-size dog."

I lean down to pet the bouncing Leonard. The beams of the cottage are so low I have to duck to pass through doorways. In the front room Ed and Hester look up at me, resembling a Boden picture, side by side, in their chunky jumpers and crackling firelight glow.

"Evening, Eve!" they singsong, as Leonard resumes his place on a chair nearby. I toast them with my glass. I'm relieved the fight at the wake is long enough ago we can simply pretend it never happened. Ed flashes me a slightly discomfited look, and I smile to assure him things are normal. As normal as they can be.

Justin brings me a plate of stew and mash, and I'm asked for a summary of Edinburgh between mouthfuls.

I keep it brief and positive.

"How was the brother, did he keep up the Nosferatu levels of affability?" Ed says.

"More of a Yes-feratu for me," Justin says.

I hadn't considered how to handle this very obvious line of inquiry. My mind has been on larger matters. Like recalling the way Finlay Hart looked down at me in a darkened hotel room.

"He was . . . fine, actually. I ended up quite liking him. I think he was on the defensive when we met him, because he knew we'd have a low opinion of him."

"We had a low opinion of him because Susie told us he was a total turboshit. Checkmate."

"Who do you think you're checkmating, me?" I say to Ed.

"Him, mainly."

"Well, I know him better."

"What, on the basis of a few days of going up Arthur's Seat, you're saying you know him better than his own sister did?" Ed scoffs.

"Maybe, in a way, yes, I do," I say, watching Ed's scowl of incredulity deepen.

"What?!" he spits.

"Do you know him better in the sense Susie never slept with him?" Justin says to me, pressing his hands together in prayer. "Did you, in fact, 'go up Arthur's Seat'? Please say you did, and bring me news from the wild erotic frontier. My love life is up on bricks, here."

"Sorry to disappoint, but no," I say, and avoid looking at Ed, and thus gauging his response or relief. This is a shift. I don't care if Ed cares? Ed caring has been my lode star for a long time. I test my feelings on this matter again . . . *he's jealous, don't you care?* Nope, nothing.

"Hahaha, she wouldn't tell us if she had, Justin," Hester says.

I look over at Hester and she's twirling a piece of golden hair by her ear, shapely legs crossed in black skinny jeans, her vivid mouth painted with her favorite Mac Lady Danger lipstick. Hester is so damn decorative.

In the sarcastic twitch of her crimson mouth, I can perfectly easily see that Hester hasn't forgiven me for the spat at Susie's wake, and instead a different level of enmity has been unlocked. *Challenge accepted.* In female fights, never trust the wishful interpretations of men.

Ed is frowning, knocking back wine.

"I would tell you. Why wouldn't I?" I say.

"Because everyone thinks he's awful." Hester shrugs a cable-knitted shoulder, unwinds, and sloshes some more wine into her glass.

"If I wanted to sleep with him I wouldn't care if you thought he was awful," I say, and as I speak, I can hear that the mood has plummeted from carefree chatter to loaded subtext, flying in every direction.

"If you say so," Hester mutters, plumping the sofa cushions with one hand before rearranging herself against them.

"Yes, I do say so," I say. "Given I know my decision-making process better than you do."

"You got that right," Hester mumbles, under her breath.

Justin looks disconcerted at this immediate descent into warfare.

Ed's still staring furiously ahead at the fire, chinning his wine down. I don't think he thinks I slept with Finlay, which must mean he's this mad at me merely approving of him. How much control of me does he think he's owed?

"Susie despised him," Ed says.

"You asked me for my opinion of him, not hers," I say, tone sharp as a dagger.

"Why would you think she'd got him wrong?"

"She wasn't right about everything," I say, staring levelly at Ed, and he senses danger, and says nothing in reply.

"Didn't she say he used to model?" Justin says, hastily, desperately.

"I thought he was a psychiatrist?" Hester says.

"He was a *what*?!" Ed says, delighted at being given a new line of attack, eyes dancing with a Satanic pleasure. "He's a model-slash-shrink. Tell me about your relationship with your . . ." Ed turns his head away, then snaps back with an exaggerated pout. ". . . *father*."

"He's a psychologist, and to be fair, seems like he's done brilliantly at it. He's not short of a few quid," I say, relinquishing my empty plate to Justin. "He treats some really famous people, so famous he couldn't tell me who they are."

"*Convenient*. Rich kids always prosper."

"By that logic, Susie was a rich kid."

"She was, but I don't think she denied it," Ed says.

"How has Finlay denied it?"

"He's going to be richer still when Dad goes. Ever find out whether there were shenanigans going on with changing his will?" Justin asks me.

"No," I say. I'm agnostic on that. I can't imagine Fin standing over dotty Mr. Hart, encouraging him to write his name on a dotted line, but equally a lot of things that have happened are things I couldn't have imagined.

"God, that poor old man," Ed says. "Lost his wife and daughter and his marbles, and the decision whether to switch off his machines one day will be made by *that* bloke."

"Dessert, Eve?" Justin says, in a *let's lighten the mood shall we* perky housewife voice. "It's spotted dick with pink custard."

"Are you kidding?" I say.

Leonard jumps down from his chair and starts barking.

"I'm not joking and nor is my greedy son."

ED AND HESTER turn in first, to the master bedroom with the en suite at the front of the cottage, enough of a distance we don't fear disturbing them by staying up.

Justin has carried a storm lantern to a picnic table outside in the freezing dark, where he can have a cigarette. He encouraged me to bundle in a coat and refilled my glass. "Ten minutes, max. It's my *birthday weekend*."

"This welcome is as warm as the one I got from Ed and Hester," I whisper, teeth chattering, petting Leonard, who makes plaintive noises and then goes back indoors.

"There's a bit of an atmosphere between those two," Justin says, voice quiet, blowing smoke from the side of his mouth. "Last night was all *'can you pass the salt, PLEASE.'* I get the feeling that planning a wedding in a few months flat is taking it out of them. I don't see why it has to be so fast? Hester's drinking plenty, so it's not *that*."

"Do you know about my fight with Hester at the wake?" Justin shakes his head. "Brace yourself . . ." I fill Justin in on it all, from the letter when we left for university that got lost with water damage, so long ago, to my seeing the Susie letter in the box of secrets the day before the funeral, about the Rock City shagging. "I know you knew, but I didn't know all of it," I say. I don't find this disclosure difficult, possibly due to practice with Finlay. For the first time, I truly and fully comprehend that I should've told Susie, and Justin, and even Ed how I felt, back when it mattered more. This information's eternal power source was in part in its unsaidness.

Hang on. Again, I test my feelings: imagining Ed and Susie wound around each other in a toilet stall, her long legs gripping him, his carnal grunting. Nope . . . nothing? An anthropological kind of curiosity, but no pain. Yes, I feel foolish for being protected from the truth, like some Mrs. Rochester fragile hysteric. But I don't feel that sensation of my stomach being scooped out by a doctor with cold hands. Maybe it's having had this much red wine.

"You didn't know about that? I thought we all knew but were never going to mention it again. The most macabre coupling since Steve Coogan and Courtney Love. Brrrr."

"No. Susie never told me as she thought I was in love with Ed."

"Were you?" Justin asks.

"Yes," I say.

"Are you?" he says.

". . . I don't know."

"Eesh, let me get an ashtray for this," Justin says, now a late-night deep-and-meaningful is getting going. "Why did I choose a no-smoking cottage? I prioritized WiFi. Ain't nobody needs that 'tranquil and peaceful haven, completely cut off from the world' shit."

"Surely they're all no smoking these days. Also didn't you just quit?"

"I took it back up the day Susie died."

Justin returns with a coffee mug receptacle and taps his cigarette into it.

"Let's dig into this Big Undiscussed. I thought it was mutual, and so did Susie," Justin says. "Susie and I used to say, *Why doesn't Ed tell her? Why doesn't he*"—Justin points upward—"*see which side his bread is buttered?*"

"Really?" This patches up my ego somewhat. "Why did you think we were in love? Was I that much of a transparent dickhead?"

"Hahaha." Justin takes a deep drag. "No, no one thing. The way you looked at each other, the sexual tension. Ed was absolutely obsessed with you in sixth form. Partly why I was so shook by him cuffing himself in our first year, I took it to be a rebound from missing out on you. And then . . . well. The rest is history. The rest is *Hestery*."

"Why didn't Susie say anything to me about it, ever?"

"I'm guessing because she thought it would've embarrassed you? And once she'd drunkenly diddled Ed, far too politically hairy. I mean, if I've done anything I'm ashamed of, I just avoid it like the plague, job done. Denial is a very underrated coping mechanism."

"I suppose so. Why do you think it happened? Ed and Susie, I mean."

"'Cause twenty-four-year-olds are horny? I dunno. I thought it was nailed on that Ed would end up with one or other of you at some point, from the day we met you. We all loved each other, and love can get messy and squirty."

I laugh. I wish I'd spoken to Justin about this sooner.

"Suze liked to know she could have anyone she wished, and Ed's not someone to reject female attention."

"Even though it hurt me?" I say, more of a statement than a question. "I know I had no rights over him. It's not upset or anger anymore; it's only not understanding why."

"Hmmm yeah, but Suze had a ruthless streak," Justin says. I look at his bloodshot eyes by candlelight. "I do too. We recognized it in each other. I want to remember her how she really was, and how she really was had its less beautiful parts."

I nod, and think about Finlay's idea that Susie was trespassing, in order to investigate. That our key differential was my being permanently hopelessly in love, and Susie not knowing what being in love felt like.

I thought losing Susie, and then finding this secret out, meant I'd never have an answer for why she slept with Ed. In my gut, I feel I have a fuller answer in Finlay's insight than I would have ever had from Susie.

I look at the ink-black of the hills around us, relieved only by the odd tile of yellow illumination in neighboring houses. I surprise myself with a distinct pang of missing Finlay Hart. Gazing at that forbiddingly handsome, closed face and wondering what he was going to say next. What was going on behind his eyes. Missing Finlay Hart, how strange is that?

I hear Susie say: *pervert*.

"I wanted to ask you if you approve of something," Justin says. "I'm going to get back in touch with Francis."

"Your ex, Francis?"

"Yeah. I've had a revelation. He was great, and I treated him like shit."

"OK."

"I wasn't ready to be someone's boyfriend. I am now. But I don't know if crawling back a year later and saying I'm older, wiser, and bereaved isn't the most monumental piss-take of someone who was capable of being a fully rounded human being by age thirty. Who had to listen to me say I simply hadn't slept with enough people to be settling down."

"Only one way to find out. Don't let your pride matter more than a shot at love," I say.

"It isn't an outrageous approach to make? The very premise isn't offensive?"

"Not to me, but that's for Francis to decide."

Justin nods.

We both startle at the door opening behind us and Ed in a dressing gown, putting his head around the door. I assume we're going to get a telling-off for making too much noise.

"Aren't you two freezing?"

"We're coming back in now, my nicotine urge sated," Justin says. "Did we wake you?"

"No, couldn't sleep," he says.

I carry the storm lantern back to the kitchen table and Justin pours out whiskies.

"I'll finish my wine, thanks," I say, holding a palm up. I didn't get to age thirty-four without knowing the law of group holidays and all hen dos—everyone completely canes it on the first night and is at reduced capacity for the rest of the trip.

"You two burning the midnight oil, then?" Ed says.

"Lots of sorrows to drown, one way or another," Justin says. He raises his glass. "To Suze. Who'd have joined me for a cigarette and right now be trying to make a snowball."

We clink glasses and I get the concrete-heavy emptiness in my stomach, because I'd passed another tiny milestone of grief—I'd forgotten to notice Susie isn't here. I'd taken her absence for granted. We're quieter without her, and the energy doesn't crackle in the same way.

We chat about this and that, but this thought has sobered me right up. Also, the atmosphere is "off," somehow.

Ed darts looks at me constantly. I get a peculiar sense that he's nervy around me, trying to get my attention, or approval.

"I'm going to leave you lads to it," I say, stroking Leonard's ears.

Ed looks crestfallen. "Not like you to fold first?"

"Pacing myself," I say.

In bed, a duvet pulled up to my chin that smells of "strange place," I hear Justin and Ed creak up to bed on the hollow wooden staircase.

I know why Ed's being weird. He thinks he has to strive to win what he once took for granted. He might be right.

37

I wake early in a constructive mood and put my hair in plaits, which I've not done for years—fearing it would be seen as a bid for male attention due to men in pubs who yanked them like bell pulls. As I fold thick sections of my hair over my fingers, I think of Finlay Hart, saying in his eyes I'd not failed at anything. He must be flying today or tomorrow. He might be in the sky right now.

In my mind's eye, the image of Finlay Hart checking the gate for his flight, throwing his leather-strap watch in the security tray, preparing to step onto a plane: it gives me stomach pain.

The twinge provokes me to run over The People vs Finlay Hart for the umpteenth time. "Poison." The Fin I met, and the one I remember from our childhood, could be aloof to the point of disconnected. Perhaps even lonely. *You looked so worried, for a kid. Maybe it takes one to know one.* All this animosity swirls around him, and all I can detect is an unbearable sadness. What was the Spanish flu about? Was he sickness or symptom? Or both?

I like him. I feel an affinity with him that I can't explain, and I think it's mutual. That's what he was getting at when he told me about the jukebox song in the New York hipster bar.

I pick my way downstairs quietly and make a mountain of scrambled eggs before anyone's awake, full of that hearty feeling of being up and useful when everyone else is asleep.

Unfortunately, Hester appears first, but it probably does us good to be forced into stiff small talk for the fifteen minutes or so it takes Ed to enter the dining room, flushed from the shower.

"You did all this? I'm in awe," Ed says to me, as I bring another plate of toast to the table, and I shrug.

"Oh well I woke up early, for some reason."

"Plus, you found time to style yourself as Dorothy in *The Wizard of Oz*," he says, and I'm careful to pass on the other side of the table and sit down next to Hester, lest he make a playful grab. "You're getting away with it 'cause you look that youthful."

Hester's eyes narrow at Ed. "They were bunches, not plaits."

"Oh right," Ed says, swigging his orange juice.

"There I am worrying about how you'd prefer my bridal hair and I bet I could wear a beanie, for all you'd care," she says.

"Hahaha. Bridesmaids in rubber promotional Guinness logo top hats."

Justin walks in in his grandad pajamas, yawning, Leonard at his feet, yapping. "Yes, Leonard, there is a tin of Chum in our luggage, if Ed hasn't eaten it. Settle down."

"Morning boys!" I say. "Eggs are keeping warm in the oven."

"Bloody hell, you on amphetamines? I thought you were Wiccan. I'd not anticipated you rising until it was getting dark outside again."

I gurgle. There's something strange about this Saturday and

I realize what it is. For the first time since I lost Susie, I feel a glimmer of happiness. It's a very qualified happy, like a flickering lightbulb, but something approaching happy blinks on and off nonetheless.

The only thing you lack is self-belief.

Is that true? I hold on to the idea, trace its reassuring contours, like a polished stone in my pocket.

After breakfast, we bundle up and go for a walk, forgetting that this time of year is completely inhospitable to a bunch of city twats wandering around in untamed nature, without sufficient rain-proofing or sensible footwear. It's larks until we get two hours in, a degree of exhaustion takes hold, and we have yet to see civilization again. It dawns on us we are significantly lost, as opposed to cute-lost.

Ed has Google Maps on his phone, Hester standing by him with her arms wrapped around herself and chin buried in her chest. Justin is wheeling in the near distance with his arms thrown wide, Leonard running in circles around him on his jumpy little legs. Justin cries: "We've gone on holiday by mistake!"

"Is he pissed already?" Ed says to me, in irritation. I miss Susie's interjection here; she'd have handled Justin's exuberance and Ed's grouchy misanthropy in a dry one- or two-liner.

Actually, while stomping up hill and down dale, I've seen the method to Justin's rural madness. When breathing in lungfuls of cleaner air and concentrating on moving my body forward, grief eases. Exercise helps.

"Right, my phone says there's a small inn or lodgings house in that direction." Ed points into the distance. "If the Lord spares us, we should make it by nightfall."

"You're joking, aren't you?" Hester says.

"Yeah, more like twenty minutes if we get a yomp on."

"Thank fuck for that."

It occurs to me I've not heard one friendly word between Ed and Hester since we arrived, and I don't know why. They should be in pre-wedding euphoria.

As Ed promised, we find a pit stop at a village pub where we eat spongy white rolls stuffed with grated cheese—as does Leonard, covertly—iceberg salad with green peppers, and a breakwater of fat, deep-fryer 1970s chips, and drink pints of brown ale that taste of biscuits and socks. In hunger, weariness, and the toll of the low-level panic before we found it, it's a majestic feast.

After getting soaked to the skin on the way back, Leonard zipped into the front of Justin's coat, head sticking out, we finally reach the cottage. Ed builds a fire and Justin gets more fizz out of the fridge.

"By the way, I know this isn't a light topic, but we need to decide what to do with Susie's ashes," Ed says, dusting his hands. Justin sets four flutes down on the seaman's chest that doubles as coffee table in the sitting room.

"It's harder to find a place with a not-outdoorsy person, isn't it?" I say. "We can't exactly spread Susie at Searcys Bar at St. Pancras. We should ask Finlay what he wants too."

"He'd not care," Ed says.

"I think he would. Either way, he deserves a say."

"If he didn't go to the crematorium to claim the urn, how arsed can he be?"

"He lives in the States. What opportunities did he have if you'd already claimed it?"

345

Ed double-takes.

"What exactly went on in Edinburgh to turn you from 'the psycho brother's trying to embezzle a fortune' to 'he would care, he's a sensitive model-slash-quack who looks great in patent meggings'?" Ed says, in a squeaky impression of my voice. "Or have I answered my own question?"

"Okay, I've had enough of this, fuck this," Hester says, voice like a scalpel through the air, making everyone's hairs stand on end.

"Enough of what?" Ed says, warily.

"You obsessing over her," Hester says, pointing at me but not looking at me.

A grisly hush descends.

38

"You're having, or have had, an affair, am I right?" she says, arms crossed.

She's vibrating in that way that someone does when on the incredible high of unleashing something destructive they've been holding back.

Ed, the color of a beef tomato, says: "No!"

"Definitely no," I say, clearing my throat.

It feels as if the whole world has hit mute on background noise while this moment plays out in cinematic Dolby surround sound.

"Oh, like I'd believe a word you say," Hester says to me, looking at me now. "With your big sad eyes and your oh-so-witty asides, trying to position yourself as the sad perma-single cat lady, a Pound Shop Velma. You're a fucking menace in polka dots, sister."

Justin, halfway through unwrapping champagne bottle foil, has bulging eyes like the time he took too many psychotropics at Glastonbury. We're collectively experiencing a sensation like we're plunging down a lift shaft.

"Woah, don't talk to Eve like that!" Justin says. "Have your barney with Ed, but don't drag us into it."

"You missed the part where she dragged her-fucking-self into it!" Hester screams at Justin, and we shrink back.

"What were you arguing about, at the wake?" she continues, looking from me to Ed. "I walked up to you, something intense was going on. Ed was looking defensive. When I reached you, you both stopped and pretended nothing was up. Then Eve was so wound up she tore a strip off me, for no reason."

I take half a second to admire how she's making sure that's not forgotten.

"It had been a long day. We were both exhausted. I can't even remember, I think it was some admin thing . . . ," Ed blusters.

"*Admin thing.* That couldn't be shared with me? Do I seem as if I'm going to be palmed off that easily, Ed? Do you think I'm stupid? It was a wake for one of your best friends. You'd done a reading, that she wrote." She looks at me, as if that in itself is suspicious. "I can't see reason for you to have had words, at a moment like that, unless it was something major."

My skin is prickling and my palms are wet. I want to try to cover, but I don't know if I should and I can't think how to.

"Are you going to tell me?" she says to me. "Or can you not 'remember what the admin thing was about' either?" She does air quote fingers. "Was the admin thing the times you met up at, oh I don't know, wild guess—The Mercure behind my back? Or did you go to her drab spinster's nest?"

I open my mouth and nothing comes out.

"It was about the fact I'd had sex with Susie," Ed says, and time stands still for a second. "Once, ten years ago."

"What?" Hester says, stunned, eyes flicking between us, try-ing to work out if this is some gambit. Blame the woman who can't deny it. "Then why would Eve be angry?"

"Because we'd hidden it from her. She found out from a letter among Susie's personal things. Eve was furious on your behalf and insisted I should tell you before we got married."

I'm awed by the speed by which Ed has invented this to protect me. Hester's clearly struggling to catch up with having the right crime, infidelity—but the wrong perp, and the wrong timeline. That I might not be involved seems inconceivable to her. That's not actually unreasonable, I think. It did to me too.

"Once, ten years ago?" she repeats.

"Yes. When you were working in Switzerland."

"I think we should give you two some space to discuss this," Justin says.

"We'll go outside," Ed says to Hester, and although I don't think she's keen to take instruction from him, she's too pole-axed to argue. They disappear off to the kitchen and the door to the garden shuts after them.

Justin sits down on the sofa next to me, and we both make a lot of air-escaping-mouth noises and shake our heads at each other.

"Is it too soon for me to say 'You're a fucking menace in polka dots, sister' was an absolutely incredible line?" Justin whispers.

"Drab spinster's nest! Can I get that on one of those var-nished slices of wood to hang outside next to my front door?" I say, and Justin cracks up.

The sound of the door opening again tells us that Ed and Hester are finished debating sooner than we expected. We in-stinctively stand up and troop into the dining room.

"I might have been wrong about the affair, but fuck both of you, frankly," Hester says, hair tousled and eyes glittering. "You were never my friends and you've done nothing but undermine me and Ed."

We stand and take it, blankly. She pulls her engagement ring from her finger, throws it on the table, and runs up the stairs, her feet thundering like someone's banging drums, Ed in close pursuit.

"I deserved that, how did you deserve that?" I say to Justin. I look over at Leonard on the chaise lounge, who's sleeping through.

"Hester! Hester?" Ed chases her across the landing. Justin and I listen with gritted teeth to his progress following her, trying to talk her down throughout her packing. Five minutes later, Hester exits the cottage like a blonde hurricane.

"You had pints at lunch, are you even safe to drive?!" Ed shouts, offstage.

We hear the roar of a car engine, the wheels spinning in mud and noise of an ex-fiancée, accelerating away.

Ed returns, eyes wide with shock, still bristling with the rush of the confrontation and the speed with which his engagement broke.

"Have you made up?" Justin says.

"Ha ha," Ed says. He picks the ring up off the table and pockets it.

"Speaking of which, I appreciate this is a lesser issue, but Hester was our ride home," Justin says.

"Could ask if she'll come back and pick us up tomorrow?" I say.

"I'm glad you two find this so bloody funny," Ed says, affronted, but without enough moral high ground to go for anger.

"Sorry," I say.

"Pardon us, we know you've had a time of it. But Eve and I got an absolute volley of verbals and I've had my birthday weekend annihilated, so I don't think we're without rights to find some laughter in this darkness?" Justin says, with both self-control and an edge.

"Yeah," Ed says, limply, rubbing his closed eyes. "Sorry. We've split up, anyway. As you may have gathered."

"She's definitely finished with you, you don't think you can mend it?" I say.

"No," Ed says, raising his embattled gaze to meet both of ours. "I ended it. It was about time."

Neither of us know how to respond to that.

"Justin. Can I talk to Eve, alone?"

Justin says, "Well, merry birthday, Justin!" before adding, "Yes, yes, I fancied a ciggy out on that bench anyway."

He puts on his coat and bobble hat and picks up the discarded Moët.

"I shall swig from the bottle, in the manner of a tramp who's won the lottery."

"I'm sorry," Ed says once Justin has left. "That was one hundred percent my mess and you got dragged by the hair into it. Sorry for the vicious things Hester said, she wasn't herself."

"Ed," I say, in a polite tone. "I think you can afford to be honest about her not liking me, at this point. I think the cat's out of the bag. She was herself. Also, I'll admit to never liking her in return. There. Sorted."

He gives a rueful smile.

"I don't blame her," I say. "I think she's justified in not liking me. I haven't ever been her friend, that's true. I was a menace to her relationship."

"That outburst wasn't your fault. It's been building for a while."

"Oh?"

Ed thrusts his hands in his pockets. "I don't know if we should sit down. Feels stupid though, doesn't it? Like I'm chairing a meeting."

"Standing's fine."

His voice is low and thick and I feel a huge foreboding. I want a glass of champagne and to salvage what's left of this weekend. Ed wants a watershed.

"At first I thought Hester and I didn't feel right after we got engaged as I'd not had much of a choice, time to think about it. I didn't feel in control. But as things got worse, the penny dropped—it wasn't the engagement that had changed us. It was Susie dying.

"Losing someone the way we've lost Suze, the brutality of it. It brings everything into sharp focus. I had a status quo that I maintained, which didn't really, truly make me happy. It felt like my job to maintain it all the same. I didn't think I had the right to be happy, not the way I wanted." His eyes meet mine. "As it would hurt people to get there. Better to stay where I was, make the best of it."

I say nothing, arms tightly folded.

"My feelings for you, Eve, they've always been there. I put them to one side. I figured I'd missed my chance, and that was that. You were my best friend, and that would have to be enough."

I still say nothing.

". . . But seeing Susie's life end at thirty-four. The unfairness of it. It strips you down to your factory parts and asks you if you're spending this brief time we have the way you want. I wasn't. Hester felt I was pulling away. It was coming to a head, and then when you arrived . . ."

He pauses.

"This is not the way or the moment I imagined saying these words," Ed says. "But then I'm not sure how I ever did imagine it. I love you, Eve. I've always loved you. It's been a constant for me since we were teenagers."

A pause. I nod, as some sort of response seems essential. A silence develops that I gather I have to fill.

"What am I supposed to say?" I ask.

Ed shakes his head. "Whatever you want. Nothing. I'd reached the point I had to tell you, that's all. There's no expectation in it."

I think on this. Once upon a time, a very recent time, this would feel like everything I'd secretly hoped for, falling into my lap. Yet it doesn't feel the way I thought it would. Not least because Ed didn't choose this moment, he's using this moment.

"There is an expectation though, isn't there?" I say. "The idea is I'll think on this and want to be with you too, at last. That's why you acted as my savior and fell on your sword over the Susie secret. It wasn't for Hester's sake. It was preparing to make this appeal to me."

Ed shakes his head. "I was protecting you from Hester's furies. I caused them, I should take them."

"But not only just now. You've always kept me at clutch biting point. I'm your Plan B. And here we are, your Plan A is halfway through the Peaks right now, and the time to tell me you love me has finally come. It's Hester who forced this decision, not you."

"Plan B? You're making me sound like some mustache-twirling, conniving rotter." Ed gives a small laugh of disbelief. "My life's fallen apart in front of you, like a fucking clown car with the doors dropping off. I've not planned any of this. As or Bs. Hester sensed I was in love with you and there was nothing I could do to fix that, because I am."

Fin's observation about Ed thinking he's only ever been a victim comes hurtling back to me.

"When you got engaged, in the pub," I say. "I didn't go home from The Gladstone afterward. I went on to a bar and nearly had a hook-up with a lad who works there."

"Right . . . ?"

"I was doing it like self-harm, so I didn't have to think about you marrying Hester. I was doing it to cheat on you, on us, our great unspoken passion. I was going to mention it, or let Susie mention it, down the line. To see if you reacted. I wanted you to be jealous. I wanted you to know I'd done it, and to feel something in return. I was prepared to have sex I didn't want to have, for the two-second vindication of the look in your eyes, before you changed the subject. Which is quite something, when I spell it out."

Ed frowns.

"I thought we were deeply in love, in the same way," I continue. "The grand delusion of it for all these years depended on me believing that. But you know why we definitely weren't? I've figured it out. This has never given you any pain. From the letter going missing onward, what happened hurt so much, for me. But until now, until Hester lost her patience with this ménage à trois bullshit, it's never damaged life for you at all. Quite the opposite, you liked it. The secret drama, the girl in your back pocket. The little romantic comedy playing out. Giving me the 'c'mere you!' consolation hug that lasted seconds too long. You loved the way I looked at you. You say you care about me, but you never cared what it did to me. You're a sensitive, perceptive person. I don't think you would've had no idea there were nights I went home and wept, not if you thought about it. But you were careful never to think about it."

I have sweat on my top lip as I pause for breath, but I don't regret a single thing I've said.

"OK, my God," Ed says. "That's quite the onslaught of things to think about. And I will think about it all, obviously."

His Nicest Guy in the Room act—in the face of me naming what's been happening, turning the lights on—is so inadequate. It's a way of him not thinking about it, again.

". . . I didn't consider our friendship as keeping you hanging on, Eve."

"I know you didn't. That's what allowed you to do it."

"You're making this sound like something I perpetrated. Neither of us spoke up. Neither of us said, what if we were together?"

"True, and I could have, but you were committed to Hester. I thought it was up to you to change your mind, because I was always available. Which is how it suited you, me tragically yearning. What did Hester call it? Perma-single. I don't think it was a total coincidence you slept with Susie right after I met Mark."

"Oh come on, why would it not be . . . ?"

"For some of the same reasons I tried to hook up with that barman the night you got engaged."

"I was a coward when it came to you, Eve. That's the truth." Ed rubs his temples. "The letter going astray ruined everything between us, didn't it?"

I shake my head.

"Hah, no, I used to think that. I was desperate to think that, it was the . . . what's the film phrase? MacGuffin of our origins myth. We were each other's soulmate, separated by circumstance. The truth is, you didn't choose me. That's it." I shrug. "That's the whole story of Ed Cooper and Evelyn Harris. You didn't want me enough, when choosing me became harder. You didn't even risk a phone call, or wait a term, to check why I didn't write back. Do you know what? That's fine. I understand, and we were kids. I own my part in victimizing myself over this, you can own yours. But let's stop blaming bad luck or misunderstandings."

"People aren't always brave. They make mistakes. You've still been my best friend."

"No, Susie was my best friend. We're close friends, with this added manipulation. Friends with drawbacks. You pulled the 'best' thing out of the bag once I found out you'd slept with her, and I needed to be thrown fresh hope of my specialness. Because you knew that men who sleep with your best mate aren't anyone's romantic hero. And that's what you wanted to be, whatever cost it had for me."

Ed looks staggered. I've kept my temper, but I'm finding this far too powerfully cleansing to pull any punches.

"I'm blown away that you'd think I'd deliberately—"

"It's not deliberate, in the sense you plot," I interrupt. "It's instinct. The trouble with your lies, Ed, is you tell them so fast and so easily, you don't see yourself constructing them. You believe them yourself. Look at the way you altered the story of our fight to Hester just now, to gain an advantage from it."

Ed doesn't speak for a moment.

"You make me sound a proper monster."

"You're not a monster. You're someone who naturally takes on responsibility, you're always the responsible adult and the map reader, but won't take responsibility for himself with women."

"Today's turning out to be a helluva day for self-discovery," Ed says, after a short pause. "I'm sincerely sorry for having hurt you. I didn't intend any of it."

I never thought of the story between Ed and me being a circle. I thought it was open-ended, it would run forever. Yet here we are—him finally declaring himself again, and me closing it. I'm glad. My life's been short of moments of closure.

"Apology accepted. I'm sure you can see why I think I'm worth more than someone who spent sixteen years making up his mind about whether I was worth the hassle."

Ed looks fairly stunned and yet is without comeback.

A heavy silence ensues. The door handle cranks and Justin appears, rubbing his hands, Leonard skittering ahead of him.

"Apologies, on the one hand you two seem to be still full *Jerry Springer*. On the other, I have shotgunned half a bottle of champagne, my battery is on twelve percent, and my dick is an icicle."

"It's fine," I say, looking at Ed. "We were finished."

39

"Think he's alright?" Justin says. "Are my onion pieces small enough?"

I crane over to see Justin's chopping board. We're making a Sunday roast while Ed is off on a "head clearing" hike.

"I think so and definitely. They're only going under the chicken."

"Ah, so they can soak up the chicken's weltschmerz."

"Do you mean schmaltz?"

"Oh. Yes. What's weltschmerz?" Justin rubs his hands on a tea towel and picks up his phone. "A German word for a feeling of melancholy or world weariness. I wish these onions could soak that up for us."

I laugh and return to peeling the potatoes.

Last night was pretty dour. We watched a film—*All the President's Men*—and pretended to discuss Watergate when everyone's minds were on Hestergate. Ed was understandably stilted around me, keeping his distance, while I tried to be as normal as possible to make it clear I didn't want any rift.

Today, Ed's spent a lot of time on the phone at the end of the

358

garden, brow furrowed, and has now gone on a solo excursion, no doubt in a state of weltschmerz.

"I think it's safe to say I was fully off my chanks to book a cottage break comprising the warring couple, and his secret amour, in the first wave of grief after losing a dear friend," Justin says. "A decent set-up for a horror film."

"I've enjoyed it. So has Leonard," I say, waving my peeler at Leonard, sitting in the kitchen's window seat.

"I take it last night's drama between you and Ed was him declaring himself your prince and offering you his hand in marriage instead? And you saying no, thank you, you would rather marry Prince Andrew?"

"Yes, pretty much."

"He could've given you the ring right then and there too," Justin says.

"I would recommend throwing that ring into the fires of Mordor."

"Fuck, I hope he doesn't get back with her."

"You think he will?" I privately and ignobly glory in the fact I can ask this, without it affecting me in the slightest. Such heady freedom.

"I dunno, but immediately propositioning you doesn't speak well of his willingness to try being single, and there's been an awful lot of talking to her today."

"They own a house and a car and had booked much of a wedding. There's a lot of disentangling."

"I don't think they're debating calling the caterer, do you?" Justin says, starting on the carrots.

"You think they could come back from the Susie sex? If I was Hester I don't think I could."

"Hester would want to kill her," Justin raises his knife. "But our wily girl Susie clearly anticipated this."

"Justin!" I gasp and he guffaws.

"She's cackling in heaven every time I drop one of these. It's my way of keeping her with us."

He pauses. "I don't think Suze will be the sticking point now. I think she'd want him to get rid of us. Or at least you."

"After the things I said to him last night, I wouldn't blame him if he decided he's best off choosing his relationship."

"I'm not so big-hearted. If he gets back with her and dumps you, he can dump me while he's at it."

I do want to stay friends with Ed, I think. But not at any cost. A very simple-sounding idea, and yet I think it's taken me my whole adult life to work that out. I have weathered the un-imaginable loss of Susie, so far, and that has given me strength, and perspective.

"How's it going? Something smells amazing," Ed says, having to practically fold himself double to get through the doorway to the kitchen.

"That's my peach cobbler," Justin says.

"Eve, can I have a quick word? It will be quick," Ed says, and Justin turns his back fast, before he says something caustic.

I wipe my hands on my apron and follow him outside, clos-ing the door after myself. My God, it's cold. Am I really going to get an official dismissal?

"I want you to know I've thought about everything you said. You were right. I did, without fully meaning to, manipulate you. I loved thinking you were in love with me, I encouraged it, and I never asked myself if it hurt you. I purposely blurred the lines between friendship and fancying and us being in love, because it felt good, and so I thought it was benign."

He takes a deep breath and I see he's teeth-rattlingly nervous.

"Then with me and Hester falling apart, and the thought of you off with that good-looking bastard last week, it started to torture me. It dawned on me"—Ed points into the middle distance—"halfway across that field, right now, while I was humping the fence, trying to haul myself over—my feeling like a complete nervous wreck when you were in Scotland, losing my appetite, the whole nine yards. That's what I've been putting you through all this time."

I smile. "Mainly hung on to my appetite, but more or less."

"Last night I said sorry, but only in a defensive way. It was the first time I'd been confronted with how I've behaved, and my instincts were to deny and deflect. But one thing I didn't lie about was you being my best friend. The timing of telling you, that had a motive I hadn't examined, maybe, but it's true for me. I want you to know, from the bottom of my heart, I'd like to still be mates. But with zero gray area or agenda. Equally I'd understand if you don't want to be."

"You articulate sod," I say, equal parts embarrassed, gratified, relieved.

"I did rehearse that for the last hour and drew hard on my school assembly practice."

"Of course I want to be friends," I say, and we hug each other, with some tears and deep breaths. "I think it takes some character to get kicked hard as you did when you were down last night, and be able to say this the following morning."

"It took character to tell me the truth."

I put my hand out for Ed to shake, and he does, after we wipe our eyes.

"We've made up!" I say to Justin, as we return. I don't want him having to decode the atmosphere yet again. "Fully and completely. Nothing left unsaid."

"Good," Justin says. "You may celebrate by making the gin and tonic aperitifs. Are you and Hester getting back together?" he says to Ed.

"No?" Ed says. "What gave you that idea?"

"Fatalism," Justin says.

"Give me some credit. Especially after what Hester said to you both yesterday, over is over."

"We wouldn't want you to feel like you had to choose," I say.

"I would," Justin says, throwing his tea towel over his shoulder.

Ed lays the table for lunch and we're pleasantly drunk by the shrimp cocktail starter.

After a vast birthday feast, Ed rings around local taxi companies to get us home. "It's my fault, so I should fix it."

"They're cool with taking Leonard?" Justin says.

"They said so."

An hour later, we find ourselves having a row with a taxi driver:

"Wrap it in a towel or I will ask for a soiling charge upfront, your choice!" says Reg from Valley Cars. "I've had a Doberman shit all over the back seat and the valeting was a hundred and fifty quid."

"Does Leonard look like he has a Doberman's bowel capacity to you?" Justin says.

"If I may be candid, he looks like a Muppet that's done jail time," says Reg.

"Oh man, you're way over the line there," Ed says. "He got a suspended sentence."

"I have a towel we can use!" I interject frantically, unzipping my case, before my best chance of a lift home implodes.

40

On the journey, my phone buzzes with a WhatsApp. Finlay Hart?! My stomach does a little somersault of joy and the do-pamine floods my body. I'd been planning a polite inquiry, which was more about the fact I somehow can't resist making contact. I'm almost sure there's absolutely no significance or synchronicity in this arriving right when I was drafting the *hi so I hope your flight home was OK and everything's sorted with your dad* message. Almost.

> *Thought I'd let you know: my father's been assessed now, and the woman from the council thought he's currently safe to live at home but he'll be getting regular care worker visits. Hope you've had a good weekend. Was it Derbyshire? Finlay x*

I track back and delete my previous typing. Only beady Leonard, shrouded on Justin's lap like E.T. in the blanket, is watching my hands moving, Justin dozing.

*That's good to hear. Yes, Derbyshire! It's been quite torrid. Hester,
Ed's fiancée, accused us of an affair, Ed confessed to the Susie
fling, Hester and Ed split up, Hester zoomed off into the horizon in
our BMW out of here. Ed declared being in love with me, I gave Ed
a ton of hard home truths about having cake and eating cake. To
his credit, he's taken it well. Now crammed into a cab, radio blasting
David Bowie's Absolute Beginners, with a small dog wrapped in a
towel, praying he doesn't defecate. It's all been strangely cathartic. x*

> *Lot to unpack here, Evelyn: glad of the catharsis, hopes &
> prayers with you on the defecation. I've still got the Merc,
> I could've come and picked you up if you said! x*

The initial kiss I wrote off as etiquette, but ongoing kisses?
That's a different matter. Along with offers to do mercy dashes
into the Peaks.

*Thank you! There's three of us, luggage, and a
chihuahua Yorkshire Terrier crossbreed called Leonard,
though* ☺ *. . . wait, you're still in England? x*

> *Yeah it was going to be such a mad rush otherwise, I put my
> flight back a week. Three of you, luggage, and dogs called
> Leonard would've all been welcome. Any friend of yours, etc. x*

*That's really nice of you, Fin, thanks. By the way, I got your dad
some shortbread in Edinburgh, I forgot to say. I'm his biscuit dealer.
Am I alright to call round with it after work tomorrow? 6ish? x*

> *Yes no problem. I've been using the cleaner to facilitate my check-ins so I might use that opportunity when you're there to put my head round door? x*

Yes, please, as that was exactly what I was hoping for and conniving, like a rotter.

> *Sure! See you there. x*

> *Just to be clear, did you tell Ed you were in love with him too? This is what we call "fishing," etc etc. ☺ x*

My heart pounds.

> *No, because I'm not anymore. x*

> *Good for you. x*

> *Yeah, it feels like it is. x*

"You look very . . . sparkly, all of a sudden?" Justin says, awake and giving me a sidelong glance. "Who's that then?" He nods toward my phone. "How are you even getting a signal?"

"A friend."

"FINLAY HART?!" Justin mouths silently, with exaggerated enunciation, and I guilty-grin-blush.

My phone dings with a Justin text.

🐧🐧🐧

It's what Susie would've wanted. X

I grin some more and hum along.
If our love song /
Could fly over mountains

41

The pater familial Volvo is reassuringly present in the drive as I walk up to the door of Susie's former family home the following evening, clutching my tartan presentation tin of shortbread.

"Hello!" I say, eagerly but nervously, as Mr. Hart answers. "Sorry for appearing unannounced again. I got you this up in Edinburgh."

I proffer the shortbread.

"Oh, that's very thoughtful, Eve," he says, accepting it. "I best start watching my waistline! Would you like a cup of tea? I've put the kettle on."

I say, "Yes, please," and follow him indoors.

A quick glance around suggests everything is fine. The cleaner has left it immaculate.

He's put the kettle on, and I've taken a seat when the doorbell goes again.

"Someone with you?" Mr. Hart says, getting up to answer it.

"Oh, Finlay might be joining us," I say.

"Yes, you're right, it's your young man," Mr. Hart calls from the hallway.

"Hi," Fin says, winding headphones around his phone as he walks into the room in running gear, pushing hair damp with sweat back from his glowing face.

"Hello," I say, standing up.

"Tea for you too?" Mr. Hart says to Finlay.

"Thanks, yes. Milk no sugar, please," Fin says, as Mr. Hart bustles off to the kitchen.

"I remember!"

I stare at Finlay and he stares back. We're both fixed on each other, and as seconds pass, I realize neither of us is trying to pretend it's anything other than a heart-struck gaze of mutual longing. Everything about his face is so ridiculously, staggeringly lovely to me, in this moment, I'm unable to speak.

Beauty isn't an arrangement of features, even features as perfect as Finlay Hart's, it's a feeling. This is how it feels in the split second you suddenly become aware that you're falling in love with someone. The click of a jigsaw's last piece, the rainfall of coins in a jackpot slot machine, the right song striking up and your being swept away by its opening bars. That conviction of making complete sense of the universe, in one moment. *Of course. You're where I should be. You're here.*

"How are you?" Fin says to me, eventually, and we both break into broad smiles at the ludicrousness of having declared our feelings without saying a word. I can't wait to talk to him properly, after we leave here. I can't wait, full stop.

"Shortbread on the side!" Mr. Hart says, pushing the door open with his foot, carrying a rattling tea tray in the door, placing it on a footstool. The Hart home is the kind of home to have footstools that match the sofa.

We chat about nothing much and Fin sips his tea, looking at

me over the rim of the cup, and I've never had such a tumultuous internal response to someone looking over a teacup at me.

"Mind if I use the loo?" Fin asks Mr. Hart, after ten minutes, and I guess, even if he does have a full bladder, he wants to check for things like electrical appliances in baths.

Finlay's given directions to a bathroom he must have used for two decades.

When Finlay returns, he looks perturbed. I mouth, "What?" but he shakes his head.

After making the smallest of small talk, Fin says: "Where did you get the lamp on the landing, by the way? It looks familiar."

"Oh, the décor's my wife's concern." Mr. Hart laughs.

Fin clears his throat and darts a look at me. "It looks a lot like one from the hotel we stayed in?"

"Does it? Which?"

"The Caledonian. In Edinburgh."

"Are you implying anything?" his dad says.

"No. I . . . wondered where it was from, that's all. Can you remember where you bought it?"

Mr. Hart doesn't immediately respond.

"Are you calling me a liar?" he says, in a low, even register, one that sets a warning light flashing inside me.

"No . . ."

"It sounded like you were."

Mr. Hart stands up and, in alarm, Finlay and I stand up too.

"I'm NOT A BLOODY THIEF!" Mr. Hart roars, at a deafening volume, right up close in Finlay's face, as I jump out of my skin. I'm not sure I knew anyone could be that loud, let alone a man pushing seventy, with no vocal training or build-up. Incredibly, Fin doesn't flinch.

He steps backward, breathing heavily. He closes his eyes and stumbles slightly and for a moment I think he's going to fall over.

"Are you OK?" I say, darting over to him, my hand on his arm.

He doesn't answer, eyes still closed, and he looks as if he's gasping for breath, his face a worrying gray. Is he having a heart attack? *It's a panic attack*, says an inner voice.

Mr. Hart has turned the television on and sits back down, paying no attention to either of us.

"How about some fresh air?" I say, and Fin manages to nod with the merest incline of his head.

I help him through the kitchen, to the back door, scrabbling for the key on the windowsill.

I throw it open and we make awkward progress, me half-holding Fin up, down the deep steps into the garden. I don't want to be responsible for him fainting onto a hard surface. I'd willingly split my head open to break his fall though. That much I know.

On the patio, Fin sits directly on the stone, back resting against the garden furniture, a wrought-iron chair. I sit next to him, my legs outstretched alongside his.

"Are you feeling better?" I say to Fin, and he murmurs yes, and I slip my hand in his. He's very cold, but he squeezes it. He breathes deep lungfuls of the freezing air.

After a while, his breathing is steady and his complexion is a healthy color again.

I lean my head on his shoulder. He puts an arm around me, his hand holding my waist.

"Are you ready to tell me whatever it is you've not told me?" I say.

I don't know where these words have come from—they travel from my subconscious, out my mouth, entirely bypassing my conscious decision to utter them.

"Yes," Fin says, without hesitation.

42

The lipstick-pink hydrangeas I remember from the summers of our youth are still there, their heads now petals of rusted, brittle slate-brown in the depths of winter. There are lights on timers in the flower beds, blinking on in the falling dusk.

Fin starts speaking.

"The first time my dad beat me I was six. Maybe seven. I didn't know what I'd done wrong. I remember the sheer confusion, above all. More than the pain, or the shock of the violence. Knowing that people thought I was a *clever boy*, but for some reason I couldn't figure out what had led to me being walloped like that. Like a math problem where I just couldn't add up. *Think, Finlay.* After that first time, it carried on once every month or so, until I was eleven, or twelve, I think. When I got old enough to fight back, or to tell people—people who could've caused real trouble, like teachers. Before then, I drove myself mad thinking there were ways to avoid it, if only I could adjust my behavior accordingly.

"There was also about six months or so when I was ten that it mysteriously stopped, which afterward I put down to him screwing a secretary at his firm. My being left alone ran con-current with heated arguments with my mother, lots of slam-ming of doors, and someone called *that slag Christina* by my mum, who got fired."

Finlay gives me a wry look but I'm not ready for wry yet.

"I always knew when a beating was coming, I learned to read the signs. He'd get this malicious glint in his eye, or he'd been drinking. Or he'd come back from the office in a foul mood. He'd pick fault, work himself into a temper with me to justify it. It was like an outlet he allowed himself, but he was fastidiously careful. It was always in an upstairs room with the door closed, it was always as quiet as possible. For the most part, he never left bruises. No belt or anything. No marks. He'd already thought about how he might get caught, and in a really twisted way that gives me peace. I don't ever need to wonder if he intended me harm, if he intended me to suffer in silence, and be disbelieved if I told anyone. I know for sure he did. It might have been an irrational urge in him, but he con-trolled it in an incredibly rigid, rational way."

My face is burning hot in the extreme cold. I have to take my hand out of Fin's and rub it on my skirt.

"That day, you waited for me on a bike ride," I say. "When Susie and Gloria rode off. Do you remember that day? He hit you for that, didn't he?" My mouth's dry. Looking back, I can picture the intensity of Mr. Hart's wrath, and the limp, blank acquiescence of Finlay as he was pulled indoors.

I could easily cry but I fight it, I don't want to, I don't want to turn this into Finlay having to comfort me.

"Yes, but that wasn't because I stayed with you. If I'd left you, the thrashing would've been for that. He constructed no-win scenarios for me. Like I said, when he wanted to do it, he always found cause."

I nod. "I see." Except I don't, not at all.

"Aged thirteen, having not been belted for a while, I found the courage to tell my mum what had been going on. But my dad had established this narrative that I was malign, I was disruptive. If you demonize a child, they tend to get a bit demonic, making it easier and easier. He was clever enough an abuser to have discredited me. I could do no right, Susie could do no wrong, that was always how it was. So straight away, my mother said I was lying, that it was a disgusting thing to say about my father, and how dare I. She actually said: 'This is typical of you.'"

"She really didn't believe you?"

"No, I think she did. I'm not going to let her off the hook and say she thought it wasn't true. I think she probably knew, instinctively, it was. My mum liked our social status, she liked our house, the holidays. My mum valued appearances. Look at how the affair was handled. I bet Susie never told you about that?"

I shake my head.

"Yep. We had it drummed into us that you do not talk about the family skeletons. It getting out that my dad was violently assaulting his young son would've torn it all down. When I said he'd been viciously beating me for years, either he had to be thrown overboard, or I did. It was a straight choice. My mum chose my dad."

I get a hard, sharp pain under my ribs. "Did he hit Susie?"

Fin shakes his head.

"Never, that I know of, nor my mum. I think I would've

known. Doted on Susie. Whatever psychological fault line that I opened up, she didn't. I've asked myself many times, if Iain Hart had two daughters, would he have ever laid a finger on his offspring? Who knows. Maybe a different son would've got different. Maybe he just hated me."

"It's not your fault. Whatsoever," I say.

"I know," Fin says, clasping my hand again, and squeezing. "Took some time, and a change of continent, a spot of rehab, and a fair-size therapy bill, but I know."

"Fuck," I say. "All this time. You being spoken of as this terrible person . . ."

"Susie didn't lie to you." Fin turns to look at me. "I don't want you to blame her. I always tell clients not to use the word 'damaged,' but I was, Eve. Through my teens, I made it very clear I wanted nothing more than to be the fuck out of the family home as soon as I could. Susie saw a lot of shit behavior from me as we got older. I played it out exclusively at home, because I was smart enough to know school was my launchpad for getting out of here. Like my dear dad, I too knew to keep it behind closed doors."

"Did you never try to tell her what had gone on?"

"Yes, once. As a punishment, he locked us in a wardrobe. We were very little. That was the one time I saw him go ballistic on Susie too. She was hyperventilating that she was going to run out of air, it was horrible. That was why I didn't want her to be buried."

I know Fin isn't trying to score a point, but I feel this anyway.

"I thought that sadism might be the shred of proof I needed for her to believe me.

"We were in the pub, not long before I left for London,

I took a very deep breath and said Dad had abused me. She shrugged it off. *Come on, Finlay, don't dramatize it with the A word. You were a total bastard to him too and you know you were. I remember your arguments. Remember when you stole his credit card. Or trashed his spirits cabinet. You got smacked a few times? Well Dad's old-school, isn't he, he still thinks you can do that. Yes, he would think he could do that to a boy in a different way. Especially a hoodlum like you.* It was like watching stones bounce off shatterproof glass.

"She was seventeen and I was nineteen and I'd left it too late. Susie's opinion of her upbringing wasn't going to change in one conversation. Her view of her father wasn't going to shift to accommodate it. As she made clear, I wasn't a sympathetic victim. I know what she meant."

"It's not your fault if no one would listen," I say, slightly hoarse.

"I've had a lot of time to think about what happened between myself and Susie. You know how, if you're late to meet someone—at first the person waiting for you is confused, then they're pissed off. They get worried. Your task when it comes to an explanation and apology when you do turn up gets bigger, with each passing minute. Eventually they give up, and they leave. They're not waiting for you anymore. That was my relationship with Susie. By the time I was ready to talk and tell her why I'd been such a destructive, miserable bastard, she'd gone. I'd kept her waiting too long for her to have any interest or faith in what I was going to say. That doesn't mean I shouldn't have tried harder. I wish I had. I wondered if her diaries had any hint in there that she knew, that she ever thought back on that conversation about Dad, and rethought."

"That was why you wanted them?"

"Yes."

He has to know. He can't think he's told me all this, and I still wouldn't hand them over.

"Fuck, Fin. I destroyed them. Before Edinburgh. I was angry at Susie, and you were pushing and I thought I should do something definitive. You were right. I had no right, or idea what I was interfering with. Fuck, I'm so sorry . . ."

I find I'm not even scared of Fin's reaction, I'm too disgusted and shocked at myself, before that can crowd in. I *want* him to scold me, I deserve it.

"Hey, it's alright," Fin says, evenly. "I'd changed my mind anyway. It was an impulse, in the first wave of grief, knowing I'd never get to ask her. I don't think I should've read her diaries." He pauses. "My behavior toward you, over that—that was you getting a taste of the displaced anger that Susie got inured to."

"Susie would've sided with you, if she'd known what I do," I say, with conviction. "It would've been tough to absorb but she'd have got there. She hated bullies. Remember the shoes story, in her eulogy?"

"I hope you're right. Getting to know you has helped bring her back to me. I almost feel like it's Susie, from the afterlife, gloating—*see, Finlay?!* I'd misjudged too."

"Haha, why?"

"I thought she was an arrogant princess who, compared to me, had played life on the easy setting. My dad's divide and conquer had worked. But she'd kept you as a best friend, that tells me she was always the little sister I remember. Boisterous, bloody cantankerous when thwarted, but funny as hell and heart in the right place."

"That's a good Susie summary," I say, with the uneven, gasping tone of someone who's breaking up crying, my sight blurred.

"Every time you make one of your arch comments, I feel like I can hear her laughing like a drain. Thanks to you, I'm proud of her. You're a connection to the Susie I didn't get to be close to."

Finlay only just gets these words out before his own tears take over and we lean against each other, holding on to each other, like the ground beneath us might move.

As we steady ourselves, we realize how cold and dark the garden has become.

"Have you had attacks like that before?" I say, quietly, wiping under my eyes. "That was a panic attack?"

"Yeah, but not for years, and not many. With the cost of American healthcare, I soon taught myself breathing techniques, so I didn't land with a trip to A&E. He gave me an unexpected jolt, is all. I've never liked being inside these walls again."

I say, "Of course. He gave me a jolt." There's a pause. "There's something I still can't work out," I say. "Why are you helping him? Why not fly back to NYC saying see ya later, electrocute yourself in the bath for all I care? I would."

"For closure. Never got it with my mother, won't get it with my sister, and realized when Susie first said my father's memory was fragmenting that the bastard would evade me ever confronting him. I got the hatred and the anger and the self-righteousness out of my system in my twenties. I understand better how I remove the noose of Iain Hart from my neck now. It turns out that Christians were on to something, with forgiveness. If I treat him well, find a home, make sure he has end-of-life care—it's ultimate proof to myself that I'm not him. My conscience will be clear when he dies. That feels like a victory."

"You're a better person than I am," I say.

"Oh, I'm not," Fin says, turning dark blue eyes on me, and I wilt. Everyone should be looked at the way I'm being looked at right now, once in their life.

"Right. I need a minute alone to get myself together, do you want to say goodbye to him?" Fin says, standing up, brushing his hands. "Here's the keys to the Merc. I parked a few streets away and went on a run. Never visit here without a getaway car."

"I'm not walking out of the front door and leaving you alone with him. Not for a second."

"Come here," Fin says, and hugs me hard enough to squeeze the air out of me. "If he tried to swing for me now I'm six foot and he's senile, it'd end badly for him. I'm not in any physical danger. I had a shock earlier, that's all."

"I know I'm a pathetic protector and I'm wearing a skirt with dancing squirrels printed on it . . . but . . . let me rescue you!" I blurt, half crying, half laughing.

"Ah, but, you see—the thing is, Evelyn Harris. You already have," Fin says, putting his hand to my face.

As I PASS the front room, I hear the burble of a television show and can't stop myself from walking in and looking at him, one last time.

Mr. Hart glances up, face wreathed in smiles. "Eve! You two still out there? What are you gabbing on about?"

"He told me it wasn't him who was the poison. You are," I say, under my breath.

"I'm sorry?" Mr. Hart says, turning back to the TV.

"I wish you were," I say.

43

We don't speak much on the drive to my house, but when we park, Roger appears in the window, pawing at the glass, somehow managing a feline frown. *What time do you call this, young lady? And who is he, might I ask?*

"Hello, you didn't mention you had a lodger," Finlay says. "He's a handsome swine, yours?"

"No, I don't know how Roger 'Piecrust' got in there. He won't leave," I say, smiling. "Twee name not entirely my fault."

"Is that from some show I never saw?" Fin says.

"Longish story. For another time. Your sister is involved."

"Remember who the killer was in *Twin Peaks*?" Fin says. "The bad guy was the dad. Periodically possessed by a demonic entity. Otherwise seemed the perfect loving father."

"Shit . . . ?"

"That was why I was trailing my coat about why you chose the theme music."

"Pure coincidence, unfortunately. Except Susie had a thing about being Laura Palmer. Now I'll forever wonder what she was seeing there. Fin, I still have her phone. Do you want that?"

Fin turns the engine off and unsnaps his seat belt, shifts to look at me. "No, really. It wouldn't be right or do me any good. If anyone should have her things, it's you. As we've said, you were the love of her life."

Finlay Hart looks at me steadily, while my insides unwind. I stare at his hand resting on the gear stick.

"Do you want to come in and meet Roger?" I say, my breath feeling like it's blocked in my chest with anticipation and fear.

"Yes," Fin says, still looking at me. "Thing is, though. There's a problem with that. Remember in Edinburgh I said, what if I dropped the act, the second-guessing? What if I told you the truth about what I'm thinking? What if I stopped Gatsby-ing and risked someone really knowing me, and rejecting me?"

"That's rich, you talking about rejection! You said that right before you looked at me like you might kiss me, then went scuttling off in horror at the thought of it."

Fin bursts out laughing, one of his eye-creasing laughs that changes his whole face.

"I didn't feel any horror at that idea, quite the opposite, but don't you see how bad it would've been if I had? I bullied you into helping me search for my father in another country, I'd got you a hotel room. You'd been weeping, shortly before. Can you imagine, if anything had happened, what you might've wondered I'd been up to all along? Or the advantage you might feel I was taking in comforting you?"

"I never thought of that. I didn't doubt your motives at all."

"I know. I wanted it to stay that way."

I smile, and marvel at how my opinion of Finlay Hart has undergone such a revolution. I would trust him with my life now. Which is just as well.

"Honesty, right, I'll go first, then you can have a turn," Fin says, and I brace. "I'm trying to reconcile all the following things. If I come in now, I think you know, I won't want to leave again."

I hard swallow.

"I want you to say you feel the same way, but I don't want to hurt you: I have to get on a plane to America in a few days' time, even though I don't want to. I can't stay here because my job isn't here. I don't want to tell you to come with me, even though I passionately want you to come with me, if that's what you want. Tearing someone else's life up by the roots like that isn't fair. I don't know how we make this work, but I don't want to not try either. So yes, I want to meet Roger. But meeting Roger has a lot riding on it. Because if this is just going to be a very eventful few days, I feel like we both should agree to that. Not that it will make my leaving feel possible. OK. Now you."

There's a pause where I clear my throat and hope my voice works.

"Yeah, same," I say, casually, and in the tension breaking we both laugh so much we have tears forming.

"I think . . ." I pause. "I think when you think of all the things we've both overcome, to be sitting here in this car together, having found each other. I don't think we should let the distance between England and New York bother us. We'll work out what happens next. We got here. We're together. That's what matters."

Fin leans down and kisses me, and I twist around and put my fingers into his hair and kiss him back, soft then harder, feeling him respond.

"Might be easier if you undid your belt," Finlay whispers, pointing at it, twisted across my chest like I'm in a child harness. I guffaw.

"Know when I knew that I loved you?" he says. "When I met you in the lobby to go to dinner. You were walking across the lobby, bandy-legged in those heels like a Gumby in *Monty Python*. It was like I could hear an orchestra, and all the stars came out."

"Really?"

"Well, it was either that moment, or when you were bellowing you'd not even seen my pubic area on Leith quayside. I was very relieved about that, by the way."

"Worst thing imaginable, for me to see you naked, then?"

"My personal Vietnam. Let's never let that happen."

I laugh and reach for the door handle.

"Why do I feel we understand each other so, so well, Evelyn? I'm meant to be the one who has answers for things like that," Fin says, looking at me in some sort of awe. "It's like my whole life was about traveling back to you."

I've had time to think about this, lying awake in a cottage listening to rain on the roof. Thinking about how Finlay never abandoned me, whether it was on bike rides as children, or in hotel rooms as grown-ups.

"Because of the lesson we've taught each other," I say.

"What is that?"

"Recovery."

44

The quizmaster's booming voice cuts through the burble of chatter.

"In the BBC comedy series *The Office*, the Slough branch merges with a second branch of their paper merchant business. Where was that branch based? *Where was that, branch based?*"

Why do quizmasters always put the pause in a sentence in a really odd place?

"Reading," Justin hisses, tapping a forefinger on the sheet.

"Ricky Gervais is from Reading, that's why you think it's Reading," I hiss back.

"It's not going to be a big city," Ed whispers, fingers rifling in a bag of Frazzles. "It's got to be Slough equivalent."

He throws a Frazzle to Leonard who wakes up, eats it, and goes straight back to sleep.

"It's where the John Travolta dancing guy comes from," I whisper.

"Which was Reading," Justin says.

"It's not! Back me up, Francis."

Francis nods. "Reading's too big."

"Thank you."

"Also not funny enough, somehow."

"Is Slough funny?" Justin sniffs.

"Intrinsically, yes," Ed says. "Imagine Vic Reeves singing in melodramatic voice . . . *the whore was from SLOUGH!* Funny."

"Swindon," Finlay says.

We all look at him in surprise.

"You live in New York, you don't know our trivia," I say.

"It was on well before I left Britain, and we have the BBC over there."

"Swindon? You're sure?" I say.

"Yep," Fin says, necking more beer. He complains about the "Carrington half stone" he's put on since we started dating, three months ago. As someone who regularly spins out brushing her teeth to watch him shower, I can confirm it suits him.

"Right, that's the last question," the quizmaster says. "We'll have a short break, then I'll be back to do the scores."

"When do you fly back this time, Fin?" Justin says.

"Wednesday," he says. "I've reached the plausible limit of Skype consultations, for the time being. Eve's going to join me for her month in New York, the week after."

He reaches up and touches the nape of my neck, under my ponytail. "I'm going to show her the tourist stuff this time, which I've never had a cause to bother with until now."

"Can't wait. That's when me and Rog gonna PARTAY," Ed says, doing heavy metal horn hands. "Slash, watch a lot of *Queer Eye* and eat Dixy fried chicken."

"Really grateful to you for the house and Rog sit," I say.

"Pleasure is mine. Your house beats my flat any day."

Ed got a tough time from Hester over the sale of their home and ended up announcing his lack of interest in reentering the property market, for the time being. He's renting a flat at the moment, but it's a real manhole—dirty bike propped against radiator, no pictures up. He's on Tinder and has some tragicomic tales already. It feels quite the switcheroo, Justin and I being in serious relationships, Ed single.

"Your boss is definitely OK with your sabbatical?" Ed says.

"OK-ish," I say. "She's signed it off."

"Shhh," Francis says. "Results!"

"I smell victory," Ed says. "Breathe it in, my bitches."

"If we had victories as often as you smell them, Ed, we'd be banned from this quiz the same way Ben Affleck isn't allowed in Vegas casinos."

"Really, what for? Being rich?" Ed says.

"They certainly don't chuck you out for being rich, they do ban you for being too good at blackjack," Fin says. "That's why the house always wins."

"Counting cards." I nod.

"He wasn't counting them, he told me that . . ." Fin stops, eyes wide at all our shocked faces. "I mean, I read that he said . . ."

We all screech in delight.

"OK. Here are the answers . . . ," the quizmaster says, and we swap sheets with the next table for marking. We do improbably well, compared to usual.

"And last . . . I asked, which branch did the Slough branch merge with in *The Office*?"

"If it's Reading, I hate you all," Justin says.

"It was of course, Swindon. *Sunny Swindon.*"

"Yes!" Ed says. "Nice one, Finlay."

We exchange papers back again.

"Forty-six!" I say.

"Alrighty then! Who got . . . fifty out of fifty . . . ," bellows the quizmaster.

We're tense, Francis and I holding hands, eyes squeezed shut.

"Forty-nine!" Silence.

"Forty-eight!" Silence.

"Forty-seven!" The Packable Anoraks got forty-seven, surely. Silence.

I open my eyes.

"Who got . . . forty-six?" the quizmaster says.

We look at each other. "Us! We did!" the five us shout in unison, waking Leonard. Unfortunately the Packable Anoraks have bellowed too.

"Bring your papers up here, please," and Francis scrambles up to hand it over for verification.

Within minutes, the quizmaster says: "Ladies and gentlemen, seems we have a dead heat here. So you know what that means: a tie-break question. Can each team nominate a member to come up here. I will ask a question, only the two nominees get to answer. The first to give me the right answer, wins."

The Packables send their best man, who looks like a furious wizard, patting him on the back as he steps up. "Go on, Tony!"

We look at each other.

"Eve," Fin says. "You're equal to this challenge. Go get us that trophy."

"Oh no, I'm shite."

"Not shite. Up," Fin says, and Ed, Justin, and Francis make noises of agreement.

"Here it is, the tie-break. Remember, shout it out because it's fastest answer as well as correct answer, now. The ballad 'I Will Always Love You' was a smash hit for the late Whitney Houston in 1992, spending fourteen weeks at the top of the Billboard charts. However, Whitney didn't write it. Who did write it?"

"BARRY GIBB!" Tony from the Packable Anoraks shouts, like he's been Tasered, to football-stand cheers from his team.

"That is incorrect, I'm afraid," the quizmaster says, as the din subsides. "Would this lovely lady like to give her answer?"

I look at the hopeful faces of my team, their fists clenched in anticipation. Finlay winks at me.

"Is it . . . Dolly Parton?" I say.

"We have a winner!" the quizmaster says, and my corner of The Gladstone erupts in hysteria.

"Congratulations, to . . ." He picks up our answer sheet and squints through his readers at the name. "Susie's Losers."

45

After

You were alive again last night.

It wasn't a nightmare, Suze—and I've had plenty of those—it was just another world, exactly like this one but with a dramatic difference. Your presence. Your presence, which I took for granted.

In this place, we were cheerfully organizing a ski trip, sitting at a school desk, while next to a busy motorway. The cars thundering past made the table shake but neither of us were bothered. *How about Switzerland?* you said. We had plans.

(I wonder if Switzerland was some subconscious thing because that's where Hester was, when you and Ed . . . ? Haha, by the way, in return? You never get to complain about Finlay. PSYCH. Yeah don't argue. You know I have you.)

It will always be this way, I've come to realize. You are never behind me, Susie. You are never something that happened. You are always alongside me.

I clumsily scrabble for my phone in the blackness, scroll

down, and find the last text from Susie. Those words in a speech bubble on my handset. It still feels impossible there is no chance of any more, that it was a final word. That she's not there, behind that screen, hovering out of sight. Waiting for a cue.

I type a reply:

SO much to discuss. Speak soon. I love you. xxx

Across the room, where I'd plugged her phone in to charge, there's a firefly glow as it lights up, as if in response.

I hear her, clear as a bell, in my head.

Love you too, you iridescent beast. xxx
PS still have to say, my brother, GROSS

We make each other so happy, though! ☺

I am not sure that doesn't make it MORE gross. That's what Mr. Pulteney the geography teacher said when we found out he and his wife were nudists, remember?

I laugh to myself. I will always hear Susie in my head. It's an ongoing conversation. Lifelong.

Fin stirs awake. "You OK? Did I see a light on?"

"I'm fine."

"That cat is not only heavy, he's soaking!" Finlay says, registering Roger's presence, and Roger yowls territorially, in reply.

"Rog is as Rog does."

Finlay pushes his arms around me, and we lie in silence, side by side, for a while, listening to the swish of greenery in the wind beyond the window.

"I think the rain's stopped," he says.

I twist around to face him.

"So do I."

Acknowledgments

Much editorial gratitude with this one: first, to my editor Martha Ashby, who was not only hugely enthusiastic at outline stage, but also, before departing for maternity leave, fielded a lengthy phone call from me where I wailed I'd bitten off more than I could chew. She calmly informed me I had not, I would be carrying on, and it would be great. Without those words this book wouldn't be here, so thank you, Martha, for your faith. Further gratitude to my skilled caretaker editors throughout rocky old 2020, Lynne Drew and Sophie Burks, whose good humor and unflappable approach have made them a joy to work with. I especially appreciated being pushed to get each draft to where it needed to be, without ever feeling like I was being pushed. Cheers to you all, ladies, I look forward to raising a glass when it's legal again. And thank you to the whole HarperCollins team, both UK and USA, for their support and energies, I've missed seeing you all!

Thank you to my agent, Doug Kean, who's always a cheerful pleasure to work with. It's like a marriage now, except we don't argue over choices of coffee table.

My first-draft reading crew: Tara, Sean, Katie, Laura, I

couldn't do this without you. Special shout-out to Kristy Berry on this one for saving my sanity. Thank you to Carol Clements for her patient, legal expert advice on wills and probate. If I've mangled it, that's on me.

And thanks always to Alex, who has the not-always-joyous but completely essential task of telling me to stop catastrophizing, carry on, and that maybe it's quite late to still be in my pajamas.

About the author

About the book

Insights,
Interviews
& More . . .

Meet Mhairi McFarlane

Ruth Rose

Sunday Times bestselling author MHAIRI MCFARLANE was born in Scotland, and her unnecessarily confusing name is pronounced Vah-Ree. After some efforts at journalism, she started writing novels and her first book, *You Had Me at Hello*, was an instant success. She's now written seven books, and she lives in Nottingham with a man and a cat. ∿

Author's Note

Dear Reader,

I really hope you enjoyed *Just Last Night*, and that the British slang wasn't too impenetrable. (I never realized how many colloquialisms I use until I had international readers.)

As is probably obvious, I wanted to write about grief in a romantic comedy setting. It might at first seem like an unusual combination, given that we associate the genre with lighter topics. But in life, humor and tragedy exist alongside each other. We still laugh through the darkest times, so why not present that in a novel?

I've never experienced a sudden loss in the way the characters do in the book, but I have lost people I love. Something I'm learning is that while detail is personal, so much of what we go through is universal. One observation in *Just Last Night* that I pulled straight from my own life is the moment when Eve is startled by the realization that she is no longer shocked to think of Susie's death, because it's been absorbed into her daily reality. At the time it happens, it seems impossible that it will ever become routine. Grief is a unique pain in that it's grueling and yet, in some ways, we don't want to get past it to the point where our loss becomes normal. ▶

Author's Note *(continued)*

Perhaps in bereavement, we long to go backward instead of forward, and that resonates in the way Eve endlessly replays her missed chance with Ed. Wait, this is turning into a writing workshop for me! ☺

This is all quite heavy—if you discuss my story in a book group, I hope it's a fun evening, even if there are sad themes!

Following are the conversation points I would pick, but I'm sure yours will be as good if not better. Also, have wine. Susie would.

Love,
Mhairi x ∾

Reading Group Guide

1. The principal friendship group in the story has a special bond, in part because they met as teenagers. You "can't make new old friends," as the saying goes. "They know all the versions of you. They know how you were built. They have a map for you," as Ed says in the eulogy. Do you think long-standing friendships are different from friendships you made later in life, and if so, how? Are old friends worth hanging on to, or can they hold you back?

2. So I'm an overthinker and often a fence-sitter, like Eve, but Justin and Susie are the type to be emphatic and certain. Justin declares: "Nobody gets a reputation by accident," and yet we find out Finlay has, if not a reputation by accident, a reputation that isn't fair. Have there been times you've judged too harshly or too fast? Should we always wait to hear the other side? Does social media make the tendency to pass a verdict at a distance or on hearsay worse? ▶

3. At the start of *Just Last Night*, Eve is still in unspoken love with Ed. She's thought about him, and their situation, endlessly—though she discovers new perspectives on it during the story. She's devastated to discover his and Susie's involvement. Secrets are a theme in the book, whether among friends, family, or lovers. Would Eve have been better off not reading the letter that led her to unravel what had gone on? Why do you think Susie did it? The story offers a variety of explanations, but the woman herself can never provide one so Eve will never have a definitive answer.

4. Eve and Finlay get off on the wrong foot, but as time goes on, they find they're both sensitive and thoughtful and have more in common than they thought. Was the revelation about Finlay what you expected? Have you ever changed your opinion of someone to a dramatic degree?

5. Before writing this, I didn't realize the pub quiz is a British institution that isn't as common in the States. Which British traditions would you import to America if you could, and which can we *definitely keep?* ❧

Discover great authors, exclusive offers, and more at hc.com.